Charles Au Lavoie

Legacy of a FILIPINA

Victoria, British Columbia

Library and Archives Canada Cataloguing in Publication

Lavoie, Charles-Auguste, 1945- author

      Legacy of a Filipina / Charles Au Lavoie.

Issued in print and electronic formats.
ISBN 978-1-77302-820-0 (hardcover).--ISBN 978-1-77302-819-4 (softcover).--
ISBN 978-1-77302-821-7 (ebook)

      I. Title.

PS8573.A87L44 2017   C813'.54   C2017-903070-1
                                     C2017-903071-X

Tellwell Talent
www.tellwell.ca

ISBN
978-1-77302-820-0 (Hardcover)
978-1-77302-819-4 (Paperback)
978-1-77302-821-7 (eBook)

To the memory of Marcelina, for opening doors for me.

List of Characters

Main Characters

Carmelita Tauber, née Madridejos Baldemor
Born in Paete, Laguna. Left Philippines in her twenties. Widow of Max Tauber.

George Miller
Writer. Friend and neighbour of Carmelita. Becomes involved in Filipino community through her.

Marty Pua
Oldest child of Carmelita's sister Soledad Pua. Marty is in his thirties, teaches at Montessori school, lives with his mother.

Supporting Cast

Sandy Pua, née Surla
Friend of Marty Pua, married to Marty's younger brother Tomas.

Soledad Pua
Carmelita's sister, mother to Marty, Tomas and Susan. Immigrated to Edmonton, Alberta, with her husband Phil. After the death of their first child, the couple moved to North Vancouver, BC, where Phil subsequently died.

Tomas Pua
Second child of the Pua family; married to Sandy. Tomas owns a Pharma-Shop franchise in partnership with his father-in-law. The couple has no children.

Adela Orantes
Marty's aunt and his host in the Philippines. Lives in Santa Cruz, Laguna.

Anna Embottorio
Relative of Aurora Munda. Her husband's name is Boy. Anna and her family move in with the Puas.

Apin (Zerapin) Eneres
Friend of George Miller, lives in Victoria, BC. Born in Igbaras, Iloilo.

Argie Saldua
Nicknamed the Short One by Carmelita. Married to Manuel. Their children are Doreen and Tony.

Aurora Munda
Distant relative of Soledad Pua. Lives in Vancouver.

Betty Calder
Holy Name of Mary Church parishioner, sits on parish council.

Brother Melvin and Richard Lepage
Pilgrims of St. Michael missionaries.

Carmen Escovedo
Friend of Carmelita. Originally from Nicaragua. Twin teenage daughters Emily and Melanie and son Julio live with her.

Christie Hong
Colin Hong's niece, daughter of Peter. Lives in Los Angeles with her parents.

Colin Hong
Friend of George Miller and Keith Andrews. Born on a farm in Surrey, BC. Caregiver to his elderly mother, lives with her during the week. Colin's older brothers are Peter and Christopher Hong, both engineers. Peter lives in Vancouver, Christopher in Los Angeles.

Elina Gito
Carmelita's classmate at the Mayo Clinic. Lives in Victoria, visiting Philippines while George is there.

Father Alfred
Pastor of Holy Name of Mary Church. Born in Newfoundland.

Heidi and James Blair
Carmelita's neighbours. Their children are Finley and Lizzy.

Hilario Eneres
Apin's older brother. He and his wife Analisa live in Edmonton, Alberta, but have a house in Igbaras, Iloilo.

Jerry and Florfina Surla
Sandy Pua's parents.

Jim Goshinmon and Lukas Sterzenbach
Friends of Colin Hong. The couple lives in Vancouver.

Jimmy Habunal
Susan Pua's fiancé. Born in the Philippines. Raised as a Baptist, Jimmy converted to Catholicism in order to marry Susan.

Joel Palma
Marty Pua's friend in the Philippines. Lives in Famy, Laguna. Community organizer and *barangay* councillor.

Joey Enequia
Apin's neighbor in Igbaras, Iloilo. His siblings are Joemar, Joylin, Joven, and their father is Juan. Joey's girlfriend is Asrine.

Josefine Estrera
Friend of Carmelita. Lives in Honolulu. Former employee of Max Tauber and Phil Pua's vitamins and supplements company.

Juliet Eraldo
Apin Eneres's older sister. Her husband is Jejomar, their son is Bongbong. Their granddaughter Jade lives with them, as does Jejomar's niece Avelina.

Keith Andrews
Friend of George and Colin Hong. Lives in Vancouver. Keith's partner is Mohamed. Haroon, Sigmund and Hilde are Keith's friends.

Lilia Arcilla
Holy Name of Mary Church parishioner.

Lorin and Sherry Higa
Friends of George Miller, live in George and Carmelita's neighbourhood.

Mac and Laurene Erikson
Carmelita's neighbours. Son and daughter-in-law to Thora and Ingmar.

Margaret and Geoffrey Seymour
Longtime friends of Camelita and Max Tauber. Both in their nineties, originally from England.

Mary Hendricks
Close friend of Carmelita. Holy Name of Mary Church parishioner.

Mei-Ling Lim
Sister of Emile Lim. Her daughter Mimi studies at the University of British Columbia. Her son William lives in Toronto. Her niece Vicky, from Hong Kong, lives with her in Victoria during the school year. Occasionally cooks meals for Carmelita.

Paul and Jeanne Rose
Janitor and secretary at Holy Name of Mary Church.

Raquel Escaba (married to Isidoro) and Dolores Lastimosa
Holy Name of Mary Church parishioners

Rey Gonzalez
Teresita's older brother, married to Gloria.

Rhodrigo Opina
Nephew of Marty's Aunt Adela. Family doctor in Philippines.

Rita Walter
Childhood friend of Carmelita. Lives in Honolulu, married to Jack, a Native Hawaiian.

Rolando Ermoso
Farmer in Catiringan, a barangay of Igbaras, Iloilo.

Rose and Rex Escarmoso
Rose is Apin Eneres's relative. The Escarmosos are caretakers for Apin's sister and her husband when they're out of the country.

Ruby
Soledad's cousin and live-in cook for the Pua family.

Serena and Mio Kulenović
Holy Name of Mary Church parishioners. The couple has two sons.

Susan Pua
Marty and Tomas Pua's sister. Lives with her mother Soledad. Fiancée of Jimmy Habunal.

Teresita Lim, née Gonzalez
Carmelita's goddaughter. Married to Emile Lim, recently arrived from Hong Kong. Emile is the oldest son of a wealthy family. His mother was a friend of Carmelita's.

Thora and Ingmar Erikson
Carmelita's neighbours.

Trinidad Quesada
Grew up with Carmelita in Paete, Laguna.

Trish Hamilton
Victoria Community Care Nurse. Caregiver to Carmelita.

Wilma and Ron Hunter
Holy Name of Mary Church parishioners. Originally from England. Their granddaughter Kristel lives with them.

The soul is undiscovered
though explored forever
to a depth beyond report

Heraclitus
Pre-Socratic philosopher, 535-475 BCE

Legacy of a

FILIPINA

PART I

Chapter One

"Nowadays I eat with my eyes." Carmelita Tauber née Madridejos Baldemor urged her dinner guests to enjoy second helpings, even as she left her own plate untouched. George Miller gazed at the old Filipina with equal parts affection, exasperation and admiration. Her cancer was visibly weakening her. How had his life become so wrapped up with hers?

Earlier, when he'd arrived at the West Coast style mansion on Raynord Street, it was Rey Gonzalez who opened the door. George looked down at the man's form-fitting, faded and torn jeans. "Are those distressed jeans?"

"These skinny jeans are very popular among young people!" Rey said. "As you know, they're quite expensive." When George lifted a skeptical eyebrow, Rey added, "What you feel inside is what matters, right?"

George nodded. What could he say to a man in his sixties who was trying to look like a teenager? Rey had come to Canada twenty years earlier, and even though he made a point of watching hockey on TV and drinking beer when he was with "Canadians," he never managed to fit in.

Rey continued to bend George's ear. Rey and his wife Gloria, along with Rey's younger brother and sister-in-law, had just returned from a trip to Las Vegas. "Gloria and I just watched. The food is cheap compared with Canada, and the alcohol, too!"

George knew nothing about the cost of drinks in Vegas, but he had heard from Carmelita that Rey made a fool of himself and was rarely sober during the trip.

As Rey wandered off, George stepped into Carmelita's living room to say hello to the mostly Filipino guests gathered there. There were more than a dozen people, but they didn't begin to fill the space.

Teresita Lim, Rey's sister, saw the liquor store bag in George's hand. She took him aside and asked him not to get her older brother drunk. George was taken aback. He wanted to ask her to mind her own business. Instead, he placed the bottle of red wine in the centre of the dining table, and none too gently.

Rey was telling the others how important it was for immigrants to wear the right clothes, since police officers in Victoria could see right through people. "They look at your clothes and decide if you are correct or not."

"What do you mean?" George asked.

"They know right away if they have in front of them someone they can trust." Rey's current outfit represented his latest attempt to feel Canadian: a light grey leather jacket and a T-shirt with a complex, greyish pattern, like something a heavy metal fan or Hell's Angel would wear. A four-inch cross on a silver chain rested against the busy T-shirt.

Carmelita came over to George to collect a peck on the cheek. She hadn't missed a word of Rey's remarks about the alcohol in Vegas, and the Victoria police looking for immigrants in the wrong clothes. She noticed Rey's eyes light on the wine bottle and whispered to George, "Hide your bottle away."

"Am I supposed to drink water all evening?" he snapped.

"Of course not, professor. When you want some wine, do it discreetly. Don't refresh Rey's glass." Turning to her guests, she announced, "To drink without food is not good, as we all know." Rey didn't hear her comment. He was still looking for the bottle, which had vanished from the table.

Carmelita had told George that Rey was quite handsome in his youth. He became an excellent cook by observing and helping his grandmother, the family chef. Rey loved to dance and was always surrounded by girls, but he ended up marrying the not particularly sexy Gloria. She was so in love with him that it became impossible to refuse her.

Her talent for business made them a good match, since Rey was a dreamer, a creative personality. Gloria had studied accounting, hoping she could earn a good living when they moved to the United States, the destination their friends and relatives recommended. Instead, the couple landed in Canada, accepting that life doesn't always go according to plan. Rey certainly never expected that his sister Teresita would marry a Chinese man.

George was surprised to learn that in the Philippines, the Chinese had separate schools and newspapers, and their own cemeteries. Some Filipinos referred to the Chinese people as *chicks* behind their backs. A Filipino friend of Rey's had to date his Chinese girlfriend in secret.

Rey and Gloria were the first of the Gonzalez family to arrive in Canada, and Teresita arrived a few months later. The whole family, including the parents, eventually settled in Canada. Teresita stayed single well into her forties, and despaired of ever finding anyone to marry her. She had been considered too old for most Filipino men back home. They wanted a woman who would wait on them hand and foot, yet take pains to remain beautiful.

While still in the Philippines, Teresita hid her sadness from her brothers and sisters, who were all married with children. Her relatives, neighbours and others took advantage of her single status, making continual demands on her time. Her new life in Canada soon mirrored her old one. Emile Lim was her way out.

Teresita worked at the Lighthouse Home Care Agency and would forever be grateful to her co-worker Mei-Ling Lim for playing matchmaker. Teresita and Mei-Ling's brother Emile got to know each other through Skype. Three months later, with Mei-Ling at her side, Teresita flew to Hong Kong to meet her future husband. They were married in a Buddhist ceremony there, then flew to Victoria and settled into Teresita's three-bedroom condo.

Ate Carmelita arranged for a Catholic wedding ceremony at her parish church and for the reception afterwards. Teresita's supervisor was only willing to give the bride one day off, so *Ate* called the manager and threatened to lodge a complaint with the province's labour ombudsman. The agency relented and Teresita got one week off for the wedding and honeymoon.

Even though Teresita now supported Emile as well as herself, she would be mortgage-free by the time she retired from the agency. Emile was a good man, a wonderful husband, but Teresita's siblings had made it clear from the beginning that they didn't approve of him.

Emile had divorced his first wife, who walked out on him when their son was quite young, leaving Emile to raise the boy alone. Emile had no contact with his former wife, and their son was now married and still living in China. Emile, an artist, had made a name for himself as a set painter in the theatre and film industries in his home country; now he worked in his studio in the couple's home and struggled to find a market for his work.

The Gonzalez family sat together at the far end of Carmelita's living room, next to the floor-to-ceiling windows overlooking the deck and formal gardens. They were conversing in Tagalog. This habit was a source of some frustration for George, but he had learned to put up with it. He saw that Emile was part of the group.

Emile's in-laws were eating and chatting, ignoring the six-foot-tall, two-hundred-pound man, who looked as if he wanted to disappear into the couch he was sitting on. He had a plate on his lap and his eyes were glued to his food. Knowing her husband liked to eat, Teresita had dished out as much fish, pork, noodles and vegetables as the plate could hold. It was only fair, since Emile had prepared most of the Filipino food on offer that evening.

George carried a plate and chair over to Emile. "Do you mind?"

Emile raised his head and recognized George. "How are you?"

"Fine, Emile, and you?"

"I am fine. Thank you."

George said, "Next weekend is the Moss Street Paint-In." Emile obviously didn't know about the Paint-In. "It's an annual summer event, with painters working outdoors all along both sides of the street, from the museum all the way to the ocean. It's too late for you to get in as an exhibiting artist, but if you have pictures of your paintings, you could show them to people there. There's always a huge crowd. Would you like to go with me?" After saying, "Yes, yes, thank you" a few times, Emile went back to his plate.

Carmelita, who had been listening, said, "Let's all go together. I like paintings. You must learn the language that is spoken here, Emile. This will help you make a living with your art."

George knew that Emile's mother had recently died, and that he wanted to return to China for her funeral. Carmelita was adamantly against his plans and had already said to Emile, "You must not go! The Chinese government is corrupt. They will take your passport and forbid you to return to Canada. They will ask for money, always more money."

Now Carmelita whispered to George, "He misses his mother so much." She turned to Emile. "Your mother and I became good friends when she was in Victoria visiting your sisters. One evening she waltzed with my husband Max." She giggled at the memory. "They got along really well. The four of us went to Vancouver."

Carmelita seemed happy. She urged her guests, "Eat, have more! George, get some *pancit*. Emile made it." To reassure Teresita, who was staring disapprovingly at Carmelita's untouched plate, Carmelita repeated, "Nowadays I eat with my eyes."

Teresita said, "You need someone to live with you and cook for you. When is her next medical appointment?" she asked George.

Carmelita said sharply, "Next week. And for your information, Teresita, it's with Dr. Allan's replacement."

"Dr. Allan is on a study leave in Paris," George explained.

"She deserves it," said Carmelita. She beamed. "Everyone is so nice at the cancer clinic. They even offer you cookies and tea, all sorts of tea."

Teresita looked puzzled, so George explained, "Volunteers at the clinic."

Carmelita looked around the room, her eyes resting on each of her guests: her goddaughter Teresita and her dear Emile, Rey and Gloria, Carlo, the youngest of the Gonzalez family, and his wife; Lorin and Sherry Higa, along with George and a few other neighbours and friends. "I am not afraid of dying," Carmelita declared. Then she giggled and said, "Did I tell you? At the train station in New York City, they told me that the cabs were on strike. Can you imagine? I had two big suitcases and had no idea how I would get to my hotel on foot. I was going to the Easter ceremony next day at St. Patrick's Cathedral and my hotel was near there. But it was miles away from the train! A young black man came to me and asked, 'May I help you?'"

George had heard this story many times, so he discreetly invited Lorin outside for some fresh air. Once they were standing on the back deck, Lorin took a joint from his shirt pocket and lit it. After one meticulous puff, he offered it to George and asked, "How did the two of you meet?"

George took a puff. A few seconds later, he exclaimed, laughing, "Wow, this stuff is potent!"

"It's because of the buds."

"I see...What did you just say?"

"The buds."

George shook his head. "No, before that." He paused. "I remember now, you asked about Carmelita and me."

"Oh, I forgot," Lorin said, and both men laughed.

"John and I lived two houses away, but I never had a real conversation with her. When I saw her pushing a cart down one aisle at Fairway, I'd duck down another aisle."

"Why?"

George shrugged. "John never missed one of her barbeque parties. I said to him one day, 'That woman's crazy!' He said, 'She just likes people, that's all.'" George took another puff. "After John died, I fell under her spell. When she talks, she's like a drunk driver, weaving all over the road. She goes on and on! I'm used to it now."

The two men stepped off the deck and strolled through the neighbourhood, chatting easily. Nearly an hour later, George returned alone to Carmelita's house. He whispered in Sherry's ear, "We got stoned. I walked Lorin home."

The guests washed the dishes and cleaned up, and Carmelita sent everyone home with bags and containers of leftovers. George was still with her as she sat on the couch, watching a documentary on Pope John Paul on the Eternal World Television Network (EWTN). She joined her hands and prayed aloud, "Take me, O Lord. Take me."

She was drowsy, and as George helped her down the hallway, she said, "There is food in the fridge. Help yourself. Take something home."

"Thanks, but no thanks," George said, as they reached her bedroom door.

Carmelita shot him an annoyed look. "Why not?"

"You must be tired. Good night."

"You are so stubborn!"

"As you so often say, it takes one to know one." He bent and gave Carmelita a tender hug, the way he'd never hugged his own mother. He turned off the lights in the living room, dining room and kitchen, and let himself out of the house.

Chapter Two

"My cousin was so upset with me!" Carmelita was reminiscing, watching Carmen Escovedo bustle about getting Christmas dinner on the table. "With a pair of scissors, she cut my nice dress with all the ribbons into pieces!" George was barely paying attention.

"My grandfather was an ambassador to the US, you know." After a pause, Carmelita added, "We were the poorest of the family but Mama always made sure that there was enough food for anyone who showed up at the door."

"The girls are going to be late," Carmen informed them. "They have been working every day this week and today they have to stay to the end. You know what it's like, everyone last minute in the stores."

"You let them quit school?" Carmelita asked in disbelief.

Carmen shook her head. "Just for a little while. There was no school anyway for the last two days." Noticing Carmelita's look of disapproval, she added, "They are going back to school in the New Year, *Tia*. This was just to make a little extra money."

"They shouldn't be working on Christmas Eve. You are their mother."

George had first met the Nicaraguan family at one of Carmelita's dinner parties, and was delighted to be invited to dinner at Carmen's house. When he and Carmelita got there, the long table in the dining room was already set with white plates on a red tablecloth and serviettes with a stars and snowdrops pattern. An enormous punchbowl sat on the cabinet against the half wall dividing the kitchen and dining room.

Carmelita complimented her hostess on the Christmas decorations in the living room, including red candles on the coffee table. "George, did you see the crackers?" she exclaimed.

"It was Julio's idea," Carmen called out from the kitchen. "We made them, the twins and me. There was a video on YouTube."

"Where is he?" Carmelita asked, looking around.

"Julio is in the basement doing his homework. He will join us when his sisters arrive."

"What about mass?" Carmelita shouted. "Did they go to mass before going to work?"

Carmen shouted back, "Of course, *Tia*."

"It's your duty to teach them how to behave," said Carmelita. "When I die and meet my Judge, He will ask me about your children. Remember, I am their godmother."

Just then the front door opened and the twins burst in. They were gorgeous teenagers, and both wore the store's black blouse and skirt uniform. George could never tell them apart when they were not together. As he and Carmelita took seats at the dining table, the twins greeted them with hugs and kisses, then darted away to change out of their work clothes. As soon as they came back, Carmelita reminded them of the importance of going to church once a week. "I don't want to be blamed for not assuming my responsibilities toward you all."

Julio's head appeared over the staircase railing. A playful expression on his face, he said, "You don't have to go to church. You can pray anywhere." Then, seeing Carmelita's displeasure, he hung his head, obviously wishing he hadn't spoken.

George observed the eighteen-year-old, admiring his striking dark eyes and chiselled features. He would make an excellent magazine model, George thought. He felt badly for the boy. As usual, Carmelita was being too hard on Carmen. In George's opinion, she had done a great job as a single parent of three children so close in age. He said to Carmen, "I was thinking about you the other day, how you said you arrived in Winnipeg in the middle of winter. I was there once in January. It's an experience I'll never forget."

One of the twins urged, "Mom, tell Uncle George the story."

"My husband immigrated to Canada first," Carmen said. "One year later, he said the children and I should come, too, to Manitoba. I had no idea. A woman on the plane, sitting behind me, asked me if I knew what the weather would be like in Canada in December. I told her I don't know, but I was so embarrassed. I was wearing a cotton dress and high heels. I asked my husband on the phone what I should wear, but he said, 'Don't worry, we go shopping when you get here.' One day, he said to me, 'Things will be better in Vancouver. More jobs for me,' and he left us again."

Carmelita pursed her lips at this point, and George knew it was because Carmen's husband had gone to Vancouver with the woman he'd met shortly after his family came to Canada. "He was a fool," was Carmelita's only comment. Carmen's mother and father had settled in Florida two years before, but "the fool" had convinced Carmen to immigrate to Canada, and then deserted her and the children.

"Julio was three years old," Carmen was saying, "and the twins one and a half years. My neighbours in the apartment building in Winnipeg babysat the children when I had to go to Immigration, or shopping or work, and they invited us for Easter. They were both born in Canada, but his uncle was a missionary in Nicaragua, so they wanted to help us. They were so good to me and the children."

Her husband called her occasionally, complaining about how hard things were for him in Vancouver. That was his excuse for not sending her money.

"I couldn't take the cold, so I said no, we have to go to Victoria. I saw on TV, and I knew Victoria was where we had to go. The children would be closer to their father, and he promise they can come to him in the summer and go hiking and camping. I said okay, but not with that woman. I found out about her," Carmen said.

In Victoria Carmen met Carmelita, who at that time was a volunteer counsellor at the Victoria Immigrant and Refugee Centre, and the older woman put her in touch with a Spanish-speaking family lawyer who forced her husband to pay for her Victoria apartment.

"My husband, was he ever mad at *Tia* Carmelita," Carmen said, laughing. "I wanted my son to have a father, but my husband always complain he have no money, it's not a good time...always an excuse for not seeing his own son."

When her children started school, Carmen took courses in cosmetology and worked on her English by taping TV shows and watching them at night with her children. Years later, her command of the language was still shaky. "Julio is ashamed. He always correct my English."

"You've raised three fine children, Carmen," George said to her. "You can be proud of that." He looked at Julio, who seemed to squirm under his gaze.

"My Julio, he wants to be a professional singer," Carmen was saying. "Music is in his blood. His grandfather was a symphony conductor in Nicaragua. Julio sings tenor at the conservatory and his teachers say, 'He has the sensibility of a true artist.'" Julio reddened at the compliment.

"He's the best-dressed guy at school, that's for sure," one of the twins said, grinning at her brother.

Carmelita said, "Fashion is not the end of all." The twins and their mother just smiled, too polite to interrupt the Filipina when she was intent on giving advice.

George mentioned a composer Julio had never heard of. The youth left the table and booted up the laptop computer on the corner of the buffet table. "Ricardo Hahn," he read aloud, "a friend of several artists living in Paris in the nineteenth century. Composer of melodies...from Argentina... His parents moved to France when he was quite young... I'll ask Mr. Huntington about him," he said, returning to the dining table for the apple pie and vanilla ice cream that *Tia* Carmelita had contributed to the dinner.

"Julio love to dance with his sisters and their girlfriends," his mother was saying. "They get along so well."

"At the conservatory, everyone thinks I'm gay," Julio admitted.

"You are my child," his mother replied. "I will always love you."

George was startled when Julio said, "Mom, I don't know if I am or not."

"You can bring home anyone, I don't care," his mother assured him.

Later, George and Carmelita said their goodbyes. He settled Carmelita in the front passenger seat, then called Teresita to say he would be stopping by on the way home to pick up the *congee* Emile had made for Carmelita. As he slid behind the wheel George said to Carmelita, "It's late. I told Teresita I didn't want to go in for a visit. Emile will be waiting for us outside."

"Fine with me," Carmelita said.

Chapter Three

George pulled toward the curb on Cedar Hill Road just after nine o'clock. Carmelita looked at the condo building opposite them, where Emile and Teresita had been living since their marriage four years earlier. Emile was standing a few feet away on their side of the road, anxiously watching the passing cars. A large covered pot was on the ground beside him.

"Poor soul," said Carmelita. "He will catch a cold."

"He looks lost," George observed.

"He misses his mother."

Emile broke into a smile as the green sedan came to a stop beside him. "Come, come!" he shouted, gesturing.

George rolled down the front passenger window and shook his head. All he wanted was to complete his mission and get home. He wasn't about to cross four lanes of traffic, drive down into the building's underground parking, then gnash his teeth while Carmelita walked slowly to the elevator, then to the condo holding on to Emile's arm and slowing him down to her pace... That was not going to happen tonight. "Thanks, Emile, but it's late, and tomorrow's Monday."

He got out and unlocked the back door. Emile placed the pot of *congee* on the floor. George could see that it was filled to the brim. "Careful, careful!" Emile said to them, "Very hot!"

After thanking Emile for the powerful gruel that he had so kindly cooked for her, Carmelita said, "Tell Teresita I will give her pot back the next time you two come to my house for dinner." She ordered Emile inside the car. "It's cold and you are not even wearing a coat."

Emile sat behind Carmelita, who said, "Your mother and I were friends." Forgetting that both men had already heard the story, she said, "Your mother came in the early Nineties to visit Mei-Ling and Denise." Both daughters had emigrated a few years earlier.

"I didn't know Denise was living in Canada then," George remarked.

"Not anymore. She went back to China; she had to help her husband look after the family business. Anyway…" She burst out laughing and covered her mouth with her hand like a teenage girl. "I can still see them waltzing in our living room. Your mother and Max would talk to each other in German."

Emile beamed, but George was puzzled. "Where did she learn German?"

"When World War Two started she was travelling in Europe. She got stranded. Passenger ships couldn't go back to Hong Kong because of the Japanese alliance with Germany. All civilian transportation was cut off. Your mother was quite a beauty in her youth, very elegant," she said to Emile. She added for George's benefit, "She was the first Chinese woman to enter university. Her father was a banker."

George turned to look at Emile, who was listening closely to Carmelita. *Ate* was the only person in Canada who had known his mother. The massive man looked like a forlorn puppy.

"At the airport, we hugged. 'See you in China' your dear mother said to me." Carmelita paused again. "Max is gone. Your mother is gone."

"I must go, *Ate*. Teresita…worry…"

Carmelita awoke from her reverie. "Why on earth would she worry? You are with me and George."

After saying thank you instead of good night, Emile opened the car door. He bowed and uttered a few extra thank-yous and finally closed the door behind him. George watched Emile check for traffic, then cross the street and enter the condo building.

George said, "I wish someone would tell me what it's like 'up there.' No reaction from his passenger; Carmelita was staring straight ahead, her face a mask.

Just before he died, John had called his name. The nurse had been standing by the bedside, but she left the room as soon as George came in. The pain of John's death had subsided over the years, leaving a void that, at this particular instant, George felt a strong temptation to leap into.

George started the car and drove away.

✳

Teresita was in the kitchen rinsing the dishes. "Why did it take you so long? Where is *Ate*?" she wanted to know.

"Gone."

In the living room, Rey and Carlo and their wives were watching the Filipino channel on television, as they always did when they visited. Emile went to use the computer in the guest room. The telephone rang.

"Can someone pick up the phone? My hands are wet," he heard Teresita shout.

In the living room, a guest picked up the receiver. Emile didn't answer the phone during the day when his wife was at work. It was never for him anyway.

When the phone rang again several hours later, Emile did pick up, knowing it was his son calling from China. As usual, he was asking for money, saying that unless his father sent money, the government wouldn't free up the inheritance from his grandmother. Emile tried to explain why he couldn't help, but the young man hung up on him.

"No good, no good!" Emile said as he returned to bed.

"Tell him not to call in the middle of the night," Teresita said with a yawn.

"There is nothing here," Emile complained. Teresita didn't hear him; she had fallen back asleep.

Victoria was a village compared to his native Guangzhou. Emile often wished he could go back there, just for a few hours, just to hear people talking to one another in a language he understood. He longed to eat his favourite foods, the ones he couldn't cook because the ingredients weren't available in Victoria, not even in Chinatown.

Teresita had recently started worrying about his health, and when she convinced him to see a doctor, she had to explain the physician's findings.

"Did you have a heart attack in China, Emile, before we came to Canada?" Emile just shrugged.

In China a lot of money. Victoria, no money, he thought as he tried to get to sleep. He was mildly surprised that the words had come to him in English.

If only Teresita knew about the life he had enjoyed in Guangzhou. They were both too old to have children and really build a life together. He and Teresita were like old trees, slowly toppling.

Chapter Four

Two weeks later, Emile's sister Mei-Ling called George to say she was cooking a bone soup for Carmelita, who was refusing to eat anything except dessert. "No good for cancer," Mei-Ling remarked.

"I'm sure Carmelita will be pleased."

"Tomorrow early I go to Vancouver with food for my daughter."

"She is at UBC, right?" George asked.

"My daughter eats at cafeteria. No good."

"Will you spend the weekend?"

"No. Back to Victoria tomorrow."

"Quite a trip in one day! You're a good mother." Mei-Ling said nothing. "When the dish for Carmelita is ready, call me," George said.

*

After tidying up the house that evening, Mei-Ling turned off the front porch light. Her fourteen-year-old niece Vicky, who had been living with her for the past two school years, was already in bed. She spent her summer holidays with her parents in China, then flew back to Victoria in mid-August.

Mei-Ling had learned to cook quite young when her family was living apart. She, her sisters and her mother lived in Hong Kong while her father and brothers were forbidden to leave mainland China. Mei-Ling was the one who brought food across the border. The guards always recognized her. The communist government wanted her mother to return to China with her daughters, but she always refused, for fear of losing everything the family had in Hong Kong.

On weekdays after work, Mei-Ling cooked her daughter Mimi's favourite dishes and froze them in preparation for her monthly trip to Vancouver. Loaded down with two large insulated bags, she took two different buses to the ferry terminal, then boarded the downtown express on the ferry, and later the Broadway bus which dropped her off close to Mimi's residence on campus. If her son William lived in Vancouver instead of Toronto, Mei-Ling would do the same for him. Just before going to bed, she packed something for herself to eat on the ferry.

Mei-Ling's husband had left her for another woman when the children were young. He offered to pay for her and Mimi's trip back to Hong Kong, but he wanted William to stay with him. Mei-Ling refused. How could he expect her to leave her son to him and his new woman?

Her friend Teresita at the agency suggested she contact the Victoria Immigrant and Refugee Centre and ask for Carmelita Tauber. "She's helped a lot of women like you," Teresita said.

After listening to her story, Carmelita said to her, "You will fight back." She contacted a lawyer who discovered that Mei-Ling's husband had deserted his first wife in China before marrying Mei-Ling in Canada. "Your husband will pay, or my name is not Carmelita Tauber," she vowed.

Mei-Ling won custody of both children and her husband had to comply with the judge's order for monthly support payments. She had been supporting her children on her home care salary, and had quickly built a reputation for reliability with her employer. They always called her when one of the other caregivers took a sick day. The extra shifts helped a lot, and the money from her husband, which arrived sporadically, was a welcome bonus.

The Victoria Filipino community was abuzz with the news that Carmelita had been steadily losing weight over the past six months, and many were concerned that she was still living alone. George contacted Carmelita's friends to ask if any of them could provide some support by cooking for Carmelita, drive her to medical appointments when he wasn't available and eventually stay with her overnight. The friends made it clear they were busy looking after their own families.

When these concerns reached her ears, Carmelita asked, "Why do you all worry?"

On a Sunday night in mid-January, a dozen friends gathered at the Sun Wah restaurant to honour Carmelita. They didn't know how much longer she would be among them.

Carmelita appeared at the door of the restaurant, supported by George's arm. A few seconds later, Emile arrived with Kevin, a successful software designer, who had driven him to the restaurant. Carmelita asked why Teresita wasn't with him. Emile bowed and said, "Don't know. She is home."

His sister Mei-Ling rushed out from the kitchen to greet Carmelita and George. "I told the chef you are sick, need lots of vegetables. You too, George, you like vegetables, right? You have the corner table," she added, pointing. "Too cold by the door, you catch a draft."

Carmelita looked around her with a smile. "Are you okay?" Mei-Ling enquired. "I am fine, thank you."

Teresita came in, looking upset. As soon as she sat at the table, she turned to her husband. "Why didn't you wait for me?"

Emile mumbled something, not looking at her. Poor soul, George thought.

The restaurant owner came to welcome Carmelita and the others, then stood aside as his staff brought out a succession of steaming, fragrant dishes on large trays. Mei-Ling announced the Chinese name of each dish, followed by a description in English. She prepared a plate and handed it to Carmelita. Emile carefully rotated the tabletop toward George, who was second in order of importance among the guests. George served himself, then the others took their turn.

Carmelita rearranged the food on her plate with her chopsticks. "I am so happy to be here," she said to the group. She bowed her head and recited, "Bless us, O Lord, and these thy gifts which we are about to receive from thy bounty, through Christ Our Lord. And bless all the homeless people in Victoria."

The others bowed their heads out of respect. Mei-Ling told everyone about meeting Carmelita at the refugee centre years ago and how much she had helped her.

Carmelita listened impassively, then remarked, "One day little William came to the house. He pointed at the big recliner in our living room and said, 'Uncle Max used to sit in that chair.'" She announced, "I don't know how much time I will live, but I want to thank you all." She removed the shawl from her shoulders. "My friend Jeanne...you remember Jeanne from the parish, right? She knitted this for me."

Emile urged George, "Eat, eat!"

After several courses were sampled and some dishes re-ordered and consumed, the servers brought out the fortune cookies. By then Carmelita's head was drooping and she was snoring softly. George touched her arm, "Let's go."

"Sorry, I was sleeping," Carmelita remarked with a giggle.

George crossed the restaurant parking lot, followed by Carmelita and Teresita, who had her arm around the older woman's waist. George held the passenger door open and helped Carmelita ease into her seat. He reminded her to buckle up, then closed the door and turned to say goodbye to Teresita.

"She has lost so much weight since last time," Teresa remarked. She tapped herself on the chest and said, "This is like needles to my heart."

George walked around to the driver's side. Teresita followed him. "Couldn't you stay at night with her, in case something happens?"

"You don't think what I do is enough?" George snapped. Teresita stared at him. "The answer's no!"

"Why not?" Teresita persisted. "You don't have a family."

George recalled what Teresita had said when he mentioned his hope of visiting the Philippines one day. Teresita just happened to have a second- or third-degree cousin, George couldn't remember which, who would make an excellent wife. The cousin had looked after her parents until both passed away.

George replied with his standard, "Thanks, but no thanks!"

Chapter Five

That evening, George realized that although he had been out of the closet for nearly half a century, he was back in it, pretending that his cravings for men were secondary, almost irrelevant. Carmelita was now the centre of his life; she had taken away his past, both sexually and emotionally. He chauffeured her to the cancer clinic and to the lab for blood tests, and escorted her to events at the Victoria Philippines Centre and meals at friends' homes. Carmelita referred to him as her angel, but George felt more like her implant. He needed a break from her.

He resumed attending the monthly meetings of Prime Timers, the local association for older gays. When one of its members mentioned an upcoming gathering called Heart Circle, to be followed by a potluck dinner, he wrote down the host's number and called to register.

George opened the door of the heritage house on Chambers Street in the bohemian neighbourhood of Fernwood. A university student named Andrew welcomed him and took him into the living room, where a small group was already assembled. George looked around. There were books everywhere, on shelves and in piles on the floor. Posters of old movie stars like Greta Garbo and Marlene Dietrich in *Blue Angel* adorned the walls. Andrew explained that he and his partner Tyson were just lending their place to the shaman leading the Heart Circle. "Do you know Clive Oak?"

George shook his head. "I've never met him."

"He's amazing!" Andrew said.

The so-called shaman was an athletic, handsome man in his forties. He sat in a chair, looking up at an older man who stood before him in a trance, his whole being focused on Clive.

Andrew touched the standing man's arm. "Sorry to interrupt." He looked at the shaman. "Clive, this is George."

Clive immediately got up, all smiles, and gave George what could only be called a long and meditative hug. George felt himself melt inside. He stepped back and offered his hand to the other man, who still hadn't moved away. "I'm George."

"I'm Ed."

Another six people arrived. Four were students like their hosts, while the other two were middle-aged. After a quick hello to everyone, they sat on the floor, as the faded but inviting Fifties-era couch and armchairs were all occupied. The guests formed a circle and waited.

To open the session, Clive uttered what sounded to George like universal maxims. Clive pronounced each phrase like a mantra: "Love is like a muscle; it takes practice to grow stronger... Magic is the art of changing consciousness at will."

After a while, Clive came down from the mountain, broke into a smile and opened his arms as if to embrace everyone in the room, young and old. "The Heart Circle, my friends, is an opportunity for gays to become free."

He invited each participant to tell his story to the group. "Darcy here, for example, came out late, after his wife died."

George looked at Darcy, an elongated man in his late sixties, who was crying. Clive took Darcy in his arms.

Darcy shared his story. "After I told the kids that I was gay, I met a guy. He was married." In less than a year, the two men became best friends. But now the other man had moved to Toronto to be close to his ailing parents-in-law. "I can't see myself without him in my life," Darcy said, sobbing unashamedly.

Another older man named Dave was next. He had just come out of the closet a couple of years earlier, after a lengthy marriage that included children and grandchildren. "I always avoided gays. I was afraid that the presence of a gay man would make me reveal something about me that I hated. You have no idea of what it means to me to share this with you." After a pause, he added, "The Heart Circle is worth more than any of those other programs that cost you an arm and a leg."

Andrew thanked Dave for sharing and said, "I want to do this for a living after my graduation. Host Heart Circles, help people come together."

"I wish there were something like this when I was young. I could have saved myself so much pain," Dave said with a sigh.

Clive smiled at Andrew and Tyson and made eye contact with each man in the room. "It's magic! What a mix of people: boys and dads." His audience laughed. "Boys need dads. Young gays need mentors."

George saw that Andrew and Tyson had been holding hands throughout the session. Tyson's right foot was tucked under Andrew's left. Their intimacy brought back memories of George's early years with John, when they needed the reassurance of constant contact.

At four, the Heart Circle session ended and new people began appearing for the potluck. Clive invited Andrew to say a few words in closing. The young man pointed at Tyson. "He did all the work. I just got the table and set up the chairs."

Chapter Six

Mary Hendricks recognized Carmelita's name on call display. She picked up the handset. "Good evening, Carmelita. How are you?"

"I can't do... my back."

"I don't understand, Carmelita. What you are talking about?"

"Don't you remember?" Carmelita sounded frustrated. "I already told you, UPS brought the box of patches that my sister ordered for me."

"What does your oncologist think?"

"Dr. Allan? She is in Paris. I told my sister I won't find her equivalent in Vancouver." She paused. "But you know how Soledad is, she won't listen." Carmelita's voice became agitated. "One thousand US dollars for a six-month supply, can you imagine? Without counting the special delivery to my house from North Vancouver."

"What kind of patches are these?" Mary asked.

"The instructions are in the box." Carmelita fell silent, then asked, "Could you do me a favour and come and help me put them on?"

"Of course, love. I have an evening shift at the hospital today, but I can stop by on my way." No response from Carmelita. Mary asked, "Are you okay, love?"

"I worry about my sister." Carmelita sighed. "Her health has always been fragile."

"I can't talk, love. I have my keys in my hand. I'll be there soon."

"God bless you!"

A half hour later, Mary was in Carmelita's house, studying a diagram showing where to apply the patches. Carmelita took the sheet from Mary's hands.

"Later, Mary, I have something for you." She pointed at two plates wrapped in plastic on the counter. "Someone brought me this last night for dinner."

Mary didn't mention that food shouldn't stay all night on the counter. Mary, a registered nurse, knew her food safety rules, but she didn't think this was the appropriate time to have that conversation with Carmelita, who loved to share food. *Far too late to change her at this point*. Mary looked at the diagram again. "It doesn't say what they're for."

Carmelita interrupted her. "Don't worry about that. Just put one on each side of my spine. I can't reach the ones on my back." She sighed again. "I don't want radiation that attacks good cells. Look what happened to Theodora. The radiation killed her in a few months. I'm a nurse, I should know. But my sister won't listen."

"When is she coming?" Mary asked.

"She wants to, but I keep telling her: Your duty is to yourself and your children."

Mary's attention was on applying the patches: two on each side of Carmelita's spine, one at her waist and another on each shoulder blade. She applied two more to Carmelita's temples. "That should do for now, love."

Carmelita got up and shuffled to the kitchen. "Sit down and eat."

"I had a good meal," Mary replied. "A glass of water will be fine. I can't stay long." She put her hand Carmelita's arm. "I have to tell you something, though."

"What?"

"My son and his girlfriend don't want to get married in a church. Last night he called me to say, 'Mom, Katrina and I don't believe in God.' Instead, they will have a ring tattooed on their fingers."

"I am glad that I don't have children," Carmelita remarked with a pensive expression.

Mary said the Queen's *annus horribilis* had been nothing compared to what she had been through in the past two years. She lived alone in a house full of bad memories. One after another, her children had left home when their father started spending his evenings and part of his nights watching movies. "He accused me of not taking care of my own children." Mary wiped away tears.

She confided, "One day, in front of the children, he said I was having an affair with the parish priest." She laughed. "Father Al, can you imagine?" Her children were looked after; they had clean clothes when they left for school, and when they came back, the meals were ready, no matter what shift Mary was working. "If you ask me, people are going crazy with this Internet thing."

Mary massaged Carmelita's shoulders. "My oldest son doesn't even talk to his father on the phone anymore. I told him, you have to call your father on Father's Day."

"The back, Mary, please." Carmelita smiled and sighed. "Oh, it's so good." EWTN was on in the living room. After a few minutes, she said, "That's enough, thanks." She patted Mary's hand. "Let's join Father John."

Mary helped Carmelita onto the couch and kneeled beside her, then pulled her rosary from the pocket of her white cardigan. The two friends recited along with the TV audience: "Holy Mary, Mother of God…"

Chapter Seven

Throughout the Philippines, the feast of the Santo Niño, or *sinulog*, is celebrated on the third Sunday of January. Isidoro and Raquel Escaba came to consult Carmelita about holding a *sinulog* in the basement of her parish church.

"We are going to ask the secretary for a meeting with Father Al."

Carmelita interrupted. "Let me call him. I was on the council for many years."

When Carmelita spoke with the priest later that day, she reminded him how deeply devoted Filipinos were to the Infant Jesus, and she talked about the feasts throughout the Philippines. Father Al listened to the end, then said, "You have my blessing. I trust you."

His approval of the *sinulog* caused some awkwardness for Father Al at the next monthly parish meeting. Betty Calder reacted as soon as he announced the upcoming celebration. "I'm not speaking for myself, Father, you understand, but some parishioners are saying that these people are already taking up too much space."

Father Al was aghast. He had no idea that this hostility had been brewing.

Betty hesitated, then added, "I'm afraid I have qualms about the choir as well, Father. I'm not saying the director isn't a competent professional, but most of the members are Filipinos now, like him. People who have been in the choir for decades are being told to stop coming to rehearsals. 'You've done your share,' he's telling them."

Father Al looked around the table, but Betty was the only one who would meet his eyes. He sighed and promised to look into the matter.

✱

That Saturday evening, Raquel and Dolores Lastimosa greeted Carmelita at the side entrance to the parish church. They could hear the music playing in the community hall in the church basement. Raquel took Carmelita's arm and asked, "Did George bring you?"

"No! I can still drive myself, you know," Carmelita said. As Dolores led the way to the elevator, Raquel whispered to Carmelita, "We are praying for your recovery, *Ate*."

Dolores held the elevator doors open as the other two slowly approached. On their way down, Dolores ventured to ask, "How are you?"

"I am fine, thank you." Carmelita replied, with no hesitation. Dolores and Raquel said nothing to this.

Carmelita looked at them and said with a smile, "It's a miracle. So many people are praying for me. My sister wants me to come and live with her in North Vancouver."

"You are selling your house?" Raquel enquired.

Carmelita replied sharply, "I am fine in the house that my husband built for me."

"Are you sure it's a good idea, *Ate*?"

Carmelita looked at Raquel, either angry or shocked. "Did she talk to you?"

"Soledad cares for you, this is why she worries," Raquel said.

Stepping out of the elevator, Carmelita freed herself from Raquel's grasp. "I need to go to the kitchen to make sure that everything is in order." Without turning back, she said, "Tell my sister not to worry. I am fine."

The kitchen door opened, startling Betty Calder, who said, "What are you doing here, Carmelita? You should be with your—" Betty paused, reconsidering. "With the others."

Carmelita didn't seem to hear her. "Do we need more food? I can ask Sebastian to go to Safeway."

Betty shook her head. "Everything is fine, Carmelita. Father Al is already here."

"I must go then." Before leaving, Carmelita said to Betty, "If you need any-thing...my car is here. Do you want the keys?"

"It's okay, Carmelita, go."

Seeing his old Filipina parishioner approach, Father Alfred called out to her, "What an extraordinary spectacle, my friend!"

Father Al was born and had spent most of his life in the Bonavista Bay region of Newfoundland. When he took over the Victoria parish, he hadn't been prepared for his Filipino parishioners' colourful expressions of faith. On this occasion he watched in bemusement as dozens of brightly costumed Filipinos danced and sang. They weren't really singing, he realized, but praying for the ailing members of their community, in particular Carmelita. He recognized the words "Santo Niño" as they chanted.

"In a certain way, the parish reminds me of my native Newfoundland," Father Al said to Carmelita as he escorted her to a chair.

"Really, Father?" Carmelita beamed with satisfaction.

Father Al nodded. "Where I'm from, the church was a place for people to go when they were suffering and felt lost and close to despair. As the son and grandson of fishermen, I've seen bodies of dead men brought back from a wreck, nothing but blocks of ice, slowly melting... Women raised their children alone, not knowing when their husbands would return or if they would ever come back." The priest pointed at his heart and his forehead. "The memories are still here and I am seventy-two years old."

"You are young, Father."

Father Alfred continued as if he hadn't heard. "Men and boys would go through the village, their faces hidden and wearing costumes, singing. The custom is known as mummery—quite lively, like this celebration. Newfoundland is a place of dreams and superstitions. But they drank…they drank too much. Life was hard back then."

A woman held a statue of the Infant Jesus over her head as she danced to the rapid beat of the drum. Grown men with red ribbons in their hands and women wearing crowns of flowers walked in circles, repeating, "Pit Sinior. Pit Sinior."

Father Al watched as a group of women brought a glazed roast piglet from the kitchen and added it to the food already displayed on the central table.

"Excuse me, Father." Carmelita directed the dancers to place the Santo Niño on another table at the left side of the hall.

"Quickly, please!" Carmelita invited Father Alfred to say grace.

"Let us bow our heads." The sturdy man from Newfoundland continued, "Thank you, Dear Lord, for this bountiful food, prepared and served in honour of the Infant Jesus." Father Al blessed the piglet, the rice, the stew, and all the plates of roasted vegetables, along with the fried fish, the various types of noodles and even the dishes he couldn't identify. After a very loud *Amen*, the parishioners rushed over to admire the piglet.

"We call it *lechon*, Father," Raquel informed the priest.

Father Al repeated the word *lechon*. Everyone laughed good-naturedly. Carmelita urged him to be first in line to be served by the women standing behind the table. Father Al said, "I'll have some of the pork, of course! And a small portion of your noodles, my dear."

As she dished up the noodles, the woman said, "Back home, we call it *pancit*."

Father Al took a stab at the word, but it came out as "punch it." The parishioners laughed again, but Father Al didn't mind. Over the years, these Filipinos had become like brothers and sisters to him. He couldn't understand the uneasiness some of the other parishioners felt.

Carmelita urged the priest to eat the fish with his fingers. "Be careful, Father, milkfish have lots of bones."

Father Al laughed. "I was raised with fish bones, my dear friend." Even though she was younger, Carmelita reminded him of his maternal grandmother—a captain in control.

Because of her cancer, Carmelita had been on the parish's prayer list for more than a year. Everyone admired her strong will. Recently, though, she had fainted during a mass. From the altar, Father Alfred saw her slowly collapse and gradually slip off the front pew where she always sat.

His dear friend had summoned new vitality this evening. A half-dozen non-Filipino parishioners had come downstairs out of curiosity, and Carmelita was shepherding them toward the food table.

Father Al was aware that whenever someone mentioned that the parish needed something, Carmelita took out her bank book and wrote a cheque. A few years ago, when the Victoria diocese almost went bankrupt due to unwise investments, Carmelita purchased diocese bonds. Money was never been a problem for her. For his part, Father Al had never forgotten how it felt to go hungry. The first time he got enough to eat was when he entered the seminary to become a priest.

Chapter Eight

Betty Calder leaned against the wall, watching the dancers perform the two-steps-forward-one-step back movement of the *sinulog* dance. Men, women and children held statues of the Infant Jesus over their heads as they danced. The statues, of various sizes, had all been blessed by Father Al during the mass earlier that day. The women and girls were wearing what Betty knew to be traditional Filipino dresses, while the men and boys had on transparent shirts. "Pagans," she muttered as she watched.

"Did you eat enough?" Carmelita asked Betty, who almost jumped out of her skin. *Why was this woman always sneaking up on her?*

"If you'll excuse me, I have to go," she said, moving away from the wall.

"You are always so beautifully dressed, Betty," Carmelita persisted. "How is your youngest son? I haven't seen him."

"He's fine, thanks," Betty replied. "Carmelita, I'm sorry, but I need to rearrange the flowers. around the altar"

"Do you need help?"

"I'm okay. Thanks for the offer." Betty just wanted to be left alone.

The auburn widow waved at Father Al. She left the community hall and climbed the stairs to the main level. A few seconds later she was in the sanctuary. She crossed herself and kneeled. She noticed that the light over the statue of

Mother Mary was off. The Mother of God looked so sad in the dark. Betty got up quickly and flipped the switch behind the statue, then kneeled again.

"Holy Mary, Mother of God…"

The beating of drums and the pounding of feet came through the sanctuary floor. It was a confirmation of what Betty had been thinking for some time: the Filipinos were now in control. Betty felt like a foreigner in what used to be her church. In the choir, old Mrs. Jones and her grandson were the only non-Filipinos left.

When Betty's husband died in a car accident three years earlier, she thought her life was over. Then her hip began bothering her, and soon she developed a limp. Pills were no help and the pain got steadily worse. She couldn't understand how Carmelita could carry on despite what must be tremendous pain from her cancer.

Betty had once asked Carmelita where she got her energy. The Filipina had replied, "When I say I am okay, I immediately start feeling okay." Betty knew Carmelita suffered from high blood pressure, and she had the swollen legs that indicated poor circulation. But the woman always bore a wide smile and acted as if nothing mattered more than food and telling stories. Betty had said to her, "I don't know any other person like you." Yet Carmelita's happy nature and optimistic outlook had no effect on Betty, who struggled day and night to keep her head above water.

The parish treasurer poked his bald head through the doors of the sanctuary. He'd been to the celebration, Betty could see. He had a plate of food in one hand and a cup of coffee in the other. He mumbled something about accounting, entered the code to the office and quickly closed the door behind him.

Betty rose and walked over to the altar. She admired the new altar cloth, and her hand brushed the fine linen. If only she could have given birth to one priest! Neither of her two sons ever showed any desire to enter the priesthood, even though their father was a religious man.

She headed for the staircase, but her left hip was hurting, so she decided not to rejoin the festival. Her first surgery wasn't that long ago, and she was due for her second hip replacement. Carmelita was always reminding her to take the elevator to spare her joints. "Take it easy, Betty," she would say. "Be patient." As usual, she would end with, "I was a nurse, remember? A nurse is always a nurse."

Chapter Nine

After Sunday mass, Francka Žumer stepped out of George's car and thanked him for bringing her home. "Would you like to come in for a cup of tea?"

"I'd love to, thanks."

Francka served George soup and bread in the dining room.

"You said a cup of tea!"

"The house is so quiet when I come back from church," she said softly. "I am happy for the company."

"A few months ago, you mentioned you'd written a book," George said.

Francka nodded. "Oh yes, I told you about it, didn't I?" She felt herself come alive. "It is an autobiography. As you know, I was born in Slovenia. At the time it was part of Yugoslavia. Everyone in the country learned Serbo-Croatian, and later French and German, as well as Latin. At the Jožef Stefan Institute, I worked with Professor Leonardlin. We launched balloons carrying nuclear emulsions into the stratosphere. I wanted to go to America, which was the leader in nuclear physics."

"What about your husband?"

"He was more anxious to go than me. He didn't want to live anymore under a communist regime. After a few months in the States, we moved to Quebec City and I got a teaching position at Laval University. The university had a Van de Graaff accelerator."

Francka paused. "Carmelita is lucky."

"What do you mean?"

"So many people care for her."

George said, "One day a parishioner asked if we were brother and sister." George laughed. "I didn't know what to say. I asked, 'Shouldn't we have the same colour skin?' The poor lady was so embarrassed. She said, 'I don't pay attention to people's skin colour.'"

"At least she has you; she is so lucky," Francka repeated. "I don't have any of my children with me."

"Where are they?"

"They were all born in Canada, but now my two daughters are raising their families in the States and my son is living in Calgary."

"Do you have grandchildren?"

Without a word, Francka got up and brought over a large framed collage of photographs showing her children and grandchildren, all dressed in their Sunday best.

"What lovely pictures! You have beautiful grandchildren."

Francka smiled. She put the photograph on the kitchen counter behind her. She thought for a moment, then raised something that had been on her mind for some time. "The Catholic hierarchy does not seem to care about the poor. The parishioners seem not to care, either."

Francka decided to put her cards on the table. "I am looking for someone who would replace me as the parish representative for Development and Peace. I thought that you might be interested."

"I can't be the parish representative."

"I understand. You are busy taking care of Carmelita."

"It's not that. I'm too critical of what I see around me, Francka. The parish council uses the community hall for potluck dinners but won't open it to the homeless people in town when it's freezing outside."

Francka listened, smiling. "You remind me of my husband. He too was unwilling to make compromises; he couldn't stand hypocrisy."

"Carmelita often gets upset by what I say about the Pope and the bishops. Her theology is too basic for my taste. I have to say, though, it doesn't stop her from caring for others."

George got up and thanked Francka for the very tasty soup and the homemade bread. "Good luck with finding a replacement."

After he left, Francka stood at the kitchen sink washing dishes. As she gazed at the deck of the neighbouring house, she remembered her good friend Jane Cliff who used to live there. If Jane was outside, Francka would open her kitchen window and invite her friend over for a visit. A year ago, Jane, who was several years older than Francka and quite frail, moved to an assisted-leaving facility, as they called it. The new neighbours weren't taking care of the lovely backyard the way Jane used to.

Francka felt like crying. Her life hadn't been easy. Her husband hadn't really wanted to get married; his dream was to become a Jesuit priest. Francka was his main caregiver when he lost his sight to diabetes. A master plan, unknown to her, had been unfolding step by step over the course of her life.

Chapter Ten

After the mass, Zerapin Eneres noticed Carmelita turning around, her cane tapping the floor with every movement.

He asked, "What are you looking for?"

"I lost him."

"Who?"

"George."

"I saw him a few minutes ago, talking to an old woman with a white bun."

"Some respect, please!"

"You know, the pale woman with a strange name. She always sits in the pew behind you...?"

"Francka Žumer. Of course I know her!"

"I saw her get into his car."

"George will give her a ride home."

"What about you? How are you going to get home?"

"I am still *compos mentis*." She looked at Apin. "Have you forgotten what it means?"

Being a nurse himself, Apin knew the meaning of the Latin phrase. He was concerned about *Ate*'s brain, wondering whether her cancer had progressed that far. She was more and more impatient with people lately, and everyone was talking about it.

"I can still drive my car."

Apin was aware that the local Filipinos didn't know what to make of Carmelita's so-called angel. Was he after her money? Apin didn't care about that; he just wanted to know what kind of man George *really* was.

One day he had asked Carmelita whether George was retired, married, or what.

"Why do you want to know?" she barked.

"No reason, just...he used to have a friend. John, wasn't it? What happened to him?"

"He passed away. Now, are you satisfied? " Carmelita reacted. After a pause, still looking angry, she said, "Don't you have better things to do than gossiping?"

"What's wrong with that?"

Apin had been curious about George for some time, and the matriarch wasn't going to stop him from getting to the bottom of things. Rumour had it that that George's friend John had filed a complaint with the BC Ombudsman, after the bishop had fired him—not long before he died.

Finally, Apin got the juicy details from a friend who preferred to attend mass at the cathedral rather than the parochial Holy Name of Mary Church. George's partner was some kind of administrative assistant at the diocesan office. Apin said to his friend, "Some say he resigned."

His friend burst out laughing. "Resigned? Are you kidding? The guy was fired."

"Really? Why?" Apin couldn't keep the excitement out of his voice.

"Our bishop doesn't want gays around him. And guess what?"

"What?"

"Around the same time, another parish council let their male secretary go, too."

Now Apin seized his chance with Carmelita. "So the firing of staff, it's true?"

"How should I know?" Carmelita retorted. "At the time, I was travelling in Europe with Papa, who needed a change. He was depressed after my mother died. Papa wanted to go back to the Philippines. My sister and I were so worried. We convinced him to move to Hawaii where some of his fraternity friends had emigrated and were living."

Suddenly, Carmelita stopped talking; she was examining a Nativity painting on the wall. The scene depicted peasants kneeling, adoring the baby Jesus. After a few seconds, she made the sign of the cross. "At home, there were always guests. People would come in, Mama would invite them to the table, or if they couldn't stay, she would give them something to take home."

"My mother did the same." Apin's parents might not have had any money or connections, but they were hospitable, too. "In my family, when there was a funeral, the whole village had to be fed, you know?"

"What's wrong with you?" Carmelita interjected.

Apin didn't hear. He was remembering how reluctant he'd been to leave the farm as a child because the other boys made fun of him and pushed him around. For a number of years, he had stayed with an aunt whose house was close to the school, and walked to class. The bullying continued. The same thing happened when he went to Iloilo to study nursing: the head nurse hated his guts and made his life hell.

Once in Canada, Apin's life took a different turn. By then he had accepted that he liked men, and he was able to have all the sex he longed for. Then he got sick, with a fever and aching muscles. He could hardly walk. Terrified, he confided his symptoms to Carmelita. She told him to get tested for AIDS, and when he was speechless with shock, she added, "Don't look at me like an idiot, I am a nurse."

"So what?"

Carmelita had slapped his face, yelling, "Show some respect, young man!"

By the grace of God it wasn't AIDS, but rheumatism. Nevertheless, Carmelita's slap still burned. Who did she think she was?

Apin volunteered at the Bayanihan Community Centre, serving food and taking photographs of the various events held there, then posting them on Facebook.

That summer, the Philippine Madrigal Singers came to Victoria and Apin attended the concert at the Royal McPherson Theatre. He photographed the ladies in their colourful gowns with butterfly sleeves and the handsome men, all wearing *barongs*. After the concert, the president of the Victoria Philippines Association invited Carmelita, the association's founder, up on stage to be photographed with the choirmaster and the singers. She insisted on having George with her.

After the photo session, Apin invited George to the monthly lunch at the Bayanihan Centre the following Sunday. "Do you like Filipino cooking?" he asked.

George laughed. Pointing at Carmelita, who was following the conversation, he remarked, "She trained me to like it."

When he saw George arrive at the centre that Sunday, Apin came over. "Glad you could come!" He introduced George to his sisters, their husbands and their children.

George asked Apin, "Do you have a wife?"

"No. I'm looking for a husband," Apin replied with a laugh.

The two men agreed to meet for coffee.

Chapter Eleven

In mid-October, George was in the room when Carmelita received the good news from her oncologist: "You can go to Hawaii during the holidays."

"Did you hear, George?" Carmelita smiled, then ventured, "Could I go to the Holy Land?"

The oncologist shook her head. "In your condition, it's too risky. Hawaii's safe, as long as you go with a companion."

Carmelita turned to George. "I suppose you're too busy, as usual." George rolled his eyes. "I will ask my nephew Marty. I will take a travel insurance coverage, too."

"That would be wise," her oncologist said, nodding.

As expected, the old Filipina had more to say. "Quite expensive, if you ask me. My husband and I always took insurance when we travelled to Hawaii. He refused to come with me to Europe. He could still remember the horrors of World War Two."

✱

The news of Carmelita's travel plans spread quickly through the Filipino community. One day, her sister Soledad's phone rang. It was Lilia Arcilla. As soon as Lilia hung up, Soledad phoned her older sister in Victoria.

"Good morning," Carmelita answered.

"Good morning to you, too," Soledad said. She got right to the point. "If your doctor says it's okay for you to travel, I guess you don't need my advice."

"Remember, you are not my mother." Carmelita retorted.

"I am sure you will find someone in the parish to go with you," Soledad resumed. She wanted to help her sister, not argue with her.

Carmelita reacted. "What's wrong with asking Marty?"

Soledad remained silent. Then, keeping her voice neutral, she said, "It would be so much easier if you would come and live with us in Vancouver."

"I already told you: I am going to die in the house that my husband built for me," Carmelita declared. "Anyway, all the parish people are busy. Mary Hendricks has her children coming home for Christmas, so I can't ask her."

"What about the church secretary? What's her name?"

"How many times do I have to tell you?" Carmelita sighed heavily. "Her name is Jeanne."

"So...?" Soledad asked.

"So what?"

"Couldn't she go with you?"

"She and her husband are spending Christmas and the New Year on Salt Spring Island looking after their son's horses. The son and his wife are going to Mexico again."

Soledad couldn't help herself; she burst into tears and said, "I worry about you."

"I am fine, I am surrounded by people." Stressing every word, Carmelita said, "Do you understand what I am saying, Sol?"

"You are my only sister."

"Every day I drink four litres of the alkaline water you recommended. It's amazing! It does me good, I can feel it."

Soledad was pleased. She was a firm believer. "Alkaline water is what you need in your condition; it is essential. Acidity in the body is so bad for cancer."

"I am a nurse, Sol, remember?"

Soledad remained silent for a few seconds. "So explain to me why you don't have any energy!"

"If you keep that tone of voice..."

"Are you taking the dietary supplements I sent you? You never told me. "

"I have so many pills to take," Carmelita replied with a sigh. "I have no room left in my stomach for food."

"I am not saying that the doctors in Victoria are not good, but a second opinion might be wise."

"Why should I go to Vancouver? I am fine."

"I worry about you. With all the old stuff in your place, I wouldn't be surprised you have fungus in the house."

"Fungi," Carmelita corrected her.

"You see how you are? You still treat me as if I were a child."

"Let's not fight," Carmelita said. "Anyway, I wouldn't be able to stand the noise and the pollution." She paused. "And the church is too far."

Soledad counterattacked. "The message is clear to me. You prefer strangers to your own family!"

"I need to rest. I will call you back."

Realizing that Carmelita had hung up on her, Soledad blew out a frustrated breath as she walked into the living room, where her cousin Ruby was watching TV.

"How is *Ate*?" Ruby asked.

Soledad replied, "I am so upset. I need to talk. Can you please turn off the TV?"

Chapter Twelve

Marty had his coat on, his backpack over his shoulder and was leaving the house when the phone rang. He rushed to pick up.

"Marty, what are you doing there?" It was his aunt from Victoria. "Are you sick?"

"Mom's still in bed. I was going to call you."

"Let me talk first. Are you still coming to see me?"

"I can't this weekend, *Tita*. I'm sorry."

"What's the problem with you?" His aunt sounded irritated.

"I'm making up my students' report cards."

"Are you paid overtime for the work on weekends?"

"It's part of my job."

His aunt said, "You should do something else. You are a professional, sweetheart, don't forget."

"What's wrong with being a teacher? It's better than the future Dad had in mind for me, working with him in the business."

"Let's not talk about the company. I'll get upset. Anyway, would you like to go to Honolulu for Christmas?"

Surprised, Marty asked, "Have you talked to Mom about this?"

"I am old enough to run my own life, young man."

"I didn't mean to upset you, *Tita.*"

"What's the reason for not coming this time?" his aunt asked, changing direction as she often did. "What's so important, can you tell me?"

"I already told you, *Tita.* The report cards."

"You and I will stay with Josefine."

"You mean in Hawaii, right? I don't know her."

"She was an associate of your father and Uncle Max way, way back. Go now, you will be late."

"Bye, *Tita*, I'll tell Mom you—" His aunt had already hung up.

A week before Christmas, Carmelita and Marty were at the Victoria airport, waiting for their WestJet flight to Honolulu.

"*Tita*, we're getting the VIP treatment," Marty remarked, as an airline staffer came over to them, saying there would be someone to help them board the plane.

"It's because we requested a wheelchair," his aunt whispered to him.

Marty laughed. "Next time I travel, I'll request one for myself."

"Where would you like to go?"

Marty thought for a second. "I wish I knew."

"Now is the time for you to travel, while you are still young. Go to Europe."

"I don't know what Mom would say."

"Or, simply, go to the Philippines." His aunt shook her head. "Don't worry about your mother; she can go and visit you," she added, while massaging her legs.

"Are you okay, *Tita*?"

"I am fine, don't worry."

"You sure?"

"I am sure." Carmelita took her nephew's arm. "You are sweating, sweetheart. I think that you worry too much, like your mother."

As soon as their flight was announced, a staff member came over to collect their carry-on luggage. Carmelita's wheelchair was surrounded by colourful bags in all shapes and sizes. He joked, "You're a living Christmas tree, with all the bells and whistles!"

"They are presents to my niece and my friends at St. Philomena Church," Carmelita said.

The man set about consolidating everything into two bags. "Don't want you to get in trouble for having too many carry-on items, do we?" he said with a smile. He grasped the handles of the wheelchair and their little procession moved into the corridor leading to the plane. Marty carried both bags. He felt like a beast of burden, and joked, "I'm your *carabao, Tita*."

As they made their way through the passengers at Honolulu International Airport, Carmelita said, "There she is!" Josefine Estrera spotted them at the same time and signalled that they should stay where they were. They could barely see Josefine as she threaded her way toward them through the sea of travellers and greeters.

"It's so nice of you to pick us up," his aunt said as the two women hugged.

Josefine smiled, "You look well, *Manang*. I wasn't sure..."

"The pain is under control."

"Was the trip tiring? You can take a nap when we get home."

Carmelita shook her head vigorously. "Let's eat first."

"Okay, but I need to go to bed early. I'm in charge of preparing food tomorrow at St. Philomena—."

"Tomorrow is day six of the Misa de Gallo," Carmelita said to Marty. "We have to get up at four o'clock for the five a.m. mass."

"We're going to be jet-lagged. Can't we skip tomorrow, *Tita*?"

There was a knock at Marty's door. "It's four o'clock, Marty. Time to get up," his aunt said.

Marty groaned. "The mass isn't till five," he said.

"Your aunt Josefine needs our help."

"Okay, but I need a shower."

"Hurry. Josefine is waiting outside."

✳

Sitting in Josefine's minivan, Marty asked, "Why is it called Misa de Gallo?"

His aunt was shocked. "Where is your Spanish, Marty?"

Josefine smiled at Marty in the rear view mirror. "It's Rooster's Mass in English. There are nine days of dawn masses leading up to Christmas. In 1669, the Pope ordered that the mass be heard before sunrise since it was harvest season in the Philippines. The farmers needed to be in the fields before the midday heat."

The city of Honolulu was still dark when they arrived at St. Philomena Church, but there were already several cars parked at the back of the white adobe structure. Marty got out and grabbed some of the plastic bags that were piled up in the back of the minivan.

"Out of curiosity, how many people are you expecting?" Marty asked Josefine.

"Approximately one hundred and fifty. Yesterday we had one hundred and thirty-five."

As soon as they saw Carmelita enter the church hall on Marty's arm, several volunteers came forward to hug her. "So glad to see you," one said. Another woman offered her condolences. "We heard about the loss of Max!"

Carmelita made the introductions. "This is Marty, my sister's oldest son. My sister lost her husband too, not long ago. That's why she is not here with us. I promised to give her regards."

She shuffled among the long and narrow tables, leaning heavily on Marty's arm as well as her cane. More than once she muttered, "Five years. It has been five years since I was here."

Anicia Solinap, in charge of the liturgy at the church, invited Carmelita and Marty to her birthday party later on that day. "We will pick you between five and six p.m. and take you to the restaurant," she said.

Agnes Estologa, visibly moved, remarked, "If you are not too tired."

Carmelita announced, "My nephew will help you; just tell him what he has to do." Noticing that members of the Misa de Gallo committee were draping tablecloths over the tables, she said to Marty, "Can you help them place a bouquet of flowers on each of the tables?"

The two visitors from Canada entered the church and walked up to the front row. One of the pews bore a card labelled Ate *Carmelita and family*. Marty helped his aunt kneel. She joined her hands and closed her eyes, her lips moving as she prayed. Marty looked around and noticed the band at the right side of the altar; the musicians were going through their scores and murmuring to each other.

"How are you, my dear?"

Carmelita jumped, then recognized the old friend who had softly tapped her shoulder, "*Manang* Rita! Marty, help me, please."

Rita Walter objected. "What are you doing? Don't get up."

Carmelita got to her feet and greeted the other woman. Rita looked at Marty, "And who is this handsome young man?"

"My nephew Marty, Soledad's oldest son."

Rita's face saddened. "Your aunt told me about your father, Marty. I would have liked to go to the funeral but Josefine couldn't take days off to come with me. I knew your father well."

Carmelita invited her friend to sit beside her. "How is Jack, *manang*?"

"More stubborn than ever," Rita replied with a shrug. She laughed. "He plays golf and that's it."

"How is your daughter?"

"Still living in Las Vegas."

Manang Rita squeezed Carmelita's hand and whispered, "You look well. Josefine told me the bad news. I hope you don't mind."

"Of course not. There is nothing to hide."

The two old friends began sharing memories. Max would sunbathe on Waikiki beach or drink with his business acquaintances and friends at the Sheraton Hotel's beachside bar, while the two women drove around Honolulu, sightseeing and shopping.

"Speaking of the hotel," Rita said, "If you don't have other plans, we could go to the Sheraton for lunch."

Carmelita touched Marty's arm, "Your uncle and I always stayed at the Sheraton when we came to visit Papa."

"Let me warn you, the place has changed a lot since your time. We will go tomorrow. I will pick up the two of you."

Without looking at her nephew, Marty's aunt said, "Wait till you see *manang's* car. Do you still have the Lincoln Continental?"

Manang exclaimed, "Of course! There is no better car." She laughed.

The women laughed and chatted as if the intervening years were only days. Rita looked to be about ten years older than his aunt. He sensed some complicity between the proper, convent-school-educated Carmelita and wild Rita.

"Jack was quite a handsome man back then," Rita said, sighing happily. "He is a Native Hawaiian, you see. This is what they do, if you know what I mean." She winked at Marty.

"*Manang*," Carmelita said, her hand to her mouth. "We are in church."

"I didn't invent sex," Rita said. She pointed toward the altar. "He did."

Marty chuckled softly. "When's the last time you two saw each other?"

"After Papa's death, Max and I never came back," his aunt replied.

Manang Rita shook her head. "Don't forget that I visited you in Victoria once."

Carmelita smiled. "I completely forgot. It was so kind of you to come. You were with Josefine."

Rita grinned. "Yes, and you wanted her to meet a certain bachelor friend of yours. We met a lot of your friends at your place."

Carmelita beamed. "Father Al was at the dinner, and Jeanne and Paul." She paused. "George was there, too."

Rita exclaimed, "That's his name! Do you still see him?"

Carmelita said, "I don't know what I would do without him. I never had a brother, you see."

Marty interjected, "He is *Tita's* angel." He turned to his aunt. "Wait, were you trying to hook Auntie Josefine up with George?"

"What's wrong with that?" Carmelita looked at her nephew with a stern expression.

Just then the priest, in black cassock and white surplice, appeared at the back of the church. He was flanked by four altar boys bearing lighted candles. As the band struck up, they walked up the aisle and the congregation stood.

Marty attended all the remaining Misa de Gallo masses with his aunt. He was continually swept up in helping the church committees, comprised mostly of women in their sixties and seventies. One of them welcomed him and his aunt with *lei* made of dark fluorescent blue beans the size of Marty's thumb. As she placed the garland around his neck, the woman asked Marty, "Your wife couldn't come with you?"

"I'm not married."

The woman apologized for being nosy. "You are still young." Another parishioner who was listening took up the baton. "Don't you like children?"

Thanks to his aunt, Marty caught up with old friends and acquaintances he used to play with during Christmas holidays. His cousin Jilbert had become a professional photographer and his friend Benjie was now working for an international consulting company.

One day, while they were at Jilbert's parents' house, Marty's cousin showed him albums of photos he'd taken for a wedding in the Philippines the year before. The bride was born in Hawaii and the boy was from Cebu. "Marisol and I were classmates," Jilbert explained. "She asked me to be their photographer."

Sitting next to Marty, his aunt Carmelita became interested into the photographs. She kept asking, "Who is this one? Who's that one?" She suddenly recognized a face. "Esperanza is fat."

"Don't say that, *Tita,*" Marty objected.

"In the Philippines this is a compliment."

Tita Rosemary, Jilbert's mother, added, "You won't believe it, *Manang*, but she still drives her big red Mercedes."

"Why shouldn't she?" Carmelita reacted. "She is the same age as me."

Marty was going through the pages of the first album documenting the wedding. One photo showed six pairs of sponsors. Another image showed two secondary sponsors – one to hold the traditional cord and the second, the veil. "A marriage is taken pretty seriously, isn't it?" he commented.

"Yeah, as you know, Filipinos spend a lot of money on weddings," Jilbert said with a laugh.

Marty said, "When my younger brother Tomas got married, we had two hundred and fifty guests."

"I've seen bigger ones than that," the photographer said. "Still, you can't invite everyone."

When she heard that the wedding had taken place in Santa Cruz, where the bride's family lived, Carmelita remarked, "We have relatives there."

"Where's Santa Cruz, *Tita?*" Marty asked.

"In Laguna." She sighed and said to the others, "He doesn't know his ancestors' country."

A woman named Amelia had joined the group. "My own husband never comes with me when I go to the Philippines, nor my children," she said. "Too much pollution, they say."

Carmelita looked Marty in the eye and, waved her finger under her nephew's nose. "If I were not sick, I would take you to the Philippines."

"Why don't you?" Rita asked.

Slightly embarrassed, Carmelita whispered, "They don't want me to travel that far."

Seeing that Marty's attention had shifted, Jilbert asked, "Have you had enough of the albums?"

Marty said, "Sorry, we got off on a tangent. So all the guests flew to the Philippines?"

"We almost filled up the plane," his cousin replied with a smile. "I don't know about you, but I like Filipino food."

"Look at me," Marty said, pointed at his protruding stomach. "This isn't a beer belly, believe me."

"Man, you should have seen it! I don't know how many pigs they slaughtered for the feast. A caterer took care of everything so no one would get upset that they weren't asked to cook anything. Do you miss the Philippines?"

Marty said, "I was not born there." He paused. "Maybe I should go, you know, reconnect with my roots."

"Do you want to hear the beautiful story of Rio and Marisol?" *Tita* Rosemary interjected, her voice animated. She turned to Marty. "They had a long-distance relationship on the Internet for four years. They met only once and got married!"

"Only once?" Marty asked.

"Yes, sweetheart," Rosemary replied, "They fell in love just like that!"

"What about planning the wedding?" Marty laughed. "Did they do that over the Internet, too?"

With her hand on Marty's arm, Rosemary said, "Yes. The bride in Honolulu, the groom's older sister in the Philippines, they planned the whole ceremony according to tradition: the choice of sponsors, the list of guests, the music at the church and the reception."

"Where are they living now?" Marty asked.

Jilbert shook his head. "Marisol came back alone. She had to apply to sponsor her husband."

"So what happens next?" Marty asked.

Tita Rosemary's expression turned sad. "All that money! It goes to lawyers, immigration consultants and the government before Rio and Marisol can be together and start a family. It should be simple, right? She wants to sponsor her own husband. They are married. Life is not always fair, if you ask me."

Marty went back to the photo albums. There was one for the church ceremony and another depicting the reception. It was as if the images—young men and women with their arms around each other, uncles and aunties smiling with satisfaction, the bride, the groom—were shouting at him: *What are you waiting for?*

Distraught with envy, Marty was close to tears. He excused himself and headed for the washroom.

Marty felt dampness under his armpits. He slid his hand under his shirt and then sniffed his fingers, grimacing at the scent.

Later that day, he had no qualms mentioning the sweating to his aunt, since she'd brought it up at the airport. She repeated her diagnosis: "You worry too much, sweetheart."

"Sandy tells me the same thing."

His aunt sighed. "This morning, at the church, I gave money to Father Efren for a mass to Tomas's and Sandy's intentions."

"For what, *Tita?*"

"You know what I mean," Carmelita replied, without looking at her nephew.

✱

Ten days later, Josefine drove her guests back to the airport. Marty watched as she hugged his aunt with more affection than before. *She knows this is probably be the last time they'll see each other.*

As soon as she sat on the plane, Carmelita took Marty's hand. "Let's pray to God for a safe journey home." She closed her eyes. The two passengers recited in unison, "Hail Mary..."

Hearing rustling from the row ahead of them, Marty opened one eye to see a little girl, her face squeezed between the seats, watching them.

✳

The following Saturday, Marty and Sandy stood on the stage of the reception hall at St. Patrick's Church on Main Street in Vancouver. They were to perform for that day's wedding, but the other members of their ensemble had yet to arrive. The group was in demand, playing for Filipino weddings, graduations and other events at community centres and outdoor venues.

Relatives and friends added final touches to the decorations under the supervision of the mothers of the bride and groom, who were double-checking the names on the place cards.

As they waited, Marty gave his sister-in-law a report on his Hawaii trip. "I swear, Sandy, every single one of *Tita* Carmelita's friends asked me when I was going to get married. What should I do?"

"Don't ask me, you know the answer to that." Sandy never beat around the bush. "Sooner or later, you're going to have to tell your mother."

Whenever Marty worried about something and felt at loss, he would call 911 Sandy. They had known each other since they were born. In their teens they used to exchange love letters. Soon enough though, Sandy realized that Marty was different from his younger brother and the other boys in the band they had formed a few years earlier. They stayed friends and regularly shared their plans for the future.

"What's wrong with me?" Marty asked.

"There's nothing wrong with you," Sandy began. Just then, they saw Romeo, their violinist, and their cellist, Lewis, approaching the stage. Sandy whispered to Marty, "We'll talk about it later."

Marty nodded. He helped carry Sandy's harp onto the stage. The players took their places, tuned their instruments and warmed up with the opening bars of Mendelssohn's *Wedding March*.

The guests were mingling, waiting to take their seats for the ceremony. The women and girls wore formal gowns, while the majority of the men and boys were dressed in the traditional *barong*, some with a T-shirt underneath. Others wore white shirts with the collar buttoned up. The groom was wearing a white suit with a pink necktie.

"Wait till you see the bride's dress," Sandy whispered in Marty's ear.

"You've seen it?"

Sandy giggled. "The bride's sister is a friend of mine. How do you think we got this gig? Anyway, she showed it to me and said, 'Don't tell my sister, she'll kill me.'"

Marty kept an eye on the door through which the bride was to appear. When his younger brother Tomas got married, his mother had cried a lot, but their father had been overjoyed. The bride was an only child and her father owned a Pharma-Shop franchise. Tomas, a pharmacist, was already an associate in his father-in-law's business, and hints had been dropped that he could take over the franchise when the older man retired or get a franchise of his own.

As soon as the bride, her parents, and all the sponsors made their entrance, a family member standing in the wings gave the signal and the musicians began to play.

Chapter Thirteen

Argie Saldua's husband Manuel invited nearly a hundred people to celebrate her fiftieth birthday in February. Manuel and the children had spent weeks secretly preparing a slideshow to honour Argie. It was set up to run in a continuous loop on the living room TV screen. Manuel showed it to his wife the night before the party, which was just as well, as Argie was moved to tears. There was a blurry picture of herself as a baby lying on a small blanket, her buttocks exposed; and several pictures of her parents. Her father had died so young! Also, there was her mother at her seventieth birthday party, her hair styled for the occasion; Argie on the beach at thirteen; shots of her and Manuel when they were courting; and of course, their wedding photos.

The slideshow included an image of Argie in a classroom, taken in the Philippines when she had just started teaching accounting courses. Manuel couldn't remember who the photographer was. "Probably that student who was crazy about you."

"Mom, you never told us!" her daughter Doreen teased.

Laughing, Argie asked her husband to move on to the next slide. Argie was leaning against the trunk of a tree, wearing a body-hugging dress and showing a lot of cleavage. Her son Tony was amazed. "Mom, you look like a movie star!"

Argie's tears continued to flow. Manuel held her hand and said, "You haven't changed a bit, honey. You're as beautiful as ever."

"Dad, what's wrong with Mom?" Doreen asked.

"I'm okay," Argie assured her. She wiped her tears and hugged her family.

The next day, the front doorbell never stopped ringing. There was so much food—both Filipino and Canadian dishes—the table surfaces were barely visible. Carmelita was there with George, her constant companion these days.

"When she opened the door, I didn't recognize her," Carmelita said to Argie.

Argie knew Carmelita was referring to Doreen, who had begun wearing makeup. "All her friends go to school that way."

"That's no reason." The old Filipina shook her head. "Doreen should focus on her studies."

Two of Argie's high school classmates entered the house. Argie was overjoyed, as she hadn't seen them for twenty years, even though they had lived in Vancouver for most of that time.

"How did you reconnect?" George asked, after the women finished catching up.

"On Facebook," Argie replied. "It was pure luck."

"And how did you come to know Carmelita?" George asked.

"Whenever she entertained, before her cancer, she called all the women of the community to do some cooking for her. She had a nickname for me: *the Short One*. I made whatever she wanted. Sometimes I had to take a day off," she said with a laugh. "*Ate* would set the table with expensive plates and cutlery from Europe. After the guests left, Teresita and I would stay and clear the table, do the dishes and make sure her house was back to normal. Since we came to Canada, she has always been kind to me and the children, so I was glad to help."

Argie didn't mind chatting with George, but like other Filipinos in the parish, she felt it was a family's responsibility to care for its loved ones. The day George called her to ask for help in finding a Filipina live-in companion for Carmelita, Argie said, "You will find no one who will do it for free."

"Just for a few hours, and not every day."

To which Argie had replied, "Canadians are different."

Now she moved away and muttered to her husband, "When I think of *Ate*, my heart hurts. I can't look at her."

"Don't look at her, then," her husband replied.

"She must feel so lonely."

Shortly after, Carmelita and George walked to the door. George was carrying a bag of Styrofoam containers in each hand. Argie accompanied Carmelita, stroking her back all the way to the car. As George held open the passenger door, Argie said, "You need to eat, *Ate*."

Back in the house, Argie went to have a quick word with her daughter. "When you go to church, don't wear any makeup."

Doreen looked at her mother, her eyes wide open, "Why not?"

"Out of respect, Doreen. You know how *Ate* is."

"I don't care what she thinks!" Doreen replied.

Chapter Fourteen

Father Al parked in Carmelita's driveway and climbed the steps to her front porch. He transferred all the jugs he was carrying to his left hand and rang the doorbell. He was there to refill the jugs with alkaline water from her kitchen tap.

The day Carmelita was diagnosed with cancer, her sister Soledad ordered a Japanese water filtration system for her and convinced her to use it exclusively. "You just push a button to get the right pH," she explained. Carmelita soon became an evangelist for alkaline water. "Too much acid in one's body is not good," she would say. She had issued a standing invitation to everyone she knew to bring empty containers and fill them with tap water that had gone through the ionization process.

Carmelita learned that Father Al didn't have any containers, so she bought him several four-litre jugs, enough to hold two weeks of drinking water.

"I am coming, don't go away," he heard through the door. Several minutes passed before his parishioner peered through the curtains, then opened the door.

"Good morning, Father. I've just made coffee, would you like some?" She was having obvious difficulty walking. In the kitchen, she said to him, "Please, have a seat. One or two sugars, Father?"

The priest lifted a stack of magazines from a chair and settled at the table. He looked around the room. The counters were piled with jars of coconut oil, canisters, utensils in stainless steel vessels, open recipe books and all manner of general clutter. He marvelled that she ever found anything in all that mess. *But what a wonderful person she is!*

"This is so kind of you, Carmelita," Father Al said as she joined him.

"Would you like some cake, Father?"

The priest looked at the Black Forest cake covered with a two-inch layer of icing.

"I had never seen icing before I went to the seminary," Father Al said. "A small portion, just to taste, please. I just had my lunch."

"You can always come back again," Carmelita said with a smile.

"My father, his father and his grandfather were all fishermen, like Jesus's disciples."

Carmelita poured, not the slightest tremor in the hand holding the coffee urn.

"Fishermen in Newfoundland are as poor as ever, you know."

"Same thing in the Philippines, Father."

"In the old days, Newfoundlanders ate cod day after day. I shared a room with my brothers. In the winter, I would wake in the middle of the night to see the walls covered in frost! We were three boys to a bed, shivering all night. None of us wanted to take the side closest to the wall."

Father Al ate the last bite of cake and Carmelita immediately offered him more. He grinned and said, "Another thin slice, then. Thank you."

Shortly after, Father Al rose, carrying his containers to the water filter, a white box next to the kitchen sink. Pipes connected the filter to the tap.

"Let me help you," Carmelita said, holding on to the edge of the table as she stood.

"My dear Carmelita, my mind seems clearer after I drink your water."

"It helps eliminates the toxins. Wilma and Ron are coming tomorrow to get some water."

"Amazing, quite amazing." Father Al tightened the cap on the second jug. "I have to go, my dear."

"You are like George, always in a rush." Carmelita picked up two grocery bags by the door and insisted on accompanying the priest out of the house, deploring the fact that she could no longer carry the full jugs. "I am not as strong as I used to be, Father."

Father Al shook his head. "This is not what I see, my friend," he said as he placed the jugs in the trunk of his car. Carmelita handed him one of the bags, which turned out to be full of Ambrosia apples. "These are my favourites, thank you!" he exclaimed. The second bag contained six frozen chicken pies. "You are too generous, my dear. I will have one tonight for dinner."

"One is not enough, Father. You should have two."

Women had served Father Al all his life: first his mother, then the nuns at the seminary. After he graduated, there was always a good Newfoundland widow to cook and clean for him and do his laundry. Last year, the Catholic Women's League treated him to a birthday lunch at Il Terrazzo. He was grateful, but found the place a bit fancy for his taste.

Father Al made the sign of the cross before starting up his car. Backing up, he saw George waving at him. He rolled down the car window. "Visiting our friend?"

George shook hands with Father Al and said, "I'm driving Carmelita to an appointment at the cancer clinic."

Father Al was surprised. "She didn't tell me. Oh dear, I may have stayed too long." Once again, the priest realized that he was not as perceptive as he should be. All he knew was what people confided to him in the confessional.

The following day, Wilma Hunter gathered her empty containers and took them to the car. Before leaving, Wilma decided to check on Kristel. The girl was becoming more unpredictable by the day. Kristel was a permanent reminder of their only child Ben, who had died five years earlier.

When he met Kristel's mother, their son's previously stable, normal life descended into chaos. They lost touch with him until the RCMP turned up at their door to inform them that their son was in hospital in a drug-induced coma. She and Ron kept vigil by his bedside. There was no sign of his partner. A day later, their son died.

His partner showed up two days after that, hollow-eyed and shaking, a grubby seven-year-old girl hiding behind her. "I'm leaving for Saskatchewan, but I can't take the kid. Her name's Kristel." Wilma's heart went out to the child and they took her in willingly, but they were both in their seventies and not as strong as they used to be.

It was late, past noon already, and Kristel hadn't emerged from her bedroom. "Aren't you going to eat something, dear?" Wilma spoke through the closed door.

"Go away!" Kristel screamed. "I hate you!" The words were a knife to Wilma's heart, and she sank to her knees in the hallway.

Ron found her there, eyes closed, praying. "What are you doing? I thought we were going out to get some water." He put his arm around his wife's shoulders.

"I'm praying for the repose of Ben's soul."

Ron knocked on the bedroom. "Come and eat your lunch, Kristel. You can't stay in there all day."

"Get lost!" Something heavy thudded against the inside of the door.

Ron took his wife's arm. "Let's go, love. Carmelita's expecting us." He helped her up.

In the car, Wilma asked her husband, "Are you keeping something from me? You've been so quiet since your appointment last week. When you came out of his office, I heard the doctor say he was worried about you."

Ron leaned his head against the headrest. "I haven't had the courage to tell you."

Wilma became agitated. "What is it? What's wrong?"

"The doctor says I have lung cancer. How can that be? I've never smoked a day in my life."

Wilma burst into tears as Ron continued. "I've been praying every day that he's mistaken."

The couple held hands. "It's a good thing we're drinking the water," Ron said. "It's supposed to be good for seniors like us. Carmelita told me they've used it in Japan for thirty years. People with cancer have been cured, she says. She's had cancer for three years and she still drives."

Wilma stared out the passenger window. *How could I possibly cope with Kristel without him?*

As soon as Wilma entered Carmelita's, she confided to the Filipina, "Our granddaughter is barely eating. She thinks she's fat."

Carmelita listened to Wilma, but she was scrutinizing Ron's face as he took their containers to the sink. He hit the power switch on the filter and pushed the button to select the pH level. When the mechanical voice announced, "pH level 9.5," Ron inserted the white plastic tube into one of the jugs and turned on the cold water tap.

Wilma sat with Carmelita at the dining room table. "I was telling Ron that it's all those television shows, especially those dreadful reality programs, where all the women are skinny."

As Wilma launched into a comparison of Catholic schools in Canada and England, where she and Ron were from, her husband placed the last container by the door and joined them at the table. "The quality of education was better at home, I dare say," Wilma said.

She noticed Carmelita watching Ron. "You know, don't you?" she said. Carmelita admitted that Ron had confided in her after mass one Sunday. "I have been praying for him ever since."

Chapter Fifteen

"Mother, I love your hair." Darlene Simonson was busy aligning her three plastic jugs on Carmelita's kitchen counter.

Carmelita called everyone niece, cousin, aunt or mother. *It's part of their culture, I guess.*

When Darlene's ex had passed away, she didn't bother spreading the news around about a man she hadn't seen for nearly a quarter of a century. Why would she? *She* wasn't his widow.

"Does your hairdresser make home calls?" Carmelita asked.

"Sorry, my mind was elsewhere. I'll ask her." Darlene let out a deep sigh. She wished that this could be the last episode of a series that had run for far too long. "My car needs repairs, again."

"Come and sit." Carmelita pointed at the cookies on a plate. "Someone brought them yesterday."

Darlene shook her head. "Thanks, but I'm not hungry."

She turned off the water filter and went to join Carmelita who, she suddenly realized, had shrunk even more over the past six months. The cancer was taking its toll.

The two women had served on the parish council together for more than twenty years. Quite often it seemed they were the only ones with any money sense—or common sense in general.

"Do you remember the day you banged the table with your fist, when the council didn't want to accept the pews the Esquimalt base commander wanted to donate to us?" she asked her old friend.

Carmelita laughed. "I told the people around the table, 'If you refuse, I will purchase the benches myself, with my own money!' Then some parishioners complained that the Protestant benches were not as comfortable as the Catholic ones. You and I applied for government funds to build the new community hall. Thanks to us, the church always paid its debts…"

Darlene was only half listening at this point. Carmelita touched her friend's hand. "What is it, Mother?"

Darlene awoke. "He won't give me money."

"Who?"

"My son! When I think of all the money I've given him since he was a child."

Carmelita was aware of how hard Darlene had struggled to raise her child by herself. "You should be proud of yourself. He is now a successful business man."

Darlene said, "Last year, at Christmas, he asked if I could pay some of his daughter's university fees."

"She's just a child!" Carmelita interjected.

"Not anymore, she's taller than her father."

"I remember what a doll she was, and so well-behaved." Carmelita smiled.

The coffee was fresh, and when Carmelita again offered cookies and ice cream, Darlene repeated that she wasn't hungry. She felt tears well up.

"What's wrong with your car?" Carmelita asked.

"They've had to tow it to the garage twice in two months because it wouldn't start. Once it was in the parking lot of the parish church. I was so embarrassed! I need a new car, and my son won't help me. He's threatened to take my driver's licence away."

"Is this a good idea, Mother?"

Darlene said nothing.

"What about your ears?"

"I can't hear as well as I used to, I'll grant you that, but I can still drive. Look at you, you're still driving." Noticing Carmelita's expression, Darlene added, "I'm not stupid. I never drive at night, for instance. But I need to be able to get the bank, go shopping and visit my friends when I want to. Is that asking too much? Can you loan me the money?"

"Let me think about it. I'll let you know in a day or so."

That was not the answer Darlene had been hoping for. On her way to her old friend's house, she'd been confident that Carmelita would say, as she always had over the years, "How much do you need?" Darlene had always managed to pay her back; she'd made certain of that.

The bank had already turned her down. If her best friend said no, she would have to use her savings again or go to a casino. It would not be the first time. She had been through worse. "He's not going to stop me," she said aloud.

Chapter Sixteen

In March, Carmelita called George to report that she had been receiving phone calls at seven in the morning. "Every day, they call me."

"Have you been hanging up?"

"I told him, 'Don't call me when I am resting,' and I said it takes time for my medication to take effect."

"Don't answer when the phone rings in the morning."

"'I am sick,' I said. 'I don't travel alone anymore.'"

"Carmelita, nobody you know would call you at seven o'clock. Your sister wouldn't; I wouldn't."

Carmelita wasn't listening. "He couldn't say my name correctly. 'My name is Tauber,' I said. 'Do you want me to spell it for you?' I said '*T* as in Toronto, *R* like Romeo...' Then the caller asked me to write down a number and call him right back—"

"You must never do that, never!" George interrupted her.

"The reception was fine. Why would I need to call him back?"

"If you do, you'll be billed for long-distance calls that you never made."

"I said, 'I can't do it now, there is someone knocking at my door.'"

"Good for you. Was that true?"

"I said, 'I have to go. Call me another time, but not when I am resting.' He agreed."

"Who was at the door?"

"It was Mother."

"Who?"

"You know, Darlene Simonson. I was so pleased to see her. Are you coming today?"

"Did I say I would? I don't remember."

"You have too many things on your mind, professor. Don't forget to bring your plastic jugs for the alkaline water."

"Right. The miracle water, can't miss that," George teased.

"There are times I would like to punch you! Miracles happen only with God's will."

George knew that Carmelita was enjoying the steady stream of visitors. For months, parishioners and friends had been making the pilgrimage to refill their water jugs and to check on the old Filipina. The visits kept Carmelita's mind off her illness and gave her a chance to dispense medical and personal advice, however unsolicited.

Chapter Seventeen

How can human beings forget that life comes with death? George wondered. *We start dying the moment we're born.* Carmelita's cozy childhood, her marriage, her globetrotting, her good works in Victoria—it was all vanishing, along with her awareness of her situation. More than once, visitors left her house wondering whether she'd been told she had cancer. When she couldn't perform a task or remember someone's name, she would say, "What's wrong with me?"

George was often around as the visitors came and went, but their numbers diminished as the weeks went by. George wondered if she even realized that some of her friends could no longer bear to be around her, watching her die.

Because of the morphine she was taking three times a day, her brain couldn't always respond to what was being asked of it. She was repeating herself even more often. "In Vienna, Max's friends were so good to me. Oh, George, I was in such pain after my fall."

In her mind, the old woman was still on the road, a resilient traveller, but George barely listened anymore.

One day in June, she was marvelling at what a wonderful life she had had. "When I was a nurse, one of my patients wanted to marry me instead of the girl his old mother wanted him to marry. I advised him: 'Don't marry her, just to please your mother.'" She remembered the expensive jewellery her husband had showered her with, including an elegant ring Carmelita said was "worth more than a down payment for a house." She sighed contentedly and said, "Someone should write a book about my life."

Coming back to reality, she noticed the plastic jugs on the kitchen counter. She had put them there for George to fill and take home, but they were still empty. "Why don't you want any water?" she demanded.

"Carmelita, I have my own water filter. It's in my basement. You might not have seen it, but it does exist."

"You are so stubborn." Carmelita sounded exactly like what she was: a dying woman pretending she was still alive and well. "Let's not fight. It's not good in my condition."

George wanted to shake her and shout, *You're not fooling anyone!* He was ready to leave.

"Bye, Carmelita."

"You are forgetting something. Always in a rush!"

To part from the old woman was never an easy operation for George. A new story would be announced, one that would inevitably begin with, "Did I tell you...?" Heidi, her next door neighbour, had sent Finley over to give her a kiss while she was watering the plants on the front deck. "I gave a banana for him and his sister."

George sensed that another story was simmering, ready to boil over. He had to get out of the house, *now!* George's hand was on the doorknob when she said, "You see how you are? You are forgetting the *congee*."

George clicked his heels, saluted and said, "Jawohl!" Carmelita stuck her tongue out at him.

Arguing was a waste of time; there would be no end to it. George opened the fridge and pulled out the pot of *congee*. Because of its fat content, he would probably throw the food away as soon as he got home.

In the past, he used to offer good reasons for not taking the pork and black bean stew, or the sweet rice desserts that had been in her fridge for an indeterminate number of days.

What was behind Carmelita's warm feelings for him? The old woman seemed to see something in him, God only knew what, that she liked or approved of. Was it because he had taken care of John and never talked about it?

George was already in the street when he suddenly remembered the original purpose of his visit. He climbed the steps again and rang the bell, then took out his key and opened her door. "It's me," he called out. "I forgot to tell you something."

Carmelita turned back from the hallway leading to her bedroom. "Why did you come back? Wait, wait I have something else for you." She headed for the kitchen.

"I don't have time. I just wanted to invite you to my house. Remember I mentioned Colin Hong in Vancouver?"

"Of course, he is your friend. He looks after his old mother."

"Right, well, they're coming over next Thursday. Would you like to come for tea?"

"I will bring a cake."

"You don't need to bring anything; I'm inviting you."

"How about some Philippines spring rolls? You like *lumpiya*, don't you? I will get some."

George agreed to the *lumpiya*. "Nothing else, though, okay?"

"Jawohl, professor," she said, grinning.

When he arrived to pick up Carmelita, George saw her on the porch, weeding her flowerpots. He complimented her on her long cotton dress and her enormous hat covered in ribbons and flowers.

"What about my kiss?" she asked with a smile.

George kissed her on both cheeks, the way her husband used to greet female friends.

"I will finally meet your friend Colin."

Carmelita was having trouble getting into his "sports car." George burst out laughing. "What a name for an old American compact car!"

At his house, he helped Carmelita free herself of the seat belt. She tried to lift her feet out of the car, but the floor was below the level of the sidewalk. Frustrated, she snapped, "Keep my car with you! How many times do I have to tell you?"

George helped her through the garden gate and got her settled at the outdoor table he had set earlier. "Thank you. What would I do without you?" Carmelita sighed. She admired the fresh flowers and brightly patterned china as George brought out a vegetarian paté and crackers, and set them next to the *lumpiya*.

Just then they heard, "Mom, we're here." George excused himself and walked back through the gate to greet his guests from the Lower Mainland.

Colin's mother, a frail woman in her mid-nineties, leaned on her son's arm. "Mom, do you remember George?"

"Of course! George from Victoria," Mrs. Hong shouted. There was nothing frail about her voice.

George introduced Colin and his mother to Carmelita. "Nice to meet you," Mrs. Hong said.

Carmelita bowed slightly. "George often talks about you. He tells me that you like flowers."

"Mom, tell Mrs. Tauber about your passion for orchids."

"I order them from Japan," his mother said with pride.

Carmelita hugged Colin, after complimenting him on the way he was holding his mother's arm. "Not everyone knows how," she said.

"If you'll excuse me," said George, "I'll get the tea and everything else."

"Need help?" Colin asked.

"Sure, come on in."

Colin looked out the kitchen window. "Mom's chatting with your friend. I've never seen her talk so easily to a stranger."

"Carmelita is generous with her love."

"Most people are selfish," Colin said, "including me."

"Why do you say that?"

"Everyone tells me how wonderful it is that I look after my mother, but honestly? I feel like a prisoner who can't wait to get out of jail. Isn't that awful?"

"No, not at all," George said quietly.

Neither woman wanted the paté and crackers or the *lumpiya*, but brightened up when George appeared with a glazed lemon cake with some jelly. They tucked into the dessert immediately, and both smiled when he offered second helpings.

"Mom, remember what your doctor says," Colin warned. "Too much sugar isn't good for you."

Carmelita nodded. "Canadians eat too much sugar. Mind you, I am the last one to speak." She smiled mischievously, then looked at her host. "Your cake is excellent, George. My husband and I loved desserts. A cook used to bake strudels for us, tortes…"

Mrs. Hong was restless, fiddling with the buttons on her cardigan. "Mom, would you like to see George's garden?"

She nodded. Colin took his mother's arm while Carmelita took George's arm. We must be quite a sight, George thought as he saw passersby glance their way.

The garden was a dense collection of raised beds, arbours, trellises and dwarf fruit trees, separated by meandering paths of finely crushed stone. Mrs. Hong wanted to know the name of every plant, often forgetting that George had already supplied the information.

"Colin is a good man," Carmelita whispered to George. "You deserve good friends."

When the tour of the garden ended, Mrs. Hong rubbed her hands together and refused to sit down. "Guess Mom wants to go," Colin said.

"Pleasure to meet you," she said to Carmelita. Bending toward her son, she shouted, "This woman's skin is dark. Where is she from?"

The question shocked Colin, who immediately apologized on his mother's behalf. Carmelita giggled and said, "I take after my mother." She shook hands with Mrs. Hong. "I will pray for your good health."

As George moved toward the gate, he looked back to see Carmelita leaning on her cane, examining the sweet peas. She bent toward the trellis and grasped a stem to sniff the delicate flowers. Then she asked about the bountiful fruit on the adjacent apple tree. "What are they?" she called out to George.

"Jonagolds," George shouted back. "Wait there, I'll be right back."

George walked Colin and his mother to the Volvo station wagon that used to be Mrs. Hong's car. Colin explained, "Mom doesn't like my Ford Focus; she thinks it's too small."

George shook hands with Mrs. Hong and hugged Colin. "The visit was too short. We didn't get a chance to talk, you and I."

Colin got behind the wheel and rolled down his window. He asked George, "Does God talk to you?"

"What makes you think God socializes with me?"

"You Catholics seem to know about these things." He chewed his lip. "Has Keith told you I hear voices? I want to know if it's God talking to me."

"Let's talk about it on the phone. I'll call you tonight or tomorrow. Your mother's tired, you should get her home."

Mrs. Hong's head was bouncing softly. Waving at her, George said loudly, "Thanks for the nice visit." Mrs. Hong remained silent, her eyes half-closed.

"Mom, say goodbye to George."

"Nice meeting you," she mumbled. She sat up with a start. "George, from Victoria. I know who he is."

Colin blew a kiss to George and drove off.

"Mrs. Hong is a very nice person," Carmelita said when she saw George coming back. "She has a bad memory, but I've seen worse, a lot worse."

"What do you think of Colin?"

The expression on Mrs. Tauber's face suddenly changed. "He reminds me of my nephew."

"Which one?"

"Marty, of course. Not Tomas."

"Why do you say that?"

"Marty loves his mother too much. That's not good."

"According to Keith, Colin has been depressed for quite a while. Nobody seems to be able to help him."

"You must not take Colin's pain upon you."

"I worry about him."

"He has his own family to look after him. They are the ones who should be worrying."

George made no mention of Colin's voices, for fear that his old friend would start worrying. Not about Colin, but about him.

Chapter Eighteen

The phone rang in the parish rectory. Father Al glanced at the call display and picked up. "Good morning, Carmelita."

"Am I calling too early, Father?"

"It's never too early; I have already had my breakfast."

"I don't know what's wrong with me, Father. I am feeling weak since I woke up."

"Would you like me to call an ambulance for you, Carmelita?"

"Please don't, Father."

"Is something bothering you, my dear?"

"God has been good to me. I've been lucky, when I think of it." Then there was silence. Carmelita's voice came back, this time almost normal. "I must have pressed the button of the Medic Alert. It's only when I heard the girl from the speaker on the kitchen counter that I looked at my alarm clock: it was six o'clock in the morning. She said the same as you, 'Do you want me to call an ambulance?' I said: 'Are you kidding? I haven't had my medication!'"

"Carmelita, please hang up. I'm going to ask Paul to go to your house."

Ten minutes later, Paul Rose was on Carmelita Tauber's front porch, holding a key in his hand. Carmelita had given the key to his wife Jeanne, along with the code for the security system. Paul knocked but didn't wait for an answer. He stepped into the house. "It's me, Paul."

A voice came from Carmelita's bedroom. "I am watching the rosary on the TV. Make yourself some coffee."

When Paul pushed open the bedroom door, Carmelita was getting out of bed. "Do you need help?"

"Yes, please. Are you hungry? A girl woke me up this morning."

"Was it a nurse?"

"No! It was someone from the alarm company." Peering up at him as he gently lifted her up, Carmelita said, "You look so much better than four years ago."

"Thanks to your prayers."

When Paul was diagnosed with gallstones, he shared the news with Carmelita, just before she left on her pilgrimage to Lourdes.

"You said you'd pray to the Mother of God for my recovery."

"You were in my prayers all the way to Lourdes."

"And I've been stone-free ever since." He helped Carmelita to a chair at the dining room table. In the kitchen, while he was scooping coffee into a paper filter in the coffee machine, he added, "Unfortunately, Jeanne isn't doing as well. Her blood sugar is spiking and dropping. It's frightening."

"Tell her to come and get some of my water. Father Al is feeling stronger, he says."

"Jeanne will call to set up a time with you."

"Don't be silly. Just come, you have a key to my house."

Carmelita and Paul were drinking their coffees when George entered the house. "What are you doing here at this time of the day?" Carmelita looked at him, puzzled.

"The Medical Alert company called me this morning. They said you refused when they offered to send an ambulance," George replied.

"I was half asleep when they called me. I could hardly hear anyway. She kept saying, 'Do you want us to call an ambulance?' What an idiot! But I didn't say it, of course. I said, 'Call me later. I must eat something before taking my medication.'"

"Did you call the Victoria Community Care unit, too?" George asked.

"As a matter of fact, I did," Carmelita replied. "Trish was not there. I left a message."

"So how are you feeling?"

"I am fine. Have you had you breakfast? Come and sit down, Paul and I are getting ready to eat."

To Paul, George looked ready to explode, and Carmelita noticed. "Sit, sit," she said. "I told you, I'm fine. The receptionist told me that Trish will call me as soon as she arrives at work. She put me on hold for almost one hour. For several months they did nothing for me and now I am the one who has to call them." She was playing with her teaspoon and staring into her cup.

She started to push back her chair, ready to set the table for breakfast. Then she launched into a story about her visit to the president's palace in Manila as a child. The next moment she was reliving her trip with parishioners from the Victoria diocese to attend the Fifth Eucharistic Congress in Quebec City. "At the Toronto airport, someone touched my shoulder and said, 'Mrs. Tauber, is that you?' It was the former Canadian finance minister, the Honourable Michael Wilson."

Paul and George looked at each other; both men were reluctant and silent actors in Carmelita's movie. There was a knock at the door.

"I'll get it," George said. He opened the front door and called out to Carmelita, "It's Trish."

Carmelita introduced the community care nurse to her guests, forgetting that George already knew her. Trish had been paying monthly visits to Carmelita's house for more than a year.

"Would you like some coffee?" Carmelita asked.

"No, thanks," the trim young woman said. "I've already had two this morning." Trish also held up a hand when George passed around a box of chocolate bonbons, on Carmelita's orders.

Paul looked in disbelief at Carmelita and wondered, What's wrong with her?

Carmelita told Trish that Paul's wife Jeanne was the church secretary. "Jeanne used to take me to Costco. We both love shopping." Then she added with a giggle, "But not professor George—"

George interrupted her. "Can you please tell Trish what happened this morning?"

"Oh, thank you, George. He is my angel."

Paul didn't know what to say or think. It seemed that from the moment she woke up that morning, Carmelita had been sending out SOS messages. The world had responded, but now it was as if she'd forgotten all that, and was just begging for attention, using coffee, chocolate hedgehogs and the promise of breakfast to keep them all there.

"I said to Father Al, 'What's wrong with me?'"

Paul was tempted to take Carmelita's head in his hands and say: *You're dying, love!*

Chapter Nineteen

Tomas got out of his car in front of the pub and thumbed the lock button on his key fob. Michael Power was walking in his direction. He was a slim man in his early thirties, a nervous energy in his walk. The two men were high school pals who lost touch when Tomas went to university. They had bumped into each other recently and set up a lunch date.

Displaying his customary grin, Michael said, "Twice in two weeks. Not bad, eh?" They hugged and backslapped. Michael pointed at Tomas's car.

"Wow, a Lexus LX 570!" he exclaimed. "Business must be good."

Tomas was embarrassed. "It's my father-in-law's car," he lied. "So, how's everything going with you? We didn't get to talk much last week."

"Same old, same old," Michael replied. "Working for that computer place on Marine Drive for the past ten years. I'm hoping to start my own company someday." As they walked into the pub, Michael said, "Hope you like this place. Quick service, not too noisy."

Tomas asked for bottled water and Michael ordered a beer. Tomas asked after Michael's parents, but as soon as the words were out of his mouth, he remembered the couple had divorced before Michael reached his teens. "I forgot, Michael. I'm sorry."

"Don't be. In the Eighties, all my friends' parents divorced, one after another. Was it the same with Filipinos?"

"No, they held the fort," Tomas replied with a smile.

Michael burst into laughter. "Your father used to use a bell to wake you up! Do you remember?"

"Part of his early training at the Jesuit school," Tomas replied with a laugh.

Michael's expression changed. Tomas couldn't tell if it was pity or envy. "Every time I was in your parents' house—God knows I was there often enough—I didn't want to go back home. Your parents were so nice; mine were never there." He paused. "Your mother was gorgeous, like a fashion model with her high heels."

"One day, she was pulled over for speeding. 'Sorry, officer,' she said. 'It's because I'm not wearing my high heels today.'" Both men laughed.

"Sandy's the opposite of my mother," Tomas continued. "We live in the same building as her parents," he added.

"My in-laws are someplace in Ontario. I met them the day of our wedding and haven't seen them since. Fine by me, actually." Michael gulped his beer. "You sure you don't want one?"

"No thanks, I have a big afternoon ahead of me."

"You've got more self-control than me." Michael's expression turned serious again. "I always admired you, you know."

Tomas went back to his noodle salad and said nothing. There had always been a wall between him and Michael, and they'd just hit it again. His father had the first and last word on everything, and his attitude to non-Filipinos had made it impossible for Tomas to emulate Michael's easy camaraderie. Tomas pushed his empty plate away and said, "My mom quit her job to raise us."

"Really?" Michael looked stunned.

"In Edmonton, she worked in a medical lab, but after they moved to North Vancouver, she stayed at home. Dad travelled a lot, and she felt someone had to be around for us." Tomas tapped his iPad on the table to check the time. "Sorry, Michael, I have to get back to work."

When the server arrived with the bills, Michael grabbed both. "My treat, buddy."

Outside the restaurant, Michael said, "The four of us should go out for dinner." He pulled Tomas into a hug.

All the way to the pharmacy, memories kept coming back to Tomas. His parents, like many immigrants, had an *us and them* view of the world. All events—joyful or sad—were lived among Filipinos. In the community, everyone knew each other intimately, including which families were well off and which were struggling financially. Every year the Pua family would go to Honolulu for Christmas, even though this meant the children would be away from their school friends. Tomas used to cry all the way to the airport.

"They will wait for you," his father used to say to console them. Tomas vowed things would be different for his own children.

"Do you think Marty is gay?" Tomas asked. He and Sandy were in bed watching a broadcast about the first same-sex marriage in Spain.

"Why do you say that?"

"He's older than me and he's never had a girlfriend."

"He used to have me," Sandy said with a laugh.

"I'm serious. Do you know?"

"You're asking *me*? He is your brother."

Tomas stared at his wife. "I worry about him. He's put his life on hold out of love for Mom. That has to stop!"

"So talk to him."

"Don't we have enough problems of our own, you and I?"

Sandy remained silent; she knew what her husband was referring to. After eight years of marriage, the baby's bedroom was still empty.

"There is nothing I want more than to have children," Tomas said. He started crying.

Sandy embraced her husband. "It will happen; so many people are saying novenas."

Tomas was shaving the back of his neck when the telephone rang. Sandy knocked at the bathroom door. "It's your mother."

"Tell her I'll call her from work."

The door opened and Sandy gave him the handset. "You should talk to her, it's important."

"Anything wrong, Mom?"

Soledad got right to the point. "I want you to call your *Tita*. She needs to see a specialist here in Vancouver."

"Mom, I have to get to work."

"She won't listen to me."

Tomas sighed and rolled his eyes at Sandy, who was standing close. "Mom, I have an 8:30 appointment and I can't be late."

"Will you call her?"

"I will."

"When?"

His mother had more to say, but Tomas cut her off. "I'll call her before lunch. I promise." After he hung up, Tomas looked at his wife. "Maybe if she was working, she wouldn't feel so lonely."

Sandy shook her head. "Your mother can't work in a lab after all these years. Think of all the new technology she'd have to learn. It'd be too stressful for her."

Tomas picked up his iPad and his keys from the table in the front hall. "Take my friend Michael as an example. He and his wife live their own lives."

"They're Canadians."

Tomas shook his head. "You and I are Canadians, too."

"Give me a kiss and go. You'll be late."

Chapter Twenty

After dinner at Teresita and Emile Lim's house, George finally lost it. Teresita's brothers and their wives were in the living room watching CNN news, while Mio and Serena Kulenović remained at the dining table with Teresita, George, Carmelita and a few other guests.

"What about Canadian politics?" George said loudly.

Without looking at George, Carlo, who was the youngest of the Gonzalez family, remarked "Politicians are the same everywhere. All corrupt."

Irritated by Carlo's reply, George turned to Carmelita, trying to bring his temper under control. "You're looking quite elegant this evening." Carmelita was wearing a deep blue jacket threaded with gold, a pearl necklace and a black stone on her ring finger.

"Max and I used to go out regularly," she replied with a drowsy smile. "This was an outfit he bought for me just before he died."

George moved into the living room. His intention was to have a discussion, an exchange of ideas, with Teresita's siblings, who had been living in Canada for twenty-five years. He didn't sit; instead he stood facing the television screen, both hands in his pockets. Someone had changed the channel to the Vancouver CTV station. *The Conservative government wants to give more power to the police,* the anchor announced.

George decided to toss a bottle into the sea to see what would happen. "In Ottawa, the opposition parties are outraged by this decision. Canadian citizens should be angry, too."

He heard a snore; Carmelita had taken a morphine pill for breakthrough pain a few minutes earlier and the drug had kicked in. In the living room there was silence. George realized that they disapproved of his outspoken attitude. He threw his hands in the air, conceding defeat.

Tonight's dinner had been arranged in honour of Teresita's cousin Graziella Casile, who had recently arrived from the Philippines with her husband and their little boy. They were staying with the Lims while they looked for a place of their own. The day after his arrival, the husband had contacted the Lighthouse Home Care Agency where Teresita worked, and was offered a job immediately. Five-year-old Nathan was registered at a day care to improve his English.

"He is learning songs," Graziella said to George. At her urging, the boy sang "O Canada." His pure voice roused Carmelita, who applauded with the others when the anthem ended.

"I'm impressed," George said. "I wish you luck."

Carmelita said, "Very good, very good." The boy seized her right hand and brought it to his forehead as a way of receiving her blessing. He did the same thing with "Uncle" George's hand as his mother looked on proudly.

"Your son is musical, and smart, too," George said. Graziella thanked him. "He won't have any problems adapting here," George added.

Carmelita was reminiscing. "During the holidays, the international students, young doctors and nurses, we all stayed on the campus near the Mayo Clinic. Every time someone asked me where I was from, I would start crying. I missed my parents. I was so young! One day, Dr. Mayo gave me his handkerchief so I could blow my nose. He said to me, 'The next time you are homesick, just call my wife and she will send someone to pick you up.' I came here to help. I never took anybody else's job," Carmelita said. The other guests listened politely, but without showing great interest.

"I heard you are writing a book about Carmelita," Lilia Arcilla said with a smile. George nodded. "My life is a book, too. You would be surprised. I went to Singapore as a live-in maid to help my parents and my sister and brothers. Every time there was a new baby, I sent more money home. I had to cook food I didn't like. I've built a house for my sister, who lives in Ilocos Norte. Last winter, one of the grandchildren got a virus and almost died. I paid for the doctor, the antibiotics, everything." Lilia's face took on a thoughtful expression. "Some Filipinos leave their country and never look back. I wish I could, but I can't." She paused. "Anyway, thank you for looking after her."

"I'm not looking after her."

"You shouldn't be the one to do it," Lilia whispered. "Don't get me wrong."

Mio stabbed the elevator button. "This woman is so stupid!"

"Who?" Serena asked.

"Did you hear what Lilia said about Max tonight?"

Mio took the whiskey flask from his jacket pocket and tipped it to his mouth. "Carmelita chose Max because he was born in Europe," he said, mimicking Lilia's whiny, nasal voice.

Serena pressed the button, wondering what was taking the elevator so long. "I don't know what you've got against her." Mio was born in Zagreb, part of the old Austro-Hungarian Empire. Serena knew it was easy for her husband to sympathize with Max, an Austrian.

"Max was a womanizer, yes, but in a gentlemanly way," Mio said. "What's wrong with kissing women's hands?" He was about to light the cigarette he was holding, but Serena stopped him.

"Can't you see?" Mio continued. "The woman never set foot in Europe. She must think Carmelita is a snob because Max drank red wine and played classical music at parties." Once inside the elevator, he lit his cigarette, despite his wife's protests. "Carmelita was intelligent enough to go and get what she was missing."

Finally, the doors of the elevator opened; the couple exited the building, and Serena rushed to the driver's side of the car. "I'm driving," she said, pulling her set of keys from her purse.

Her husband took an eternity to unlock the door on the passenger side. Serena watched impassively; she wasn't about help him.

Just before he threw himself onto the passenger seat, Mio froze and stared at her.

"I really miss Max. I enjoyed having a drink with him."

"Yes, it was so nice for me, too, the two of you drunk, making fun of everything around you." She started the car and merged into traffic.

Mio looked through the side window and yelled, as if to the driver in the next lane, "I hate all this yakking in Filipino!"

Serena would have loved to possess enough self-control to calmly say, *Well, stay home then, instead of hiding in the bathroom and drinking*. She decided to pretend she was alone in the car.

If it weren't for their two sons and her grandchildren, she would file for divorce. It would kill her old mother, though. Mio, slumped in the seat next to her, had become a caricature of the man she fell madly in love with many years ago. When she was with her girlfriends or her walking group, Serena referred to him as her ex. Occasionally one of them would ask, "Why don't you divorce him for real?"

Mio was singing, "*Casta Diva, che inargente*." His voice gained power as he continued, "*Queste sacre, queste sacre antiche...*" This was his favourite aria; it usually preceded his passing out.

Serena never responded to her friends' urgings. There was always another woman who replied for her, "Because she is married." Like in a musical, her girlfriends would then recite, "For better, for worse, in sickness and in health..." They would all laugh, but they knew that for Filipinas, the words *till death do us part* represented much more than ritual.

Suddenly, her husband awoke and trumpeted, "Max and Carmelita always fought. Do you remember? Like you and me. Ha!"

Serena looked at her husband, who was staring at her with an ugly smile on his face. He wanted a confrontation, but she wasn't about to fall into that trap.

After Mio collapsed onto the bed, Serena continued her musings. If only she could be free again, and go out with a man for coffee! She wasn't looking for sex, just for a chance to talk about something besides Filipino food and the community fundraising events. If only she had someone she could talk to about what she was going through. Not even her girlfriends knew how desperately she wanted to get away. Her children didn't seem the least bit curious about what was happening between Mio and her. *They must feel the tension.*

Mio was right about one thing: Carmelita and her husband used to quarrel.

Lying beside Mio, Serena used his snoring to cover her sobbing. She grieved the loss of the past: her memories of going to the theatre and to art galleries with her beloved Mio. They would sit side by side, reading books, often reading passages aloud to each other.

Serena's mother belonged to the Spanish elite of Manila, more interested in socializing than literary discussions. As a young girl, in Canada, Serena met Mio who introduced her to the finer things of life. Her darling Mio had been dead for half of her adult life.

Chapter Twenty-One

Carmelita called George at ten one morning. "Did I wake you up?"

"No, I was just about to go out. Anything wrong, Carmelita?"

"Since this morning, I've been checking my blood pressure; it goes up and down. I am mad at that woman."

"What woman?"

"I don't want to call by her name a woman who is a liar." Carmelita decided to provide a clue after all. "You know, the physiotherapist."

George had already heard the story about the physiotherapist borrowing money from Carmelita. Father Al and Jeanne had both urged her to call the police about it.

"I now get a recorded message saying that the service has been discontinued."

"How much did you give her, Carmelita?"

"Why do you want to know?"

"Forget it."

"She is a certified physiotherapist. I could tell by the way she was working my shoulders, my neck and particularly the back."

"Can you please finish your story?"

"You should have seen her clinic. In Calgary she had regular clients, but in Victoria she was living like a pauper. BC Hydro cut off her electricity—"

"I can't talk long, Carmelita. I have to do some errands."

"Where?"

George ignored the question. "So you gave her some money?"

"I am not crazy. It was a loan." Carmelita explained, "She was expecting some money from England. The monies that would go into her bank account. The caller gave her his name and the name of the firm in London, England."

George exclaimed, "It's a scam, one of those international scams. How could someone fall for it? The police have been warning people for ages."

"I said to her 'Be careful, crooks are everywhere. I know what I am talking about,' I told her." She sighed. "This man in the Philippines."

Here we go again! George thought.

Carmelita was referring to the loss of a substantial amount of money, supposedly intended to help with the expansion of the family's business. "Thanks God, Max didn't live to see all the financial mess."

George remained silent. He was trying to keep up with Carmelita's ramblings. One minute she was upset about the man in the Philippines who stole her late husband's money and her personal savings: "We are talking of one million of US dollars here, not a few thousands." The next minute she was laughing. "'You are good at spending money', he used to tell me, 'not at making money.'"

One fateful day, while she was relaxing under the warm hands of the physiotherapist, Carmelita had asked, "How much do you need, love?" She wrote a cheque so the woman could pay her overdue bills. "'You'll get your money back, as soon as I receive the funds from England,' she told me then. But it was all lies!"

Then, in a timid voice much more in keeping with a person whose cancer had made her frail and dependent, Carmelita asked, "Would you be kind enough to call the police for me?"

Knowing that a refusal on his part would make things worse for Carmelita, who sounded quite upset, her "angel" asked, "What's her name?"

"I have her business card, but I can't find it. It must be here somewhere."

"Can I be frank?"

"Of course, professor!"

"Forget about the loan. You'll never get your money back."

George was ready to hang up and return to his life, but Carmelita was on the road again. "When I think of all the money that we lost because of them…"

Them being the people in the Philippines who had simply pocketed the "business development" money.

When it was discovered that there was no money left and the account books had disappeared, Carmelita forbade the lawyer and the children from saying anything to Soledad.

George could hear the rustling of newsprint over the phone and the sound of papers being shuffled.

"What are you doing?"

"All this junk!" Carmelita sighed. "I can't stand all that mess on my table."

"Your sister's right, after all," George ventured to say.

"Soledad shouldn't worry about me. She has her own problems. She called me last night. She wants me to start saying a novena at our church."

"For what? They're coming over this weekend, right? Her and Tomas and Sandy?"

Carmelita remained silent.

"What, have they cancelled?"

"They have to postpone." As if she were psychic, Carmelita said, "Don't give me that look, Mr. Miller."

"What look? We're on the phone."

"I know you better than you think."

Carmelita suddenly lowered her voice, as if she thought someone walking their dog down her street might hear. "This is a very critical time for the couple."

Tomas and Sandy were both working at Mr. Surla's pharmacy, and Carmelita had recently mentioned that her nephew might soon get a franchise of his own. George assumed that this was the critical matter.

"It's not the right moment for Sandy to travel," Carmelita said.

"What are you talking about, for God's sake?"

"George, don't swear."

"What are you are trying to tell me?"

"You are a man. There are certain things that a man—"

"Carmelita, don't call me to tell me there's something that you can't tell me."

"You are like a younger brother to me." She sighed. "They are trying hard to have children." After a pause, she explained, "You might not know, being a man, but stress is bad in a case like this."

George then learned that the last time Carmelita was in Vancouver, there had been an open discussion about ovarian temperatures.

"I told them, 'You must put everything on your side.'" On that day's agenda were artificial estrogen drugs that cost less in the US, sperm counts, and things to avoid, such as hot tubs. "They have one in their building. I told Tomas not to wear tight underwear."

"You said that to your nephew?"

"Why shouldn't I? I am a nurse. I told them, if it's God's will, it will happen."

She said on both sides of the family and both sides of the Georgia Strait, people had the young couple in their thoughts and prayers.

"If they can't have a child, why don't they adopt one?" George asked.

"You cannot trust government," Carmelita yelled. "Too much bureaucracy!"

Chapter Twenty-Two

Brother Melvin abandoned the strawberry cheesecake and rose from Carmelita Tauber's dining table to examine the collection of religious artefacts in her living room. The statues of Mary included Our Lady of Lourdes and Our Lady of Fatima. The middle-aged missionary named the other saints as his companion Richard Lepage looked on from the dining room: "Francis of Assisi, Ignatius of Loyola, Thérèse of Lisieux, Teresa of Ávila, Padre Pio, Queen Elizabeth of Hungary..."

Carmelita had created a multi-tiered arrangement of shelves and up-side down clay pots to display the statues and crucifixes of various sizes. "It's my shrine," Carmelita explained.

Brother Melvin and young Richard had left the headquarters of the Pilgrims of Saint Michael in Rougemont, Quebec a month earlier. They were travelling across the country to spread the word about their organization and its philosophy of applying Catholic principles to all aspects of life, including monetary reform.

"It's sad to say, but outside Quebec, most people we meet in Canada have never heard of us," Brother Melvin said to Carmelita.

"How can I help?" she asked.

"One way is to tell people about our journal." Brother Melvin handed Carmelita the current issue of *Michael*, which was dedicated to Canadian saints. The cover photo depicted Marie de l'Incarnation and provided a list of other saints that were featured in the leaflet: Monseigneur de Laval, Marguerite d'Youville, and several Jesuit martyrs.

"Are you both from Quebec?" Carmelita asked.

"I am from Montreal," Richard said in his accented English. "Brother Melvin was born in the US."

Carmelita said, "I studied at the Mayo Clinic in Minnesota, but I came to this country to serve. I supported Pierre Elliot Trudeau, our late prime minister. He was an exceptional man. My best friend returned to Montreal after her training in the US. A couple of times, I visited Montreal. When my contract in Dawson Creek came to an end, I thought of going to Montreal instead of Victoria." Carmelita said she had always wanted to learn French, a romance language like Spanish. "You see, my ancestry is Spanish."

"I'm confused," Brother Melvin confessed. "I thought you were from the Philippines."

His hostess was more than willing to provide details on her family background. She started with her mother, who was from the north, while her father, but Brother Melvin interrupted her.

"Brother Richard and I must go out for a walk and to pray."

"Of course. Feel free to come and go as you please. This is your house."

Before they left, Carmelita insisted on showing them the guest bedroom, which she had assigned to Brother Melvin. Richard would sleep on the living room sofa, under the eyes of saints, popes, the Virgin Mary and Our Saviour on the Holy Cross. He brought Carmelita's walker closer to her chair and offered his help.

"I am fine, thanks."

When they entered the guest room, the six-foot-tall Brother Melvin said, "I'm going to appreciate the king-size bed."

"If you don't mind being surrounded by my late husband's videotapes."

Richard saw that the walls of the guest room were lined with bookshelves full of VHS tapes, all labelled. Most were recordings of musical performances and biographies of Beethoven, Bach, Caruso, Maria Callas and other composers and classical singers.

As the young man pored over the tapes, Carmelita complimented him on his outfit: grey flannel pants and navy blazer, with white shirt and blue tie. She remarked, "My husband always wore a blazer and a white shirt. After he died, I gave everything away, but I still have his shoes. I think they would fit you."

"Oh! Thank you."

Richard kneeled to get a better look at the tapes on the lower shelves. These were history programs on Rommel, Mussolini, Churchill and other figures from the Second World War. Richard pulled out one tape and saw that the back was labelled with the recording date and details of the contents. "This is quite a collection, Mrs. Tauber."

"Pick anything you want, there is a machine in the living room."

Richard couldn't understand everything the old lady said, but she reminded him of his grandmother. He stood up and noticed a portrait of a man with a severe expression.

"That is Wagner, the German composer," Carmelita said. She touched Richard's arm, "When I would come home from work, my husband would tell me to sit down and be comfortable. He would put on some music so I could relax."

Brother Melvin cleared his throat. "If you'll excuse us, we must go for our walk."

On their way back to the front of the house, Richard noticed some old long-playing records on the lower shelf of a hallway cabinet. Stacks of LPs were piled on the living room floor. Carmelita walked her visitors to the door, thumping along behind them with her walker.

She unlocked the front door. "I will leave the door unlocked. Don't tell George, but I often forget to set the alarm." Covering a giggle with her hand, she added, "I am warning you, I snore."

As the two men descended the porch steps, Richard inhaled the fresh spring air and thought about his parents. The life of a Pilgrim of Saint Michael was much easier now than when they were active in the organization. In the Fifties and Sixties, the Pilgrims were persecuted in Quebec. Homeowners would spit on them as they went door to door, and they were mocked for their white berets and the statues of the Virgin Mary and the Archangel Michael they carried during their processions.

They had just reached the sidewalk when Brother Melvin sneezed. "So many flowers in Victoria." He sneezed again. "I'm allergic to pollen."

Richard was curious to know what Brother Melvin thought of their hostess, but didn't say a word. Brother Melvin pulled a rosary out of his pocket. "Let us pray."

The two men walked for a few blocks, praying aloud. A few passersby glance at them, intrigued. An hour later, they returned to Carmelita's house.

Before they went in, Brother Melvin warned Richard, "Tomorrow will be a busy day. We'll start calling on people by nine."

As soon as they opened the door, they were greeted by the sound of snoring. Richard smiled. "She is such a warm person, don't you think? She is the first Filipina I've ever met."

Brother Melvin didn't reply. He was struggling to untie his shoelaces—no easy feat, given the size of his belly.

✳

The next morning, Richard was already sipping a glass of water at the kitchen table when Carmelita came in. He rose and offered to help her make coffee, but she waved him back to his seat. She went to prepare the ingredients for an omelette.

Brother Melvin appeared, and after a brief greeting, he said, "Several priests and bishops were supporters of economic democracy." He checked to see if he had Carmelita's attention.

"Keep talking, Brother Melvin, I am listening. I can do multitasking."

"Clifford Hugh Douglas formulated our financial principles and since then, Louis Even and the Pilgrims of St. Michael have been spreading the doctrine. We believe that the government's role is to distribute debt-free money to all members of society. This isn't welfare, but a dividend. Whether the money comes from a capitalist institution, a co-operative or a nationalized institution, it's a gift from God. What do you think, Mrs. Tauber?"

"I am listening," Carmelita said as she whisked eggs in a bowl and poured them into the pan. "I use butter, if you don't mind. Margarine is not good for you."

Carmelita removed English muffins from the toaster and put them on a plate adorned with a delicate floral pattern. "My late husband ordered this china from

England for our wedding." She handed the plate to Richard and with his help, served the rest of the breakfast.

After they ate, Carmelita asked Richard to get the pecan pie from the fridge. "Would you like ice cream?" she asked her guests.

Richard felt overwhelmed by Carmelita's generosity. He felt that through her, he could see God.

Brother Melvin asked, "Would you be interested in attending our international conference in Rougemont next month?"

"I will check with my oncologist, but I don't see why she would say no."

The two Pilgrims of St. Michael stayed at Carmelita's house for the duration of their three-day mission in Greater Victoria. Every morning, before heading off to knock on people's doors and distribute their pamphlets, they shared a meal with their hostess. In spite of the regular "yo-yo," as she called the ups and downs of her blood pressure, Carmelita woke early to cook bacon, eggs and toast for her guests and pack fresh fruit and granola bars for them to take for the day.

"You need to gain weight, young man," she kept telling Richard.

One day over breakfast she told them about an acquaintance who had applied to become a member of the Equestrian Order of the Holy Sepulchre of Jerusalem, but was not accepted.

"I'm curious. What is the Order's mission?" Brother Melvin asked.

Richard nodded. "I'm curious, too."

Carmelita seemed pleased to enlighten her guests. "We are helping Christians living in the Holy Land by supporting schools and monasteries. Every year at Christmas, Father Jerome, who is in charge of one of the schools, sends photographs of the children standing in rows." She asked Richard to look for Father Jerome's annual report in the drawer of a small cabinet close to his chair.

Carmelita filled the silence as Brother Melvin read the report. "My husband and I always stayed at the Sheraton Hotel in Waikiki." She burst into laughter. "He used to lift me up. I was thin, would you believe me? I'm getting thin again," she added, pulling at her dress. "I can wear the same clothes from my twenties. Would you like to see my designer's clothes?"

Richard, who had never seen designer clothes from the Philippines, wanted to say yes right away, but he waited. Brother Melvin was still immersed in the annual report.

"Let's do it next year, when we come back to Victoria," Richard replied.

"If I am still of this world."

Richard got up and kissed the old lady on the cheek. Her skin was soft and wrinkle-free, unlike his grandmother's lined face. Tears rolled down Richard's cheeks.

Carmelita seized the young man's wrist. "Don't! I had a wonderful life!" she said, stroking his hand.

Chapter Twenty-Three

From the moment she learned that her husband Geoffrey had invited a dozen friends to help celebrate her ninetieth birthday, Margaret Seymour was beside herself with excitement. She felt like Mrs. Dalloway in Virginia Woolf's novel. Her mind was buzzing with images of the hugging and kissing that would take place the next evening. It had been a while since they'd thrown a party.

Geoffrey reminded her, "Don't forget to take your heart medication before our guests arrive."

"I promise." Margaret smiled. "Anyway, Dolores will remember. It's Tuesday tomorrow, so Dolores will be here," she said, referring to one of her two caregivers from Lighthouse. "Nathy comes on Fridays. It's all she can do, because her mother is unwell..." Geoffrey nodded where appropriate as his wife chattered on.

Margaret didn't sleep well that night. She lay awake trying to decide what to wear to her party. Her wardrobe was spread throughout their three-bedroom condo, including what used to be Geoffrey's office before he retired. Every closet held an assortment of garments in protective see-through bags.

Selecting an outfit had become more of a challenge for Margaret in recent years. She liked having Geoffrey around for consultation. Often, he simply laughed indulgently at her indecision.

As she stood in front of their bedroom closet the next morning, she said, "I was thinking, Geoffrey." Getting no reply, she looked around her. "Where are you?" Still no reply.

"Dolores," she called out.

Dolores appeared in the doorway. "Yes, Mrs. Margaret?"

"Hello, love. Would you go and tell my husband to turn on his hearing aids, please?"

"His batteries are dead, ma'am."

"He is so forgetful. Could you get some for him, love?"

Dolores gave a series of nods. "Yes, Mrs. Margaret."

That evening, Margaret felt surrounded by the love of her dear friends, most of whom she had known for decades. When her Filipina friend entered the living room, leaning equally on a cane and George's arm, Margaret tried to get up. Carmelita said, "Mother, don't do that. It's your turn to be spoiled for once."

Like two teenage girls in a dormitory, Margaret Seymour and Carmelita Tauber sat holding hands. "Do you remember the reception at the Shaughnessy country club in Vancouver?" Carmelita asked.

"Of course. You could see the water from the gardens."

For George's benefit, Carmelita explained, "Geoffrey was a member of the club. My niece Susan had her debutante party there."

Margaret smiled at George, "Thanks so much for coming. It's always a pleasure to see you, George." The birthday girl asked her husband to introduce George to the others.

Terri Moore joined Margaret and Carmelita on the sofa and joked, "Andrew and I are fresh from the boat." Margaret was confused, so Terri added, "We're just back from a Mediterranean cruise."

"Really, dear? Do tell us all about it," Margaret urged.

"It was wonderful. But hard at times, too."

"Did you fall ill?"

Terri laughed. "No, but we rode on a donkey. It was scary. The paths were narrow, right on the edge of a cliff. Only the women were on this adventure; our husbands preferred the hotel bar. This was somewhere in Italy. Andrew, what was that village called?" Her husband was chatting with another group and didn't hear her. "He's so good with foreign words. My granddaughter Alison has the same flair for languages. I'm trying to persuade her to do an exchange trip to Europe."

"I always loved Italy," Margaret commented. "My parents would take us there during the holidays." A sudden memory made her feel sad. "The war changed everything, I'm afraid." She brightened and said to Terri, "You remember Carmelita Tauber, don't you, dear?"

"Of course. How are you, Carmelita?"

"I am fine, thank you."

"Andrew and I have never been to the Philippines. Where do you suggest we go?"

"You have the choice." Mrs. Tauber replied, "There are more than seven thousand islands and we have one hundred sixty-five languages."

Terri laughed. Pointing at her husband, "That would keep him busy for some time. Andrew and I feel that now is the time to travel. At sixty-five, we're still young enough, but in ten years, who knows? One's health can fail. Mind you, we have a friend who's eighty and trekking all over the world. She's fearless."

"I always loved to travel. When I was young—" Carmelita didn't complete her sentence; her head down, she was examining her fingernails.

Leaning toward her, Margaret whispered, "Are you comfortable, dear?"

"It's so nice to see familiar faces. All friends, good old friends." Carmelita looked lost.

Margaret sighed. "The only one missing today is Max."

Andrew, who had wandered over by this point, said, "Max Tauber was an astute businessman, and such fun to be with."

Margaret noticed that Louise Elford, a radiologist at the BC Cancer Clinic that Carmelita attended, seemed to be avoiding the Filipina. Louise's husband

Oscar was also a former associate of Max Tauber. Margaret realized that Louise was bothered by how thin Carmelita had become.

Carmelita, unaware of Louise's discomfort, said to her, "I love your dress."

Louise smiled her thanks and seemed to relax. "I love your dress, too. How are you, Carmelita?"

At some point in the evening, at Carmelita's request, Margaret asked her husband to dim the lights in the living room for a better view of the inner harbour.

"You might not know, but a developer from Alberta is planning to build a giant marina for yachts in the harbour, right under our eyes," Geoffrey said.

David Jones, who sat on the condo's strata council, said, "We're opposing the project, as you can imagine. We're meeting regularly with politicians and bureaucrats from Victoria. And Ottawa as well, since the ocean is under federal jurisdiction."

Oscar reminded the group that he and Louise lived in another condo building on the harbour, then added, "We're fighting tooth and nail to stop this monster project from going ahead."

Margaret hadn't heard a thing about the plan, and looked at her husband in dismay. Geoffrey reassured her, "Don't worry, darling. It won't happen."

Margaret introduced George to an athletic man who looked younger than the others in the room. The man sat down next to them. "George, this is Daniel Sherman. He lives in our complex."

"But my condo is bigger," Daniel joked. When George asked what he did for a living, Daniel replied, "I used to be an investment banker, like Geoffrey and Max, but I retired early. I decided that two million was enough for me to live on."

As soon as the elevator doors closed, Carmelita said in a low voice, "I never liked that man, and after listening to him tonight, less than ever." Shaking her head, she snarled, "My condo is bigger. How could a woman love such a man?"

"Who?" George asked, "Daniel Sherman?"

Carmelita refused to acknowledge the man's name. "Really, George, how could a woman fall for a man like him?"

"Why don't you like him? Is it because he's a Jew?" Carmelita looked at him in astonishment.

Outside the high-rise, they walked toward the row of parking spots marked with a wheelchair logo.

In the car, Carmelita turned her head in all directions. Agitated, she tried unsuccessfully to grasp the seatbelt behind her. "Where is it?" she said, irritated.

"Wait!" George got out and walked around to help her buckle the belt.

"What's wrong?" George asked when he was back behind the wheel. The old Filipina was silent, staring out the window and still distraught.

Finally she said, "Could you turn on the engine, please?"

"Anything you want to say?"

"I don't want to talk," Carmelita replied, in a rather aggressive way, George thought.

At her home, George helped Carmelita climb the stairs and take off her coat, scarf and hat. "I'm off. Are you going to be okay?"

"Can you walk me to the bedroom? I want to lie down."

George saluted. "Jawohl!"

Carmelita stared at George, stricken. When they arrived in her room, she pointed to the chair at the foot of the bed. "Sit down. I need to talk to you."

"About what?"

"I wouldn't have married a Nazi!"

She lay down on the bed and fumbled with her rosary, her eyes on the ceiling. She had taken refuge in a place where a caregiver's good intentions were irrelevant. George felt trapped. He sensed that although she was in her bed, the afterlife was where Carmelita longed to be. A young Max was in the room, too, in theatrical garb with a small harp in his hands, gazing out from a charcoal portrait over the bed. Next to that was a large photograph of Max as an old man, a proud giant smiling at the camera.

Carmelita saw him looking at the images and tilted her head back so she could see them. "His professors were all predicting that he would end up singing at Bayreuth."

Carmelita's eyes moved to George, who now sat on the bed next to her. "My husband was not anti-Semite."

"It was just a joke." He was surprised that the same word she had laughed at a few weeks earlier now caused her such obvious distress. "I'm sorry if I upset you."

She squeezed George's hand nervously. "He was able to come to Canada."

"How old was he when you met?"

She gripped his hand even harder. "I said to him: you should marry a woman of your kind. He was more than a husband, he was my friend, my teacher." George had heard her refer to Max this way many times.

"There was always someone to ask him whether he knew about the concentration camps back then. He never cared for politics. He was a good man!"

George could feel Carmelita's nails digging into his palm.

"I wouldn't have married him, if he had been a Nazi."

George gently freed his hand, hoping Carmelita wouldn't notice that he'd had quite enough of the conversation. "I have to go," he said, rising.

"Five minutes, please!"

George sat.

"Mama said to me that she would rather have me marry a cart driver, a *carretero*." George checked the time on the alarm clock by the bed. "For Mama, Germany and Austria were all the same."

Once the five minutes that he had agreed to were over, George got up again. "Try to get some sleep." After reminding her to call him the next morning, George closed the bedroom door and left.

Once outside, he paused on the front porch. He could see the Fairmont Empress Hotel and the BC Legislature in the distance, but his mind was inside, in Carmelita's bedroom. He could still feel her bony fingers in his hand. She was wrestling with her ghosts, alone. He felt as if he, her angel, were abandoning her to her mysteries and secrets, unable to provide the answers that would give meaning to her life. He refused to bear witness. It was *her* fight, after all.

One day it will be your turn. George walked down the steps and headed home.

Chapter Twenty-Four

Heidi Blair had reluctantly agreed to their neighbour Mrs. Tauber's invitation to Easter Dinner to please her husband James, but she was still grumpy about it as they were getting ready to go next door. "Why did she invite us, anyway?"

Cool as ever, her husband said, "She likes our children."

"I know. Whenever she sees them, she gives them sweets—"

"She lives alone and she's sick, from what I hear." Her husband's philosophy was simple: smile and be nice to everyone.

"Don't expect me or the children to eat pork."

"There'll be fish, I'm sure. Asians eat a lot of it."

"Deep-fried, probably."

James kissed his wife. "We won't stay long. Everybody knows she's not well."

Heidi persisted. "You don't know how eccentric she is, the fuss she always makes over the children, as if they were related to her. Of course, you don't see that, do you? You're away six months of the year."

James made regular trips to the United Arab Emirates, where he served as a consultant to the royal family.

"Religious people give me the creeps!" Heidi said with a shudder.

James hugged her and whispered, "I told you, we won't stay long. What could I do? She asked about our plans for Sunday, and I said we weren't going anywhere."

"There'll be chocolate all over the place."

As soon as he heard the magic word, little Finley tugged on his mother's hand. "Please, let's go, I'm hungry."

James laughed. "See? He loves Mrs. Tauber."

"I know, I know." Heidi sighed. "I guess she has some good qualities."

James locked their front door. The family walked up their neighbour's driveway and climbed the steps to the porch. The front door was wide open.

Mrs. Tauber gave them a joyous welcome. "Come in, come in!" Tightening her grip on her cane, she leaned toward Finley. "Hello, Finley. How are you? And how is your sister?" She straightened up and caressed Lizzy's cheek. The baby stirred in her mother's arms.

Carmelita walked the young family into the living room and introduced them to the assembled guests.

Heidi nodded to the brightly dressed men and women. Suddenly she realized that she was by herself; her son Finley was on an expedition, holding Mrs. Tauber's hand. Her husband was chatting with Mac Erikson, their neighbours across the street. She was relieved to see several Caucasian faces.

Mac's mother Thora came over and whispered, "Don't feel obliged to eat everything."

Heidi shifted Lizzy to her left arm and picked up a bone china plate decorated with tiny flowers. She couldn't help admiring the design. Mac's mother said, "Her late husband was a wealthy businessman."

"What kind of business?"

The older woman looked at her son, who had joined them. "Do you know?"

"Max had a vitamins and supplements business," her son replied. "Pretty successful, I'd say."

The ten-foot-long dining table was buried under an assortment of platters and pots. Heidi glanced into the kitchen and saw a Chinese man in a sleeveless T-shirt sautéeing vegetables in a wok.

Carmelita said, "This is Emile, the husband of my goddaughter Teresita. Where are you?" she asked, looking around her.

A woman in her mid-fifties wearing an apron appeared at the summons. Carmelita introduced Teresita and Emile to Heidi, saying, "Her husband James is over there. And the young man with me is their son Finley. Help yourself, eat," she urged, with an emphasis on *eat*. To Heidi it sounded more like a command than an invitation.

She examined the offerings on the dining table. There was a monstrous roast turkey, a huge piece of ham covered with pineapple slices, spring rolls, and several bowls of noodles.

"There is no red meat, Heidi. I told Teresita that you were vegetarian."

"How thoughtful of you, Mrs. Tauber!"

Teresita indicated which noodle dishes were Filipino and which were Chinese. Carmelita looked around, "Where are the vegetables?"

"Coming," they heard from the kitchen.

Teresita held a serving dish while her husband poured the vegetables onto it. When the dish arrived, Heidi recognized some of the vegetables and thought they looked quite tasty. Teresita put some food on a plate and offered it to Carmelita, who had taken a seat at the head of the table. "I am not hungry. Later, thanks."

Her neighbour had lost a significant amount of weight, and Heidi marvelled that she was willing to exhibit her deteriorating health to strangers.

Most of the Filipino guests were eating in the living room, their plates on their knees, chatting in their own language as they watched TV. Heidi realized that there was an invisible wall between the two groups. *Why should I be the one to break the ice?*

Heidi noticed the unopened Christmas gifts piled up against the living room walls. To amuse herself, she began counting the crucifixes all over the walls of both rooms. How could a normal person have so many Virgin Marys? On each statue Mary had red spots on her cheeks and wore exotic clothes. Some figures were made of wood and others of plaster. The room reminded her of a cemetery. And all those candles and dead flowers in vases with no water! Heidi walked over and looked at the thermostat. Thirty degrees!

Mrs. Tauber walked slowly to the thermostat and turned it down. "Let me know if it is too warm. I feel always cold."

Her investigation completed, Heidi rejoined her family and the Eriksons at the table.

"Have you been here before?" Heidi asked Thora, keeping her voice low. She didn't want to be heard by the other half of the room.

Thora nodded and smiled. "Oh, yes, on several occasions. New Year, Thanksgiving, that type of thing, you know. We used to live outside Port Alberni. When Mac got married, he bought the house across from you, and soon after that, we bought our house next to him so we could be close to our grandchildren."

"How long have you lived here?" James asked.

Thora looked at her husband Ingmar. "How many years has it been?"

"I'm not good with dates," Ingmar said. "Max was still alive."

"What kind of man was he?" Heidi asked.

"The day after we moved in, Max crossed the street with a bottle of really good wine and introduced himself."

Thora said, "He was a handsome man who loved to party. They had someone who would cook and bake for them. He had money, apparently." Whispering in Heidi's ear, Thora added, "No children."

"Time for us to go," Thora announced. When she stood, Mac and Laurene rose with her and thanked Carmelita for the dinner. They waved at the Filipino TV watchers in the other room.

"Bye everyone," Thora said. She got a few nods in return.

Her hostess excused herself for not getting up. "My legs have had enough," she said. "Where is little Finley?"

"They had to go," Thora replied. "Heidi asked me to say goodbye for them. You were busy talking with someone else."

"I was going to give Easter eggs in chocolate to Finley. He likes chocolate, I can tell you."

Thora noticed the disappointment on Carmelita's face and offered to drop the gift off on her way home.

"That's very kind of you," Carmelita said. "Chocolate is good for the brain, as you know."

"Please eat more," Carmelita urged Lorin and Sherry Higa. George had told her that the couple, his neighbours and close friends, were leaving early the next day to visit Lorin's mother in Alberta. "How is your mother?" Carmelita asked.

"She's still going strong, it's amazing."

"Did your parents get sent to internment camps during the war, like so many Japanese families?" George asked.

Carmelita admonished, "You don't ask that type of questions."

"I don't mind," Lorin replied, laughing. "My parents were born in Lethbrige, and I grew up there. Memories of the war were still fresh in people's minds when I was a kid."

George noticed that the Filipino guests had torn their eyes away from the television screen and were following the conversation.

"Sherry and I are going to spend a week with Mom. We're really looking forward to it. We'd love it if she moved in with us here. The day after my dad died, I started converting our garage into an apartment for her. We're still trying to convince her, and it's starting to sound like she wants to make the move."

"I would love to meet your mother," Carmelita said.

"My older brother doesn't like the idea, because Mom would be alone while we're both at work."

"Does your brother live with your mother?" George asked.

Lorin shook his head. "No. He's been a missionary in Central America for years."

"Catholic priest or friar?"

"Baptist preacher. We don't see eye to eye on religion or much of anything else. Sibling rivalry, I suppose."

"I have a sister, too," Carmelita commented.

"My mom now lives in a seniors' home. She seems happy, but she wants to be closer to us."

Carmelita asked Lorin to pass on her regards to his mother. "You are a good son, I can tell. Your mother is lucky to have a daughter-in-law like you, Sherry."

Later, when she said that Teresita was her goddaughter, Lorin seemed puzzled and asked, "Are you related?"

The woman sitting next to Sherry said, "In the Philippines, everyone is related. My name is Gloria. I am the wife of Rey." The short, chubby woman pointed at a man sitting with the TV watchers. "The one with a baseball cap of the Canucks."

When Sherry mentioned that she worked downtown at the Bank of Montreal, Gloria said to her, "I work in a bank, too."

"Which one?" Sherry asked.

"CIBC, downtown."

Sherry suggested meeting for coffee someday.

Gloria said excitedly, "Yes, this would be so nice." After a pause, and looking shy, she added, "This will be the first time I have coffee with a Canadian."

"Aren't you Canadian?"

Looking even more awkward, Gloria corrected herself immediately. "Someone not from the Philippines, I mean."

Once again, while she was clearing the table, Teresita reminded Carmelita, "You must eat, *ninang*."

"Later, I promise." Then, louder, she said, "Someone please turn off the TV. I want to tell you something." The Filipinos gathered in the living room dropped everything to listen to *Ate*. "I met Senator Lucille Jolicoeur in Quebec, and we became friends. It was during the Eucharistic conference in Quebec City. Rey, Gloria, or someone else, when did we all go to Quebec?"

"Four years ago, *Ate*," Gloria replied.

"Her husband Marcel cooked the breakfast every morning for us. He used to be a judge. Days and evenings, we sat together, attending mass and listening to bishops from various countries, in particular Cardinal Ouellette. He will be a pope, one day. I asked for his blessing. Senator Suzanne just came back from a trade mission to China, with the prime minister."

Carmelita continued, "It was pouring rain, do you remember?" She turned to George. "Would you be kind enough to get the card from the past prime minister of Canada and pass it around?"

George got up and stretched to reach the large Christmas card on top of the glass-fronted cabinet. It bore a photograph of the former prime minister sitting under a tree in front of 24 Sussex Drive, flanked by with wife and children.

"When the senator's secretary asked me where to send the Christmas card, I gave her other names to add to the prime minister's mailing list, including yours, George. My sister has received one, too. The secretary told me that the senator is praying for me."

George hadn't received a Christmas card from the prime minister. Those niceties were reserved for *ethnic* citizens, he thought. The old Filipina and the other Filipinos were impressed by the gesture, but George saw it as a cheap way to buy votes.

Chapter Twenty-Five

George almost choked when Serena reported the rumour was going around in the Filipino community that he was Carmelita's boyfriend. The two were having tea at George's house.

"What are they thinking?" George asked her. "Hasn't it ever crossed their minds that a man of my age who is single might be gay? Are they blind, or stupid?" He shook his head in annoyance. He was aware of Serena's love for gossip and ferreting out people's secrets, but he didn't care.

"Did you tell her?" Serena asked.

George laughed out loud. "What makes you think we share our sexual experiences?"

Serena threw her line into the river. "How did the two of you meet?"

"I met her through John." Serena looked puzzled. "John, my partner. I keep forgetting he was already dead when you and I met. John was an administrative assistant."

"Was he one of the staff in the diocese that the bishop fired?"

"Yes, right before he died."

"They had no right to do that!"

"Don't ever tell Carmelita; she likes the bishop."

"Philippine women have a reputation for spoiling priests."

"You're quite outspoken for a Filipina."

"In the family I have a reputation of being a rebel." Serena laughed.

"How is Mio? Are you still living together?"

"Why are you asking?"

"Don't you remember? The other day, at the restaurant, you asked me to find a man for you."

"Yes, I was serious. I am not looking for sex with a man." She laughed again. "Not like you, George. I just would like to have someone to go for a coffee with, and talk."

"You don't do that with your husband?"

"It's over between Mio and me."

"He's still living with you, though, isn't he?"

"As a matter of fact, he is now at my brother's house."

"What's he doing there?"

"Housesitting. My brother and my sister-in-law are away for a month."

"And the man you call your ex is looking after their house?" George couldn't help it, he burst out laughing.

"What's so funny?"

"Nothing, Serena, nothing. Let's make a deal. If you can find a man for me, I'll find one for you."

"I don't have gay friends."

"I don't have straight friends."

"Too bad for both of us!" Serena smiled. "Change of topic: Are you a friend of Carmelita, really?"

"Of course! Why?"

"I have difficulty imagining you and her together, as friends."

"In a certain way, she reminds me of John."

"You must be kidding."

"No, Serena, I mean it. Carmelita doesn't have hang-ups about social appearance and convention. She doesn't seem to regret anything." George paused. "Like her, John always trusted life."

George felt like he was living on another planet. In the eyes of the neo-Canadians, he was the foreigner. The inevitable question came up when he met new arrivals from the Philippines. Why was he living alone? This was followed by the inevitable offer of introducing him to a single or widowed female relative back home.

Someone had recently offered to connect him with an unmarried cousin, describing her skin as being "almost as white as yours. She's on Facebook, do you want to see her?"

As usual, George bit back what would have been his preferred response: Would you happen to have a male cousin? He figured Asia had already had its share of tremors, so he made some vague remark praising the candidate's appearance and promised to think about it.

He was angry with himself, and ashamed that he felt unable to be honest with the Filipinos. He couldn't understand it, since he'd never been bullied in his youth for being more interested in books than cars. With an older brother who was openly gay, George's sexual preferences had never been an issue for his parents. They didn't reject him when he told them he had a boyfriend and was in love.

Born in Clinton, Ontario, George knew what a close-knit society looked and felt like, and resented it. Religion had never made any sense to him; it was a way of postponing happiness or hoping that someone or something would take care of your destiny for you. Early in life he had decided that life was to be enjoyed to the fullest.

He'd been happy teaching at the University of Toronto, where he had a wide network of friends. He travelled to Europe as often as he could: London, Berlin and Amsterdam, of course. Wherever he went, there were people like him. He worked hard (publish or die!) and gratification was plentiful.

The day he was diagnosed with AIDS, he moved to Vancouver, where the expensive cocktail of drugs he couldn't afford in Central Canada was available for free. Soon after, he met John. Together, they bought a two-story house in Victoria, on a street near the reclaimed rail bed called the Galloping Goose Regional Bike Trail. It was also across the street from Carmelita and Max Tauber. From his living room window one day, he could see the short Filipina with her finger poking the chest of a tall Caucasian man. Her husband, he assumed, and it looked like they were arguing.

In 1996, Carmelita became a widow; in 2014, George became a widower or a widow, depending on one's view of the world. It was only after John passed away that Carmelita invaded his planet like an alien power, her reasoning being, "You and I have no family here."

One day, she asked him to accompany her to a fundraising gala for the Victoria Immigrant and Refugee Centre.

The reception hall of the McPherson Theatre was full of people of Asian and Southeast Asian descent. Carmelita appeared to be at ease with the various cultures and knew what to say to each individual. She continued to ask him to escort her to similar events, and after a time, people in the parish and the Filipino community began inviting them to private dinners as if they were a couple. When they found out he was single, the matchmaking attempts began.

Carmelita only did it once. The day she tried to set him up with some relative from Hawaii who was visiting in Victoria, he exploded. "Is matchmaking part of the Filipino culture?"

His new friend didn't take offense; she simply said, "What's wrong with that?"

At times, what Carmelita called *our* culture would drive George crazy. It seemed to him that Filipino culture consisted of eating rice three times a day and praying to the Santo Niño, as they had been doing for centuries back home. Along with that came a deep-seated fear of expressing an opinion on any political, social or personal matter, as if there were spies in the room, ready to report on them. When they did open their mouths it was to compare Canadian manners with their own, not the other way around. The younger generation didn't talk at all; they texted, and tended to avoid adult company.

In Carmelita' house, George learned to eat a mango by dicing the pulp of the fruit into small cubes with a small knife and to indulge in cheesecakes and chocolate truffles. One day, not long after her cancer diagnosis, while she was watching on EWTN a bearded Franciscan friar, who praised the Lord while deep-frying samosas, George heard Carmelita mutter, "You can take me, O Lord. I am not afraid of dying." This became her spiritual leitmotif.

For nearly half of a century, the old woman had given her time to the Bayanihan Victoria Community Centre. Filipinos would extend personal invitations for her to attend birthday parties, wakes and other special events that required a multitude of both prayers and food. Her status of elder meant that adult men and women refrained from challenging her, while children and teenagers bowed to her.

The media's lament over the loss of the sense of family in North America didn't include the so-called ethnic communities. For the Filipinos, to fully exist as a person, an individual was first and foremost the sister, uncle or second-degree cousin of someone else. To George, this aspect of their traditional world was both exotic and beautiful. He wanted to experience more of this, and gain from it.

When he was Carmelita's escort at a social event, people extended him the same courtesy and respect they bestowed on the old woman. Then he began to see the dark side. For one thing, although they seemed to love the old lady, saying, "How are you, *Ate*?" upon her arrival at a party, a minute later the questioners would return to their clan.

For years, George opened doors for Carmelita, handed her the metal cane, helped her walk with the support of his arm and stood close by to steady her on stairs, and his actions were noticed. Carmelita knew everyone in town, it seemed, and George had hoped to make new friends through her. Among the Filipinos at least, it turned out that no one was interested in him. He felt like the proverbial tree falling in a forest with no one to hear. Filipino gatherings were family affairs, and among them, George felt lonely, without purpose and invisible.

When she was still able to do her own shopping, Carmelita would buy large quantities of fruits and vegetables. She would arrive at the cash register with her overloaded cart and ask the cashier to call the manager. When this individual arrived, Carmelita would introduce herself and shake hands. The manager would order one of his staff to carry everything to her car and load the bags into the trunk.

Over the following days and weeks, Carmelita would distribute the contents of the dozens of shopping bags among friends and neighbours who dropped in for a visit, starting with the parish priest. The rest would eventually rot in her extra-large stainless steel fridge, on the kitchen counter or on the large table on the deck. Things changed when her illness advanced and her energy diminished. After swallowing half a dozen pills, all she craved was an end to the swallowing. She could no longer carry groceries down to the basement and add to the piles of food on the rows of shelves or in her freezers.

Now Carmelita claimed she only felt hungry when she had someone by her side. "I've always been a social eater," she would say to George, who made a point of visiting her at noon. As soon as he set foot in her house, he could hear her voice from the bedroom, "Let's have some breakfast."

George would cook for both of them. "Your breakfast; my lunch," he would say. After the first tiny bites, she would utter her customary, "You are my angel," then dismiss him after the meal with, "I am sure you have things to do."

One day, while she was walking in the direction of her bedroom to rest, Carmelita said, "My sister called last night. She was telling me what to eat and what to do to get better." A second's pause, then she added, "If they don't want to see me, fine with me!"

"But every time they call, you tell them not to come." George mimicked Carmelita's voice. "I am okay...No need to worry...I am surrounded by people." Carmelita remained silent. "They love you. All of them, they care," George said.

"I don't want to be a burden."

Before closing the front door, George shouted, "I love you!"

A soft reply came from the master bedroom: "I love you, too." The voice was muffled by her morphine vapours and the heaps of clothes draped over the bed and the backs of the chairs and the aggregate of bulging plastic bags and boxes on the bedroom floor.

Chapter Twenty-Six

"I'm so excited!" George exclaimed as he and Colin Hong stepped into the elevator. Colin pressed the button for number 40. "I'm glad I decided to come over for the weekend; tonight the closing of the international fireworks competition, then tomorrow the Gay Pride parade. I can't wait."

"Think of all the handsome men showing their wares," Colin remarked.

George laughed. "Yes, it's like standing in front of the Casa Gelato on Venables, trying to pick a flavour."

"Wait till you see the view from Jim and Lukas's condo. The place is worth over a million dollars now."

"You're paying for the view and the prime location." George asked in a low voice, "What kind of business are they in that they can afford this place?"

As the elevator doors opened, Colin explained, "They've been buying, renovating and selling properties in Greater Vancouver for decades."

The condo door opened and Colin introduced George to Jim Goshinmon and Lukas Sterzenbach. Both men treated him to a warm BC hug.

George's eyes widened as he took in the view of North Shore mountains and seagulls floating over the bay.

"Let's go out on the balcony," Jim suggested.

"You're not afraid of heights, are you?" Lukas asked.

George peered over the railing at Coal Harbour; the tiny specks moving along the seawall were joggers, he knew. Awestruck, he said, "You can't tell if the jogger is a man or a woman."

"There are no units above ours," Jim remarked.

Sunlight flooded the interior of the condo, which was minimally furnished with a contemporary eggshell leather couch and chairs, sleek lamps, a huge wall-mounted flat screen TV and a wide bookshelf with rows of alphabetized DVDs. The living and dining rooms and the kitchen shared the open-concept space.

George studied the brightest decor note in the room, a rug styled with geometric motifs and a central medallion. "It's from Azerbaijan," Jim said. "We got it from a merchant on Granville Street, north of Broadway."

"I know that store," Colin said. "It's near an antique dealer off 7th Avenue that Leonard and I used to go to."

Now that Leonard's name was out of the bag, George thought, Colin will make sure that it stays out.

"Do you remember Leonard's house in White Rock? You and John came once, right?"

George nodded. "I remember. There was also an Asian guy."

"I don't remember him." Colin's expression suggested there was more to come. "Leonard's always been attracted to younger boys, especially Asians."

Jim and Lukas looked at each other. Like George, they knew Colin hadn't recovered from the breakup with his ex.

The sun set as they stepped back into the condo. "Let's eat before it gets dark," Jim suggested. He pointed at the dining table, set with elegant cutlery and plates on a white linen tablecloth.

Lukas set a dish of raw vegetables and fruits on the table, while Jim brought a platter of salmon steaks with a delicate sauce drizzled over the fish. "There's no cream in the sauce," he said.

George congratulated the chef, who he learned was Lukas. Jim said, "I cook on weekdays, but on weekends, he does."

Colin stared at Jim, whose sculpted muscles rippled as he served his guests. "I wish I had a body like you two," he said plaintively. "I'm so out of shape!"

"Just go to the Y," Lukas said. "They'll assess you, build a fitness program for you, and you just go from there. You can get a personal trainer to keep you motivated."

Jim followed with, "Lukas and I jog on Monday, Wednesday and Friday and on Tuesday, Thursday and Saturday mornings, we meet our private coach and train at the gym."

When Jim got up from the table and bent to retrieve something from a lower cupboard, Colin stared openly. "That's the kind of ass I want."

"Colin, stop," Lukas said, laughing.

"You're not my type; I don't go for Asian guys," Colin retorted.

Jim changed the subject. "George, Colin tells me you have a garden."

George nodded. "Yes, a vegetable and fruit garden. I'm not very good with flowers."

Lukas said, "We both love gardening. Before we bought this condo, we lived next door to an old lady and looked after her garden. We ended up buying her house. Jim had metal stakes labelled with the names of the plants. I'm not kidding; he had one for every single plant." He smiled at his partner.

Jim explained, "I used to design computer programs for Telus. I guess I need order."

George noticed how connected the pair seemed to be, their eyes rarely straying from each other.

His craving for some kind of intimacy led him to question, even interrogate the couple, prefacing his questions with, "I hope you don't mind…"

At one point, Colin reported being bullied at school because he was of Chinese descent. Lukas interjected, "Jim was, too, being of Japanese descent. You should hear what he had to endure from the cannery workers' kids in Steveston. What a place, nothing but the smell of dead fish everywhere." Turning to his partner, he urged, "Tell them, Jim."

George would have enjoyed hearing Jim's childhood stories, but his host just stared at his plate and smiled. Unable to figure out what Jim's reaction meant, George smiled, too, and said nothing.

Colin resumed, "My dad raised animals. I can still remember the smell when he came into the house for a meal."

Colin had more to say about his childhood in Surrey, but Lukas didn't want to hear it. "This is depressing! Okay, it's almost dark, we should get going."

Before heading out, Jim took George to see the guest room. "This is our office, as you can see."

Against the wall was a metal table with a computer, two monitors and all sorts of peripheral devices, interconnected through wires and cables of various colours. Several levers on the chair adjusted its seat, back and arms. The Scandinavian-style bed-sofa was made up with silky cotton sheets.

Jim indicated the wool blanket folded at the foot of the bed. "In case you get cold."

"I doubt I will. Thanks for everything, Jim. It's such a pleasure to be with creatures of my own denomination," he joked. George's sense of being a foreigner in his own land had melted away as soon as he'd stepped off the ferry at Tsawwassen.

Jim and Lukas put on hoodies. "It might be cold when the fireworks start," Lukas warned.

George went back to his room to grab a sweater.

Colin, wearing a long-sleeved shirt teased the others, "Sissies, all of you."

"You grew up on a farm, Colin, so you're tougher than the rest of us," George replied with a laugh.

On the way to the beach, the streets were thronged with young parents carrying children on their backs or in strollers, teenagers holding hands, and groups of men and women carrying blankets and folding chairs. Lukas leaned toward George and whispered, "I know you're curious. One day, Jim left Steveston and never looked back."

"What about his parents?" George asked.

"I've never met them. I don't even know what they look like or whether they're still alive."

He added that Jim's parents had been among the legions of immigrants who never made it and deprived themselves of everything to give their children a chance at a better life. George decided that Jim had turned his back on them in every way. His shaved head and urbanite clothes and lifestyle were the opposite of George's image of the parents: worn out, a permanent stench of fish clinging to them.

Lukas walked ahead to rejoin his partner, and Colin strolled along with George. "Lukas and Jim met at a club. They danced all night, then Jim invited Lukas to his apartment. The next day they moved in together."

"Is that true?" George asked, raising his voice so the couple ahead of him could hear.

"Neither one of us had ever been with someone before," Jim said.

Lukas added, "We've been living together for nearly thirty years."

Colin looked at George. "Like you and John, right?"

Lukas slowed and his face took on a sympathetic expression. "When did he die?" George gave him the briefest possible response.

They reached Kitsilano Beach, where the sky was exploding with fireworks, to the amazement and delight of the crowd. Jim and Lukas held hands, and Colin seemed lost in the visual orgy. George was remembering how happy he'd been with John. Standing there with Colin and his new friends, he felt overwhelmed with joy. He had loved and been loved.

At ten the next morning, George, Jim and Lukas waited outside the condo building. As soon as Colin arrived, they headed for the Gay Pride parade.

The procession included tattooed women holding hands and young boys with hair dyed in Day-Glo colours. Colin seemed spellbound by the extravagant beauty of hundreds and hundreds of creatures shouting, jumping, and exposing every part of their anatomy for the crowd. It was as if a playful giant had spilled cans of bright paint all over the West End of Vancouver.

George and Colin stood on the shady side of Beach Drive. As the parade wound past them, they caught glimpses of Jim and Lukas on the opposite side, both wearing baseball caps to protect them from the July sun.

"I feel like a dinosaur," George said, laughing.

Colin said, "I wish my niece were here."

"Which one?"

"Christie. She's a lesbian."

"She told you?"

Colin nodded. "My brother wants her to be an engineer."

Half-naked boys and men were waving at the crowd and blowing kisses from a float sponsored by Vancity.

"It's like a vibrating rainbow," Colin said, ecstatic.

The next float bore the logo of a local TV station. George recognized the young Filipino anchor, whose first name was Tony. "He's originally from Victoria. I've seen him on TV a few times."

The music was loud, the volume changing as each float went by. The city's mayor zigzagged past on rollerblades, shaking hands with the boys and girls on the floats and glad-handing the spectators on both sides of the street.

Police officers were vigilant but friendly, smiling indulgently as they patrolled amid the flamboyant crowd. On this day, the truth was on display.

The parade over, people folded their chairs, picked up their children or dashed to the portable toilets.

It was like when the lights came back on at the end of a movie. You saw the people sitting next to you and behind you. In the darkness, they were just a no-brand crowd; you barely noticed the back of a head, or the sound of fingers digging into a popcorn bag. Now the Gay Pride actors had metamorphosed into creatures that had only one thing on their minds: to urinate.

Colin touched George's arm and pointed out a man in his late thirties walking toward them. "That's my type," Colin said, licking his lips. "Yum, yum!"

The bars along Davie Street were packed. Jim and Lukas spotted an empty table at the back of the Pink Club. The four of them moved closer and the bouncer let them in.

Colin whispered to George. "The last time I was here, he smiled at me." When George asked who he meant, Colin, said, "The bouncer. He's attracted to me."

Lukas wanted more details. "Have you talked to him?"

"No!" It was evident from Colin's outburst that things weren't that simple.

The four men ordered fruit juice—pomegranate for George and Jim, orange for Lukas and Colin. Colin, a teetotaller, didn't mind being among people who drank alcohol, but he couldn't tolerate it. Alcohol made his face blush.

Looking around the room, Jim said, "Lukas and I rarely come here."

"Why would you? You have each other," Colin said. He added, "Oh, I just remembered, today's bath day for Mom. This morning, I called to remind her caretaker. She's completely senile, but she's easy to take care of. When I say, 'Mom, it's time to eat,' she just gets up from her recliner and comes to the table. She'll be ninety this year."

"She doesn't mind your going away on weekends and staying at your house in town?" Lukas asked.

Colin shrugged. "She watches TV all day long. She used to garden but she can't look after the plot anymore."

"Do you take care of the garden, then?" Jim asked.

Colin said, "Why should I? My brothers will sell the house as soon as Mom dies."

"Would you like to stay in your mother's house?" Lukas asked.

Colin stared at him. "I would rather die than live in Surrey. My parents only built that monster house to boost our inheritance."

Chapter Twenty-Seven

"George, did you know?" Carmen Escovedo's frantic voice rang in George's ear as soon as he answered the phone.

"Know what?"

Carmen was agitated, but managed to tell him she was calling from Vancouver. "I am here with my children. My sister visiting from Miami. George, *Tia* Carmelita was in a hospital!" Then, as if she could sense George's disbelief, she added, "This is true!"

"How did you find out?"

"I knew *Tia* Carmelita was with her sister, so I call there, and Ruby told me *Tia* Carmelita, they take her the *emergencia* because of some blood pressure problem and that Soledad is in this moment in Victoria."

George had some difficulty following Carmen, who reassured him, "This has nothing to do with her cancer."

After she was discharged from the Burnaby hospital, Carmelita told the doctor that she wanted to return to Victoria. That was when the situation worsened, according to Carmen. "George, very bad."

"How?"

"Soledad want Carmelita to come and live in North Vancouver with her own family."

"Yes, I know all about—

Carmen interrupted. "Yesterday, I go to Soledad's house. *Tia* Carmelita herself open the door. I didn't know her, George, she lose so much weight! She say 'Soledad went to Victoria to clean my house.' *Tia* Carmelita say to me, 'I call, but they don't answer me.' She say, 'Take me back to Victoria.' George, she was so angry, she was shaking. I was scared. She say to me, 'She has no right to go in my personal belongings. My car is in my sister's car port. Here are the keys, let's go.' I didn't know what to say."

George remained silent.

"I couldn't do it, George. I don't have the Canadian citizenship. If I kidnap her, I could go to jail. But I owe her so much. You remember how she help me with my divorce."

Carmen was distraught, feeling she had failed her children's godmother. "I am so ashamed, George. What will happen to her? We have to do something."

"Carmen, this is a family matter. We can't interfere." He stopped to think. "I guess I could go to her house and see why no one's answering the phone."

"George, thank you so much!"

Chapter Twenty-Eight

"The woman has lost her brains." Susan Pua's fiancé was gazing at the jumble that was Carmelita's house. The living room was a sort of oratory with crucifixes and statues of the Virgin Mary, monks and nuns. Plastic flowers, covered with dust, were everywhere. His family in Iloilo would have been shocked by the knickknacks. Jimmy had been raised as a Baptist but converted to Catholicism in Canada, shortly after he met Susan; it was the only way he would be accepted by her family. As a child, he was taught to believe in the power of faith only, not images.

For the past two days, Soledad had been calling around to Carmelita's friends, begging them to come and help clean the house. All had made excuses. Teresita Gonzalez worked nights and had to sleep during the day, but suggested Soledad call her sister-in-law Mei-Ling, who often cooked for *Ate*. Mei-Ling said she was cooking for an old woman due to return to China to die. Mei-Ling kept apologizing, but said she was working seven days a week. Jeanne Rose, the parish secretary, worked all day and into the evenings, and on the weekend they were going to Salt Spring Island to help her son and daughter-in-law build a barn.

Finally, Soledad called a company that rented dumpsters and had one delivered to Carmelita's driveway.

That day, a woman from the parish church showed up at the door. She was shocked to see Jimmy and Soledad. "Where's Carmelita? Is she worse?" Soledad explained that her sister was in Vancouver, and that she and Jimmy had come to clean the house. Although supposedly a good friend of *Ate*, the woman didn't offer to help. She pointed at her husband, who was leaning over the porch railing, staring into the dumpster. "I'm sorry, we have to go; my husband is waiting. Please tell Carmelita she's in our prayers."

"Jimmy, can you come and remove the boxes?" The voice came from the basement.

"I'm coming."

Soledad, who he called Mom even though he and Susan weren't yet married, was in the basement, separating Carmelita's belongings into piles. When he reached the bottom of the stairs, Jimmy's eyes widened. Soledad could barely turn around in the space.

There were rows of boxes containing dozens of old shoes, and an armoire with men's suits, shirts and jackets. Floor-to-ceiling bookshelves were crammed with cans of corn, peas, water chestnuts, stuffed black and green olives, sauerkraut, home-made pickles, fruit jelly, crushed packages of noodles, homemade wine, rice wine for cooking, and pouches of powdered sauces from various cuisines. Packages of candied ginger were heaped on top of chocolate bars.

Soledad staggered when Jimmy removed two large boxes from the first freezer and lifted the lid. "Oh, my God!" she wailed. Without the boxes, the lid wouldn't have stayed closed.

The freezer overflowed with frozen packages of salmon, trout, lobster tails, Italian and other smoked sausages, trout, milkfish, meatballs, a whole Peking duck, blocks of various cheeses, frozen green, yellow and red peppers, and bundles of asparagus spears.

Soledad picked up a bag of pirogies and her eyes welled up as she showed it to Jimmy. The best-before date was 1989. Another package of wontons was twelve years old.

Jimmy was desperate to escape the nightmarish mess. "I have to go out for a minute," he said. "I need to get something at the hardware store."

"Before you go, can you please bring me one of those big suitcases, and some big garbage bags? I will start emptying the deep freeze."

In the driveway, Jimmy recognized Mac, the neighbour who had introduced himself the day he and Soledad arrived. Mac held up a six-pack and asked, "Want to join me for a beer?"

As a former Baptist, Jimmy had avoided alcohol, but after his conversion he developed a taste for beer. He and his construction buddies often had a brew or shared a joint at lunch. He smiled and said, "Sure, thank you, sir."

Mac burst into laughter. "For Christ's sake, call me Mac."

Mac's wife Laurene came out of their house to say hello. When she asked about Mrs. Tauber, Jimmy explained that Carmelita was in Vancouver and that he and his mother-in-law were cleaning her house. "She can't stay here alone. It's not safe." Jimmy gulped his beer and wiped his mouth with his sleeve. "Thanks, this is just what I needed. Mom says *Ate* needs someone 24/7, not people who come when they have nothing else to do."

Jimmy felt he could finally breathe again. He'd been alone with his mother-in-law for forty-eight hours. "She's still in shock from her husband's death," he confided.

"How did it happen?" Laurene asked.

Jimmy told them how Soledad's husband had been felled by a stroke the day before he was to travel to the Philippines on business. When he mentioned the nine-day wake, Laurene looked puzzled, then said, "Interesting custom."

"The body isn't always there. Relatives and friends pray for the dead person. Back home, people drink and eat and play cards, but not here in Canada."

Laurene asked, "When is she coming back?"

"We don't know. Maybe never, depending..."

"We have a friend who'd be interested in buying the house." Mac seemed embarrassed. "Not our business, you know, just for your information. We can't predict the future, right?"

"I'll tell Mom." When Jimmy mentioned the overstuffed freezer in the basement, Mac and Laurene were shocked. "We're dumping everything. It'll be the same with the second freezer, probably."

"Man," Mac said. "One dumpster might not do it." He handed another beer to Jimmy, who shook his head, saying he had to get back inside.

"C'mon, let's drink to the memory of Max Tauber, who was a true gentleman." Jimmy smiled. "If you insist. Cheers."

"Max often invited me and my father for a drink," Mac explained.

When Jimmy returned to the house, his mother-in-law was talking on the phone.

She put her hand over the mouthpiece and said to Jimmy, "Tomas wants to know how things are going here."

Jimmy headed to the washroom; he was bursting. Soledad was in the middle of her report. "The first container is almost full. I am telling you, we need another one before the weekend."

Jimmy opened the bathroom, then quickly turned back to zip up. "Mom, Mac who lives across the street says that it shouldn't be hard to find a buyer for the house."

Soledad was heading back down to the basement. "I told Tomas that I will have a look at the second freezer before calling for another container."

A few seconds later, Jimmy heard a cry. "My God! How could this happen?"

"What?" He trotted down the stairs and walked over to her.

Soledad replied, "I can't believe it. Lamb chops. Look, this is also from 1989! I thought she might be a hoarder, but not with food. She was a nurse for so many years!"

Strangely, Soledad seemed energized by her mission, as if her duty to her sister were clear. She got on the phone to order a second dumpster. "They're coming the day after tomorrow to replace the first one," she said to Jimmy.

"Good. That'll give us another day to fill it." He spent the next hour pulling down the two dozen neglected flower baskets from the porch railing and ripping up dead plants in the front yard and along the driveway. All of it went into the container. He and Soledad had lunch, then returned to the basement.

Soledad inspected the contents of a box: napkins from the Sheraton Hotel in Honolulu, coasters from French cafés, theatre tickets, a tiny envelope with neatly folded Godiva chocolate wrappers. She gathered up Christmas garlands and plastic bags full of plastic bags. "Throw all this into the bin, Jimmy. I don't want to see this junk." When Jimmy seized one bag it shredded, the pieces littering the concrete floor like confetti. "We can use this for our wedding."

"This is not a joking matter!" Soledad said, angrily. "Where is everyone? In Vancouver, things would be so different. Do you remember what the people of our parish did for us when Phil passed away?"

"Yup!"

"They brought food, did all the dishes, they even took the garbage out. My sister keeps talking of her good friends in Victoria, but look, there is no one to help us!"

The door bell rang. Both of them seized the excuse to leave the depressing basement. Soledad parted the curtains, then smiled as she opened the door to George. "Come in. I am so glad to see you. Please, come in."

"No, thanks. I don't have time. Here's an extra key. You might need it."

Soledad seemed surprised to learn about the key, but said, "You are part of the family. My sister talks about you a lot." She repeated her invitation, then said, as if George had invited the confidence, "I am not very well; I really think that my older sister is in better health than myself. My husband's death was such a blow!" She took George's arm and stepped out onto the porch. "Your presence at the funeral meant so much to me and the children."

Jimmy stood nearby in silence.

George repeated, "Sorry, I really need to go." He freed his arm. "Allow me to say something: Victoria is home for Carmelita. She's lived on Vancouver Island for half a century! All her friends are here." After wishing them good luck, he left.

Soledad closed the door and exploded, "Did you hear what he said? Why did he say that?" She had tears in her eyes. "I know that my sister lives in Victoria, but family is family." She headed to the phone. "I am calling Vancouver."

"Call Susan; she's working from home today," Jimmy suggested.

"Can you dial her number, please? I am shaking."

After a few "I'm fine, I love you's" to his fiancée, Jimmy handed the phone to Soledad, who reported her conversation with George. Apparently not hearing unqualified support from her daughter, Soledad changed the subject. "You should see the mess here. It's not safe for her. The dust, the smells, all the junk..."

When she got off the phone, Soledad said to Jimmy, "She said Tomas is the only one who can convince her to move to Vancouver."

The phone rang later that day. Soledad's number came up on the call display and they heard the voice mail recording, then Carmelita's command: "Sol, pick up the phone and talk to me. What's going on?" Not a trace of weakness in the voice. "Vacuuming shouldn't take a week."

Soledad stopped Jimmy's reflexive movement toward the receiver. They both breathed a sigh of relief when Carmelita finally hung up.

"Are you going to call her back?" Jimmy asked.

"She needs to rest. I will call her tonight. You and I have more work to do." She said, "What would I do without you?"

Soledad opened the basement door and once again, they trudged down the steps, preparing themselves mentally for what awaited below.

Chapter Twenty-Nine

George's phone rang. It was Carmelita, reporting that she'd just returned to Victoria. "I am so glad to be in my own house."

"Did you drive your own car or did someone bring you home?"

"I told my sister, if there is no one to chauffeur me, I will drive."

"So, who chauffeured you?"

"Tomas."

"Is he still with you?"

"He just left; I called a cab for him for the Greyhound terminal."

"How did your sister react when you wanted to leave?"

"I told her, 'Sol, I am sorry but I am going home!'" Carmelita paused. With a sigh she added, "She never fully recovered from the loss of her first child, and her husband's death made things worse—"

"Wait a minute. She lost a child?"

"The little angel was hit by a car. My sister saw it from her window."

"That's awful!"

"A little girl, her name was Susan."

"So she named her second daughter after her?"

"George, keep it to yourself, please! None of her children knows. "

"Of course, Carmelita."

"Mama came to look after her. My sister never went back to work again."
Carmelita sighed heavily. "It's so sad! She graduated with the top marks.
Her first job was in the microbiology lab in Edmonton. It was owned by an
American company. In just a few years, she became head of the lab. Don't tell
anyone, George, please."

George heard the sound of running water. "Carmelita, I can't hear you."

"Her health has always been fragile. Anyway, I don't want to be a burden
to anyone."

"What are you doing, Carmelita?"

"Max couldn't stand dirty dishes on the kitchen counter."

"Get some rest, you've only just arrived. Oh, that reminds me: I'll call the
Lighthouse agency to let them know you're back."

"I can't stand those people!" Carmelita exploded. "What are they paid for?
There is one who just sits at the table with me and talks. The last one, when I
asked her to change my bed, the girl refused for fear of ruining her manicured
hands. I said to her, 'I can't afford to get a manicure.'"

Over the next few days, George learned that Carmelita was refusing to answer
the phone when her sister called. When he asked about it, Carmelita flew into
a rage. "My sister had no right going through my personal papers! No right!
And now guess what?"

"What?"

"The dishwasher is not working! He must have done something to the
dishwasher, and now I can't use it."

In Carmelita's vocabulary, Jimmy Habunal had various names, *he, him* or *that
man*. Refusing to be drawn into the family squabble, George asked, "What's
wrong with the dishwasher?"

"I have done it all my life: remove the thing and connect it with the faucet."

"Don't worry. I'll have a look at it next time I come over."

"I brought mangoes for you. When are you coming?"

"When you stop asking questions and let me hang up, Mrs. Tauber."

As soon as he entered, Carmelita shuffled over with her walker. She sounded like a beggar on a street corner. "Can you help me? Please?"

The bulky portable dishwasher had to be rolled to the kitchen counter and connected with the tap. Carmelita had managed the operation for decades, but now she couldn't find the part to connect the appliance to the faucet.

"Why don't you call your sister to find out whether it was working properly when they were here?"

"I don't want to talk to her."

"Have you two talked at all since you came back?"

The old woman shook her head violently. "No, I haven't forgiven her yet."

The next time George stopped by, Carmelita asked, "Where have you been? I haven't seen you for a week."

"For the record, my dear Mrs. Tauber, I was here two days ago for the dishwasher, and since then, you and I have talked on the phone several times."

"I don't want to fight. Come and give me a kiss." Carmelita then switched to a crucial topic: "Eat! There is something for you in the fridge."

"Later."

"Now!"

"On one condition: sort through all that junk mail on your dining table."

"You're always giving me orders. You remind me of someone else."

George invoked the name of Trish. "Remember what she said? There's too much stuff on the table." He noticed a pile of old community newspapers, thick with flyers and advertisements, at the other end of the table. "Let me put these into the blue box."

"Can you please sit down and stay quiet? Try to relax for once."

George started examining the photos on the front pages of the newspapers. Carmelita was still standing at the sink, her walker next to her as she rinsed the dishes. George heard the Japanese water filter announce the pH level. Suddenly his old friend bent over the sink and laid her head on her arms.

"What is it, Carmelita?"

"I cannot take it. Before you arrived, Teresita called to say that she was worried because I didn't answer when she called last night. Twice, I told her, 'I was sleeping.'"

Earlier, Teresita had left a message on George's answering machine, expressing her ongoing concerns about *Ate* living alone. Rather than simply leaving a message, the caller repeatedly shouted, "George, are you there?"

George found the whole situation absurd. Like Soledad, Teresita was upsetting Carmelita with her constant worries and tears.

"I am okay. Why don't they understand that?"

George reported that Teresita had offered him a big couch. "Thanks, but no thanks, I said to her."

"Why don't you take the couch? Carmelita asked. "You could put it in your office."

George replied with a laugh, "Am I supposed to tear down a wall to accommodate Teresita's couch?"

Carmelita was not amused. "I can't stand it when you talk nonsense."

"Do you mind if I get something from the fridge? I'm hungry." Carmelita looked at him, angry or suspicious, he wasn't sure. "You don't have to ask permission. There are times I would like to strangle you."

Carmelita continued fussing in her kitchen and dining room. Everything needed to be touched, changed, re-arranged to suit her. Carmelita expressed her annoyance with all the people who were trying to help her. George figured there would be no end to the litany of complaints, so he changed the subject. "The Catholic Church just announced that the next Eucharistic congress will be in the Philippines, four years from now."

"You should go, George."

"I might be dead by then."

"How can you say that? You are young." Carmelita became animated. "We could ask Teresita to come with us. She still has the house of her ancestors. We could stay there."

"Why didn't you go back to the Philippines after you left the States?"

"Stop asking questions!" Carmelita apologized and said, "It has nothing to do with you." She was back in the kitchen, moving objects around, as if trying to find homes for them.

Carmelita walked back to the dining table and sat at one end. She used a knife to open one of the letters she had received in the past few days. "I won a million dollars. Ha!" She opened another envelope.

George took her hand. "Are you okay?"

The old Filipina shook her head. "I cannot think properly. I don't know what's wrong with me. I am so thankful that you come and check on me."

George was standing by the door, ready to leave. Carmelita asked him to go to Teresita's house and pick up the *congee* that Emile had cooked for them again. "In the Philippines, we call it *arroz caldo*," she added in a whisper.

The old woman's eyes were fixed on a wooden carving of a *nipa* hut that was on the wall opposite her. The massive piece, two feet by three feet, was hanging above the buffet, which was covered with birthday cards, tins of Walkers shortbread cookies, and a bowl of tiny chocolate bars left over from Halloween. "Papa and Mama brought it with them when they came to Canada. An artist from Paete carved it." Then, without looking at George, she said, "Go to the Philippines!"

"I will, Carmelita." George felt tears in his eyes. He quickly opened the door and left. *And you will travel with me.*

In fact, they had already embarked on a journey together.

For several years, he had half-listened as she reminisced about the famous head physician at the Mayo Clinic, who had a chauffeur; about her soft-hearted papa, who cried so much when his wife died; Prime Minister Trudeau's convertible Jaguar and her own spending extravaganzas that followed her tantrums. George was at her bedside in hospital when she received her cancer diagnosis and, on that day, their friendship was born.

Whenever he was with Carmelita now, George asked questions and took notes. He worked hard to make sense of her memories and daydreams. He was hugging her even more often these days, and did his best to let her know how much her friendship had meant to him over the years.

*

George drove to Teresita's house, then rushed back to Carmelita's with the *congee*. With a laugh, he reported that this time, Teresita had offered him two chairs; they were making her living room look too small. "What makes her think I want everything she's trying to get rid of?"

"Why not? They would look nice in your garden," Carmelita remarked.

George looked at her. The old tiger, notwithstanding her wounds, was still fighting.

For months, Raynor Street had been invaded by a steady stream of non-resident vehicles, Carmelita's caregivers and visitors taking up parking spaces on both sides of the street. Neighbours like Thora Erikson were concerned about accidents. It was no longer safe for her grandson and his friends to play street hockey. Drivers used to slow when they saw the children, who would move their nets and replace them when the cars passed. One day, an impatient driver simply dodged around the players before they could react. Thora called 9-1-1 to file a complaint: "The stupid man zigzagged right through a dozen children!" The receptionist gave her a number to call.

On a Thursday evening, James Blair, just back from the Emirates, learned from his son Finley that Carmelita hadn't been outside her house for some time. James decided to inquire about her condition. He rang the bell at 611, and a woman opened the door. She stared at James, puzzled. "Oh, I thought you were the paramedics."

James introduced himself. "I live next door. My little boy was asking about Mrs. Tauber. How's she doing?"

"I am her caregiver. You have to talk to her family." As she started to close the door, she added, "I just called for an ambulance."

As he was walking down the steps, James heard the siren. He watched from his front door as the ambulance turned onto their street and parked in

Carmelita's driveway. The paramedics got out, removed a stretcher from the back of the vehicle and hauled it up the stairs.

James said to his wife, who'd been watching through the living room window, "That's the end, I'm afraid."

PART II

Chapter Thirty

In the last days of his life, John used to share stories of his childhood exploits with siblings and friends. Carmelita now seemed unwilling or unable to share anything with anyone. George was surprised by her silence, and was taking it personally.

A parishioner whose name he couldn't remember had suggested to George, "Do as I do, pray for her."

When the head nurse entered Carmelita's room one day, he asked, "Why won't she talk to me?"

"I'm not sure she can. The cancer has spread throughout her brain. Hold her hand; that's all you can do."

The nurse left. Then, out of the blue, Carmelita sighed. Her eyes were wide open. George moved his chair closer and seized her hand. The dying woman looked at him with a blank expression.

After a few seconds, her eyes focused and she began to speak. "There was always someone coming to the house from the street, from early in the morning till late at night." Then, abruptly, she said, "Why don't you go home?"

George kissed her forehead and was headed for the door when she spoke again. "There was a crazy man who had no family. He would go from one house to another house, begging for food. The poor soul would collect branches along the road and bring them to Mama. The beggar would not come in; he would eat outside, on the steps of the side porch. If Mama was not there, one of my aunts would give him a cup of coffee."

Leaning against the door frame, keys in hand, George didn't dare change position for fear of breaking the flow of reminiscences. He had already started working on his book about the old Filipina. Every word from her was a precious gift now.

"My mother would buy a pig or a cow. The neighbour would raise the animal until it was ready for the slaughterhouse. From the selling, Mama would get one part of the benefits."

Notebook in hand, George went over what he now knew about Carmelita. Many of his jottings were direct quotes from her. He thought he would use them verbatim in the book.

She had been surrounded by love in her childhood, which she had described as one of pure happiness. Her grandfather, the Philippines ambassador to US, had never cashed his salary, she once said. When he retired, the country's president honoured his achievements with an official reception at the Malacañang Palace. Young Carmelita watched the whole ceremony, peeking through the banister with the other children. Her grandmother wore an elaborately embroidered gown, made especially for the occasion.

"There were always people coming in asking for food or money. Papa would tell them, 'Go and talk to my wife. She is the one with money.' He used to say, 'Amor con amor se paga' (Love is repaid with love)."

"So you got that from your father. The generosity, I mean."

"It's our culture!" was Carmelita's response.

She had told George about her mother's reaction when Carmelita announced she wanted to study to become a nurse. *"'People treat nurses as servants.'"* Her mother eventually gave in and Carmelita registered with the College of Nursing at the University of Santo Tomas in Manila.

While working in the Manila General Hospital, she wrote a community nursing guide as part of a UNESCO project.

After her training at the Mayo Clinic in the US, Carmelita didn't return to the Philippines. She accepted a nursing job at a clinic in a remote northern BC community, helping First Nations women give birth. The snow had surprised her, and she endured a constant fear of being buried in an avalanche.

"One evening, I was busy looking after two mothers, and someone brought another woman ready to give birth. I called the doctor who was in charge of the clinic; he refused to come. He said, 'I am sure you can manage.'"

"Did you manage?"

Carmelita beamed. "Of course." Then her face became sad. "So much poverty among Natives. It shouldn't be so." She paused. "Iona Campagnolo and I became friends. She was an activist!"

"Where did you meet her?"

"While I was in the North or maybe in the south...She was a close friend of the prime minister of Canada."

"Pierre Elliot Trudeau?"

"The prime minister after him!"

Over the years, Carmelita would say to other Filipinos in Victoria, "You should travel in Canada, the country that welcomed you."

She had told George, "Their relatives in the Philippines keep asking for money."

When George ventured to say it must be hard to refuse, given the poverty in the Philippines, Carmelita had said, "There is poverty in Canada, too. Don't forget."

Carmelita's proud, strong voice and her stamina were all gone. Her hand was now a thinly sheathed bundle of bones. There was so much he still had to learn, and his old friend was abandoning him when he needed her the most. Soledad was no help; she had no access to her sister's past.

One day, George heard a knock at the door. It was the head nurse. "Did you close the door yourself?"

"Yes, because of the noise."

"How was she when you arrived?"

George got up to talk to the nurse. He stepped outside and closed the door behind him. "Actually, she's quite agitated."

"I'll call the doctor."

George went back into the room. "Carmelita, this is George. Can you talk to me?" The old Filipina looked at him, frightened.

George placed his index finger in Carmelita's palm. "If you can hear me, squeeze my finger."

He was repeating what he had learned six years ago with John: maintain physical contact. That was all that was left.

When John was sick, George wanted to know and feel what he was experiencing. Night time became their meeting place. John's habitual reserve meant he hadn't been very good at showing his emotions. Toward the end, he was finally able to say: "Here's my heart, here are my feelings."

When he awoke, John would share his dreams with George.

"I was on a boat..."

"Was it pleasant?"

"Yes."

One morning John whispered to him, "Two men were walking together."

"Did you recognize them?"

John looked at him. He smiled. "Guess who?"

Leaning against the bed and with his face close to John's, George asked, "You and me?"

John nodded and smiled.

George had once read a book or poem called, Alone with the Alone. *His lifelong friend, the man who had been at the centre of his life for thirty years, was setting out on a journey and he, George, was being left on the shore. Day after day, night after night, George was at John's side, waiting in vain for the slightest sign of life or emotion coming from the person he had loved from the day they had met. By that point, John was alone.*

Carmelita's slow breathing seemed to come from a deep, faraway place. George watched as her eyebrows moved and a winkle creased her forehead, like a sharp cut from a knife. *What's happening in her mind right now?*

Someone opened the door slowly; it was Betty Calder, the secretary of the Catholic Women's League. George had noted Betty's attitude toward Carmelita over the years, so he was surprised at the visit. "How is she?" Betty asked.

"No change."

Betty stroked Carmelita's hand and prayed, "In the name of the Father…" The words sounded like a lullaby. George got up, but Betty said, "You can stay and join me, George, if you want."

George shook his head. "I just stopped by to see how she was."

Closing the door on the sound of whispered prayers, George left.

Another day, it was the large, warm-hearted Jeanne Rose, walking with obvious pain. "How is she?"

"Same as usual. Where's Paul?"

"He's trying to find parking."

"I have to go. Please say hi to him for me."

Jeanne nodded. "Have you heard from the family?"

"They said they're coming."

Outside, Paul greeted him with, "Any change?"

"No."

Placing a hand on George's shoulder, Paul muttered, "Thanks for being here for her." The man was slimmer than his wife, but just as caring. "All we can do is pray for her."

George wasn't so sure about that, but he didn't want to offend Paul. He zipped up his jacket and left. As he walked to his car, he remembered another stream of reminiscences from Carmelita, which she called chapters of her life.

"Back then, at home, there were always visitors. A woman would arrive with a basket full of pandesal*. Another one would come carrying a pot of chicken* adobo *that she had cooked early in the morning when her family was sleeping. My mother was an ingenious woman. She could help a midwife deliver a baby, rescue a sick uncle or a cousin who had nobody to take care of him… My uncles and aunts were rich, not my parents; they were the poorest of the family."*

These bits of conversation, with names of people and places, were now knocking at the door of George's mind. From the storyteller herself, there was nothing but irregular hisses of air, interspersed with moaning.

When Mary Hendricks visited, she was shocked at the morphine protocol Carmelita was on. "They keep increasing the morphine whenever they want. It's euthanasia! The head nurse used to have to call the family doctor to increase the dosage, but not anymore."

George held back his response. He wanted to say, "Are you crazy? Our friend was diagnosed with cancer four years ago. Look at her! What makes you think she's going to live for another four years?"

As if reading his mind, Mary continued. "She's a strong woman, with a strong will. She could have lived longer. They put her on the protocol too soon."

Carmelita had sunk into a coma. Watching her, George relived John's death. He treasured the words and memories he had shared with him. As for Carmelita, everything George thought he was hearing from her came from his own head. Leaning toward her, he rested his palm on her forehead to let her know that he was there, caring for her. He could hear the old Filipina's words: *"Papa loved to sing "Besame Mucho" to Mama."*

Toward the end, John would say, "I'm bored, there's nothing to do." He wanted to die. One morning, he asked George to call his family doctor. "There's something I need to know."

Dr. White came to their house the next day, after his shift at the clinic. When he saw his doctor standing at his bedside, John looked at him, surprised. "Why are you here? Did George call you?"

"I've been meaning to come and see you for some time."

John woke up in the middle of that night. "Now I remember what I wanted to ask him: How can I unplug?"

The Palliative Care Pavilion became the scene of a living wake for Carmelita. Parishioners stopped by at all hours to hold Carmelita's hand, feel her forehead and rearrange her hair while muttering prayers. One day, a caregiver wheeled in a small table with a CD player on it. She chattered to Carmelita in Tagalog as she plugged in the machine and searched through a stack of CDs.

"She can still hear us," she said to George. "You are good for her."

George remained silent as the caregiver, Estrella, told him she was from a mountain province in the northern part of the Philippines. "There are rice terraces. You should go the Philippines."

He laughed. "That's what Carmelita used to say to me. I wanted her to come with me, but she was already sick by then."

Estrella opened the door and said, without looking at George, "Thanks for coming."

A few minutes later, a young Filipino man brought in a thermos of coffee and a plate of cookies and set them down next to George. "Let us know if you need anything."

"Where in the Philippines are you from?" George asked.

"I was born here. *Ate* helped my parents when they first arrived."

George's visits were always short. As soon as a mourner showed up, he would excuse himself and go home.

When Gladys Estopacia—George had seen her a few times at Carmelita's house, refilling her containers of water—stopped by, she wasted no time in venting her frustration. "Forgive me for saying it. The people who regularly come to see her are strangers."

"At least she's not alone," George ventured.

"Don't get me wrong. It's wonderful what you are doing. This is very generous of you, considering you are not related."

"She's my friend."

For a moment, Gladys seemed at a loss, then regrouped. "Carmelita and I often quarrelled, but we were family."

"I didn't know you were related."

"Carmelita's mother was my father's second cousin."

"Say that again," George asked.

Gladys repeated herself, but it didn't make any more sense to George, who found this business of unlimited numbers of cousins a complete mystery.

The room was set up as if for a Catholic funeral, even though the patient was still alive. There were pictures of the Virgin Mary and a wide array of saints, and a small candle burned on a side table. The CD player had been taken away to make space for the mourners, who prayed and whispered. Most of them were women; George wondered whether they believed that keeping vigil was not a man's job. When they addressed the dying woman, it was in Tagalog. The room was hot; visitors were told to keep the door closed for privacy.

On Wednesday, Soledad called George from the ferry; the family was en route to Victoria. "We will go directly to the hospital. It's a question of days, the head nurse told us last night." Before hanging up she added, "We will stay with her as long as needed."

Time to return my angel's wings, George thought. "See you tomorrow at the Palliative Care Pavilion," he replied.

The following day, George went to the hospital to whisper "I love you" in Carmelita's ear for the last time. He took a moment to caress her cheek, then said goodbye to the next-of-kin and walked to the door.

On Friday, George learned by phone that the old woman's breathing, which had been intermittent for the past few days, had stopped altogether in the evening.

Bill Howard, owner and director of Howard's Funeral Service, had one objective in mind; to honour his old friend's last wishes. Bill operated the only Catholic funeral home in Greater Victoria, and had known Carmelita for ten years. If there was a Filipino funeral, she was usually involved, often taking over the arrangements when the relatives were too distraught.

He remembered the day a few years earlier when he got a call from Carmelita. "I need to see you," was all she said before hanging up.

As soon as he set foot in her house, she commanded him, "Eat first." The story of her cancer diagnosis came out, interspersed with, "This is your favourite dessert, lemon meringue… Coffee or tea?" and "Go ahead, I am not hungry." Carmelita said she was ready to die, but she wouldn't entertain the idea of cremation.

"I've explained everything in my will."

Bill became a regular visitor. Carmelita would ask after his health and tell him to drink lots of water and not to work too hard. Not a word about her own health. She listened attentively as he confided that his wife had died when his children were young; one of them was in trouble with the police. She never pressured him with questions and invariably sent him home with fresh fruits and vegetables and cookies for his grandchildren.

One day he asked Carmelita, "Where are you getting your strength?"

"As soon as I say 'I am okay,' I feel better."

He was up late the night he got the call he'd been expecting. Tomas, who was the executor of Carmelita's will, got right down to business. "*Tita* has just passed. Can you come and meet with us? All family is here, at her house."

Chapter Thirty-One

After a nearly one-hour delay due to the frustrating Colwood Crawl, Maud and Sebastian Nieman finally reached the Holy Name of Mary Church. Carmelita's sister was already walking up the aisle toward the front pew, her sons supporting her on either side. Knights of Columbus, striking in their white uniforms with white ostrich plumes on their hats, served as pallbearers.

Maud and Sebastian were still debating where to sit. Maud recognized some of the Filipino parishioners, who politely bowed their heads in greeting. One lady invited them to take the empty space beside her.

Over the years, Carmelita had helped Maud and Sebastian feel comfortable with Filipinos.

"Our parish won't be the same without her," Maud said to the woman beside her. The parishioner had tears in her eyes. Maud opened her purse and handed her a tissue. "Here, take one."

"Thanks," the woman said, dabbing at her tears. "She loved so much her family in Vancouver. She would mention their names over and over!"

*

"*Ate* would be proud," Soledad whispered. A dozen Knights and Ladies of the Equestrian Order of the Holy Sepulchre of Jerusalem were seated in the front pews near them. Each was draped in a long ivory cape bearing a red cross, symbolizing blood. The men wore berets and white gloves, and the women, black mantillas and black gloves.

The Archbishop of the Diocese of Vancouver was officiating as Grand Prior of the Provincial Lieutenancy. In the family, they all knew about the prestigious Order, whose main mission was to support the people of the Holy Land. Like all the female members of the Order, Soledad's older sister had held the title of Lady. Bishop Henry of Victoria was co-celebrating the funeral mass that would be sung in Latin, with Gregorian chant throughout.

The church was filled to capacity, but Soledad's heart felt empty. She'd had a good cry in front of all the friends gathered at last night's wake. Sitting less than a metre from her sister's body, Soledad said, "I am not saying that they didn't do a good job in Victoria, but can someone tell me why she didn't have any radiation?" She approached the open coffin. "Look at her. She is minuscule."

Tomas and Sandy got up to stand next to Soledad. Sandy handed a tissue to her husband, who was holding his mother's arm. "She had such a strong will!" Sandy said.

The void created by the death of Soledad's husband had deepened. Even though she was surrounded by her children and her friends, the pain was too much. "All those years, she refused to let me look after her. I shouldn't have listened to her. On the phone, I would beg her to come and live with me."

Susan and Marty had joined them next to the coffin. "She always said, 'I want to die in the house my husband built for me,'" Susan said.

"She didn't die in her own bed," Soledad cried.

Prayers ceased as the assembled mourners focused on the tableau at the coffin.

"Mom, you held *Tita's* hand till the end," Marty said, crying openly. "You have nothing to blame yourself for." His words made no difference; Soledad was inconsolable. "Mom, please, I—we're all here."

"Our friend Carmelita was a warrior, spiritually and communally." His Grace, Bishop Henry, was delivering the eulogy, in accordance with his promise to Tomas when he was informed of Carmelita's death.

"Her faith helped her bring happiness to everyone around her, especially her dear sister, her loving niece and her nephews." Mentioning each of them by name, the bishop said, "Your sister, your aunt continue to look after you as before." His words were greeted with quiet sobs and discreet blowing of noses.

"Even though she was ill, Carmelita's deepest wish was to travel to the Holy Land and pay homage to the Patriarch Grand Master of the Order of the Holy Sepulchre. She once told me: 'If God wants me to go, He will give me the health and the strength to go.'" The Bishop concluded, "This is how our dear friend was."

The service over, the mourners gathered in the community hall beneath the Holy Name of Mary Church. Gone were the Archbishop of Vancouver and his assistant, who planned to catch the two o'clock sailing for the Mainland.

As George walked toward them, Tomas said to his mother, "Mom, here's George."

George shook hands with Tomas, hugged Soledad and offered his condolences to the family. Soledad said loudly, "George brought so much comfort into my sister's life." With her three children at her side, this was Soledad's *official* thank-you to George.

In contrast to her two brothers, Susan looked radiant; the six-foot tall woman, who must have been in her thirties, hugged George with so much passion, he felt like a fly about to be consumed by a carnivorous plant. "We're going to miss her, like you, I'm sure," she said. Susan confided that she and Jimmy could finally marry, something they had been postponing for a long time.

"Mom told me you plan to write a book about *Tita*."

George nodded. "Your aunt often said, 'My life could be a book,' so I said I'd write it."

"A biography?"

"No, it's going to be a novel based on her life. It's about friendship and things like that," he said, determined to keep the details to himself.

"That's cool." Susan smiled.

While he was conversing with Susan, George was aware of the dozens of people that had gathered in the hall. They were mostly older men and women, and all were standing or sitting with a heaped plate of food in their hands. *Did they fast for the occasion?*

"Your aunt introduced me to the Philippine culture," George said to Susan. He suddenly realized that these Filipinos he had wanted so much to connect with on a personal level, now represented ideas and feelings to be scrutinized, even dissected, for his book. Acceptance and love were no longer his focus.

From a few feet away, Erliza Maligson waved at George. She would never cross the room to speak with him. Even after twenty or thirty years in Canada, the old customs were still observed: a woman doesn't shake hands with a man; a man doesn't start a conversation with someone who is not *one of them*.

"George, could you come, I would like to ask you something." Soledad's voice travelled over the buffet table, now densely laden with cakes, pies, squares and other sweets, and over the heads of the people chatting over dessert and coffee.

As soon as George came close, Soledad asked, "My sister wouldn't allow me to be with her. Can you tell me why?" She burst into tears.

To Marty, George looked like he wanted to run away. "I have no idea, Soledad. Could it be that she wanted to protect you in some way?"

"I don't know what I would do without my children."

George said nothing. He raised his head and looked around.

"Are you looking for something?" Marty asked.

"I came with a friend. I'd like your mother to meet him. He met your aunt once." His eyes still scanning the room, George added, "He seems to have disappeared. I'll go find him." He turned to Marty. "Can you come with me? Let's check outside."

Reluctantly, Marty followed him.

Moments later, they stopped at the gate to the small garden at the back of the rectory. George waved. "Colin."

Seated on a wooden bench and absorbed in his sketch pad was a man who looked Chinese to Marty. The man wore an unbuttoned jacket with a white shirt and no tie, and a pair of black jeans. Marty noticed the vintage glasses, which made the man look like a prep student, except for the strands of grey in his hair. "I don't think he heard you," Marty said to George.

George opened the gate and walked up to his friend. "Colin Hong, I'd like you to meet Carmelita's nephew, Marty."

Colin stared at Marty with expressive eyes, then put away his sketch pad and got up to shake hands. "I'm gay." After a pause, he added, "Now you know."

Marty remained silent, so George said, "Marty's an artist, like you, Colin."

"I'm just a teacher," Marty corrected him.

"You're a musician, aren't you?" George asked.

When Marty heard that Colin had arrived on the first sailing from Vancouver for the funeral, he asked, "Did you know my aunt?"

Colin nodded. "We met at George's place. I'd come over for the day with my mother." Colin laughed. "Mom and your aunt really connected. Which surprised me; Mom doesn't care much for people."

Marty smiled. "My aunt liked everyone—"

"Do you like everyone?" Colin interrupted him. Without waiting for Marty's reply, he added, "I don't like people."

"C'mon Colin," George interjected. He shook his head. "I don't believe you."

Colin turned back to Marty. "Do you like people or not?"

Marty hesitated. "It depends on who they are, I guess."

Colin burst into laughter. "You're as bad as me."

The three men were being observed by the mourners leaving the hall and heading to their cars. Some carried plastic bags of leftover food.

"Let's go back to the hall," George suggested.

As the three of them stepped inside, it dawned on Marty that this man he had just met was fearless, and willing to say exactly what he thought. He felt an attraction to the man and, without acknowledging it, hoped to meet him again. This realization became *real* when Marty noticed a smile on Sandy's face; his brother Tomas was looking in their direction. He, too, was smiling.

Soledad, who was seated in a circle with friends and acquaintances, exclaimed, "Oh, George. I thought you had already left. Come and join us."

"Give me one second," George replied. He didn't seem keen on joining the mourning circle.

"Do you still live at home?" Colin asked Marty.

Marty nodded. "My sister has a fiancé and will be leaving soon."

George interrupted. "Could we meet for a coffee sometime?" As if just realizing how strange this sounded, he added, "The next time I'm in Vancouver."

"Why don't you guys come to Mom's house?" Colin asked.

For Marty's benefit, Colin added that he was taking care of his mother on the old family farm in Surrey. He described his days with her: "I warn you, Mom's confused most of the time. Would you like to come to Surrey?"

Marty asked nervously, "When?"

"I don't know. The next time George comes over."

"That sounds good," George said. "What do you think, Marty?"

Marty readjusted his belt, noticing that his hands were damp.

Parish volunteers took possession of the community hall, now almost empty, to clear the tables and remove garbage bins. There was a lot of noise. Teenage helpers folded tables and stacked chairs.

Marty held the back door of the church for his mother, his siblings, and the Surlas.

"Are you okay?" Sandy's voice startled Marty.

He was not fine, and his sister-in-law had figured it out. She repeated, "Marty, what's wrong?"

"You remind me of *Tita*."

"Why do you say that?" Sandy asked.

"She would sit next to me and say, 'What's wrong with you, Marty?' Her tone of voice when she would interrogate me."

"I remember that tone," Sandy remarked. "It was pretty intimidating."

"She'd massage my neck with her sharp fingers and say, 'Talk to me, sweetheart.' I never figured out what she was after."

Chapter Thirty-Two

"They don't care!" were Carmen Escovedo's first words when George picked up the phone. "*Tia* Carmelita would be so mad!"

"What's going on?"

"The family is having a yard sale, *pero* it's inside. I came over with Emily, Melanie is working today. I just want to see her place one more time, you know, before everything is gone and they sell the house. I just want a prayer book or a statue, you know. Something *Tia* touch and hold in her hands."

"Are you inside now?"

"No, we are sitting in my car. In *Tia's* bedroom, the closet is open, the drawers... you could see her stockings. Emily was shocked, she said 'Mom, let's go.' She had tears in her eyes. The twins and Julio, they all loved her so much."

Whenever she was upset, Carmen's speech became a mix of Spanish and English. In the middle of a sentence, she would ask, "What's the English word for this?" making it difficult for George to follow her.

"Did you buy anything?" George asked.

"Emily got some bowls. She pay one dollar for a set of three; there was also a blender still in its box, brand new; she gave $20 for it."

George remained silent.

"Christmas lights, rows of shoes, nurse uniforms wrapped in plastics, Uncle Max's suits and ties, and a big suitcase full of photographs. Not everything had a price tag. You just make an offer. Wood carvings from Africa, geisha dolls from Japan. Do you plan to come, George?"

"Are you kidding?"

"I guess you are right. Don't come, it's so sad." Carmen paused. "I just wanted a little souvenir. I was ready to pay. There was a little Santo Niño on a bookshelf, I ask 'How much?' Her nephew say to me, 'Take it. This is a gift from *Tita*.' I am so happy, George."

"Which nephew? The tall one or the chubby one?"

"Not very tall."

"Marty."

"Are you coming?"

"I don't want any of her stuff. It's not hers anymore. She's dead. Who else is there?"

"All Filipinos, I recognize a few from the parish, Serena, Lilia—

"How about Teresita? She should be there."

Carmen apologized for not mentioning Teresita, "She is upset. She took a pill in front of me, for blood pressure, she told me. Do you want to know what she said to me, in front of Soledad?"

"What did she say?"

"'How could they do such a thing to *Tita*?'"

"She was very fond of Carmelita."

"I am going back into the house. Can I call you later?"

"Sure."

Lilia Arcilla stepped inside Carmelita's house and looked around. She waved at Argie, the Short One, who waved back. Her husband was on his way out, carrying a box full of old pots and pans, rusted cookie sheets and muffin tins.

"On Monday, Manuel will take this to the Salvation Army," Argie explained. "They need help. There is so much stuff they need to get rid of."

"How about the couch, how much are they asking? There is no tag."

"Mom has promised it to someone already," a woman replied.

"You are Carmelita's niece, right? I forgot your name."

"Susan."

A tall, muscular Filipino man was bringing a box up from the basement. When he walked by Susan, he smiled at her. Susan introduced him. "My fiancé, Jimmy."

"Congratulations. Where are you from?" Lilia asked, but Jimmy had already stepped outside.

"He's from Iloilo," Susan said, adding, "Sorry, he's in a hurry; he has to get to Home Hardware before they close."

"When is the marriage going to be?"

Susan whispered, "Ask Mom."

"Where is she?"

"In the basement. Come with me."

The basement made a big impression on Lilia: the ceiling was higher than the one in her condo on Hillside. Daylight spilled through six large windows on two walls, with the back-door window adding to the brightness of the space. "This would make a nice apartment."

"We think so, too," Susan said.

The family will get a good price for the house. Lilia said aloud, "It's close to a Safeway, a post office, a walk-in clinic..."

"So you know the neighbourhood?"

"Of course, Carmelita and I have known each other for nearly thirty years."

Lilia was distracted by the sound of clothes banging inside a washing machine. She suddenly saw Soledad on a small stool, her back to the machine; she seemed distraught. Seeing Lilia, she said, "Give me a hug, Lilia."

Lilia put her arms around Soledad. "We didn't talk at the funeral. I didn't want to disturb you and the children."

"You are family to us."

"How are you coping?"

"I cleaned once already, but I didn't know that my sister had all this stuff."

Lilia nodded. "I know. But now you have a lot of help."

Leaning toward Lilia, Soledad said quietly, "Susan is getting married in December."

"That is wonderful!" Lilia noticed Soledad's sad expression. "I'll go and congratulate her."

"Later. Keep me company, if you don't mind, my friend."

Lilia sat next to Soledad. Together, they waited for the end of the rinse cycle.

Just then, Teresita Gonzalez came down the stairs and said to Soledad, "Emile just got a call from his sister Denise in Hong Kong. She wants to buy the house."

"From Hong Kong?" Soledad repeated. "I can't think properly. Talk to Tomas."

"Where is he?"

Soledad turned to Lilia. "Can you go and find Tomas?"

When the two women found Tomas supervising the cleanup and sales on the main floor, Teresita asked him, "Can we talk?"

"Of course," Tomas replied with a smile. Lilia headed back downstairs.

"Emile's sister Denise used to live in Victoria, but when her husband David had to go back to Hong Kong to look after his father's construction business, she and the children left with him. They liked *Ate* Carmelita very much. Anyway, this morning, when Denise called, she said to Emile, 'Tell the family that David and I want to buy the house.' That's good news, don't you think?"

Tomas didn't react.

"Denise says that *Ate*'s spirit is still in the house, since she died just one month ago."

Like the rest of the dozens of visitors Tomas had seen coming and going, Teresita believed that his *Tita* belonged to her, and that the family was supposed to be grateful for their love for his aunt.

"Denise is making an offer," Teresita whispered.

Tomas couldn't focus on what she was saying, as they were constantly interrupted. One person wanted a rebate on something; another asked whether there was just one bedside lamp or a pair.

"Do you have CDs?" Tomas looked down at the little boy, whose mother was standing behind him, a brand new set of pillowcases in her hands, along with some cloth.

"Do you see the man in a striped shirt over there? That's my brother; he knows the price of everything. Go and ask him."

"Thanks, sir."

"This is not the place for this discussion," Tomas said to Teresita, not hiding his annoyance.

"Let's go into *Ate*'s bathroom," Teresita immediately replied.

"You know your way around, I see." Tomas remarked as Teresita preceded him into the room.

Teresita quickly closed the door that Tomas had left ajar, "Denise is offering five hundred thousand dollars."

"US or Canadian?"

"I don't know." Teresita looked embarrassed. "Call her. Anyway, she said to Emile, 'I can pay cash.'"

"This can't be done under the table," Tomas warned.

"*Ate* said to Denise one day—she was not sick at the time—'If I decide to sell my house, you will be the first to know.'" Tomas just looked at her.

"Your mother could stay with Denise when you come to Victoria. The house would be her home, this is what Denise says."

Someone knocked at the door. "One minute, please," Teresita called out. She handed Tomas a piece of paper. "She is waiting for your call."

Tomas looked at the number written on the back of an envelope. "I'll give it to our Realtor."

"Not the Realtor!" Teresita protested. "They charge a commission, you know."

Tomas pulled out his iPad. "I have to make a phone call."

"Are you calling Denise?"

Tomas shook his head. "No, my wife. She couldn't come today; she's working."

Chapter Thirty-Three

George began calling Carmelita's friends and acquaintances, asking if they'd mind being interviewed for his book. His request seemed to take everyone by surprise.

"What could I tell you? She is gone," one of the board members of the Victoria Philippines Association replied.

Lisa Navarro, a nurse who had worked under Carmelita's supervision, told him the best way to do justice to the dead was to move on. After suggesting that he call the family in Vancouver, she, like all the others, wished him luck with the book and hung up.

George called Josefine Estrera in Hawaii. He reminded her that they had met at Carmelita's during her most recent visit to Victoria. He didn't mention Carmelita's hope that there would be a spark between the two. He informed her about his project and announced that he was thinking of spending a few days in Honolulu. "Would you be willing to talk to me about Carmelita?"

"Sure. What do you want to know?"

"She went to Honolulu every year for many years. Did you see her when she was there?"

"At the church, mainly. I knew her father, too. He lived here for several years, as I'm sure you know."

"Also, there's another friend of hers that I'd like to meet."

"Who?"

"I don't remember her name. She was with you when you came to Victoria that time."

"That's *Manang* Rita."

"Are they related?"

"No, just friends."

"Do you still see her?"

Josefine laughed. "Regularly. We are both on the parish council."

"Do you think she'd be willing to meet with me?"

"Of course! When are you coming?"

"I was thinking sometime next month. Will you be in town?"

"Yes."

"Okay, I'll book my flight and find a hotel. Can you suggest a reasonable one?"

"You are welcome to stay at my place. But let me warn you, I don't cook."

Josefine's condo was situated on the twelfth floor, the ocean just visible in the distance. On George's first morning in Honolulu, they sat on the balcony sipping fruit juice and chatting about Carmelita's connection with Hawaii.

When Carmelita's mother passed away in Vancouver, her father wanted to return to the Philippines. Instead, his two daughters opted for a retirement home in Honolulu, where several of the residents were his former classmates, or at least alumni of the same university in Manila. Every year, Carmelita would visit her father at the home.

"Carmelita would hide herself under a *muumuu* and wear large hats," Josefine said. "She didn't want her skin to get any darker. She would take her father for walks on the beach while Max was schmoozing with the tourists at the hotel."

That Sunday, George attended mass with Josefine at St. Philomena Church. While congregation members chatted, a band comprised mostly of teenagers rehearsed until the priest and the altar boys and girls arrived. It was an early mass, and many of the youngsters were stifling yawns.

After mass, Josefine introduced him to Rita Walter, a strong woman in her nineties who walked unassisted by the cane or walker so common to people of her advanced age. Josefine went to catch up with friends, and George sat with Rita at the back of the church.

Rita beamed. "We had so much fun together. We used to go to restaurants, shopping and parties, always by ourselves. Who wants men to tell you what to do?" she said, winking at George. "Anyway, all Max wanted to do was drink and talk business, and my husband Jack just watched TV all the time."

George was surprised to learn that Rita still drove. "My husband always criticizes my driving." With a serious expression, she added, "He is the bad driver, if you want to know."

Being the eldest of a big family, Rita had to work at an early age. Her parents opposed her marrying a Native Hawaiian. "My husband was quite a lover in his early years." She laughed. "Carmelita was a prude with regard to sex; I am not. You see, I was not brought up by nuns, like her."

"Did you see her the last time she was here with her nephew?"

"Of course!" Rita nodded smiled. "Josefine told me that you are writing a book about her. What kind of book?"

"It's a novel, not a biography, actually. I'm basing it on her memories as a child in the Philippines, her time as a nurse, and her travels. There's a lot I don't know about her early life."

"Her sister must be a great help."

"Not so far. There's a huge age difference between the two sisters; fourteen years."

"Josefine says you have questions for me."

"Could we meet some time? I'm here most of this coming week."

"I know a nice restaurant near Josefine's place." The old woman stared at George intently; a question was obviously burning in her. She whispered, "Did she suffer at the end?"

George reassured her, describing the steady procession of visitors and how gracious Carmelita remained with everyone. Rita knew about Soledad and the children, but when George asked whether she knew Phil Pua, the vivacious old woman shut down. She stood and said, "I need to go back home."

He watched Rita get into her huge white Lincoln Continental. It was several minutes before she started the car and drove off.

Josefine was courteous, but George had the feeling she was also keeping her cards close the vest. All George knew about her was what Carmelita had told him: she was estranged from her husband, who had returned to the Philippines, and she had a daughter in Miami.

In keeping with her general view of men who abandoned their wives and children for another woman, Carmelita's comment had been, "Her husband was an idiot." She had also lamented how many Filipino men split their time between a wife in North America and another wife in their country of origin.

George asked Josefine about the business relationship between Max Tauber and his brother-in-law Phil, but his hostess was reluctant to get into the subject. She did confirm that through personal contacts, Max Tauber and Phil Pua had imported nutritional supplements from the US to be sold in North America and Asia.

"Is it true that they lost all their investments in the Philippines?"

Josefine hesitated, then said, "After her brother-in-law's death, *Manang* went to the Philippines, hoping to get back some of her husband's money. Soledad would know."

By the time George met Rita Walter for lunch, it was clear she had decided to be open with him. She willingly shared numerous stories about Max Tauber, who liked wine, food, and especially women. "This is not a sin," she joked.

"What do you know about the family business they had here?"

"Max and Carmelita were happy together, but there was some tension between the two, precisely because of that business."

"Can you explain?"

"One day, I was visiting. Carmelita took off her sunglasses and threw them on the floor. The more Max laughed, the more upset she got. We went shopping; it was her revenge. You should have seen her! She came back with an extravagant dress, with matching purse and shoes."

Rita Walter's shoulders were shaking with laughter. She pulled out a Kleenex from her purse and dabbed at the tears in her eyes.

"What about the business in the Philippines?"

"A sham! There were politicians involved, she told me." She took George's hand and added, "There is so much corruption over there. It may sound harsh, but it is true. I am a Hawaiian first and a Filipina second. But let's talk about you. Do you have a wife?"

"No."

"How come? You are in good health."

"It's a bit complicated."

Rita frowned. "What do you mean by that? Are you homosexual?"

George found no reason to beat around the bush. "Yes, I am." He told her a bit about John.

"Oh, I am sorry. Can I give you a hug?"

His head still on Rita's shoulder, George confided, "I never told Carmelita."

Rita rubbed George's back. "She knew, deep inside, I am sure."

George, still in Rita's embrace, said, "Whenever Carmelita talked about Max, I could feel that her love for him was still burning, even after all those years."

"You are a poet."

"Can I ask you a question?"

The old woman pulled back and looked at him. "About Carmelita and Max, you mean?"

"Yes. A few times I heard her say, 'He was my lover and my mentor.'"

"Don't forget, she married late. I don't know how old she was."

"Forty-six," George replied.

"I don't think she had been in love before."

"Why would a man marry a forty-six-year-old woman from a Third World country, no offence?"

Rita seemed not the least offended. She leaned toward George. "You want my opinion?"

"Of course, Mrs. Walter."

"Call me Rita, please! My guess is that the man needed to settle down; he was tired of flirting with his business friends' wives."

"Some say he was a Nazi in his youth."

Rita's expression turned inward, as if there were a newsreel running behind her eyes. "People became monsters under Hitler. Children, not just grown men, burning and destroying, tormenting and killing..."

"What are you thinking?" George asked when she fell silent.

"Sorry. Where were we? Don't put this in your book, please! Carmelita loved that man; he taught her everything a woman learns sooner or later."

George asked with a wicked grin, "When you say everything, do you mean *everything*?"

The old woman gave him a mock slap. "I love men who are outspoken."

Chapter Thirty-Four

Carmelita was lying in a computerized hospital bed that had cost the hospital several thousand dollars. She seemed agitated. George greeted her but got no reply. She was plucking at the bedding, looking for the cord that would summon the nurse. "They are so slow," she said.

"What do you need?" George asked.

"I need someone to raise the bed. My neck hurts."

"Don't call them; I can do it." George got up to study the icons on the monitor at the foot of the high-tech bed. It took a while for him to figure out which button corresponded to which position of the bed. His trial-and-error approach did nothing to calm his old friend, who had found the cord and kept yanking it.

"Why do I have to wait for them? They are paid to take care of us." Then she said, "I haven't seen you for weeks."

"I was here yesterday, don't you remember? You asked the nurse to bring me a cup of tea with cookies."

Carmelita said plaintively, "Your friend's brain is not working properly anymore. You must forgive her."

For months her memories of the past had become increasingly tangled with more recent events in her mind, and toward the end she could hardly recall anything. When she did speak, she sometimes contradicted what she had said to him before. George knew there were stories that he would have to make up.

He remembered her going on a shopping spree a year earlier. Despite the daily dose of morphine, she was still driving. George happened to be there when she got out of her car in her driveway. He helped her unload the trunk and carry the dozens of plastic Fairway bags into the house. When he asked why she seemed so pleased with herself, the old woman pulled a small plaque out of her purse. The plaque read: *Live, Laugh, Love.* "*When I saw that, I said to myself: 'That's you, Carmelita Tauber!'*"

The old Filipina's memories of the pastries in Vienna, eating escargots in Paris and visiting the fashion boutiques on the Champs-Élysées were easier for her to access than those of her childhood under the Japanese occupation. Still, George had managed to piece together parts of her early life, bit by painful bit.

Carmelita Madridejos Baldemor was a child when the Japanese invaded the Philippines. For months prior to the invasion, Japanese soldiers disguised as street vendors had been seen drawing maps of the area. Carmelita's father, an engineer, had figured out what they were doing and warned the authorities.

When George kept asking questions about her father, the old woman said, "I didn't sleep well last night," or "I already I told you: he was in charge of the safety of public roads and bridges." One day, she said, "Ask Trinidad Quesada. Her father was in the guerrilla."

Soon after the occupation began, the poorly supplied Japanese soldiers began ransacking houses and businesses in search of food. One of the businesses was the grocery store owned by Carmelita's mother. At night, the townspeople could hear the squawking as the invaders caught chickens.

At the convent school, the nuns spoke Spanish among themselves and to their students. They called Carmelita *caprichosa* because she wouldn't eat lukewarm food. Her mother visited once a month, bringing boxes of homemade dishes.

One day a Japanese soldier slapped her father's face, and George wondered whether that was the catalyst for the family's escape. Even though the Japanese had commandeered all public and private vehicles, Carmelita's family was able to leave Paete. They stayed with relatives who owed a large property, but George never found out where it was.

"My father would never, never go outside the property."

To questions such as, "When did you leave Paete?" or "Who took care of the house while you were away?" her answers remained vague. "They were nice to my mother," or "They never touched the children," she would say.

"How long did you stay there?"

With her eyes half-closed, Carmelita said, "Maybe my father would dress as a woman, I never asked."

Instead of proper answers, she told him that although meat was scarce, people ate pineapples, oranges, mangoes and the *lumboy* that grew wild, and pomelos.

As for what came later, the decades-long corruption of the Marcos regime, she would only say that Imelda was not the bad one of the pair. When someone made fun of Imelda Marcos's ridiculous collection of shoes, Carmelita sprang to the defence of the bejewelled and stiffly coiffed former beauty queen. She wouldn't tolerate any attacks against the country's "steel butterfly," who had famously said she had to look beautiful so that poor Filipinos would have a star to gaze at from their slums.

Once in North America, Carmelita followed her family edict of *amor con amor se paga* (love is repaid with love). As if she were a channel, her parents' love permeated all her relationships. George, the child of emotionally uncommunicative English parents, was drawn to Carmelita's warmth.

In George's family, when strong feelings arose, his father would say, "Let's leave that to the French." His mother might have felt otherwise, but her inner life remained a mystery to George.

Only once did George venture to ask Carmelita about her love life. "George Miller, there are times I wonder about you," she said.

Carmelita did tell him she'd gone to a movie with a date in her teens. Her aunt sent an older cousin along to chaperone. In the next moment she talked about her parents' courtship. "My grandparents said to my mother, 'You cannot marry someone from the south.'"

In her youth, Carmelita wasn't considered pretty, as there was nothing Spanish about her appearance. She was short and plump, with a dark complexion, flat nose and full lips.

At the nursing college she learned the ins and outs of human reproduction. When did she make up her mind to defer the whole process in her own life? Once, when her friends and relatives were discussing the normal course of womanhood, Carmelita stood up and declared that she didn't need a man to tell her what to do.

"What did your mother say?"

"Mama was shocked."

A youth from her own province courted Carmelita briefly, until she introduced him to one of her cousins. The two ended up marrying. Not long after that, when Carmelita left the Philippines in her mid-twenties, she learned from her mother that the couple had a baby boy.

"I sent her a complete Johnson & Johnson Baby Pack."

The ugly duckling remained uninterested in men. She was obsessed with becoming an excellent nurse and couldn't stand the laziness or indifference she saw in other medical professionals.

In her forties, Carmelita met Max Tauber, a tall, blond, blue-eyed, handsome man fourteen years her senior. *"Could any woman not fall for him?"*

All Carmelita knew about her husband was what he told her. *"Max's mother had an important position at the Imperial Court. Like the top housekeeper."*

"Doing what?"

"She was an exceptional woman, Max used to say."

Max would accompany his mother to the palace. There, he would catch glimpses of the Imperial family as they entertained officials and diplomats from other countries. Later, he had a girlfriend whose father was a high-ranking officer in the army. The day Germany invaded Austria, Max tried to run away, but was caught before he could cross the border.

"The girl's father saved my husband's life."

After the war, Max emigrated to Canada, first settling in Toronto. He worked his way up to a sales position at a Mercedes Benz dealership, where he quickly became acquainted with the city's elite. A born charmer, Max was soon being invited to parties, where he would dance with the ladies and sing "You'll Find me at Maxim's," Danilo's aria from *The Merry Widow*.

Max moved to Calgary and opened his own Mercedes dealership. His only niece came for a visit, but took an instant dislike to Canada's oil capital, where men wore cowboy boots with their business suits. She moved to the West Coast and Max followed her there. The economy was booming in the Sixties and Seventies, and Max made good money in the stock market. He later became an investment advisor.

He and Carmelita met on Easter Sunday at St. Andrew's Cathedral. She seemed to know everyone in Victoria, and soon he was escorting her to receptions at Government House or the Philippines Consulate General. He introduced her to opera, and the couple often entertained at home.

"The day Max proposed to me, I told him, 'Go and marry one of your lady friends.' I didn't want to marry him."

The niece was Max's only family in Canada. She couldn't understand her uncle's interest in a nurse from the Third World.

"What happened to her?" George asked.

Carmelita shrugged. "She disappeared."

During the day, while Carmelita worked, her husband socialized or watched live opera broadcasts on PBS and History Channel documentaries. He would meet for drinks with the bishop and his accountant, whose financial schemes almost ruined the Diocese of Victoria a few years later. Max had been brought up Catholic, but believed that religion was a personal affair between an individual and God, and not a social one, like it was for Filipinos.

As a nurse, Carmelita had held sick and frail men in her arms, but before Max, no man had ever held her. After their marriage, Max continued to flirt openly with other women, and she knew that many in the Filipino community felt sorry for her. Carmelita never pitied herself, though; she had given Max her hand and her heart, once and for all.

Most of the relatives she had left behind in the Philippines were still alive, and Carmelita corresponded with them, but she seldom talked about them with George. He occasionally saw a thick envelope bearing Philippines stamps on the dining room table. When he asked whether she would ever visit her home country again, she would quote Gen. Douglas MacArthur's famous pledge, "I shall return." To George's knowledge, she only went back once, after Max died.

When George kissed her for the last time, the day before she passed away, he knew—and had known for quite a while—that only fiction could express who this woman was, and the world she had opened up for him.

Chapter Thirty-Five

George called Trinidad Quesada, who was born in Paete. He briefly outlined his project and was relieved when she suggested meeting the next day at a café near the Victoria Filipino Community Centre.

"I have some books that might interest you. I will bring them."

The next day, as soon as she sat down, Trinidad opened her grocery bag and pulled out a book. "It has a lot of pictures; you will see Paete before the Japanese burned it, and after. You can borrow it if you want."

There was a colourful painting on the cover of a second book. Inside were portraits of people from Paete who now lived abroad. "The artist is from Paete, but now he lives in Vancouver."

Trinidad had bookmarked the pages showing her family. "My parents' wedding. Here's our house. You can see the mountain with the three crosses at the top. The mayor has them illuminated at night. Will you be going to the Philippines for your book?" When George said he wasn't sure, she offered to go with him and give him a tour of Paete and the province of Laguna. She talked about the carvers, the *lanzones,* and the Catholic Church that still contained many old paintings.

"You should see the St. Cristobal painted on wood. He needs to be restored. In the Philippines, there is never any money."

George interrupted her. "Carmelita never talked about the Japanese occupation."

"They knew that they were losing." Trinidad paused. "The leaders of the guerillas were singled out."

"I've read about a Japanese strategy called *zona*, what did that consist of?" George asked.

"It was like a dragnet, you know, what fishermen use?"

"What do you mean?"

"The local males were herded in one place." Trinidad sighed. "They were searching for guerrillas."

They used the parish church to incarcerate and torture suspected guerillas. Prisoners were slapped, kicked, deprived of sleep and subjected to water torture. All day long, moans and screams emanated from St. James the Apostle church; its sacristy and even the baptistery were filled with prisoners. For days, the Japanese kept a white priest hog-tied to the post supporting the choir loft, refusing to give him food or drink.

"Like Christ tied to the cross." Trinidad stared at the books on the table and the mugs of coffee.

"Were there Japanese in your town before the war broke out?"

Trinidad came back to life. "There was a Japanese boy in my oldest sister's class. When the teacher announced that the Japanese army had invaded the Philippines, he rose and said to his classmates: 'Even if I am Japanese, I will not hurt or kill you. I am your brother.'"

Entire families fled the Japanese invasion, hiding in the mountains surrounding the town; others ran farther away.

"How old were you then?"

"Three years," Trinidad replied. "A pity my sister has passed away. She could tell you a lot more than me. She was already a teacher when the war ended."

As she spoke, Trinidad ran her hands over the books, as if she were polishing them. The motion seemed to have the effect of resurrecting the past. "The Japanese were looking for my father."

"Was your father in the resistance?"

Trinidad corrected him, "In the Philippines, we called it guerrilla."

"Sorry."

Trinidad explained, "There was a bad guerrilla, too."

"What do you mean?"

"We called them *makapilis*. With a bag on their head with slots for the eyes, they would point out the Filipinos who were anti-Japanese."

The Quesada family had lived on Adea Street just at the foot of the mountain facing the river that divided Paete into north and south.

"So one day, your family went to live in the mountains?"

"Only my father. My brothers and sisters and I, we stayed in town with our mother. Mama was so scared. The Japanese soldiers kept knocking at the door."

"Asking for your father?"

"He was on a wanted list. They were asking for food, too."

"Were you afraid of them?"

"They were nice to the children. One day, a Japanese soldier put me on his lap."

"Was your mother there? What did she do?"

Trinidad shrugged. "He probably had a family back home and was missing his children. Mother must have reported the story to my father or someone else, because shortly after that we joined my father."

"How did you survive all that time in the mountains?"

"When people realized the Japanese were coming, they prepared to go into hiding."

"What kind of preparations?"

Months ahead of the occupation, Paete families started planting fruit trees, vegetables, and tobacco plants for cigarettes. Trinidad offered George a list of what she and others ate during their time away from their homes in Paete. There was a shortage of meat, but they never lacked protein.

"My grandfather dug a pond to raise fish. Unlike the people in Manila, we didn't starve."

"Were you in contact with the population in town?"

"There was a conduit."

"Did you know that at the time?"

"I learned about these things from my older sister."

Trinidad had bookmarked specific pages in the first book. George examined the photos of the devastated town. "Yesterday on the phone, you mentioned a fire."

"The Japanese couldn't burn it all on the first day. On the following night, they returned and burned the remaining houses. When we got back to town, we all stayed in one of the stone buildings that didn't burn. We were like sardines; at least twelve families stayed there."

"Why did they do that?"

"The Americans were already in Manila by then."

"What happened to Carmelita's parents' house?"

"They had already left."

"Where did they go, Trinidad?"

Trinidad looked surprised. "Pasay, south of Manila; she didn't tell you?"

"She never gave me a straight answer."

"That must be because of her medication." Trinidad crossed herself. "May she rest in peace! You should talk to her sister in Vancouver."

"She wasn't even born until after the war."

Less than 24 hours later, Trinidad's list arrived in an email with the word *Diet* in the subject line. The list contained a mixture of Tagalog, English and local words. She said she would be happy to answer any other questions George might have.

Carbohydrates	Cassava roots (*kamotengkahoy* as we call it in Filipino); corn; sweet potatoes; cooking banana (*sagingsaba*)
Vegetables	Long green beans (*sitaw*); squash (*kalabasa*); chayote (*sayote*). Tips of squash and sweet potato leaves for our greens like spinach; turnip (*singkama*); jicama
Fruits	Papaya; avocado; banana (*lakatan & latundan*); mango; *Dalandan* (a species of citrus); *atis; Santo; Chico; Sapote;* guava; *lanzones;* jackfruit (*Langka*); pomelo (*Suha*); cocoa beans for chocolate
Proteins	Fish: *Gurame* (fresh water), *biya* (goby), *dalag* (mush fish), *Ayungin,* carp (*carpa*) Meat: Hunted wild pig and deer

Chapter Thirty-Six

After much hesitation, George called Soledad, who sounded stressed when she answered. "Am I calling at a bad time?" George asked.

"Of course not!" she replied emphatically. Her voice became warm, almost intimate. "I am so glad you called." The house in Victoria is still not on the market. You knew my older sister. So much cleaning has to be done before contacting any realtor—"

"I've just come back from Honolulu. I saw Josefine Estrera."

"If you want my advice, you should go to the Philippines instead."

Soledad had opened the door, and George walked right in. "Do you know anyone in the Philippines that I could contact?"

His question either hit a wall of indifference, fell into the deep sea, or simply disappeared into the Bermuda Triangle. He could hear Soledad's breathing; she was busy with something. Was she having a snack or playing with the telephone cord? She remained silent. George persisted. "Anyone I could interview, say a childhood friend?"

"My dear friend, I was not even born when my sister left the country," she said with a sigh—of relief, it sounded like to George. "I'm sorry."

George refused to let her off the hook. "A few years ago—she was well at the time—she showed me wedding pictures she'd just received from the Philippines.

The bride was the daughter of some relative. I didn't write down the name, unfortunately. It might have been the daughter of a second or third-degree cousin. On your mother's side, I think."

"You know more about my sister than me."

"I wouldn't say that, Soledad."

Silence again. George tried again. "A few times Carmelita suggested that I contact one of the relatives back home."

"My sister must have told you, I have always been closer to my in-laws." Soledad crushed George's hopes with her next comment: "There is nobody left in the Philippines." She added, "We are all getting old."

Soledad changed the topic, enumerating her physical miseries, which began the day her sister got sick. "My children are so grateful for what you did for *Ate*." She went on to a jaw-related ailment that was affecting her left ear. She might need to consult an eye specialist on another matter. "I can hardly walk. Last week, I was in so much pain." Her voice changed again, to that of an efficient, pragmatic person. "Now that I have you on the phone—"

"What can I do for you?"

"My children and I would like to offer you a small souvenir from my sister, something from the Philippines or one of her many trips abroad. As a token of our gratitude. What can we give you?"

"I'll let you know if I think of anything. Thanks." He hung up.

Shortly after, George visited Carmen Escovedo and reported his frustrating conversation with Soledad. "If she's to be believed, everything Carmelita referred to as *back home* vanished into thin air the day she passed away."

"They don't want you to discover their little secrets. The guy was a *ladrón* (thief)."

"What guy?" George asked.

"The man in the Philippines." Carmen looked puzzled. "I am sure *Tia* told you about the business bankruptcy."

"Not really. One day she started talking about it, and I told her, 'Those are family matters and I don't care.' She got angry, but she understood why I didn't want to know."

"*Tia* told me the whole story before she got sick. Do you want to know?"

"I do now!"

The vitamins and supplements company included a warehouse in Hawaii, from where the products were distributed in Canada and the US. The business was going smoothly until they decided to have an associate in the Philippines and distribute the goods throughout Asia. "People are more health-conscious, as you know. We don't know what's in what we eat. Do you watch CNN?"

George shook his head. "Coming back to the company..."

"*Es un caso de malversación.*"

"I'm George, remember? In English, please!" he said, smiling.

"Sorry." Carmen seemed embarrassed. "Julio keep telling me, 'Mom, you should take English lessons.'"

"I was joking."

"In your book, are you going to talk about the...?" Carmen searched for the word. "*¿Como se dice?* Corruption. That's the word!" she said, with obvious relief.

George had never given it a thought. "My book is about Carmelita, not the family, or the Pope for that matter."

"Don't talk like that, please!"

"Sorry."

"Anyway, she had to go to the Philippines. This is when she found out about the whole mess. Instead of expanding the business, the senator put the money in his pockets."

"A congressman, wasn't it?"

"Whatever. So, you knew about it?"

"Bits of the story, yes, but I wasn't prepared to dig any further. I was much more interested in her and what kept her moving from the day she was born..." While he was talking, George looked at a painting on Carmen's living room wall depicting men and women harvesting. "Her late husband's reputation had been tarnished. That was the tragedy in Carmelita's eyes."

Carmen said nothing.

"One day we were standing on her front porch," George resumed. "Carmelita started crying. She said, 'You cannot trust those people back there.' Can you imagine? She, a Filipina, was criticizing her own people? What's more important than blood?"

"We Nicaraguans feel the same way," Carmen remarked.

"There's another thing, I think."

"What?"

"She felt ashamed by proxy."

Carmen looked at George, her eyes wide open. "What does it mean?"

George laughed. "I don't really know, to tell you the truth. What I mean is, she was ashamed on others' behalf: first for her sister, who didn't know, and secondly for her brother-in law, who was a well-respected man in the community."

"It's like reading a book, George."

"Shame might not be the right word." Suddenly, George was on his laptop, writing. "Carmelita's whole existence revolved around others."

He looked over. Carmen had tears in her eyes.

"On top of that, she belonged to the Equestrian Order of the Holy Sepulchre of Jerusalem, an association connected with the Pope himself."

Carmen giggled. "You know what? One day, Julio beg her to show us her uniform. She put on the cape, the veil, everything. She looked so happy, George."

"When was this?"

"I don't remember, George. Years ago; she was in good health at the time. The children were curious, they wanted to hear about it. *Tia* explained what the symbols meant. I think I took a picture."

"She was quite proud of being a member of the Order."

"Only wealthy people are accepted, I think."

George laughed. "The day I made a similar remark in front of her, Carmelita got quite upset. She was unconditional in her loyalties." *That could be the subtitle of his book.*

Chapter Thirty-Seven

It wasn't until he retrieved his carry-on bag and walked down the steps from the Philippine Airlines plane onto the tarmac that George realized he was actually in Asia for the first time in his life. The hot, humid air that took his breath away outside followed him into the terminal. Buffeted by the shoulder-to-shoulder crowd around him, George struggled to see over heads as the herd shuffled through seemingly endless corridors.

At the luggage carousel of the main terminal, he recognized some of the giant suitcases and huge boxes he'd seen being checked in at Vancouver airport some fifteen hours earlier. What he'd heard was true: Filipinos did not travel light! The giant maw behind the carousel continued to spew out evidence of the underground economy. There were cases of toilet paper and family-size jars of vitamins, microwave ovens, toasters and other small appliances, purchased no doubt at Costco or Walmart. The multinationals were God's gift to Filipino ex-pats returning home for holidays.

After picking up his suitcase, George looked around in hopes of finding the departure gate for his flight to Iloilo, which was to leave from Terminal 2. He could not see any signs or information for passengers in transit, nor find staff willing to direct him; this despite the dozens of uniformed and badged men and women wandering around or chatting with each other. He approached a few of them, but instead of responding to his questions, they smiled and carried on with whatever they were doing.

The crowds were no thinner here. Heat radiated from the doors. Windows in the ceiling towering above him were wide open. It was chaos, anarchy. No, mayhem—that was the word. George decided he was going to enjoy this trip, at whatever price and effort.

Behind the arrival doors, he saw a colony of greeters, each one holding up a cardboard sign with names on it. Some bore the logo of a hotel or travel agency. They were trying to get his attention, but he turned his back to them and kept looking around. He struck out down a passageway and, thanks to the affectionate ghost of Carmelita, finally found the designated gate for domestic flights. He heard the announcement for his flight to Iloilo, the provincial capital, on Panay Island.

Three hours later, as he was waiting—again—for his suitcase to be ejected onto the carousel, he recognized Apin Eneres from Victoria. Apin had helped him plan his trip to the Philippines and invited him to stay at his family's ancestral home. His head was freshly shaven.

"How was your flight?" Apin shouted as he approached.

"Fine, thanks."

"Is that all the luggage you have?"

"Let me check." George looked at the green suitcase at his feet and put his right hand on the carry-on bag on his left shoulder; his laptop hung from his right shoulder. "Yes, I have everything," he announced, reassured.

Apin introduced the man standing at his side. "This is my nephew, Bongbong."

"Nice meeting you." George shook hands with Apin's nephew, a man in his thirties who looked as if he had blood spots in the whites of his eyes. His face was a lot darker than his uncle's, almost burned. Without a word, Bongbong picked up George's suitcase, while Apin reached to take both George's laptop and carry-on.

"Let me at least carry my laptop," George protested.

The three men walked out of the building. Apin said, "We can take a cab or a jeepney, your choice." He pointed at a line of hybrid creatures, half-jeep and half-van. "Jeepneys were originally made from US military jeeps from World War Two."

"My *Lonely Planet* book mentions them."

"These days they're built with Japanese engines and parts."

George saw passengers inside the jeepneys, peering through narrow open slats in the curtained windows, staring at him. "Why not?"

Apin looked at him. "They're crowded and not too comfortable," he warned.

"Don't worry about me."

"Are you sure? Expect black fumes from the diesel fuel they burn."

George smiled. "I'll be fine."

Bongbong loaded George's luggage and sat in the back. Apin and George found seats on the bench behind the driver. The interior of the vehicle looked like a waiting room, with passengers sitting facing each other on two long, narrow benches. The plastic covering that was supposed to protect the seats had seen better days. Some passengers covered their nose with a handkerchief or simply the collar of a T-shirt.

During the trip into the city, paper money and coins would travel from new passengers to the driver, who collected the fare by reaching back with one hand as he checked out the new passenger through a wide and narrow rear view mirror. The jeepney remained in motion during this operation, and the driver never turned his head. If there was any change due, it would pass from the driver's hand to the nearest passenger and along the bench until it reached the now seated passenger. All this took place with a minimum of words.

The streets were a mass of vehicles: buses, jeepneys and tricycles, the local term for motorcycles with sidecars welded to them. The sidecars looked like strollers, with two back to back seats. Because of the fumes, and to protect them from the dust, several tricycle drivers, mostly young men, wrapped T-shirts around their head, leaving a slit for their eyes. Drivers jockeyed for position on the road, routinely cutting in front of each other and honking for no discernible reason.

Apin was observing him. "Would you have preferred a private cab?"

George shook his head and smiled. "No, I'm actually enjoying this." He was happy to be in *her* country.

"Welcome to the Philippines," Apin said with a laugh.

A couple of times, George made eye contact with Apin's nephew. Like many of the other male passengers, Bongbong was wearing Bermuda shorts with a coloured stripe on the side, and a jersey.

When new passengers got on, they would glance at George, then turn away. He was the only Caucasian in sight, even outside their vehicle. Everyone was obviously aware of him, but he was studiously ignored. Only children stared openly; their parents pretended they had better things to do than to keep an eye on the alien in their midst. Under George's striped blue shirt and long cotton trousers, he felt like the invisible man in the classic movie.

Four jeepneys and tons of black fumes and dust later, the three passengers arrived in Igbaras. Rather than going directly to the Eneres's ancestral home, Apin suggested having a quick look at the two-story house that his sister and brother-in-law had built for themselves. "They live in Canada, but they're in Mindanao on business. They'll be here tomorrow."

"Shouldn't we wait until then?"

Apin shook his head. "My cousin Rose and her husband look after the house when they're away."

At the house, George introduced himself to Apin's cousin. "My name is George."

Rose smiled without saying a word.

George then offered his hand to Rose's husband, who was working on a new motorcycle in the yard. "I'm George. What's your name?"

"Rex." The man's head was completely shaved except for a rat tail hanging from the back of his skull.

"What's your family name?" George asked.

"Escarmoso," Rex replied with a smile.

"Another name starting with the letter *E*," George remarked. "Are you from Igbaras?"

"Of course he is," Apin interjected. Everyone was laughing.

"How is it elsewhere? Do the names start with the same letter?"

Apin named some neighbouring towns and said, "In Guimbal, the names start with *G*; in Tubungan, with *T*—"

George interrupted him. "On our way into town we passed a place called Miag-ao that had a beautiful old church."

"Did you want to stop? We can go back there if you like."

"Sure, but not today."

The main floor of the house consisted of a dining room and a huge living room, along with a modern kitchen, separated by an island topped with what looked like marble. Throughout the house, the furniture was made of mahogany, carved patterns covering the surfaces.

"It's all made here in Igbaras," Apin said. "If you're interested, Bongbong can show you the factory. It's on a property that belongs to my other nephew who lives in Victoria."

"It's three times the size of my house in Victoria," George exclaimed. "This is a mansion."

Also on the ground level was the master bedroom, complete with walk-in-closet and private bath with German-made toilet and sink. They climbed a staircase. The second floor had three bedrooms.

When they arrived at Apin's house later that day, family members were just returning home for dinner. George told his hostess Juliet that he needed to sleep.

"But you haven't had your dinner," Juliet said.

"I'm really jet-lagged. I'll be fine tomorrow after I've had a good night's sleep."

Sleep didn't come easily, though, as dogs barked and cocks crowed through the night. George kept checking the time on his cell phone. He thought sunrise was the designated time for cocks to crow, but he later learned that these were fighting cocks, and that they went by a different set of rules. Public transport vehicles passed by all night as well, honking to alert anyone waiting to board. There would be a brief interval of silence, then the symphony would resume: dogs, cocks, jeepneys and tricycles.

At 5:00 a.m., George gave up and went downstairs. Apin's sister Juliet was busy in the so-called *dirty kitchen*, a huge room with several wood- and charcoal-fired stoves where the family members took their meals when there were no visitors.

"Are you hungry?" Juliet asked.

"I certainly am," George replied with several nods.

"Sit down." Juliet removed the aluminum pans covering plates of fruit, dried fish and *pandesal*. "Eat."

At around seven, the family gradually came in and joined George at the table: cousin Rex, Apin, his older brother Phil, Bongbong and his wife. Juliet's granddaughter Jade said grace. Plenty of food was on offer: rice, fish, and soup with *munggo* beans and pork.

Apin reassured George, "Don't feel you have to eat everything."

"It's all delicious," George said, delighted.

"Well, you're easy to please," Apin said. The others laughed.

When George stepped outside, the heat was almost overwhelming. It was only nine in the morning.

"You can take a nap after lunch," Apin said. "Everyone does."

As they walked, Apin made a point of indicating anything that could be labelled a sign of poverty, as if to pre-empt George's comments.

"Look there, open sewage. The central government allocates money to clean-up projects but when it's time to do the job, the locals find that the money's already gone, siphoned off by a politician to a bogus company."

George said nothing. On both sides of the dirt road, a ditch two feet deep was filled with stagnant water and garbage.

"This wouldn't be tolerated in other parts of the world," Apin continued. "The politicians here are so corrupt!"

"Not all of them, surely."

"You're naïve. Just wait till you've been here for a while. Companies belonging to local politicians get the contracts that they themselves award. The rest of the population starves. Schools don't have money to buy resources for the children; some schools have computers, but only a few. Teachers are so badly paid, some of them are called volunteers."

"They don't get a salary?"

Apin shook his head. "They're like second-class teachers. They live with their parents because the salary isn't enough to feed their own families. Meanwhile, the rich just get richer. Sometimes I say to myself: that's enough, I can't take it anymore. Poverty is everywhere and they all want you to give them some money. You be careful; they'll probably hit you up for cash, too."

"Would you ever move back here?" George asked.

"Canada's my home now."

"Everyone I talk to smiles at me," George said. "People here are so friendly."

Apin laughed. "It's not what you think. They smile because they can't speak English."

Later that day, Apin took George to meet the mansion owners, Lea and her husband Erwin. George asked Erwin about his life in Canada.

"Canada has been good to us," Erwin said.

"Do you come back here every year?"

Erwin nodded. "When we both retire, we will come back to the Philippines permanently."

"When will that be?"

"Two years from now."

"You won't stay in Canada?"

"What would I do there? Spend my days at the mall and go home to eat?"

Cousin Rose and her husband didn't speak English. The way they were dressed, their overall behaviour, even their missing teeth were a reminder that they were dependent on relatives like Apin, Lea and Erwin and thousands and thousands of men and women like them, the so-called foreign workers.

At the end of the visit, Apin asked George, "Are you tired?"

"No. Why?"

"Then let's go and meet another one of my cousins. He's the one I said might be able to help you with your book."

They entered the Igbaras Municipal Hall. At the front desk, Apin asked for the accounting officer, Pedro Sarmiento. While they were waiting, Apin remarked, "This is how things work in the Philippines. If you know someone, then you're okay."

A staff member escorted them across a courtyard and into a small building, then to Pedro's office at the end of a corridor. Apin and his cousin exchanged a few words in Ilonggo, the local dialect, but quickly switched to English.

"Is it your first time in the Philippines?" Pedro enquired.

"Yes."

"Do you find it hot here?"

"I've just arrived, but I don't find it too bad."

"What can I do for you?"

George explained. "I'm working on a book about a woman born in the Philippines."

"Are you a journalist?"

"No. This is a work of fiction."

Pedro looked surprised. "So how can I help you?"

"I'm trying to get more information on the Japanese occupation."

Pedro pulled a book from one of the shelves behind him and handed it to George. "You are welcome to borrow it."

"Thank you!" *Legend, Story and Literature* was the book's title, with a small illustration below each word. George read the back cover and noticed that the author, Ambrosio Eiland Gotero, lived in Toronto. As the cousins chatted, he read the table of contents. Chapter Five was entitled "War Memories." At the end of the chapter was a photo of the epitaph of a certain Father John Kauffman. He showed the picture to Pedro. "Sorry to interrupt, but have you ever heard of him?"

Pedro nodded. "A parish priest. He was accused of collaboration with the Japanese. He was German, you see."

"Thank you very much for the loan, this is going to be a big help."

"I am honoured," Pedro said.

They shook hands, and the municipal officer suggested that George meet Fruto Saavadra, a former mayor of Igbaras.

Hearing the name, Apin remarked, "He's my cousin, too."

"The circles are very small here, it seems," George said.

Pedro wished George luck and added, "Come any time if you have questions. I will be honoured."

Apin said, "I don't need to be here next time, now that you two have met."

Pedro repeated, "You can come any time."

Once they were outside the building, George asked, "Do you think I could meet your other cousin, the former mayor?"

"I'll ask my sister to invite him for lunch tomorrow. I have something for him, anyway."

George spent the rest of the day reading Pedro's book to prepare for his meeting with the former mayor. The so-called memories were more or less hearsay. The author hadn't provided many specifics; he'd simply quoted his interviewees' fragmented memories.

In a different place, a fearful person refused to leave the foxhole where she was hiding. She died of fear and hunger there. When the family returned after the war, they covered the hole.

Japanese soldiers would force women to take off their clothes and dance without music. They would take turns raping and abusing them. If a woman refused, they would skin her or cut off her breasts.

Young children and babies were tossed into the air and impaled on the tips of the soldiers' bayonets.

Peoples or places were not identified; nor were any dates attached to the incidents. Shuddering at the violence depicted in the stories, George thought, No wonder Carmelita didn't want to talk about the war.

Chapter Thirty-Eight

The following day, Fruto Saavadra, the former mayor of Igbaras in the province of Iloilo, turned up for lunch at the Eneres family home. The elderly man had been briefed about George's project and said he would be glad to be interviewed after the meal.

The former politician seemed to relish every dish on the table, particularly the crab soup.

Apin said, "In Canada, the crabs are quite a bit bigger. You should see them." To George, he said, "These are really spiny, be careful."

There was a big plate of *pancit* on the table, and a stuffed fish cut into slices. Juliet explained, "You scoop out the inside of the fish, then you fry it with onions and garlic."

"How do you cook the fish itself?" George asked.

"On the charcoal."

George was ecstatic. "I had this once in Victoria, but this one tastes a lot better. Everything is delicious, Juliet, thank you!"

Apin said, "You're easy to please, George."

George protested. "Stop staying that. I just say what I think."

After the meal, Apin gave a pink backpack to his cousin. "This is for your granddaughter."

He also handed Fruto a family-sized bar of Toblerone chocolate. "Yesterday was your birthday, right?"

"How do you know?"

"Juliet told me that last Sunday after mass they sang "Happy Birthday" at the church."

"Thank you."

After lunch, George and Fruto withdrew to the living room. George immediately opened his notebook.

"I was born from poor parents," the mayor began. "Did my cousin tell you?"

"He told me that you're a historian."

The man shook his head. "I am just a lover of history. For years I researched the history of Igbaras, which was founded around 1615. I am in the middle of revising my *History of Igbaras*. It took me twenty years to write it!"

Fruto reported sadly that the local church's gilded tabernacle had been stolen a few decades earlier.

"Because of that loss and so many others throughout the province, the government ordered that all artefacts of historical and cultural importance have to be sent to the capital. Iloilo is the capital of the province. I am sure my cousin told you."

George nodded.

"In the country, nobody is allowed to photocopy original documents. The central government has the rights on everything. Despite this, I was able to get the permission to read and copy the old documents related to Igbaras. Archivists used hardener to keep the pages together."

"What kind of hardener, if you'll excuse my ignorance?"

All smiles, the amateur historian explained, "Thanks to the cans of hair spray that someone at a beauty parlour donated, we can turn the pages without damaging them."

George was dubious about the impact of hair spray on ancient documents, but kept his concerns to himself.

Given his extensive research, Fruto knew a great deal about the flooding of Calle San Augustin in 1979, the terrible actions of the bandit Montor, who killed Don Mariano Benedicto in 1890, and other stories. As the man talked, George couldn't stop looking at the ill-fitting brown toupee on the history buff's head.

"Forgive me, but what can you tell me about the Japanese occupation?" The man suddenly looked lost.

"Let me explain," George said. "In a book that a friend from Canada loaned me, the author distinguishes good and bad guerrillas."

"May I see the book?"

"I didn't bring it with me; I was afraid I'd lose it."

As soon as George mentioned that the book was mainly about Paete, Laguna, Fruto's face brightened. "That explains it. You see, things were different in Laguna."

"Have you ever been there?"

The man shook his head. "It's far from here and my parents were poor."

To forestall Fruto's reminiscences about his family's poverty, George told him more about the book he was writing, about a Filipina friend who had fled Paete with her parents when the Japanese occupied the town.

"Is your friend presently in the Philippines?"

"No, she died not long ago."

"May she rest in peace! I am sure you miss her."

George brushed off what sounded like a pure formality. "You said things were different from one place to another. In what way?"

"Here, I mean Panay Island, was in direct communication with General MacArthur, who was based in Australia. This was his fifth column, so to speak."

"Could you explain?"

"There were Filipinos working for the Japanese, but in reality they were spying on the Japanese."

"According to what I read in preparation for my trip here, everyone was spying on someone else during the war."

His interviewee leaned toward George and muttered, "There was a secret agreement."

"What do you mean?"

"The puppet government didn't want an armed conflict."

George suddenly realized that it was better not to ask questions; the man's answers only deepened the mystery. Also, he had some difficulty understanding everything the former mayor said, as he had the common Filipino tendency to say *he* when referring to a woman, and vice-versa.

"Life in Igbaras was somewhat easier than in other parts of the country, where there was a Japanese garrison," Fruto said.

"So the civilians didn't suffer as much here?"

Lowering his voice again, because there were children in the dining room, Fruto said, "There were comfort women."

"What did people say about them?"

"Filipinos love their country. Because they were so close, the women knew a lot about what the Japanese were doing and passed the information to the resistance."

George noted the use of the word resistance, when other Filipinos referred to guerillas. He asked Fruto about this, but got a cryptic answer.

"Under all circumstances, the locals always worked for the sake of the country."

"I apologize if my questions seem ignorant. We Canadians have no experience with the horrors and atrocities of war on our own soil, certainly not the way people in other countries are. What is your most vivid memory of the Japanese occupation?"

"I was not born until 1945."

An enormous silence followed. The former mayor stared at the wall. George wished he could disappear or at least hide somewhere. He had taken the toupéed man for a much older person.

"Do you have any more questions?"

"Not at the moment." George accompanied Fruto to the door and thanked him profusely. It was too bad that the man's view of the world was extracted from archival material and hair-sprayed documents. He knew the names of the celebrities of the war, and for the two hours of the interview, had simply repeated what he'd read over the years.

Apin handed his relative a Styrofoam container of leftovers from lunch. "My cousin is looking for sponsors," he said to George.

"Sponsors for what?"

"For a revised edition of his book."

"How much do you need?" he asked his interviewee.

The author uttered the ultimate sales pitch: "The sponsors' names will be at the beginning of the book." He named a figure.

George went to his bedroom and came back with 3,005 pesos. After a quick look at the bills, Fruto said, "It's 3,500 pesos."

"Sorry. I heard three thousand five."George rushed back upstairs. A few seconds later, with a 500 pesos bill instead of five pesos of coins in his hand, he said, "What's the publication date?"

With the attitude of an expert in the matter conversing with a colleague, Fruto said, "You know how these things are... It's an important topic."

Darn fool! George thought, but he was referring to himself. The amateur historian, who was *in utero* during the Japanese occupation, was going home happy: a free lunch, an Italian chocolate bar, and approximately sixty-five US dollars from a total stranger, for a revised edition that would probably never happen.

George retired to his room after lunch. At the end of a two-page photocopied article entitled *A Brief History of Igbaras*—provided to him with the compliments of Fruto—he read about the extraordinary accomplishments of former Congressman Oscar Garin (the cementing of Guimbal & Igbaras roads), the important infrastructure projects overseen by the current congressman, the beloved son of the previous congressman, and the good deeds of the current mayor. The text ended with: *Under the present leadership, with Divine Providence, Igbaras will surely march forward to progress.*

As he and Apin walked the next morning, his host told him about the habits of local politicians, which included plastering their names and faces on welcome arches at the outskirts of towns and on every other conceivable public surface. George saw this for himself on school buses and ambulances, and on banners announcing sporting events and food programs.

Apin continued to vent. "They want you to believe that all this is paid for out of their own pockets. The truth is, politicians are in election mode all year long. The priests are just as bad, if you ask me."

Later that day, the family headed off for their afternoon naps. Apin's brother Phil saw that George was moving toward the front door. "Don't go out for a walk now. You are not used to the heat, you will get sick." Phil added, "The storms are the cause of the poverty in our country."

Apin exploded. "The politicians are the cause, not the storms!" George decided to take a nap, leaving the two men to their dispute.

✳

After dinner that day, George and Apin went for an evening stroll. The street was still busy with young men in uniforms and workers getting out of jeepneys, back from their jobs in the city. Apin recognized one of the neighbours and said hello to him in Ilonggo. He then introduced George to the man, who asked in English, "What do you think of the Philippines?"

"I've only been here for three days, so I don't know what to say. I like Filipinos. Everyone's been so nice to me."

"You are a good person."

"How can you say that? Did we meet in a previous life?" George intended it as a joke, but the other man's expression changed, and George realized that he put him on the spot. The neighbour stared at him without speaking. George mentally kicked himself, then tried to make amends by changing the subject.

"How long is the trip to Iloilo?"

"In kilometres? I don't know."

"I mean, how long does it take you to get to work?"

"One and a half hours."

"You must be tired when you come home."

The man's face brightened, and George realized that the commuter would rather talk to a foreigner than go home for dinner. Since his arrival in Igbaras, people had been asking George how old he was. Apin had advised him not to take it personally, so George decided to follow the custom. "How old are you?" he asked the neighbour.

"Forty-five."

"Wow! You look younger."

To George's surprise, the guy took George's hand and put it on his chest and announced proudly,

"No fat."

"You're right. You don't have any fat. Do you a jog?"

The guy nodded a few times.

"It must be hard to jog in this hot weather."

"It's okay."

All this time, Apin had been chatting with another commuter in a white uniform, a college student who lived across the street from the Eneres family.

Back in the house, George gave Apin a report of his exchange with the forty-five-year-old jogger. "They all leave early and come home late in the evening; they must be exhausted. He told me he wants to go to Canada."

"They all want to go abroad. I grew up poor, but from the moment I left the Philippines, my life changed for the better."

"I admire you and your siblings," George said, as he wondered whether he was putting his foot in his mouth again with such open praise. "You've helped so many people and you keep on helping."

"I've been lucky," Apin replied matter-of-factly.

"Life is hard for Filipinos, it seems—"

Apin interrupted him. "They're good at begging; that's why I warned you to be careful."

George snapped back, "Why do you say that?"

"I'm serious, George. If one of my relatives asks you for money, tell me. I'll kill him."

Chapter Thirty-Nine

George joined Apin, Lea and Erwin for lunch at Hilario and Analisa Eneres's home. There was another couple from Iloilo, friends of Hilario's. In all, there were seven Filipinos around the table. All of them had lived in Canada for at least twenty years, and were back in the Philippines for their annual visit.

After a few niceties about Hilario's gardening and farming pastimes and inquiries about George's experiences in the Philippines, the conversation continued in Tagalog. Thanks to the odd English word, George was able to guess that they were comparing the Canada Pension Plan and disability benefits. Apin was receiving disability benefits from a private insurer, and told the group that the cheques would keep coming until he turned sixty-five.

The man from Iloilo suddenly switched to English, saying to George, "Foreigners always say that the Philippines are over-populated, but if you look around you, you see only rice fields, with cows and goats everywhere." Everyone laughed.

George commented on the plentiful food and on how much he was enjoying the variety of dishes.

Analisa said, "This is how we are here. Filipinos are hospitable." She added, "At home in Edmonton we eat brown rice, but here we eat white rice."

When George enquired about a particular dish, she said it was called *kadios.*

"It's delicious. What's in it?"

"Boiled pork, onions, garlic, jackfruit and black pepper. Just a small amount of pepper."

"Do you like it?" Hilario asked.

"It's very tasty." With a laugh, he said to Apin, "Don't say I'm easy to please."

At the end of the meal, George took some slices of mango, a fruit that Carmelita had introduced him to.

Hilario cleaned the plates and went outside to dump the leftovers into the compost container. He beamed with pleasure when George asked for a tour of his garden. He pointed out a small tree that was loaded with big papayas.

"A few weeks ago, that tree was flat on the ground due to winds."

"It seems to have recovered."

"Apin told me that you have a garden in Victoria."

"A small one. No comparison with yours here."

They walked among rows of eggplants, mung beans, squash and yellow bell peppers. At the back of the property stood a chicken house with cocks and hens wandering in and out of it, chicks following close behind their mothers.

"I want to raise goats."

"Here?" George asked, looking at the unfenced, empty field beside them.

Hilario said, "That's not mine. I have a lot that is close to our ancestral farm. We are in the process of building the fence so the goats can come." Hilario suggested meeting at four the next morning for a walk. "After that I will prepare a continental breakfast." He laughed, displaying his row of strikingly white teeth. "No Canadian bacon."

The next morning George woke up at a quarter to four. Once dressed, he went downstairs to wait for Hilario. It was black as pitch when Apin's brother showed up at the gate wearing an orange T-shirt with silver reflective bands on the front and the back. "Where did you get the T-shirt?" George asked.

"Costco." Hilario then looked over George's shoulder. "Where is Apin? Is he coming?"

"No, he left for the city after we came back from lunch yesterday. He's visiting some old classmates."

"Then let's go. You have a flashlight, right?" George held up his torch and they set off.

Soon George and Hilario left the asphalt streets of Igbaras and started climbing a hill. The narrow path forced them to walk single file. As the grade steepened, Hilario asked George, "Are you okay?"

"Yes, thanks. I like to walk and it's nice and fresh at this time of day."

Hilario used his flashlight to point out the occasional tree or shrub along the way. The beam revealed a light bulb trailing wire and attached to the branch of a tree. Laughing, Hilario said, "There are no construction codes here." He continued, "This is what I miss back in Edmonton. Listen."

George could hear the tall bamboo stalks tapping each other as they stirred in the soft breeze. He said, "The last time I was in Huntsville, Ontario, to spend Christmas with my relatives, I rediscovered the sound of crunching along on a snow-covered road at minus twenty Celsius."

"Same thing, right?"

George noticed a pile of three-foot-long strips of red wood tied into a small bundles with string. "What kind of wood is this?"

"*Sibukaw*, sappan tree. The *carabao* hauls the bundles on a sled we call a *karusa*."

George said he'd seen a similar sled built with bamboo sticks a few days earlier. "The *carabao* was moving faster than I expected."

"Yes, they are quite strong and fast; you have to get out of their way or they'll mow you down."

Others were walking the same path, and Hilario called out greetings to the men and women they met.

"Where are they going?" George asked.

"To the market."

The soon-to-be-retired nurse was back in his birthplace. The farmers he met on the path seemed to have forgotten him, but as soon as he mentioned his father's name, it was as if he had never left the country. "They still remember me," Hilario said, sounding pleased.

✳

Hilario opened the gate to his property and led George to the *dirty kitchen*. The building, separate from the house, was spic and span, the rays of the rising sun filtering through the venetian blinds. Both Hilario and Analisa were registered nurses, and the cleanliness of the room reflected the standards of their profession.

Analisa greeted George. "Where is Apin?"

"He went to Iloilo."

"How was the walk?"

"I enjoyed it immensely."

"Good!" Analisa seemed relieved that George was finding everything to his satisfaction. As she set the table for breakfast, she said, "Scrambled eggs. Is this okay for you?"

"Perfect! I'm hungry after the long walk." He looked at the wall clock. "We walked for almost two hours!"

"No bacon." Hilario's loud voice was accompanied by a big smile, the ultimate communication tool in the Philippines, George thought.

More than once, Carmelita had stressed, "The Philippines are in Asia but we are not Asians." George was convinced that his old Filipina friend was wrong. The Filipinos' way of expressing what they thought and felt was a challenge for a Westerner like himself to decipher.

George was growing fond of Hilario, a healthy-looking man in his sixties, whose skin, according to his wife, had darkened since their arrival.

"You look like someone who never left the Philippines," George said. When Hilario made no reply, George wondered whether his comment was too personal.

"You are not like the other Canadians; you seem to be at ease here," Analisa said to him.

George replied, "Why shouldn't I be? Everyone has been so nice to me."

"In Canada, it's so different. You have to call first before visiting someone. You have to set a time. Here, you see us as we are. Because we've been away so long, I now find it difficult here, that people show up any time."

"Like who?"

"Neighbours. Here they don't seem to realize that we need our privacy." She quickly added, "But George, you can come anytime. We all love you here."

George looked at his hostess. She was wearing Bermuda shorts, shorter than what he'd seen on local women, and a tank top with a tiny daisy pattern. "You're very kind, Analisa. Thank you."

"You see, George, I am a city girl." She paused. "When you get married, you follow your husband, right? We bought this house because we wanted to have a place in the Philippines for us and our sons when they got married. We first looked around Bacoor, Cavite, where I was born. There is new development all over the region but we couldn't find anything to buy. How do you like your coffee?"

George replied, "Strong."

Analisa smiled. "Same as my husband."

George looked at the items on the kitchen shelves. The oversize tin of coffee was from Costco, along with the sugar and powdered cream. Everything in the larder, including the pots and pans, was brought here from Canada. Even the calendar had a Royal Bank logo.

Analisa was intently watching George drink his coffee. "Do you like the Philippines?"

"Yes, but mostly its people." He could tell this was not the expected answer. What was he supposed to say? He looked down at his coffee mug, which bore a Canadian flag.

"You are a well-educated man, George." Analisa said. "There must be something that you don't like."

Now I'm on the spot, George thought. "It's hard to say." He blurted, "At times I find it hot. Mind you, it's not unbearable in Igbaras, but in Manila it must be terrible."

"There is so much pollution in Manila. My husband and I never go there."

"With the black fumes, the drivers and passengers must all have lung problems," George said.

"When you go to the city, take a bus, not a jeepney, and never a tricycle. Cover your face with a small towel. I can give you one. This is what they do here." George noted her use of the word *they* when referring to her own people.

Hilario put a plate with scrambled eggs and sautéed potatoes in front of George. George thanked him. "You see, George, Canada has regulations," Hilario said. "Here, they let people use vehicles that would be illegal to run anywhere else. Nobody cares. Take the water, for example. Did you notice how dry everything is in the fields? When I was a child, there were two harvests of rice. Not anymore. You know why? In the old days, you would get the water from the springs in the mountains. But in this *barangay*, someone built a dam to keep the water to himself."

"How can they do that? The water belongs to everyone!"

"In Canada, George, the people would say let's do something about it. Here, they don't. I don't know who stopped the water from the mountains coming down to the fields below, but I wouldn't be surprised if it was a relative of the mayor who built the dam."

After they ate, Hilario got up from the table. "I am in the middle of pruning all the shrubs around the house."

George said, "I need to go, too. Thanks for the walk and the wonderful breakfast."

"Anytime," Hilario replied.

Analisa walked George to the door. She hugged him. "Come any time."

Chapter Forty

After his second week in Igbaras, George had become comfortable with taking walks by himself. He carried a cheap pocket-sized camera. He photographed ordinary humans unaware of their eternal significance, making their simple actions sacred by freezing them in time. His images reflected his conviction that a system is reflected in all its components.

He captured a man ploughing his field with a well trained *carabao*; seniors playing *mah-jong* on the veranda of a retirement home; kids in the street tagging each other with a flip-flop sandal, girls in plaid skirts and white blouses adorned with a small necktie and boys in black trousers and short-sleeve shirts, all piled into a tricycle on their way to school.

In contrast to George, Apin always travelled with an expensive digital SLR camera. Back in his home country, he became the self-designated official visual recorder of the life and events of his birthplace. George spent an afternoon looking at Apin's photos. There were shots of children forming the letter *V* with their thumb and index finger held under their chin; teenage girls in large sunglasses mimicking celebrities; grandparents with missing teeth; and young mothers with children dressed in fancy clothes.

He posted the photos on Facebook, after a lengthy and meticulous editing process, for the benefit of Filipinos of all ages living abroad. When he returned to Canada, he intended to create photo albums and ask people planning to visit his hometown to present the albums to his relatives and acquaintances.

"You're very generous," George commented.

Apin laughed and said, "Shut up."

"I mean it."

"What can you do? I feel privileged; they're poor."

Since his arrival in early November, Apin had taken photographs at the parish church (the baptism of the grandchild of an elementary school classmate), in the municipal plaza (a gala for the seniors of Igbaras), on the street where his family lived (a New Year's Eve block party), and at a soccer tournament.

Among Apin's hundreds of photos, some showcased male curves and lines, images that some viewers might have tagged as erotic.

One day, a young man named Diego Ferrer came to the Eneres family house and asked Apin to photograph the candidates for a regional beauty pageant in Riro-an. "No problem. I'll do it."

"Where is Riro-an?" George asked.

"Another *barangay* of Igbaras, past Sign-e; you and I walked through there other day."

Diego, who had been listening, said, "Will you come, sir?"

"Are you inviting me?"

"We would be honoured." The youth was dressed in a black T-shirt and long trousers, with a rosary around his neck. George noticed the man's large watch and remembered hearing that copies of Rolex and Louis Vuitton goods were everywhere in the country. "Nice watch," was all he said to Diego.

"Thank you." Contrary to other young adult men George had seen since his arrival, Diego exuded confidence.

After he left, George asked Apin, "What do you think of him?"

"Who?" Apin looked puzzled.

"Diego."

"He dyes his hair."

"So?"

"He's one of the effeminates," Apin replied with a shrug.

"I have a question for you, Apin. In comparison with the ones that you call effeminates or the ones who roll their hips as they walk, where are we, you and I, on the sexuality spectrum?" George looked Apin in the eye. "What about the pink Bermuda shorts you're wearing?"

"They're salmon, not pink."

"If you say so."

"Are they too...?" he asked, sounding like an insecure teenager.

"You mean flamboyant?" George replied with a laugh. "I want to stay alive, so don't expect me to say what I think."

The day after the pageant in Riro-an, Apin left on his own to photograph a basketball team from the town of Igbaras. That evening he invited George to look at the images he was editing. The youths were standing in the middle of a shallow stream, wearing nylon swimsuits and flexing their muscles for the camera. Their left arms were encircled by what looked like a daisy with a big number at the centre.

"What's the number for?" George asked.

"They're the candidates at the Miss League Macho Chareeng on Saturday."

"What's that?

"The players dress and act like girls."

"A drag show?"

"Of course not!" Apin nearly choked. "It's a family event."

"You've got to be kidding."

"It's a fundraiser for the local basketball teams."

In other images, the young men, in their late teens or early twenties, were splashing around in the water, or perhaps pretending to play at the photographer's direction. "Are they conscious of what's going through your dirty mind?" George asked.

"What do you mean?"

"Come on, you know what I mean."

Apin's face remained on the screen. "I still have a lot of photos to transfer from my camera, and my laptop is full."

George got up. "I'm going to bed." As he climbed the stairs to his room, George heard a loud "Good night!" from Apin. He flinched, as the rest of the household was asleep. "Have fun!" he replied softly.

Chapter Forty-One

For several days, George had been having difficulty breathing. At night, a persistent cough kept him awake. His hosts noticed.

Analisa was the first to comment. "Excuse me for saying it, George, but you look tired."

"I haven't slept well for the past few days."

"Did you get a flu shot before leaving Canada?"

"No."

"You should go see a doctor."

"Maybe you're right."

Apin said, "There are a few doctors in town. I know one who's excellent." He offered to take George to Dr. Jaime Villanueva right after breakfast.

"Is he one of your relatives?" George asked.

"No, he's just someone I know. Do you want to walk, or would you rather take a tricycle?"

"How far is it?"

"Close to the market."

"Let's walk."

Dr. Villanueva's clinic, on a dead-end street, had an outdoor waiting room under a metal roof with direct access to the street. George watched shoppers go by, carrying bags and chatting with one another, and tricycle drivers enticing clients by honking at them. Apin directed George to one of the patient benches, made of roughly assembled bamboo stems. Apin went to talk to the doctor's assistant, who waved George over and told them both to go right in.

"What about the people ahead of us?" George asked.

"It's okay," Apin assured him.

"I'm not a celebrity."

"Don't worry about it."

Once inside the clinic, the rather delicate assistant, who had a stethoscope around his neck, pointed to a chair next to a small table covered with papers. He sat behind the desk and asked, "What's your name?"

To save time, George handed over his passport. The doctor's office had no door. All the time he was giving information to the assistant and holding a thermometer clamped under his left armpit, George could see the doctor with his patient, less than half a meter away. The language they were speaking was unknown to George, so it was as effective as a partition. As soon as the patient left, the assistant invited George to take the chair next to Dr. Villanueva, a man of indeterminate age. Once again, George decided it would be impossible to guess his age, since wrinkles seemed to be nonexistent among Filipinos.

The doctor immediately enquired about George's impressions of the country. "Do you like the food?"

"Yes but what strikes me most is people's kindness."

"You are in good shape for a man of your age," the doctor said, then added, "How is your love life?"

The question took George aback. He looked at the family doctor and said nothing. Apin, who was in the room with him, said, "He wants to know about your sex life."

George laughed. "Thanks, I'd already figured that out. You want to know if I get erections? The answer's yes." George, sitting close to the doctor, couldn't help admiring his smooth skin.

The doctor gently probed around George's throat. He checked George's lungs, pronounced them sound, and said, "You are fine. This cough will go away. It's from the pollution. You're not used to it yet. I'll give you a prescription for some things that will help."

Apin chimed in, mentioning that Dr. Villanueva was a recent mayor of Igbaras, then launched into his usual lament about the pollution in his native country. "You see plastic bags of garbage on the streets, in the fields, everywhere. The dumpsites are in the open. That needs to change, right?" he asked Dr. Villanueva.

"I tried to convince the council to do more about the garbage collection, but the opposition voted against me."

A few times, George tried to get up and go, but the doctor kept talking. Now it was about the municipal budget process and relations with the national government in Manila.

"How much of the municipal budget comes from Manila?" George asked.

"Ninety-two per cent."

George was shocked. "What about the remaining eight per cent? From municipal taxes?"

The former mayor smiled. "That's a big problem. It's quite difficult. People hate bureaucracy."

Touching George's hand, Dr. Villanueva said, "In Canada you have the best health care system."

"Have you been to Canada?"

"Yes. I went to Toronto for a conference."

George stood. "I'd love to hear more about your experience as mayor, but I don't want to interfere with your work. You've got a lot of patients waiting outside. Could we meet some other time when you're not so busy?"

Walking them out, the doctor checked with his assistant, then said, "I can see you next Friday after three p.m."

"I'll be here, thanks." George shook hands with Dr. Villanueva. Then he and Apin went to the pharmacy that was under the same roof, to fill his prescription.

George had to cancel his plans to go to the *Dinagayan* Festival in Iloilo with Apin. Sickness being a full-time job, George stayed home, resting and taking his antibiotics and other medications that were supposed to dissolve and eliminate phlegm, dilate his bronchial passages, etc. One pill was to be taken on an empty stomach, another one with food... Juliet nursed him with papaya and mango smoothies, and drinks made from *kalamansi* (lime).

Apin told George he wanted to photograph dancers pretending to be *Ati* people, the indigenous people of Panay Island, whose land had been taken from them."

"Sounds like Canada."

"Some have been relocated to Boracay Island."

"Are you kidding? Boracay Island, one of the most popular beaches in the world?"

"I am not sure. Look on the Internet."

By that Sunday, George was feeling much better. He sat on the Eneres's front steps, watching the goings-on in the street. One of the Enequia sons came over from across the street where his family lived. His mother and Juliet were good friends, he said to George. "Would you like to go to the family farm?"

"Is it far?" George asked.

"No."

"Sure. Let me put on my boots."

Juliet saw George preparing to go out. "Wait, George." She shouted something to her granddaughter Jade, who was making another beaded bracelet in the living room. One second later, Jade appeared with a flashlight.

"It might be dark when you come back," Juliet said. "Be careful."

"Thanks. See you later."

Little Jade stayed at the gate, smiling as George walked away.

As George approached the teenager who had invited him on this expedition the youth asked, "Can I have your nose?"

Puzzled, George laughed. "What do you mean?"

Grabbing his nose with his hand, the boy pressed it down. "You see? Mine is flat. I want a nose like yours."

"Sure, you can have my nose, but you have to take my old face, too." Both laughed.

"What's your name?" George asked.

"Joey."

As soon as George and Joey set off, the youngest Enequia boy came running over. "Where are you going?"

"Can my baby brother come?" Joey asked.

"Of course."

A few doors down, a young girl appeared on the front steps of her house. Like others along the gravel road, the structure was made of bamboo. "Are those banana leaves covering the roof?" George asked his guide.

"Not banana, *nipa* (palm)."

The girl smiled at George and asked, "Where are you going?"

Joey answered in Ilonggo; George was now able to distinguish the local dialect from Tagalog, the national language, with its Spanish-sounding words.

By now the rest of the Enequia offspring had joined their party. All their names started with the letter *J*. There was Joemar, the oldest boy; Joey, the second oldest; the youngest brother Joven; and Joylin, the only girl in the family. Joylin was holding the hand of the girl from the bamboo house who, George guessed, was the girlfriend of one of the Enequia boys. The group left the gravel road and struck out across a field. The half dozen boys and girls who had watched them pass by ventured to join them, but followed at a polite distance.

"They are my cousins," Joemar explained. Because he was fluent in English, Joemar took over from Joey as George's official guide.

George took out his camera, but one of the watchers refused to be photographed. Farther up, an old man who had been sitting in the shade got up and approached George. He introduced himself. George thought the name was Alerto, but he wasn't sure. The man offered him a shot of *tuba*, made from the sap of a coconut tree, supposedly a stomach twister. George shook his head and smiled. The entire Eneres family had warned George against drinking the local spirits.

For a time, George considered walking barefoot; his hard-soled boots weren't made for this rock-hard, lumpy soil. The old man took George's hand as they walked through the ploughed-up field.

"Thank you," George said, but his helper didn't reply.

Joey and his girlfriend walked behind George, each carrying a cell phone. The younger children were running around in all directions

Joemar said to George, "I am a college student."

"What are you studying?"

"Tourism. I want to work on cruise ships."

"Interesting. Where's the college?"

"Miag-ao."

"How long is the program?"

"Three years."

"What happens after that?"

"When I get a job I'll send money to my parents for my brothers' studies."

"What do you want for yourself?"

"Help my parents. My parents are poor."

"And later?" George asked.

"Have children."

One of the Enequia boys mentioned that Joemar's birthday was coming up soon.

"When?" George enquired.

Little Joven rushed up and whispered in George's ear, "Next Friday." Everyone laughed. Joven held his older brother's hand.

"If I'd known, I would have brought something from Canada. What would you like? I could send you something after I get back."

"Something silver," Joemar replied.

A few minutes later they arrived at the family farm. George shook hands with Juan, the father. The children followed as Juan wordlessly toured George around a thatched house. Joemar mentioned that they used the structure as a guesthouse and for large family events. Chickens roamed in the yard and two goats were tethered to pickets in the ground.

George pointed at the cow in the adjacent field and asked Juan, "Do you have other cows?"

The man smiled at George, and Joemar said, "My father doesn't speak English. The cow belongs to *Ninang* Juliet."

Joemar explained that people with money would buy a pig, cow or *carabao*, which would be tended by a local farmer. When the animal was slaughtered, the money was divided between the owner and the farmer who had raised the animal.

✻

The next morning, George repeated Joemar's explanation about the cow to Juliet, who was sorting mung beans at the outdoor work table.

"It's a way of sharing," Juliet explained. "The Enequias have no money coming in. There are days that Joemar goes to college without breakfast. His mother takes care of *lolo* (grandfather)."

"Her own father?"

"No, her husband's father. He is an invalid."

"I saw him once, on the doorstep. He's paralyzed, right?"

"A stroke." Looking up at the street, Juliet muttered, "The Philippines is a poor country."

"Did you know that Joemar's birthday is next Friday?"

Juliet shook her head.

"When I said I'd send him something from Canada, he said he wanted something silver."

"Boys here like jewellery," Juliet remarked, with a smile.

A man named Nonoy walked by. He came to the Eneres house twice a day to pick up kitchen scraps for their pigs.

When George said, "Good morning," Nonoy just smiled.

After he left for the Eneres farm, Juliet remarked, "He is a hard worker."

"Is he married?"

"No. He takes care of his sister and her little girl."

Chapter Forty-Two

One morning Juliet asked George, "Are you coming to the fiesta?"

"Which fiesta?" George asked. "There seem to be fiestas every few days." Reading from his notebook, he said, "January 17th: Mantanyan at 8:00 a.m. and Tighanabrar at 10:30 a.m. January 21st: Riro-an; January 25th: Jovellar; January 29th; Babacayan; January 30th: Igcabugao; January 31st: Alamida."

"How do you know all this?" Bongbong asked.

"It was on a billboard outside the church." Every at the table seemed amused. "I always carry my notebook. So why are there so many fiestas?"

Bongbong replied, "It's a way for the parish priest to get money, uncle Apin says. More fiestas mean more money for extra masses."

George had recently attended two fiestas in the same week. He could see they provided Filipinos with a break from their routine, a chance to eat and enjoy each other's company. Today's fiesta was going to be in the *barangay* (municipality) of Jovellar.

"My friend Carmelita from Victoria always told me, 'If you really want to know the Philippines, go in January.'"

Juliet's husband, Jejomar, who spoke very little English, touched George's shoulder and said, "Fiesta." He mimicked eating and drinking. "Food...Good."

At ten o'clock, the front and the back gates of the house were locked. Avelina, the daughter of Jejomar's first cousin, was staying behind to hold the fort. Apin had told George that although her cheery personality and physical attractiveness made her an appealing prospect to local men, thirty-one-year-old Avelina had no plans to marry or have children.

George asked her, "Why don't you come with us?"

Bongbong answered on her behalf. "She doesn't like fiestas."

Jejomar joked, "Pretty? Good wife."

To George, Jejomar looked quite old, but in fact was younger than him. The message was clear: the man was trying to *sell* his niece. In addition to washing dishes, doing laundry and sweeping the floor, Avelina helped family members who were having trouble with their cell phones.

She was equally handy with making repairs. One night, George woke up in the wee hours, freezing and feverish. One of the French doors in his room had jammed open. He spent a fruitless half hour trying to secure the door, then moved to another room for the rest of the night. The next morning, the wonder woman fixed the door in no time at all.

Earlier that week, George had gone to the market with Avelina. A Filipino man in his sixties was boasting about having one wife in the US and another in the Philippines. George glanced at Avelina, whose expression revealed nothing.

"A woman for one half of the year and another one for the other half?" George asked the man, who promptly offered to help George find a wife.

"Are Filipinas cheaper than Vietnamese or Thai women?" he asked. The man glared at him.

✽

The family was still at the table when Hilario arrived with his wife Analisa on a tricycle. As was common in the Philippines, Analisa was in the sidecar while her husband was seated sideways behind the driver, his feet dangling.

"George, come and sit next to me," Analisa called out. As George got in, Analisa said, "People open their doors to everyone. Filipinos are hospitable, have you noticed, George?" They roared off.

The *barangay* Jovellar was located a kilometre from Igbaras. George would have preferred to walk but it didn't seem to be the norm. To get to school, neighbourhood children preferred a tricycle ride to a ten-minute walk.

Traffic on the highway (the local name for any unpaved road) was overwhelming. Two-way traffic shared a single lane, as the other was closed due to construction.

"To be completed by next year," Hilario shouted in George's ear. "The money will be gone before the end of the project. There's a disco tonight, by the way."

"Where?" George asked.

"On the playground of the school," Analisa replied. "Do you dance?"

George sighed. "In a previous life, I used to."

A few minutes later, the passengers dismounted by the side of a house. At the back, a group of men were standing around a huge wok at least a meter wide, its contents sizzling over a wood fire. Boyet, who looked after Hilario's property when he and Analisa were back in Canada, was in charge of the cooking. With a smile, Boyet invited George, "Come, come. Eat."

"What are you cooking?"

Boyet removed the lid from the wok. A layer of banana leaves covered the food.

"What are the banana leaves for?" George asked.

One of Boyet's helpers replied, "Heat...cooking."

George had mentioned to Carmelita that the aboriginals in Canada used to roast corn with the husks left on over a charcoal fire.

"In the Philippines we use banana leaves to keep the heat in so the food cooks faster. You will see when we go. People are poor, but there is always food for visitors."

Boyet seized a long-handled shovel to stir the mixture under the leaves. He said the dish was called *valenciana*. He scraped the sides of the wok and turned over the slightly burned rice from the bottom of the pan.

"Want some?" he asked with a big smile. The gathered crowd watched closely to see how the *cano* (foreigner) would react.

George had tasted the dish before, so he knew it was turmeric that gave the rice its signature yellow colour, in contrast to the saffron used in Spanish *paellas*. Valenciana consisted of *pilit* (sticky rice), small pieces of pork liver, bell peppers, corn, and chickpeas. "I'd love some," he said eagerly.

One of the extras handed him a square-cut banana leaf, and Boyet scooped a big spoon of *valenciana* onto the leaf with a warning: "Hot. Hot."

George blew on the steaming food and took a bite. "It's delicious!" he pronounced. This brought smiles all around.

When he'd finished eating, Analisa invited him inside the house.

"Whose house is this?"

"It's Juana's."

"Is she an overseas foreign worker?"

"Yes."

George learned that Juana was in the Philippines for her annual holidays. Like many of the houses belonging to foreign workers, this one was made out of concrete blocks covered by cement. It was three times bigger than the surrounding bamboo homes.

Juana's living room was filled with guests watching a broadcast of the *Dinagayan* Festival in Iloilo. George watched the screen for a moment. Young men and women in colourful costumes, the boys shirtless, danced and played musical instruments in a street closed to traffic.

George looked around the room. The cabinet against one wall had shelves that almost reached the ceiling. The shelves were filled with dozens of photos of men, women and children, all grinning broadly. George exclaimed when he recognized Apin in one of the photos.

Juana, who was standing nearby, commented, "Apin and I are cousins."

"Everyone in Igbaras seems to be related."

Juana asked, "Do you want to see the rest of my house?"

George followed his hostess into a large dining room with several tables pushed together in a line. Several guests stood in the room, waiting to be called to the table.

"The food won't be ready for another hour," Juana said. "Go and see my cousin Rosalie's house."

"Is she there?"

Juana shook her head. "She just returned to Canada. She lives in Victoria."

"I don't know her."

"She is building the house for her parents."

"How do I get there?"

Juana called one of the dozen children scampering around the house, and said to the delicate-looking girl, "Take George to *Tita* Rosalie's house." She said to George, "Everything will be ready when you come back."

The little girl, who was as tiny as a mouse, shouted, "Let's go!"

George had noticed that Filipinos often said "Let's *go*" with the emphasis on the last word, making it sound like a command, as if they were becoming impatient. Was the stress always on the last syllable in Tagalog? he wondered. He would have to consult Apin on the matter.

Boyet saw him leaving the house and asked, "Where are you going?"

"To Rosalie's."

"She is not there. Eat. Eat."

"I'll be back."

Following his mouse-guide, George climbed the narrow path behind the house. When they reached the top of the hill he halted, overwhelmed by the scenery below. "I want to take a picture."

This was the epitome of a rural setting: mountains surrounding fields divided into plots. In some fields, the peanut plants were just a foot high. Other fields were ploughed, ready for the planting of rice during the rainy season. Cows stood apart from each other in several fields, each tethered to a picket by a cord through their nostrils.

George was so overcome by the tranquil scene that he wanted to hug the little girl standing next to him. He settled for whispering, "You live in a beautiful country." He could hear Carmelita's voice again, *"You will see when we go."*

His thoughts were interrupted by the familiar "Let's *go*."

They arrived at a big cement house with no doors or windows. A woman in her seventies welcomed them. Her face was emaciated. Rosalie's mother, he assumed.

"How old are you?" the woman asked.

George didn't hesitate. "Sixty-five. And how old are you?"

"Sixty-four. You know Rosalie?"

"No. I live in Victoria too. When I return, I will contact her to say that I met you." With his eyes, George indicated the spacious living room with its wide doorway, and the unusually high ceiling. "Your house is big." The woman remained silent.

The house was a striking contrast with what he thought of as the Third-World desolation of the region: traditional *nipa* huts, cows, wandering chickens and dogs, the ground littered with wood and metal scraps mixed with plastic jars and bottles. Farther down the dirt path, children were playing a game that he had seen before in the Eneres's neighbourhood.

"What is that game called?"

The little mouse replied, "*Pog.*"

"What does the word mean?"

"I don't *know.*"

"Do you know how to play the game?"

"I don't *know,*" the child replied.

Rosalie's mother took him through the house. The *dirty kitchen* was one of only two functional rooms. The other was the living room, occupied by, or rather invaded by, a large-screen television and an array of audio equipment.

Women brought a variety of dishes from the kitchen and set them on the dining table. One looked like some sort of stew. "Do you like pork?" one of them asked George. Without waiting for his answer, she handed him a spoon and commanded, "Eat. Eat."

George took a small portion, then looked at the young man in the living room. The twenty-something wore camouflage fatigues and a ball cap in the same pattern. Tall and heavily built, he was manipulating the buttons on some sort of gaming device, his eyes glued to the TV screen. "Are you in the army?" George asked him.

"Yes."

"Where?"

Without looking, the man pointed toward the mountains behind the house. "Over there."

"What do you do there?"

"Fight the bandits."

George asked, "Who are the bandits?"

"The enemies of the government."

"Terrorists?"

"Rebels." The youth said these opponents of the government called themselves the National People's Army.

"What do they do?"

"They tax business people."

"You mean business people pay taxes to the bandits as well as to the government?"

The military man nodded. "On Mindanao there are terrorists from Afghanistan and Libya. They are recruiting."

"There's violence there, right?"

"Don't go; they kidnap foreigners."

"Does this happen a lot?"

"They are Muslims and want to be governed by Muslims." Someone called from outside the house, and the military youth asked George to excuse him. "They need me."

The soldier walked out and George watched through a window opening as he helped two men push someone in a wheelchair out of a bamboo hut and along the dirt road toward the house.

The woman who'd served him earlier said, "That's *Tita* Rosalie's father. He had a stroke."

The men lifted the wheelchair into the platform at the back of the house, then pushed it through to the dining room and settled its occupant at the head of the table.

George introduced himself. "I'm George, a friend of Junior's."

The older man remained silent. George wondered whether he was unable to speak English or couldn't speak at all because of the stroke. The man's eyes travelled between George and the food on the table in an invitation to eat.

The children were playing video games on hand-held devices. The little mouse danced with a toddler. In the TV and audio room, the bandit fighter was adjusting the sound. The unfinished house was suddenly full of the sounds of shrieking children and adults chatting and laughing as they dug into the feast. George sampled a few dishes out of politeness, but said he had to get back to Juana's house.

On the way back down the hill, they joined a procession of others heading to the village below. Juana's house was full of guests, each holding a plastic plate. Juana said grace, then handed George a plate along with a fork and spoon wrapped in a napkin.

"Come and eat," she said.

At the centre of the table was a big porcelain bowl of *KBL*, an acronym for a dish whose ingredients were beans, pork and jackfruit. George helped himself. Both the living and the dining room were filled with women and children tucking into their food. He walked outside to join the men who were talking and laughing loudly. The explanation was on the ground: dozens of empty bottles of Red Horse beer and Emperador brandy, and many more bottles and cans waiting to be opened.

When George appeared, the men stared at him with stony expressions. This had often happened to George when he encountered large groups of Filipinos: the women welcomed him and asked him how he liked the Philippines, but the men froze him out. He would have liked to join them and talk with them, not drink but simply talk—they were human beings after all. He waited for a few seconds, hoping for an invitation, but none came.

George promised himself that one day he would crash the men's group, with or without an invitation.

On that day, the population of Jovellar went from one house to the next, eating and drinking. There were boys and girls of extraordinary beauty and old folks with missing teeth. They ate obsessively, as if in a trance; as if the goal was to blot out the hunger and the injustice of their entire country, not just their own individual hunger. They would ingest noodles, fish, and *dinuguan,* the dark brown stew made of pig organs and blood, jokingly known as *chocolate pudding*, then walk to another house and fill their plates again. From dawn to dusk, they ate for their starving ancestors.

George recalled Carmelita's words: *"This is part of our culture: poor and rich eat at fiestas all over the country in January."* George felt he was exactly where he was supposed to be, and was gratified to be witnessing something his old friend had grown up with.

Born in a country where poverty and hunger were daily realities for most of the population, Carmelita had come to love chocolate, ice cream, cheesecakes and any dessert prepared with half a dozen eggs. She loved watching male chefs on TV, flirting with the audience as they mixed ingredients for whatever dish they were featuring on the show.

When Carmelita entertained and told her guests, *"Eat. Eat!"* she was echoing what she had seen and heard as a child. In this way, she stayed in touch with the poverty and hunger of her own people. All her life had been payback time, to her native self and, later, to the people who surrounded her in Canada—people she loved and was determined to care for.

George's eyes drank in the scenery. Far away he could see the mountains where the bandits lived and fought against government troops, while here he was under the playful radar of children intrigued by the presence of a *cano*.

He suddenly heard, "I'm not afraid of dying," but it was his own voice, not Carmelita's. He laughed out loud and said, "I know, Carmelita. You reap what you sow."

Chapter Forty-Three

Apin suggested they visit Elina Gito the next day. She had been living in Victoria for nearly half a century, but was visiting her home town of Janiuay, about thirty kilometres northwest of Iloilo. "She knew Carmelita well; you might want to ask her some questions," Apin said.

"I'd love to meet her! How did you get the invitation?"

"Through Facebook."

George laughed, "Of course. In the Philippines, Facebook is the equivalent of the telephone."

"What's wrong with that?"

"Nothing at all."

They were up at five the next morning. Apin had only been to Elina Gito's ancestral home once, several years earlier. While they were waiting for a jeepney, he confided, "I hope I recognize the house."

"You don't have the address?"

"No."

"Seriously?"

"Don't worry, we'll get there."

The jeepney stopped across the street and the two men got in. "How far will this take us?" George asked.

"To the jeepney terminal in Ioilo."

The trip lasted an hour. The vehicle soon filled to what George assumed was its capacity, until the driver started getting out at each stop. He walked along the vehicle, reached through the windows and pushed on people's backs to make room for more passengers.

"There are limits," George whispered to Apin.

With a smile, Apin reported that there were already passengers clinging to the roof. "This is the Philippines; you'll get used to it."

Dust was coming from the road construction that seemed to be happening everywhere.

"They're widening the roads. It's supposed to be finished in 2017, according to the politicians. Don't hold your breath."

"Instead of widening roads, they should invest in public health," George said.

"The problem is, diesel's cheaper than regular gas."

George's nose and mouth were covered with a handkerchief. Apin remarked, "I should have brought surgical masks from Victoria."

At the front, the driver held a facecloth between his teeth and covered his nose and mouth with it when the fumes or dust got too strong—a regular occurrence.

To George, the jeepney terminal looked more like a disposal site for scrapped vehicles. Dozens of jeepneys were parked in disarray, waiting to take on passengers. Drivers called out to newly arrived travellers. It was a picturesque chaos, with drivers chatting, spitting on the ground, stretching their legs and smoking cigarettes. Several had wrapped T-shirts around their heads, or wore a rag tied around their neck. Passengers came and went by the dozens, carrying shopping bags or chickens in boxes. Vendors sold peanuts, boiled corn cobs, and pop in small pouches tied in a knot with straws inserted.

Apin studied the routes printed on the sides of the jeepneys to decide which one to take next. He finally pointed at one, then said, "I have to use the washroom."

"I have to do the same, but you go first."

Apin came back saying, "There's no toilet paper. Next time I'll bring some."

Some travellers didn't bother with the washrooms; instead, they urinated behind one of the vehicles or against the nearest wall.

"We have to take three jeepneys to get to Elina's house," Apin was saying.

"What can you tell me about her?"

"She's Joaquin's sister."

"And who's he?"

"You know him," Apin replied. "He has cancer."

George felt guilty for not remembering. He looked down at his greying handkerchief, knowing there was more dust and pollution to come.

"Keep an eye on your wallet," Apin warned him. "There are pickpockets everywhere. The week before you arrived, someone stole my wallet."

More than two hours later, the two men arrived in Janiuay. As in Jovellar two days before, the streets of the town were busy with people walking or travelling on tricycles or scooters, wishing each other happy fiesta.

"Do you know the name of the patron saint here?" George asked.

"Elina will know."

To George's surprise and relief, Apin immediately recognized the house. When they opened the front gate leading to a garden full of trees, shrubs and other vegetation, George exclaimed, "All these flowers; what a beautiful garden!"

Elina came to greet them and invited them into what she called the rest house. A woman in her seventies, she spoke with a strong voice, one accustomed to be in charge. She said she had built the rest house, adjacent to her own home, for her brother Joaquin, the year he was diagnosed with cancer. "He didn't come this year. Do you know him?"

"According to Apin, yes," George replied, laughing.

Elina invited her guests to sit on a low, narrow bench, while she perched in a sturdy-looking bamboo chair above them. "Would you like some coconut juice?" she asked.

"I'm sure George would like to try it," Apin said. Their hostess gave the order to her son.

While they waited, George asked, "Which saint is Janiuay honouring today? Apin couldn't tell me."

Elina replied with a laugh, "There are so many saints in our country. Saint Julian is our patron saint."

The hostess's son brought in a *buko*, a young coconut with its husk removed. Noticing the various cuts in the coconut, George said, "It's like a sculpture."

"It makes it easier to hold it in your hand," Elina said.

Using the straw inserted through the opening cut at the top, George drank some of the white juice inside the fruit. "Very refreshing," he said.

While drinking, he looked around the house. It was an elegant version of a traditional *nipa* hut. The walls were made of overlapping bamboo slats that allowed for air circulation; the floor was built on the same principle; you could see the ground underneath.

Noticing that George had seen what was beneath the floor, Elina said, "They are going to remove the boxes. I don't want anything there. Last year, some water came from the river that is very close to my house."

"What is the roof covered with, *nipa* leaves?"

"Yes."

"Not banana leaves?"

"*Nipa* last longer than banana."

"The house is beautiful," George exclaimed.

"Thank you."

Apin mentioned that George was writing a book based on Carmelita Tauber's life.

"I would like to ask you a few questions, if you don't mind," George said.

Elina stared at him, as if in shock. She then burst out laughing. "Carmelita was always telling us what to do!"

"I can imagine," George replied. He told her how he and Carmelita had met and became friends.

"Did she have chemo?"

"No, she told the doctors, 'No way!' She said it killed her best friend and she wouldn't even consider it."

"She could be difficult at times."

Both Elina and Apin fell silent. George felt he needed to explain his motive for writing the book. Because she had been such a dominant personality, he wondered who would read the book. "When I met her, she was in a different phase of her life."

He could hear talking outside the house; guests were arriving. Tricycles and jeepney drivers honked as they drove past. Inside, though, there was only silence and Carmelita's ghost.

"I was there when she was diagnosed with cancer. And I was there years later when she was lying in a hospital bed at the Royal Jubilee and she realized she'd never return home."

"She was lucky to have you," Apin said.

George shook his head. "No, I was the lucky one all those years. She opened doors for me." He looked directly at his hostess. "Do you have any memories of Carmelita that you could share with me? Apin told me you met as students at the Mayo Clinic in Minnesota."

"She was not that much older than us." Elina laughed. "One day, all our team refused to do what she told us to do." After a pause, she added, "I must say that she was great at organizing parties and getting everyone to pitch in."

"Parties for the nurses from the Philippines?"

Elina shook her head. "For everyone. The idea was to meet boys." The "boys" were doctors, many from Latin America and other countries, attending the clinic on internal medicine or surgical fellowships.

Elina's tone of voice changed. "During the holidays, the whole town was a desert. We were all missing our families. Carmelita started an association for international students and we had parties."

"Were there boyfriends?"

"Do you mean, for Carmelita?"

George nodded.

"I don't know. She was strict, that's all I can say. She was friendly with the son of one of the founding doctors of the Mayo Clinic. A chauffeur would come and pick her up from the residence."

Apin said, "Really?"

"When a patient didn't speak English, we were asked to help."

George asked, "When you say 'we', what do you mean?"

"There were patients from Latin America, mostly wealthy, of course. The sisters knew we spoke Spanish, so they would ask us to interpret before and after a surgery."

"I can easily imagine her doing some bedside talking."

"Good for making contacts," Elina said.

George repeated what he had heard from Carmelita: "An Argentinean or a Chilean businessman, I can't remember where he was from, proposed to her and wanted her to go and live in his country."

Elina laughed. "She told you that? It could be."

"It seems he was quite serious. They corresponded for a while. She always spoke highly of the training there."

"It was the best in the world. The mere mention of the Mayo Clinic would open doors." Laughing, Elina asked, "Did she tell you about the Canadian guy who opened some fancy clinic calling himself Dr. So-and-So Mayo?"

"No, she never told me. Where?"

"Sorry, I forgot where. He was the busiest doctor in town until the authorities suspected him of performing abortions, and guess what? He was an ex-convict."

Apin and George laughed. Elina abruptly stood up. "Let's go and eat."

The men walked Elina to her home, just a few feet from the rest house. "This is our ancestral house," she said, ushering them inside. The structure could not have been more than a decade old. Like most overseas foreign workers' homes, it was covered with dark concrete, giving it an austere, bunker-like feeling.

Visitors were filling the house. More were coming through the gate, calling out "Happy Fiesta! Happy Fiesta!"

The living room furniture was made of sturdy bamboo. There were two long, wide buffet tables covered with food in the adjacent dining room. Apin began snapping photos. Elina described the various dishes to George, listing their ingredients. Some of the fish was dried, some fried with a vegetable garnish. He saw grilled fish on a stick, a paella with shrimp and mussels, and *lechon* on a plate, along with shiny, brittle crackling. His hostess handed him a plate, fork and spoon and said, "If you have questions about a certain dish, let me know."

"I will, thanks."

George walked around the table, pausing to examine each dish. A few minutes later, he was on the front porch with a full plate in his hands. Apin was still inside, clicking away with his camera.

A skinny young man appeared in front of George. "Do you like coconut? I cut it."

"Thank you. Your aunt Elina mentioned a river. Is it far from here?"

"Want to see the river?"

"Yes, I'd like that." He put his plate and bottle of Coca Cola on the low table in front of the bench he'd been sitting on, and followed the man. "What's your name?" he asked.

"Ferdinand."

George pulled a notebook and pen from his pocket. "Could you write it down for me? Your family name, too."

Behind the ancestral house, his guide pointed beneath a *nipa* hut, his parents' house, and said, "My workshop." He opened the door and George went first, feeling like Alice falling down the rabbit hole. Piles of steel bars and rudimentary tools covered a roughly built worktable: a hammer, a machete and string, with a few firearms leaning against the wall.

"Are you a hunter?" George asked.

Ferdinand shook his head. "I repair guns."

On the wall, George noticed a newspaper clipping with a photo of a group of hunters.

"How many are you?"

Ferdinand smiled and said, "My friends." He explained how he built the firearms, using alcohol to feed the spark and shot. George had no idea about any of it. The man's gums looked ravaged, as if they'd been carved up with a sharp knife. George refrained from asking whether this was the result of some disease.

"When the door is closed, nobody comes."

George nodded. "You need peace to focus."

"Do you want to see our house?"

George hesitated. "Are you sure?"

Ascending a steep and narrow staircase, they entered the main part of the house. The floor was made of bamboo slats. A woman somewhere past sixty welcomed George and invited him to sit on a bamboo bench against a wall. She was wearing a long, dark dress in a lightweight fabric. She introduced the old man standing next to her as her husband, and George shook hands with the man.

"My father built the house himself," Ferdinand said.

George studied the combination of different sizes of bamboo slats forming the walls and roof of the house, and the geometric patterns. Bending his head, he could see through the slats to Ferdinand's workshop below.

"It must be nice during the day, with the breeze coming through."

"My father and I will replace it soon," Ferdinand said.

Noticing the photo of a young man wearing a military uniform on the wall, George turned to the woman and asked, "Your son?"

She smiled and said, "Gone."

"My brother," Ferdinand whispered.

"Where is he?"

"He is gone. Lymphoma."

"I'm sorry." Next to the first photo was another picture, this time of a young girl with beautiful white teeth.

Again Ferdinand's mother said, "Gone."

The room was silent. George, who regretted having opened old wounds, told her some of his own story.

"Life...difficult," she said.

George saw the *National Geographic* magazines on the table. Ferdinand said, "I like books."

"Is that how you learned to repair guns?" Ferdinand just smiled.

When they left, the mother put her hand on George's arm; she looked directly into his eyes. "Next time...you stay here."

On their way to the river, Ferdinand pointed at a grove of banana trees, saying, "My father and I planted them." He waved at another tree. "From Canada...chestnut."

"How did you get it?"

"*Tita* gave me the seeds."

"Do the *National Geographic* magazines come from your aunt, too?"

"Yes."

A little boy and girl followed them on the way to the river.

"Your children?" George enquired.

"No. The children of my sister."

"Where is she?"

"In Singapore. I am their father."

"What about the real father?"

"Not here anymore. Gone." Was the children's father dead or had he abandoned them? George chose not to ask.

Ferdinand suddenly lifted his T-shirt, exposing the marks of an operation he had gone through three years earlier.

"Sick pancreas... They remove it."

"Which hospital?"

"Don Benito Lopez Hospital in the city."

George understood that Ferdinand was referring to Iloilo, the provincial capital. He bent to examine Ferdinand's skinny torso. He felt a sudden impulse to touch the scar, to connect with the suffering that was associated with it.

Ferdinand broke the silence. "It's my second life."

Near the river, Ferdinand pointed out the plastic bags lying on the grass and littering the banks. The water level looked low. He said this was due to new development on the nearby mountain. Soon he was talking about the melting of glaciers, the heating up of the planet and the chemicals building up in food. George interrupted him to ask about a small fish pond in the middle of the field.

"Did you build this?"

Ferdinand nodded. "I want a bigger one, to sell fish. I need a new generator."

"Can't you fix the one you have?"

"Too old."

"How much would it cost to get a new one?"

Ferdinand shook his head. "Don't worry, my friend." The short, skinny man seemed to possess exceptional inner strength.

George stroked Ferdinand's shoulder and said, "Thanks for showing me the river, the fish pond, the garden. I'm impressed." He was thinking about what it took to accomplish all this given the family's poverty and lack of resources. He kept those thoughts to himself, and said, "You have a good vocabulary in English."

"I like books."

"How old are you?"

"Forty."

"You look a lot younger. Do you plan to get married?"

"I have my mother. She is too important. It's my second life."

George didn't know what he meant by a second life, but was reluctant to press for details. "We have to go back to your aunt's house; they must be looking for me by now."

Ferdinand smiled at him. "Thanks for being my friend."

The two men walked back in silence. Inside Elina's crowded house, George interrupted Apin, who was chatting with some Filipinos who lived in the US. "Could you take a picture of me and Ferdinand?"

"Sure."

George looked at Ferdinand. "Do you think your mother and father would agree to a picture with us?"

Ferdinand spoke to the little boy and the little girl who had accompanied them to the river. As soon as his mother and father arrived, Apin took several pictures. Then it was time to leave.

"I have to go, Ferdinand." The two men hugged. George sighed and said, "I am sad."

Ferdinand looked straight at George. His eyes were smiling. "No, you are not sad. You are happy."

George felt as if he were being torn away. The house, the river, the pond... A stranger had introduced him to his world and become his friend. When Ferdinand said his mother was too important, was he saying that his mother couldn't bear to share him with another woman? George wondered if he would he ever see this place, or this man, again.

"Yes, I'm happy, I suppose."

Once they were on the street, George told Apin, "When I get back to Canada, I'm going to mail him some literature on fish farming and hunting and a few how-to books."

"Are you in love?" Apin asked, bumping his shoulder.

"Don't be silly. I've made a friend, that's all. We connected."

"You really are in love." Apin laughed.

Chapter Forty-Four

When Juliet suggested that he accompany Avelina to a birthday party, George asked, "Where's the party?"

"It's in the mountain." She immediately reassured him, "With Avelina, don't worry. It's okay."

"Are we going right now? Where's Avelina?"

"She just went out to get Bicol."

"I know him. The other day when he saw me walking, he gave me a ride to the market. When I asked how much I owed, he said nothing."

Juliet simply remarked, "He is married to Avelina's niece."

Now I get it. George ran to his room to pick up his camera and notepad, stuffed them into his backpack, then waited on the front step. Avelina showed up a few minutes later. She was seated in the sidecar of a tricycle, but the driver wasn't Bicol. Jade was with her, and a toddler sat on Avelina's lap. The child was singing.

"Who's she?"

"Bicol's daughter."

"Juliet said we'd be going with Bicol."

"He is in Iloilo."

"What's the driver's name?"

"Pato," Avelina replied.

"What's his real name?"

"I don't know," Avelina replied with a smile.

While Pato was checking the traffic, George went to sit at the front of the vehicle, which he assumed was for VIPs. Easier said than done! The roof was quite low, with limited leg room. George inserted his behind first, then pulled his legs inside.

"Okay?" Pato asked.

With his backpack and his knees under his chin, George shouted, "I'm fine, thanks." The little girl with Avelina was still singing.

They quickly passed through Jovellar, the community next to Igbaras. A few minutes later, George saw a sign on the side of the road, a rough board with *Catiringan* painted on it by hand; that was their destination. When they came to a narrow, shallow stream, the driver said he wouldn't cross it. "Too slippery."

After taking Avelina's money, Pato smiled at George but said nothing further.

Avelina shouted the marching orders, "Let's go."

He asked Avelina whose birthday party they were headed to.

"Angela."

"A relative of yours?"

"My cousin's daughter."

They crossed the stream on small rocks laid out like a winding path. Avelina led the way, the little singer and Jade behind her, with George at the rear.

Jade turned toward George. "Don't be afraid, *lolo*."

George didn't mind being called *lolo* by seven-year-old Jade, but took offence when someone not that much younger than he was called him *grandfather*. He managed to cross the stream without getting water inside his boots. "I should have worn flip flops instead."

No reaction came from his companions. They had been joined by a number of other children, coming back from school, walking ahead of them and behind George along a bare path. With the rainy season still months away, the dirt was like concrete. A girl in her teens had joined them; she kept turning her head to check on George. "Are you okay?" she asked.

"Yes. What's your name?"

"Asrine," the girl replied.

"Have we met before?"

"Yes, we went to the Enequias's farm together."

"I didn't recognize you, sorry."

"You meet many people. It must be difficult."

"Thank you. You're very kind."

The people of Igbaras all knew George's name, but he couldn't keep track of everyone he'd met. The situation was further complicated because most people would give him their legal names, but were known by their nicknames in the community.

Asrine smiled at him again. The pretty teenager had long hair and was wearing a plaid skirt and white blouse.

George quickly pulled out his camera. A man was riding a water buffalo in a barren rice field not far from the road. Once he'd taken the shot, George waved thanks to his subject. The man stared at him with the face of a placid Buddha. Once again, George sensed that he was on *this* side of reality, *his* side. What were the purpose and the meaning of travel and meeting people if the souls didn't communicate? With Ferdinand in Janiuay, there had been a breakthrough. What happened on that day had been on his mind ever since.

A few minutes later, George was standing in the middle of a group of children still in their school uniforms. The outdoor birthday party was in full swing, with the usual bounty on the table. The children's mothers urged him to try the various dishes. "Eat. Eat." Avelina had taken Bicol's daughter to play with kids of her own age.

"Do you like the food, *lolo*?" Jade asked.

"Yes," George replied, distracted. He could hear conversation and laughter from another group a few meters away. A group of men were gathered on a plateau above the back of the house. One or another of the men would glance down at the children's party, then turn back to his companions.

It's now or never! Resolute, George put down his plate and spoon and walked up the rise toward the men.

His little chaperone ran after him, asking, "Where are you going?"

"There." George pointed at the men, and kept on walking. A few seconds later, he faced the dozen men, most between their late twenties and mid-thirties, who had stopped talking as he came close. They stared at him in silence.

"Hi," he said, almost shouting the word.

One man replied, "Hi." The rest nodded and smiled.

George pointed at the collection of bottles on the ground. "We have Fundador brandy in Canada, too."

The man next to him asked, "Do you want?"

"Sure."

Taking a glass from a small table in front of him, the man emptied whatever was left in it. He poured in some brandy and handed the glass to George.

"Are you the bartender?" George asked him.

The men burst into laughter. "Yes, I am the bartender."

George took a sip. The man gestured for him to down the whole glass. "Drink! Drink!" George drained his glass. "Can I have another shot?"

The men laughed, and the ice was broken. Even the half-asleep guy in the hammock nearby was laughing. George was pleased. After all his time in the Philippines, he finally felt visible to these men.

"What's your name?" he asked the bartender.

"Rolando."

The bartender was a real hunk. Every part of him was big and strong, including his wide feet with knobby toes; the guy was like a tree, grounded. He had the tanned skin of someone who worked day after day under the sun.

A man sitting on the ground said, "He has a relative in Canada."

"Where?"

"Vancouver." The response came from one of the younger men in the group.

"I'm from Victoria. You have to take a ferry to get to Vancouver."

George looked at the youth who had spoken on Rolando's behalf. He looked like a teenager, but exhibited the delicate constitution and nervous attitude of a child. Yet every time someone put a fresh drink in his hand, he took it without a word, as if he were the designated reservoir that day.

"What's your name?" George asked the boy.

A shout came from the hammock, "Mok."

"Is that really your name?" Mok smiled. "Are you married?"

Once again, the man in the hammock responded, "He has two children."

"How old are they?"

This time the answer came from the "reservoir": "Four and three."

George noticed that the women down below were watching, and no doubt commenting, on what was happening with him and the other men. He felt like an actor performing for two separate audiences. George apologized for not introducing himself first, but one of the men said, "Welcome, George."

"You know my name?"

Mok spoke on behalf of the group. "You are a friend of Junior."

By now George knew that they were referring to Apin, who had acquired the nickname because his father was also named Zerapin. Still, he had to think before answering the question, "Do you know anyone in Igbaras?" If he said Zerapin or Apin Eneres, people would give him puzzled looks. George decided that from now on, he would simply say, "I'm a friend of Junior's."

Since his arrival, George had felt more like a caricature than a three-dimensional human being. Children and old men would wave at him, calling him *Joe* or *Cano*.

George had been longing to meet someone who bothered to ask: Who are you? Now it was finally happening. Although the men seemed drunk—did that really matter?—they seemed to be enjoying his company. They were curious about the weather in Canada. They wanted to get his impressions of the Philippines, to find out what Canadians liked to drink and whether they ate pork. George could feel the warmth emanating from Rolando and Mok. One man introduced himself as Chum Chum.

Out of the blue, someone asked, "Are you looking for a wife?" to general laughter. The guy looked like a swimmer: tall, with a slim build and large hands.

"What's your name?" George asked him.

Another man shouted, "His name is Cano."

George laughed. "*Cano*. Like me, eh?"

"His skin is white," the reply came from the hammock.

George extended his two arms and stood next to Cano. "Look, I'm the *cano*, not you," he said, comparing his skin colour to the other man's.

George couldn't see much difference in skin tone between Cano and his companions. He remembered Carmelita saying that her relatives used to compliment Soledad on her light complexion, her Spanish ancestry more evident than in her older sister. George's mind was wandering between times and places.

He suddenly awoke when a man asked him, "Do you like cock fighting?"

"I've only been to one once. Why?"

Chum Chum said, "Cano has a farm. You should go."

Cano remained silent, so George took the initiative. "Where's your farm?"

"Banile."

"Where's that?"

"Next *barangay*," Cano replied. Then came the invitation, "Do you want to come?"

"When?"

"Not tonight, I am tired."

"Tomorrow?"

"Sure. I can pick you up."

"Do you know where I live?"

Cano smiled. Each time he did, his gums showed. Rather than being a flaw, the pink gums highlighted Cano's straight, sparkling white teeth. He spoke excellent English.

"Are you married?"

Cano didn't have to respond; a backbencher did it for him. "He is still looking." They all laughed.

In his mid-thirties, Cano didn't seem to mind the teasing. Rolando the bartender seized the bottle of Emperador and filled George's glass. He then refreshed his own drink. Raising his glass to his new friends, George said, "Cheers."

The men all raised their glasses and shouted, "Cheers, Joe."

"Don't call me Joe. My name is George."

In unison, they repeated, "Cheers, George."

Apin had warned George against drinking from another person's glass because of the high rate of Hepatitis B in the Philippines. He confirmed it was a contagious disease, and asked whether George had been vaccinated against it. George had promised to check his immunization book, but never got around to it. He'd been drinking from someone else's glass since he'd joined this group of men. Too late now, he decided.

George suddenly had a thought: the same way that, here in the Philippines he was but a shadow of who and what he was at home, the Filipinos who lived in Canada were reduced to caregivers, nannies, janitors or staff at Tim Hortons in the eyes of their employers and the population in general.

From the instant that George had joined this private club, each of its members seemed to be telling him: Look at us; we exist and can teach you a few things about life, love and the joy of being together. Forget what you think of us. We're not simpletons getting our marching orders from the priests, or victims of corrupt politicians.

George was still standing; he hadn't been offered a seat on one of the crowded bamboo benches. He could feel a longing in his heart. There had been no one in his life since John passed away seven years earlier.

Rolando said, "Do you want to see my farm?"

"Sure."

Ready to go, George made eye contact with each of his drinking companions. "Thanks for the drinks. Next time I'll bring a bottle of Fundador or Emperador. Which one should I bring?"

Cano replied, "Both." They all laughed.

Rolando and George started walking. The path was rocky and seemed to have gotten more slippery. He was quite drunk.

As they passed by the women and children, Jade asked again, "Where are you going?"

"To his farm. Do you want to go home?"

Jade shook her head and turned back to the other children.

"My wife is a teacher," Rolando said over his shoulder. He rolled up his yellow T-shirt to cool his chest. George's eyes roamed the man's body, from his ebony neck to his round buttocks.

"Here?"

"No, in Miag-ao."

"Do you have children?"

"No, my wife is no good."

"What are you saying?" George laughed. "It takes two people to make a child."

"We are going to adopt a child." Rolando wiped his face with his T-shirt. He was sweating, "It's so hot."

"You're sweating. Slow down," George remarked. He wasn't sweating, but he certainly was on fire.

Rolando suddenly exclaimed, "Wait." He left the path and walked into the field toward a black cow with white spots that was attached to a picket. After untying it, he dragged the cow behind him.

"Is this a native cow? You're taking her inside? Why?"

"Cold at night." The two men were back on the path.

"Were you born in Catiringan?"

"My house."

"Where?"

The man pointed out three bamboo houses close to one another. "Do you want to see my pig?"

"Sure."

The pigsty was nothing more than a four-by-four space with a three-foot fence and a metal roof. The pig was making noise, standing up on his hind feet.

"He recognized you," George said in amazement.

"Hungry."

"Are you going to feed him now?"

Rolando shook his head. "Let's go."

"Where?"

"Get beer."

"When does your wife come back from school?"

"She stays with her aunt during the week."

"What do you do at night by yourself?"

Rolando's answer came immediately. "I drink."

"Every night?"

"Do you have money?" Rolando asked.

"What about Jade and Avelina?"

"They know."

There was a motorbike close to the house, with the key already inserted. Rolando sat on it, quickly and with assurance, his feet, in worn out flip-flops that couldn't remember their colour of origin, on the pedals.

"What's your family name?"

"Ermoso."

"Really?" George laughed. He put his hands around the driver's waist, and squeezed hard; he was afraid he would fall off.

"I can't breathe," Rolando protested.

"Sorry."

"It's okay."

It's okay was something like a mantra here, George thought. Where he was from, things were never okay; never what they should be. He leaned toward the driver; he could smell Rolando's body odour. When they reached the river, George shouted, "Should I get off here?"

"No! It's okay."

They started crossing the stream that earlier Pato had refused to cross; maybe because of the little singing girl on board. George didn't really care whether his brand new boots got wet. Rolando's nonchalance was a lesson in how not to take himself so seriously, but to let go. George wanted to do just that, and badly! He forgot about the water level and lost himself in the here and now. He watched as they rode past a cow absorbed in her thoughts, or not thinking at all; a family of skinny goats on the slopes of the river, and fields of peanuts and munggo beans. Not only was he able to recognize the Chinese bean, but he knew its Filipino name: *balatong.*

They stopped in front of a bamboo house, where three men were sitting outside on a bench. A party was going on here, too, music blaring from inside the house.

"Money."

George handed a 500 pesos bill to Rolando, who went to talk to a man standing at the window of the "store," a small room that was part of a family house. George saw a child and an old woman in a room behind the man, watching TV. Customers had no access to the inside of the store; all transactions took place through the window. Orders were taken and products pushed through the window. A few minutes later, Rolando turned toward him, carrying five one-litre bottles of Red Horse in a plastic bag. He handed 50 pesos to George and said, "Your change."

When George offered to carry the bag, Rolando shook his head. He positioned the transparent and rather thin bag between his legs.

"They'll break."

"Do you like chicken *adobo*?" Rolando didn't wait for George's reply. "Let's go and eat."

Once back on the national road, they rode through Igbaras. George waved at Paz, Apin's second cousin, who looked surprised. "Where are you going?" Paz shouted.

George shrugged, "I don't know."

"Where is Jade?"

One member of the Eneres family had told him: In Igbaras, there are no secrets. George smiled at Paz, who was still waiting for an answer. Rolando hadn't even slowed as they went by. He was on a mission.

A few minutes later, they drove up a small hill with several farmhouses situated close together. Rolando stopped in front of one of them. "My parents' house."

George looked at the bamboo house. It was old and decrepit, like the elderly couple who emerged to greet them. George shook hands with the man; his wife bowed her head and smiled.

Rolando went hunting; there was a colony of native chickens roaming around the house. He caught one and disappeared behind the house. A few minutes later, he returned with a plucked carcass in his hands. He'd already severed the chicken's head. Blood dripped from its neck. Rolando removed his T-shirt and threw it on the rough table where George was sitting. Ignoring his guest, Rolando started a fire in the outdoor pit and held the chicken over it, turning it a few times to burn the dark roots of the remaining feathers.

With a knife, he cut the chicken into several pieces, poured oil into a pan and set it over the fire, then braised the chicken pieces. From a bottle, he took a handful of red seeds.

"What's that?" George asked.

"*Atsuwete*." Rolando said the word slowly, pronouncing each syllable clearly for his guest's benefit. George heard him, but he was lost in the movements of the cook, and the lines of his body.

Rolando seized a chair and joined George at the table. He opened a bottle of beer and handed it to George, whose attention was on the man's navel. It was shaped like a delicate flower – quite an oddity considering the size of the man facing him. This bull had once been a baby in a mother's arms.

"Cheers!" Rolando said, raising his bottle.

"Cheers!"

"Do have children?" Rolando asked.

"No."

"You don't like children?"

George replied angrily, "As much as anyone else!"

"My wife and I are going to adopt a little girl."

"What happened to the mother?"

"Her husband is gone."

"Is he dead?"

George's question got no answer. George tried a different tack. "Where is he?"

"Don't know."

Then, much as Carmelita used to do to deflect uncomfortable conversations, Rolando suddenly said to George, "I have a woman for you. My neighbour. Tall. White skin."

"What makes you think I'm looking for a wife?"

Rolando clapped both hands to his pectoral muscles and said, laughing, "Big boobs."

Rolando served the chicken adobo with cooked rice he'd warmed for a few minutes in the pan. Like his host and cook, George ate with his hands.

When they were finished, Rolando stood and said, "I will go and get my neighbour." He repeated his earlier gesture and comment, "Big boobs."

George held his hand up. "Stop it! I like men."

"Ako ay iihi."

George looked at him, "What did you say?"

"I go pee."

"Can I go with you?"

"Do you have money?" Rolando asked with a laugh.

PART III

Chapter Forty-Five

A twelve-hour sleep had helped George recover from his jet lag. Sipping his morning coffee, he checked his answering machine. He only caught "Dear George" and "our mutual friend" in the first part of Margaret Seymour's faint message. He finally figured out that she was inviting him to tea at a time that suited him. At the end, her voice strengthened and she signed off with, "We look forward to seeing you."

George dropped by the following day. After a quick report on his journey, he asked, "What were your impressions of Carmelita's funeral?" For George, the question was a pretext for exploring the significance of Carmelita's thirty-year relationship with this elderly couple, whose personal and cultural background was so different from her own.

Geoffrey Seymour, who was a young British intelligence officer during World War Two, spoke fluent German and Russian. Soft-spoken Margaret had spent several years in France working as the European contact for her father's textile business—import from India, export to Europe.

While Margaret *adored* French food, but above all, the elegant simplicity of haute couture, Carmelita was like an exotic plant with her passion for colourful fabrics and floral patterns. On festive occasions, she wore dresses with sleeves as big as elephant ears. The two women never discussed or compared their personal tastes, but they enjoyed each other's company and their friendship grew stronger after Carmelita married Max Tauber.

At the time, the Seymours were living in Point Grey, Vancouver, and the two couples would socialize between Carmelita's visits with her parents, who had moved in with Soledad after immigrating to Canada.

What a tableau, George thought. The men: a Teutonic giant, who was fond of company and a thin Englishman who collected twentieth-century paintings; the women: a South-East Asian woman prone to speaking her mind and a fair Daughter of the British Empire, whose mission in life was to please everyone, her husband first and foremost. She had retained the social graces she had been taught as a child.

Neither Geoffrey nor Max cared for Americans and Asians, and did not shy away from expressing where they stood on any issue. When they weren't teasing their wives, the two men discussed business.

Max had just moved to British Columbia. In the Eighties, the two men became partners in an investment firm, Seymour & Tauber Wealth Management. Later, when Max proposed that Geoffrey join in his new vitamins and supplements business with his brother-in-law, Geoffrey declined with a laugh. "I'm too old for that sort of venture. I get confused with my own pills; it would be a disaster."

No street sounds penetrated the overheated living room; the elevator three doors away was silent. Squeezed between Geoffrey and Margaret, who was re-arranging the plates, cutlery and serviettes on the table, struggling to stay awake, George became bored. To stir the pot, he said, "I didn't know Max Tauber. What kind of man was he?"

Margaret leaned her head toward George. Her hearing was not what it used to be, but she refused to wear "those dreadfully unattractive" hearing aids. She took George's hand and said, "He was quite dapper!"

"Yes, Carmelita told me that much."

"They used to attend events at the Philippines Consulate in Vancouver. Geoffrey and I went with them a few times." Margaret paused to take a breath. She still had a loose grip on his hand, as if she'd forgotten about it.

"She was a regular at Government House. The premier himself said to her, 'You don't need an appointment; just tell my secretary that you wish to see me.' Oh, what was his name? Forgive me, George, I can't remember."

Margaret spoke slowly, pausing often, as if to emphasise the punctuation marks in her speech. She glanced at her husband, whose chin was resting on his chest. "He had a bad night. No matter, the premier's name will come to me."

"What about Max Tauber? What did you make of him?"

Margaret's pure blue eyes widened. "Can I tell you something in confidence?"

"This is just between you and I."

"I miss her so much." She paused. "Where was I?"

"Something about Max?"

"Ah, thank you, love. Yes, Max. He had a way with women. You know what I mean, don't you?" She smiled. "What am I saying? You're a man, after all."

"Forgive me for asking: were they happy together?"

The question took Margaret by surprise. "I don't quite understand what you mean."

"I've heard people say he was at times condescending."

Margaret's expression showed her disapproval of the word, and the insinuation. "She thought very highly of her husband." Her voice adopted the formality of generations of her female forebears. "More tea?"

George realized he'd gone too far. "That was rude of me, Margaret. I apologize."

Her husband's soft, rhythmic snoring provided musical accompaniment for the pouring of Earl Grey tea. Margaret called out, "Geoffrey, would you like some tea?"

He spluttered and coughed, then said, "I would, darling, thank you." George handed him the refilled cup.

"Do tell George about the wedding in Vancouver," Margaret said.

Geoffrey looked blankly at his wife. "Would you be kind enough to refresh my memory?"

"We're talking about our dear friend Carmelita."

Geoffrey sighed. "My wife misses her terribly. We all do."

"Tell George about the wedding we attended with Carmelita and Max—"

Geoffrey interrupted her. "Dozens of guests all in a line, bringing money in envelopes. Max and I had a good laugh about it."

"Geoffrey, please!" Margaret looked acutely embarrassed.

While her husband, now fully awake, reminisced about the wedding, Margaret disappeared. Several minutes went by and George began to worry. Did she go to bed? Did she have a stroke?

His hostess finally reappeared with a photo album that she placed with great care on the coffee table. Sitting next to him, she watched George leaf through the wedding photos. In a group shot, Carmelita and Max, Margaret and Geoffrey stood with the bride and groom and their parents.

"The women looked so beautiful," Geoffrey remarked.

"Thank you for saying so, love. Carmelita used to give advice on how to apply makeup."

"I didn't know."

"She was an Avon consultant. One year she got an award. She went there, I think. Yes, she went south of the border to receive the award from the founder herself."

"Oh yes, that's right. The founder of the cosmetics multinational showed up at the awards ceremony in a pink Cadillac," Geoffrey said, chuckling.

Margaret stared at her husband. "I must say, I fail to see the humour."

Quite surprised, George mumbled, "Carmelita, going from house to house like a peddler?"

Geoffrey looked to his wife to provide the reason. "She loved being with people. She never thought it was beneath her." She turned to her husband. "You know quite well that she didn't do it for money."

Her husband set his cup down. "This direct-sales business is an American phenomenon." The old man was now fully awake. "My wife and our dear friend had one thing in common: an amazing ignorance of how the economy works. As soon as they heard the words composite index, they would rush out to do some shopping." He winked at George.

Straight men teasing the women they loved. George supposed it came with the territory, i.e. the hormones.

Memories were coming back to Geoffrey. "Max and I were business associates, as I'm sure you know."

Though Geoffrey was seven years older than Max, they had shared a love of fine wines and liquor, and enjoyed seeing their wives—and all women, really—well-dressed and looking their best. George looked at the kitchen clock and said, "Thanks for the tea, but I'm afraid I have to go."

"But you've only just arrived," Geoffrey said. "If you have no other commitments, you could stay for dinner. Would that be all right, Margaret?"

"Of course, we'd love to have you, George."

"Thanks for the invitation. Some other time."

Margaret smiled. "Yes, some other time."

George kissed Margaret's check and shook hands with Geoffrey, who looked as if he were losing his favourite playmate.

Carmelita had tried to cement a friendship between the two men. *"Like you, Geoffrey loves art."*

"So now instead of a wife, you're trying to find me a boyfriend?"

"I could strangle you!"

"Be serious, Geoffrey's thirty years older than me."

"He feels lonely. Margaret would be so pleased if you would call and visit them."

In less than a month, Geoffrey Seymour would be ninety-six. Even though she was gone, Carmelita was still showing George the way.

Chapter Forty-Six

George dedicated himself to his novel. He knew that others shared his mixed feelings for Carmelita, and he was determined to portray her virtues and flaws honestly: her generosity, her mercurial temperament, and her obsession with food.

At Costco, instead of buying one bag of potatoes for herself, she would buy two or three, knowing there would always be visitors she could share with. She bought everything in bulk: cans of tuna, herbal teas, and sweet and sour sauce mixes.

In a restaurant, other customers would stare when the dark-skinned woman cried out in ecstasy as she scanned a menu or studied the buffet offerings. At the end of the meal, she would pay for the whole table, sometimes including a lone diner she felt sorry for. In the parish or in the Filipino community, whether in Victoria, Vancouver or Honolulu, the recipients of her generosity had no choice but to *take it*. There were a few who repaid her by sticking their tongues out as soon as her back was turned.

George opened an envelope and pulled out a photo. He recognized the entrance to the Victoria airport. Carmelita, beaming at the photographer, was wearing three hats! She was on her way to Quebec City for the 49th Eucharistic Congress, thrilled at the prospect of meeting Cardinal Ouellet, the Canadian man who was in the running to become the next pope. Carmelita had hoped and prayed for it. While packing for the trip, she'd reached capacity in her various suitcases, so the extra hats went on her head.

How could anyone take her seriously? How could anyone love her? Yet hundreds, perhaps thousands did.

Her travel habits were as unpredictable as her life in general, according to Trinidad Quesada, who had gone on two pilgrimages with the old Filipina. Carmelita always packed several suitcases, then recruited a male slave to carry them down her porch steps and into the trunk and back seat of her car.

The world around her might have been drab, but she was anything but. Like a stage actor who, with a word and a single gesture, could make the audience feel that the soup in front of him was hot, Carmelita could bring her memories vividly alive. She would describe the rows of mango and banana trees on some relative's property, the Japanese soldiers bathing outside on the neighbour's property, and her rejection of the wealthy Latino American who proposed to her.

"We were in the middle of a snow storm. The angels helped us. There were two men dressed in white. They put us back on track."

To listen to her was like inhaling poppers: details came out in a head rush of intense and contradictory images.

Every July she served George a special dinner to celebrate Canada Day. The rationale: *"You and I have no family."*

The menu featured rack of lamb, accompanied by asparagus sautéed in butter, with chocolates and champagne as an appetite stimulant for the main course. *"Max and I used to do this when he was alive."* The table was elegantly set with porcelain china and crystal goblets, and 14 carat gold cutlery resting on damask serviettes.

Whatever she said aloud, George could *feel*. How could he explain that to someone who wasn't in the audience that night?

Chapter Forty-Seven

One Friday morning, a few weeks before the Easter school break, Marty's students were quietly tackling their assignments, individually and in pairs. Seated behind his desk at the front, Marty recalled his dream of the night before. *Tita* Carmelita was talking to him through a doorway. She seemed excited about something. Her self-confidence had enabled his aunt to have the life she wanted. So often she had said to him, "You are too good for your own good, Marty."

She was right. Love was burning inside him, but Marty didn't know how to let it out; he was uncertain of what love was, really. The sound of the bell interrupted his thoughts. The children stood up as one and rushed for the classroom door. Marty had to remind them to slow down.

Just before exiting, young Samuel stopped. He shook hands with Marty, saying, "Have a good weekend, sir." The boy's serious expression was comical, considering that he was six years old. He was mimicking his father, who was a diplomat.

"Don't forget, Samuel, you need to spend some time playing outside."

"Yes, sir."

Marty picked up his briefcase and left the classroom. The whole school was quiet. Once outside, he called Colin.

It was Friday afternoon, and Marty was a man with a secret. When he was at church, playing music, he was living a lie. If the priest and parishioners knew what was in his heart, they would expel him from the sanctuary.

Marty and Sandy had known each other since they were toddlers. As children, they were convinced that the two of them would be husband and wife one day. But things changed in their teens; Sandy and Tomas fell in love and got married.

Ever since she heard about Colin, Sandy had been begging Marty to let her meet his boyfriend. Marty was not pleased with the word but said he would think about it. On that Saturday afternoon, the two most important people in Marty's life met at the Prophouse Café on Venables Street, off Commercial Drive.

Sandy was taken aback and almost froze when she entered. "Wow!" She exclaimed, looking around the café. The establishment was divided into sections, separated by shelves full of books and Fifties bric-a-brac. There were old photographs and amateur oil paintings on the walls and tables covered with collectibles, serviettes, ashtrays, and children's books, surrounded by chairs of different styles and colours.

"My friend was an antique dealer. The new owner kept everything," Colin said after Marty introduced him to Sandy.

Sandy browsed through the books and faded magazines on the shelves. She touched one of the lace shawls hanging on the walls, admiring the delicacy of the work. "Wow!" she said again.

Marty remarked, "I'm glad you like it. The first time Colin and I came here, I thought of you." He turned toward Colin. "I told you Sandy would like this place as much as you do."

"Let's go order." Colin suggested.

While they were at the counter examining the selection of pastries, Sandy said, "I can't stay long. I have some grocery shopping to do. We have friends coming for dinner tomorrow."

Back at their table, Marty told Sandy about Colin's passion for art in general and pottery in particular. "You should see his work, Sandy. It's amazing."

Sandy listened, smiling. Colin downplayed the flattering comments. Half an hour later, Sandy announced, "I really have to go."

"I'll walk you to your car," Marty said. He leaned in as Sandy was about to turn the key. "What do you think?"

"Well, he's..." Sandy searched for the right word.

"Different from anybody else?" Marty laughed. "From me?"

Sandy nodded reluctantly. "Yes."

"That's why I like him, Sandy," Mary replied.

When Marty returned to the café, he noticed that the table had been cleared. Colin had his car keys in his hand, ready to leave. "Where are you going?"

Colin shook his head. "When I got up this morning, I was feeling okay, so I didn't take my pill." He covered his ears. "The music's too loud!"

Marty didn't dare ask what kind of pills Colin was taking. Instead, he said, "Okay, if that's what you want, let's go." The music hadn't seemed loud to him. All he'd been aware of was being with two people who meant everything to him.

Chapter Forty-Eight

Marty made a point of avoiding heated discussions, but today there was no escape. The Pua family was sitting around the dinner table with a single item on the agenda, in fact a question: What was going to be in George's book, for the whole world to see?

Soledad looked around at each of her children and relatives. She sighed.

Susan broke the ice. "Mom, what's wrong?"

Soledad said, "I always suspected him of abusing *Ate*'s trust for his benefit. This has always been my deepest fear."

Florfina Surla frowned, wondering what all this was about. She turned to her daughter Sandy for a clue. Sandy in turn looked at Tomas, whose attention was elsewhere; he was expecting a message from a medical supplier and had his eyes glued to the iPad on his lap.

"My sister was terminally sick," Soledad continued.

"Mom, he looked after her," Marty said.

"She was not thinking clearly! She shouldn't have encouraged the book!" Soledad was in a real furore. Mixing English and Tagalog, she shared her frustration. "Things that are private should remain private."

Susan reassured her mother, "It's *Tita*'s life. You know what she was like. She was an open book." With a giggle, she apologized. "Sorry! Bad play on words!"

"My sister was always mentioning his name, 'George did this; George did that.' He was a total stranger! Why was he doing it? At her church, some were wondering why, too. I am not the only one."

"Mom, what are you afraid of?" Susan asked.

"That he would steal *Tita's* collection of souvenirs from her travels?" Marty said, grinning.

Far from being amused, Soledad stared at her oldest son. "What do you know about the book? He must have told you, since he is your Facebook friend."

Surprised, Marty glanced at his sister-in-law, who shook her head as if to say, *I didn't tell her!*

"Yes, we talk on Facebook, but I don't know him, really."

"That's precisely my point. Why was he so...so *devoted* to my sister? Soledad looked Marty in the eye. "That man doesn't have people in his own life that he needs to look after?"

Tomas put his iPad away. "Mom, what are you talking about?"

"That's enough on the subject," Soledad said in a calmer voice. "Please, everyone, you haven't touched your custard. Eat."

Marty got up. "Excuse me."

Soledad stared at her son. "Your Auntie Ruby made the flan for you, Marty."

"I have to make a phone call." Colin was on his mind and the sky could fall, the earth shake, but nothing was going to stop him.

"It's Sunday, Marty. At this time, families are eating."

"Sorry, Mom." *Sorry for what?* Marty lowered his head.

He suddenly remembered George's last message on Facebook: *Happiness isn't easy to put on!* When Marty messaged back, *Who said that?* George replied, *Me. I just made it up.* This was followed by *hehehe.*

✳

As soon as he got into Colin's car, Marty said, as if he couldn't wait to utter the words, "Mom thinks George is trying to exploit my aunt's memory."

"So?"

Surprised by Colin's reaction, Marty laughed.

"Why are you laughing?"

"Sorry. I never know what you're going to say."

"Don't go too deep, there's nothing down there," Colin replied as he started the car.

"Where are we going?" Marty asked.

"Chinatown. I want to look at a construction site. Mom and I were there for lunch. I didn't write down the developer's phone number on the sign."

"Are you selling your house in the East End?"

Colin said nothing. He was busy looking for parking. They passed Union Station. "Parking's getting harder to find. And now they make you pay on Sundays, too."

"Look, we're in luck," Marty announced, pointing. Right at the intersection of Powell and Main, a car was pulling out. Colin drove in and parked. Marty got out quickly with the intention of feeding the meter.

Colin objected. "Mom would be insulted."

"Why?"

"She was born in Chinatown."

Marty looked at Colin's feet, which seemed to be too large for his height and weight; he had the hands of a labourer. His strong body contrasted with his artistic sensibility and refinement. "Do you know where she used to live?"

"They tore down the house not long ago."

"Was your mother upset?"

Colin laughed. "Mom only cares about sweets."

Marty regretted asking. "Sorry," he whispered.

"No reason to be sorry, she's happy."

"I wish my mom could be like her."

"With dementia?" Colin laughed so loudly that the man and the woman walking in front of them turned their heads. He then launched into a speech about architecture, mentioning well-known buildings throughout Vancouver that he knew and others that were just being built. "A house has to reflect who you are."

Marty interjected with a laugh, "Then I don't know who I am." He became serious. "Our home is like a clearing house."

Colin looked at him, puzzled.

"My parents wanted a big house for Dad's business friends, relatives from the Philippines who needed a place to stay as they adjusted to Canada, and ESL students, for extra income." Marty paused. "What about your house in the East End?"

Colin exploded. "I don't want it anymore!"

"What's wrong with it?"

"There are ghosts," Colin whispered.

"I like ghosts. I loved Halloween as a kid."

"My friend Keith says I'm crazy." Marty remained silent. "There's something happening in the basement of my house."

"You're scaring me, Colin."

The two men stopped at a construction site on Carrall Street. The project was still in the excavation phase. Colin's eyes travelled between the deep hole in the ground and the billboard showing the engineers' plan for the whole building. Pressing his nose against the metal fence, he said, "I want a two-bedroom condo."

"For friends?" Marty asked.

"No, are you kidding? I need a studio: a large table and shelves so my pieces can dry."

"I'd like to convert our garage into a studio. We wouldn't have to book a room in the church basement every time our band needs to practice."

"Do you have a pen?"

Marty opened his jacket and pulled out a pen. He handed it to Colin, who wrote down the telephone number and other information on the billboard, along with the project's tag line: *Love where you live.*

"You should add the website," Marty suggested.

"What for? I don't have a computer."

"You don't have an Android?"

"What's that?"

"You don't know what an Android is? You're not like anyone I know, Colin." He was tempted to kiss Colin's cheek.

"Let's go. I'm hungry," Colin suddenly said. "I haven't eaten since yesterday."

"Really?"

"I didn't feel like it."

"No wonder you're so thin. Look at me." Marty patted his stomach. "I'm fat because I eat too much."

✱

They didn't go to Robson Street. "Too many people," Colin said. When Marty suggested going to Metrotown Mall, Colin objected again. "Too much noise!" Instead, they headed east.

Marty held the door open at the Prophouse Café—the place he now thought of as *theirs*—and whispered, "I like this place."

A handful of customers sat along the wall, their laptops plugged into sockets. Some wore ear buds connecting them to their cell phones. Marty joined Colin at the counter. "Could we sit in the alcove?"

The young girl taking Colin's order remarked, "It's my favourite spot, too. Nice and quiet. One bill or two?"

"One," Colin said.

"You shouldn't," Marty protested, but Colin ignored him.

The alcove was a recessed space in the wall at the back of the café. A piece of fabric depicting Indian deities hung above their heads. Lamps suspended above the transparent fabric cast an intimate glow over the alcove, inviting meditation or the sharing of confidences. A worn trunk covered with tags and stamps sat on the floor by the couch. Inside, Marty found old issues of Life magazine.

A young tattooed girl with purple hair and a nose ring appeared with their coffees and desserts on a tray.

After she left, Marty asked in a low voice, "What do you think of her hair?"

"I love it," Colin replied. "She reminds me of my niece Christie, who dyes her hair depending on her mood; she's like a roll of Life Savers."

"They don't allow the students at our school to dye their hair."

"That's stupid. Christie wants to go to Berlin, but her parents are against it. It's ridiculous; they've been taking her on trips since she was a child. It never occurred to my brother that she's not a Chinese like him."

"What do you mean?"

"Christie doesn't want to be Chinese."

"But...Colin, your niece *is* Chinese, like her father and you."

"There's more to life than the colour of your skin!" Marty said nothing. "If you're satisfied with being just a Filipino, I feel sorry for you."

Not knowing what to make of Colin's remark, Marty chose to ignore it.

"You know what?"

"What, Colin?"

"My father would drag us with him when he went to castrate the bulls." Colin paused. "I had to watch him crush their testicles with pliers. The young bull would fall on its knees, screaming in pain."

"I would have fainted!"

"This was to equip us for life, my father would say. That's how things were in his time in China, and he stuck to it."

As Colin went on, Marty waited, his feelings were overwhelming. Even a glance from Colin would have been enough, but it never came. What was around vanished, leaving a wall that Marty was banging his head against.

Colin's earlier remark was like a knife to Marty's heart. "Do you want to know what it was really like to grow up as a Filipino in North Vancouver?"

"No! I don't want to hear." Silence, then Colin added, "Catholics can do whatever they want, as long as they report to a priest, right?"

"What are you talking about?"

"Sex, of course," Colin shouted.

Marty whispered, "Colin, be quiet."

"You don't know me."

"You keep saying that, Colin; don't, please."

"I'm crazy. Leonard could tell you."

"Were Leonard and you..." Marty paused.

"You want to know if Leonard and I were lovers? No, he wasn't into kinky sex."

"What does kinky mean?"

Colin was wide-eyed. "Where did you grow up?"

"North Vancouver, I already told you."

"You are so naïve." Colin chuckled. "It's sex with a twist."

"Sandy's the only friend I ever had." Marty teared up. "I've never been in love."

"You really are the lovey-dovey, I can see that." Instead of his usual distant or impatient look, Colin's expression was almost tender.

Marty hastily picked up his cell phone and said, "Let's get a picture of the two of us."

"What for?"

Marty didn't know what to make of Colin, but he was enjoying every minute of his company. "I'll post it on Facebook for Uncle George."

"Who's Uncle George?"

"Your friend George, in Victoria. We're Facebook friends. Sometimes we chat."

"You call him Uncle?"

Marty got up. "Let's take a picture, please!" He went to sit next to Colin.

"You're such a sissy."

"I love you."

"Shut up! You don't know what you're talking about."

Later, after he quietly locked the side door behind him, Marty took off his shoes. He heard,

"I am not sleeping. You can come in."

As soon as he entered his mother's bedroom, Marty noticed her reddened eyes. "Have you been crying, Mom?"

His mother patted the bed next to her. She was looking at photographs of Christmas dinners from previous years. In one image, her older sister was seated at the end of the table. She was wearing a large shawl with a floral pattern, holding a fan in one hand and smiling at the camera. Marty's mother sighed. "I miss her so much."

"I miss her too, Mom. When *Tita* was here for a visit, she would get up and sit with me while I ate my breakfast. She'd tell me stories."

"This doesn't come as a surprise."

"In Honolulu, Josefine worked during the day, so *Tita* and I talked a lot. She wanted me to travel—"

His mother interrupted him. "To go where?"

"It didn't matter to her. She said, 'As long as you go by yourself.'" Marty laughed. "Guess what, Mom. While we were at the airport waiting for our flight to Honolulu, *Tita* told me to go to the Philippines."

"Why on earth would you go to the Philippines? You hardly know anyone there." Soledad's head was down, her eyes riveted to a photo showing a happy family. "Susan is getting married." In his mother's mind, her daughter was already gone. As for Tomas, "His obligations are to Sandy." She sighed. "One day, you will meet someone." She burst into tears. "You may already have someone and you are not telling me."

Marty felt as if he'd been cheating on his mother all these weeks. He reached out to hug her, but stopped halfway; his hands were wet.

"Are you all right?"

"Everything's fine, Mom. Good night. Should I turn off your light?"

"Yes, please. Go and get some rest."

Chapter Forty-Nine

Colin relayed Keith Andrews's invitation for dinner, but Marty said he didn't want to go. "I don't know him."

"Keith is my friend."

"Who's going to be there, aside from you and me?"

"The regulars, you know."

"I'm shy."

"They won't bite you! Besides, Uncle George might be there." He laughed.

That Saturday evening, as he always did when he was meeting Colin, Marty drove a few blocks away from his house and parked on a street where no one knew him. Most of the area's residents seemed to be South Asians. A group of mothers chatted while keeping an eye on their children, who were laughing and running back and forth across the lawns. They were the same age as "his" children at school. Marty waited for Colin to pick him up.

A few minutes later, the two men arrived at a two story-house on Adanac Street, off Commercial Drive. "Keith, this is Marty," Colin said when their host stepped out to meet them.

"Glad to finally meet you, Marty. I'm so glad you could come."

Keith Andrews looked about the same age as Uncle George. His red hair, blue eyes and ruddy cheeks confirmed his Scottish ancestry. The blue eyes weren't cold at all; they were welcoming, Marty thought. "Thanks for inviting me, sir."

"His name's Keith, not sir!"

"Leave him alone, Colin. Don't mind him," Keith said to Marty. "C'mon, let me show you around."

Marty complimented his host on his good taste, noticing the brightly patterned rugs on the buffed wooden floor of the entryway, and the abstract art on the stairway walls. "You have a beautiful house."

"Thank you."

"You and Gert did a great job," Colin said.

Keith invited Colin and Marty to go through to the living room. It was only then that Marty noticed the other guests. They probably heard his lame "sir" and Colin's mocking. He wondered if they would think him stupid, as Colin seemed to.

"Guys, introduce yourselves to Colin's friend Marty," Keith said.

A tall, well-built man got up to shake hands with Marty, but was almost shoved out of the way by a short and skinny guy with a smile as wide as his whole face. "I am Haroon. What's your name again?" The guy had a high-pitched voice and an effeminate manner.

"Marty."

Haroon took it on himself to introduce the rest of the company. "Marty, this is Sigmund. Sigmund and I used to be lovers, but now we're partners. Which means I'm single and available." He brushed Marty's arm with his fingertips. "Oh, you're sweating, love." He turned to Colin with an expression suggesting he was near tears. "Ah, to be young and hot!"

Haroon walked up to a woman in a rocking chair. "And this gorgeous woman is Hilde; she LOVES opera."

Hilde gave a soft slap on Haroon's arm. "Not Wagner, though."

Sigmund remarked, "I can't stand Wagner, either. My mind is too small, I suppose." He laughed.

"Sweetie, come over here," Haroon called to a young man who had just come in and was standing in the front hall. The youth seemed reluctant to join the brouhaha in the living room. Getting no answer, Haroon marched over, seized him by the hand and brought him into the living room. "Mohammed, this is Marty." He whispered in Marty's ear, "Don't be shy, love. You're among friends."

Marty shook hands with Mohamed, who rushed to the kitchen.

"Dinner's ready." Keith announced. "Please have a seat at the table." He suddenly stopped. "Sorry, guys, I should have asked sooner, do you like lamb?"

Marty saw Mohamed hovering over the stove, waiting anxiously for the group's response. The chorus of enthusiasm seemed to reassure Mohamed. He lifted the lid of the couscoussière to check on the semolina steaming in the pan.

A few minutes later, a large shallow serving plate with lamb and merguez sausages, and vegetables heaped over the semolina was placed on the table. After warning, "The sausages are spicy," Keith invited his guests to help themselves.

Everyone complimented Mohamed for the delicious meal.

"I told you not to worry," Keith said, patting Mohamed's arm. "It's the best couscous you've ever made."

Keith then shared the bad news in his life. "The US government wants all American citizens living abroad to file a tax report covering all the years they've lived outside the country. Not just old draft dodgers like me. My friend Terry has to pay forty thousand dollars US. If she doesn't pay, they won't let her cross the border to visit her friends and family."

"I am *sooo* sorry for your friend!" Haroon looked devastated by the news.

"She's got a lawyer now, but it's costing her an arm and a leg. She's used up all her savings."

Colin reacted, "Americans! I don't want to waste my time on them."

Hilde interrupted him. "Like it or not, it's the New World Order, as Obama calls it."

Keith corrected her. "It was the Bushies who said that, not Obama."

"Well, anyway," Hilde resumed, "they don't seem to get it; people can't stand America."

Sigmund said, "It'll get worse with Trump."

Haroon, sitting between Marty and Colin, whispered to Colin, "Call me if you find him too hot," then seized Marty's arm. "I want a nice hug from you, gorgeous."

Marty returned the hug, but he was embarrassed when Haroon didn't want to let go. He remembered Colin's warning on the way to Keith's: "He drinks."

Still hanging on to Marty, Haroon asked, "Where are you from?"

"North Vancouver."

"I mean... Where were you born?" Haroon covered his mouth as he giggled. "You look Chinese to me, my dear."

"Take that as a compliment," Sigmund suggested.

All eyes were on Marty, who was feeling the heat. "I was born here. My mother's older sister was the first to immigrate to Canada. She worked at Victoria General Hospital."

Haroon said, "Oh, Sigmund and I love the Garden City. For years, we used to go..." He named all the famous Victoria sights: the Butchart Gardens, the double-decker buses, and high tea at the Empress Hotel. "Now it's the Fairmont Hotel, how boring." Haroon's expression turned sad. "It costs so much more now to take the ferry."

He moved on to the wonderful time he'd recently had in Argentina. "We toured the famous waterfalls." He couldn't remember the name of the falls, so he appealed to Sigmund.

"The Iguazu Falls," his ex replied.

After a quick, "Thanks, love," Haroon switched to their newest adventure. "We're off to Russia in two months!"

After the meal, Keith invited his guests to return to the living room for coffee and dessert. On the way, Marty's attention was drawn to an old photograph of a black woman, skinny and quite old, wearing a dark dress and a bonnet.

"Who's she?" he asked Keith.

"Gert's grandmother. You know about Gert, right?"

"Colin told me a bit. When did he die?"

"Eight years ago."

"Sorry."

Keith touched Marty's shoulder. "We can talk about it another time." Keith dipped a knife into a bowl of warm water. "Let's try this wonderful torte that Colin and Marty brought."

Marty said, "It was Colin's idea. We got it from a bakery on Commercial Drive."

"I don't cook, I don't bake..." Colin remarked with a shrug. Then, with a laugh, "Only pottery."

Keith sliced the cake and served everyone.

A short time later, Marty discreetly checked the time on his cell and said, "I have to go, sorry."

Haroon protested, "What, you need your beauty sleep? It's only nine o'clock."

"I have to do some prep for Monday. I'm a teacher."

"That's cool! There's so much that we don't know about you."

Keith walked Marty and Colin to the door. "I hope to see you again soon, Marty."

Once the two men were outside, Colin asked, "What do you think of Haroon? Did you like him?"

"No. Why?"

"You can tell he likes them young."

"I'm not young."

"You're younger than him. That's all he cares about." Colin laughed.

He was still laughing when they got into Colin's car. A sudden impulse he couldn't restrain came over Marty. "Third Avenue isn't far from here. Could we go to your house? I'd like to see where you live."

"On one condition."

"What?"

"We don't go inside."

"Okay."

They drove along East 3rd Avenue. Colin parked and pointed at a bungalow with a small front yard. "That's my house. I haven't done any landscaping."

"Let's go and sit in the park," Marty suggested, to his own surprise.

The two men crossed the street and walked into the park, which was actually a children's playground built on a small hill. They chose a bench with a view of the city below.

"Who are your neighbours?"

"People from Hong Kong. They don't talk to me, I don't talk to them."

Marty bent his head back to look at the night sky. He never wanted to leave this place. There was the sound of traffic below and all around, but he barely heard it. As content as he was, though, he saw that Colin was somewhere else entirely.

Colin awoke. "I'll take you back to your car."

"I don't want to go."

In a rush, Marty said, "I love you, Colin." Marty's entire secret life came out with the words; everything he'd held back from the moment he discovered that he was different from everyone around him.

"You're wasting your time," Colin said savagely.

"Teach me, please."

"Go to the baths," Colin snarled.

Marty was shivering. "Could we go inside?" He paused. "Please!"

It was dark in the living room. Marty's heart was beating rapidly; he could hear the neighbours conversing on the deck next door.

"I can't do it."

"Please, Colin!"

Colin headed into the bedroom. Marty was beside himself as he followed. Suddenly the visions of the faces, arms, shoulders and other body parts of men that had been haunting him all his life invaded the room. "I had a classmate..."

Colin interrupted. "Shh!"

Marty badly wanted to share what he had been wishing for, dying for all those days and nights. Instead he mumbled, "Sorry."

It was over quickly, the two coming seconds apart.

He heard his mother's voice. "Is that you, Marty?"

"Yes, Mom."

After a speedy "Good night, Mom," Marty walked down the staircase to his bedroom. He didn't want to hear, "Did you have a good time with your friend?" or "I am just curious. Where did you go?"

He heard her say, "I'm glad you are back. I will be able to sleep now."

Marty didn't turn off his bedroom lights; he undressed and went to bed. Images and fragments of conversation competed for attention in his mind. His body was still on fire, and the future was bright. Only the present was murky and hard to navigate.

Chapter Fifty

As soon as he said, "Mom, let's go, it's time for your exercises," Colin heard his mother get out of her big recliner. She walked slowly toward the front door to pick up her sneakers.

"Turn your head right, then left. Okay, stretch your arms behind your back, put your hands together and keep them there for a few seconds..." The ten-minute routine was followed by a cup of vanilla yoghourt, the only flavour she liked, and three digestive biscuits.

His mother slowly returned to the recliner in front of the TV. She liked to watch the shows that featured men and women at each other's throats in front of a live audience.

Years ago, the family had built a huge new home on the Surrey property with the proceeds that came from subdividing the farm. The subdivision left Colin with a sizable inheritance when his father died—enough that he could devote himself to his art and indulge his constant search for properties to buy. Still, he hated the monster house, with its seven bedrooms and four bathrooms.

Money is nothing. He'd been hearing that voice in his head for months.

Colin's life revolved around his ceramic sculptures. In the basement of the family house, he had all the space he needed to lay out his work and let it dry before firing the pieces in the kiln. His unconventional creations undulated like ocean waves, their shapes both soft and edgy, hinting at androgyny.

He'd once described himself to his oldest brother as a lesbian. His brother exploded. "You're a man. How can you be a lesbian?"

"I'm a male lesbian."

"Colin, you've always been weird!"

His brothers weren't interested in his sculptures. For them and their wives, art was to be found in museums in places like Paris, Madrid or New York City.

The phone rang. It was Marty, asking, "What are you doing?"

"Nothing." Colin was dicing a red pepper, his salad bowl half-full of sliced cucumber and broccoli.

"I won't keep you long. What are you doing Friday night?"

"No idea."

"After school, I could get some Chinese food and bring it to your house. We could go to a movie."

"I'm not sure about Friday."

"How about Saturday?" Colin remained silent. "I miss you, Colin. Can I come and see you?"

"What we did the other day is never going to happen again."

"You still love him?"

"Who?"

"The man you went to India with?"

Colin replied, "Leonard loves lady boys. I already told you. There's a doorman at the Pink Club on Davie Street… I am sure he's interested in me."

"Have you talked to him?"

"Mom's calling me, I have to go." Colin hung up after a promise to call back.

Chapter Fifty-One

When Keith picked up the phone, he immediately apologized for not calling George back the night before. "I got back too late."

"It's okay," George said. "I went to bed early, anyway." Keith and John used to spend hours on the phone, talking politics. After John's death, George and Keith got in the habit of a weekly call.

"What do you think of the new government?" Keith asked.

"Interesting outcome. It seems most of the country voted for change."

"Yeah, we'll see if they're able to tolerate dissent any better than the previous government. With them, if you didn't go along, you were an enemy. Not sure where we'd be if they'd gotten in again."

George didn't have the same level of interest in politics that his partner and Keith had shared. He wanted to talk about people they knew in body and soul, not silhouettes like the political figures of the day. "How was the dinner party?"

"Colin and Marty left early."

"Sorry I missed it. I had an appointment and couldn't change it. So how did it go? What do you think of Marty?"

"Nice guy. A bit shy, I think."

"Filipinos don't say much when they're among strangers."

"Haroon made me so angry!"

"Why? What did he say?"

"It's not what he said; he reminds me of a hawk."

"What do you mean?"

"He grabbed Marty as soon as he arrived and wouldn't let go of him. When there's someone he doesn't know, it's like the rest of us disappear. I'm going to talk to him about it."

"Haroon didn't do that to me the first time we met. Mind you, we're the same age." George laughed.

"Anyway, getting back to Marty, we did get to talk a bit when Haroon was arguing with Hilde about music. In a group, those two are like oil and water."

"What do think of Marty and Colin together?"

Keith laughed. "An affair between Colin and Marty? You've got to be kidding."

"Why not?"

"Colin's older than Marty."

"Keith, that's nonsense! How old is Mohamed?"

"I find that insulting," Keith exploded. "You're like my neighbour Janet. The first time she saw Mohamed, she said, 'A bit young for you, isn't he?'" Keith exhaled sharply and said, "Sorry."

"I didn't mean to upset you."

"The guy touched a chord in me the day I met him at the gym." After a pause, he remarked, "You know what? John was right after all!"

George felt lighter at the mention of John's name, as if Keith had brought his partner back to life. Over the years, friends and neighbours had overwritten John's memory with other faces and feelings. George was the only one keeping the fires burning. "What do you mean?" he asked.

"John said I'm attracted to men who have problems."

"I guess he was telling you that he fit that category, too."

"He was ashamed of his lifestyle," Keith agreed.

For years, John's "lifestyle" included drugs, and towering guilt and shame that almost killed him. There was silence on the line. George was remembering John's anguished quest for inner peace. He was certain Keith was thinking about the same thing.

Since the beginning of the conversation, George had been hoping Keith would ask, "What's going on with you?" instead of launching into a political discussion. "It's been almost eight years, and I still miss him. I can't stand it. Do you miss Gert?"

"Of course, George. Why are you asking?"

"I just want to know how you feel after all these years."

"We were captains of ships going in the same direction. That's not always the case with couples. I got lucky. And yes, I still miss him terribly."

George and John had quarrelled constantly, and Keith had witnessed the conflict on a few occasions. Painful memories, laced with shame, still woke George some nights. Better not to go there, he decided. "I'm missing my old friend Carmelita, too." Even though he was writing about her, there was nothing that he could, or wanted to share with Keith or anyone else at the moment.

Keith knew about the old Filipina. "It's amazing what you did for her when she was sick."

George replied—in fact, he was mentally writing down the words as he spoke them aloud to Keith—"What I did had its origins in me and was for my own benefit. When I sat with her as she was dying, I wanted her to tell me what to do when my turn came. Never mind. The real question is: Can one love a second time?"

Keith's voice was soft, but full of confidence. "Yes, I think you can, but the spark is different."

"That gives me hope. So what's happening with your rental house in Fernwood?"

Twenty years earlier, Keith had bought a heritage house in Victoria. He'd renovated it with the intention of renting it until he retired. John had been thrilled at the prospect of seeing his friend more often, but the move never happened. Gert had suffered as a youth under South Africa's apartheid, and Keith didn't want to expose him to that kind of prejudice again. At the time, Victoria's dominant culture was white Anglo-Saxon.

"In a big city like Vancouver, nobody cares if you're black, yellow, or pink for that matter," George said.

"In Vancouver, when you ask for Worcestershire sauce, the staff looks at you; they have no idea what you're looking for. In Victoria, you can speak English and be understood."

"And we have high tea here, don't forget."

"John and I used to joke about that." George had always been jealous of the complicity between Keith and George, who were like twin brothers.

Just before hanging up, Keith asked, "How's your book coming?"

"It's coming. But there's something missing, and I haven't figured out what. When I talk about the Philippines and Filipinos, I feel as if I'm always talking about myself."

"Isn't what all authors do?" Keith joked.

"I don't care about their food or their religious beliefs. It's like a passionate affair. I wasn't expecting that."

"What do you mean?"

George was thinking aloud. "I'm in bed with that country... Anyway, thanks for asking."

Chapter Fifty-Two

To test the waters with his book, George set up a blog with the help of a computer-savvy friend. He wanted to hear from Filipinos living abroad; any immigrants, for that matter.

He heard that the Multicultural Association of Victoria was sponsoring a cross-cultural event that summer. He immediately contacted the executive director of the non-profit organization. James Cooper suggested that George submit a proposal for a presentation at an upcoming round table, scheduled for June, on the contributions of immigrant women in the city. He also invited George to the next board of directors' meeting later that week.

On the first Monday in March, George stepped into the boardroom at the MCA. A South Asian woman in her seventies walked toward him, her right hand held up like a stop sign. "Mr. Miller?" she said, her voice ringing out. "I am Rupa Singh. Carmelita and I founded a multicultural women's group years ago."

"What was the group about?"

She ignored his question. "So you are writing a book about Carmelita." The woman beamed. "Excellent! The young generation needs to know about the past."

Unsure of what she meant, George enquired, "So you knew Mrs. Tauber?"

"You mean Carmelita?" The woman laughed. "Of course." She stared at George. "How did you meet her?"

"We were neighbours."

"When, a long time ago or just recently?"

George had had enough of the woman's interrogation. "Could we meet sometime? I'd like to talk to you about Carmelita, since you knew her."

Rupa nodded. "Sure!"

"Carmelita never told me about that women's group."

"There are good reasons, let me tell you. Carmelita and I fought a lot."

George leaned toward her. "About what, if I may ask?"

"Some people are good at getting grants from the government."

Having noticed that the other directors were muttering or shaking their heads, George suddenly felt uneasy.

Rupa continued. "Canadians don't care, forgive me for saying that. Shortly after his arrival with his wife and children in Canada, the man abandons them to start a family with another woman." She repeated, "We fought a lot, Carmelita and I."

George was confused by her cryptic statements, but he tried again. "I'd really like to hear more about this women's group. Could I meet with you at another time?"

Carmelita's war buddy didn't reply; instead, she waved at two women who had just entered the room. "Where have you been? I have to talk to you about something." Still looking at her acquaintances, the woman muttered, "My husband and I are going out of the country for a couple of months."

"Would you have time to see me before you leave?"

"I have a doctor's appointment."

"Do you have a cell phone? We could talk by phone instead."

The woman shook her head. "No. I mean, yes, I have a cell, but it is for emergency only."

George handed her his business card. The woman studied it for a few seconds, then took a seat at the table. She was chairing that day's meeting. The agenda was read; the first item was the cross-cultural event. George was invited to describe his book about a well-known Filipina activist in Victoria.

After a few complimentary remarks and general questions, the board members voted. They agreed to have George participate in the round table scheduled for early June. The theme was *Building bridges through volunteering*.

After the meeting, George tried to get Rupa Singh's attention, but she was deep in discussion with the two women she'd greeted earlier. He walked up and said, "Sorry to interrupt you, Ms. Singh, but could I have your email address?"

Rupa took out George's business card, turned it over and wrote her email address on it, then gave it back to George. Puzzled and slightly embarrassed, George said, "Thanks."

George emailed Rupa Singh that Saturday, saying he'd been pleased to meet her, and repeating his wish to meet her *at a time that's convenient for you*.

Later that day, he received a reply that read more like a diary of health-related appointments. She was scheduled for blood tests and a medical appointment that she couldn't cancel.

George sat on the stage, looking out at the audience at the cross-cultural roundtable event. Most of the participants were middle-aged women, several wearing a scarf, hijab or other head covering. There were a just a few young Caucasian women. University students, he assumed. He recognized some of the Filipino faces—women he'd met at the Bayanihan Filipino Centre.

James, the executive director, delivered the welcoming remarks, which ended with, "In Victoria, there is a British tradition, but it is essential for everyone to keep his or her identity. I am aware that some don't like the word, but the model is a mosaic."

The unsmiling young woman seated to the right side of the executive director introduced herself. "My name is Amar Abadulali." She pronounced each syllable slowly and deliberately, almost spelling the two words, then remarked on the almost total absence of men in the audience.

George couldn't help agreeing with her. How can you expect any change, if the other 'half' doesn't show up?

The young woman continued, "Volunteerism is a North American phenomenon. Here, parents get involved their children's education; residents get involved in community policing..."

George saw some people nodding, while others sat motionless, showing no emotion. Then the woman turned to George and invited him to say a few words about his book on "an exceptional Filipina who lived in Victoria for nearly half of a century."

The microphone was passed down to George who began his presentation with, "Carmelita Tauber was a nurse and a midwife who came to Canada as a missionary, without pay or very little pay. In Northern BC, she worked with Native women living on a reserve and once in Victoria, she became a political activist to help women immigrants..."

George felt he was blabbering a bit as he searched for just the right words to describe his old friend and his book.

James's eyes kept scanning the audience then returning to George. He smiled his encouragement. He was one of *them*, because of his dark brown skin, and also through the presence of his young wife, who sat nearby, breastfeeding her child. Nobody paid attention to her; this was a crowd comprised of women, after all.

During the Q & A, everyone smiled shyly, but there were no questions or comments from the audience. George felt a familiar barrier in the ensuing silence: men and women who were quite friendly with those from their own community had nothing to say to him. That evening, George was the foreigner, not them.

What a waste of time! Wrapping up, George shook James's hand and said, "Thank you for your kind invitation." He waved at the audience.

✱

In September, George received an email from Rupa Singh, the co-founder of the women's group.

"Maybe you have given up on us. We have been away and are leaving again to go out of country and will be back toward the end of November. Perhaps in December you can come over, if you would like to. Think it over."

George considered shooting back with: "December of this year, or next year?" Instead, he wrote, "Thanks, let's do that, Ms. Singh."

Chapter Fifty-Three

"Do you know why companies in America are not interested in engineers from abroad?" Curt Jergens was lecturing again. His wife stood next to him, holding a glass of wine in each hand. She handed one to her husband and said, "You have too high standards."

Curt resumed, "In Vancouver, public transit is constantly interrupted due to mechanical problems."

George wondered how the man could think this was suitable conversation just before midnight during the sixth edition of Ella and Andy Stornebrink's New Year's Eve party.

Curt's vehemently held positions on every subject under the sun were well-known among this group. He had expressed the same opinions on New Year's Eve a year ago, and the year before that. Getting no feedback from his audience, Curt moved on to the short-sighted politicians running Canada and British Columbia. "Not to mention Quebec." He added with a laugh, "Think of the corruption that they have over there."

A dozen guests were gathered in the Stornebrinks's living room, waiting for the midnight signal on the local radio. Ignoring the others' mounting excitement as they prepared to greet the New Year, Curt said, "Canada is far from being the top place to live in, if you ask me."

Unable to restrain himself, George asked the speaker on his soap box, "So why do you live here, then?"

Everyone froze. Feeling both embarrassed and ridiculous, George walked over to apologize to his hostess, who was placing flutes of champagne on trays. "I'm sorry. That was stupid of me."

"They're always like that when they come back from Germany," Ella said, to reassure her mercurial friend.

"It's not easy to uproot yourself and start a new life..." George turned toward the man who was speaking. He'd met him at last year's party and knew he was from Montreal and worked for a local investment company. "We all have expectations."

George shook his head; he couldn't guess what the guy was saying, really. All evening, the French Canadian had wandered through the living room, the dining room and the kitchen, schmoozing with everyone, his wife at his side. She suddenly opened her mouth. "In a city such as Victoria, who doesn't feel like a stranger?"

An older woman who had been following the discussion interjected, "Aren't we all immigrants?"

The investment broker looked at her, puzzled, and Ella said, "You lost me."

Her guest remarked, "Being an immigrant is the worst thing that can happen to someone." The woman had white curly hair. She was wearing an old-fashioned silver lace dress. She was another regular attendee at the New Year's parties. "My parents came from Hungary; they had a tough life... My mother wanted to be buried next to her parents and grandparents."

"Did that happen?" George enquired.

The woman shook her head. "No, we didn't..." She paused.

Her husband finished his wife's sentence. "It was a tough decision. We weren't able to follow my mother-in-law's wishes."

His wife said, "Something is lost and never recovered." She had an absent-minded expression, her mouth open, as if she was on the verge of saying something else. Then she smiled and added, "'You may try, but you never truly belong', as my mother used to say." Her husband put his arm around her shoulders.

Ella excused herself. "Andy wants me in the kitchen. It's five to..."

The guests counted down: "10, 9, 8..." At midnight, they shouted in unison, "Happy New Year!" Hugs and kisses all around, then soon after, the guests began to disperse.

George uttered a loud and non-specific "Bye, everyone" to the remaining few and headed for the front door.

Ella came with him, asking, "Is anything wrong?"

"I'm fine."

"Are you sure?"

"I miss John, that's all."

"I don't know what I would do without Andy." Ella added, "I hate the holidays. Everyone is pretending to be happy."

"Me, too."

"Let's meet downtown for a coffee. I have this week off."

"I'll call you," George replied before leaving.

A new year had begun, and here he was, still alone. He felt like a spectator watching others live their lives.

"During all those years in Canada, my mother talked of going back home to Hungary," Ella's guest had said.

To George it seemed as if immigrants never truly settled in. The tree was uprooted and slowly, imperceptibly, it died.

George didn't take a cab as he'd planned. His mind in turmoil, he decided to walk home. It took him nearly an hour. When he passed the house where Carmelita had lived, he didn't even look at it. He could hear music and laughter as the new owners celebrated the New Year.

"It's part of our culture," Carmelita used to say to explain anything that might look or sound strange to an outsider. George assumed his old friend had been referring to other Filipinos, but now he wondered whether this was her way of declaring, "I am a Filipina and always will be."

Was her last thought or last sigh in Tagalog?

That night, George had a dream. Carmelita was with a little girl who was holding on to her with her arms wrapped around Carmelita's legs. With surprising agility, Carmelita sat down on the floor. She was smiling, absorbed in running her hands though the child's curly hair and examining her plump fingers.

Suddenly, the front door of her house flew open and a noisy horde of Filipino men, women and children rushed in. The women wore Spanish mantillas, and the altar boys and girls were dressed in a white surplice over their black robes.

"I wanted to have children," Carmelita said, as if thinking aloud.

Still dreaming, George asked her, *"Should I postpone the publication of my book?"* He got no answer, yet he felt comforted. Carmelita was alive and well in the dream, and at peace with everyone.

Chapter Fifty-Four

Colin and his family had chosen the Olympic Village in Downtown Vancouver to celebrate their mother's 90th birthday. The contemporary and stylish building had its feet in water that reflected the scudding clouds overhead. Combined with the sunlight bouncing around the inner courtyard, the effect was disorienting. George recalled experiencing a similar sensory overload when he visited the Greek island of Mykonos.

As soon as George entered the ballroom, Colin took him over to his mother, who was chatting with someone seated to her right. "Mom, do you remember George, from Victoria?"

"Of course! George from Victoria! Thank you for coming."

Sitting straight up in her chair, Mrs. Hong was looking around at the others seated at the head table with her at the centre of the room.

Colin introduced George to his mother's elderly relatives. Everyone nodded hello, and George admired their smooth, translucent and wrinkle-free skin. The seniors gazed at him curiously, as if to emphasize that he was not a family member. Colin's older brothers Peter and Christopher shook hands with George and thanked him for joining the celebration. Then followed introductions to the third-generation Hong family: young men in suits with no ties and women wearing exquisite gowns. Many of them were engineers like their parents; some lived and worked in Canada, while others were based in US.

Colin said, "George, come on!" Was he upset that George was spending time with his relatives and enjoying it?

"Where have you put me?" he asked Colin.

"At the gay table."

"You can't be serious!"

When Colin invited George to the celebration, he had mentioned there would be a designated gay table. George couldn't believe he'd meant it as anything other than a joke. "Are you trying to make a political statement?" he asked. "I'd rather sit with your family. They seem welcoming and agreeable."

"They don't have a choice. They have to be polite," Colin said.

To George's relief, the table wasn't a hundred per cent gay. One of Colin's cousins from the States was there with his girlfriend. George said hello to Keith, who was putting him up for the weekend. Jim Goshinmon and Lukas Sterzenbach were there, too. George congratulated them on their recent marriage. Sitting across the table was an elderly couple.

"They're siblings," Colin said. "From Dad's side of the family."

The brother and sister had grown up on a farm close to the Surrey farm where Colin's father was born. At an early age, his parents had sent him to China, where he spent the rest of his childhood and youth. It wasn't until he returned to Canada that he reconnected with these relatives. The siblings had lived together all their lives; neither had ever married

George enquired about their childhood, and the old man said, "We played baseball... a lot. Work and more work. No money." His sister listened, an immovable smile on her face.

"Marty's not here," George said to Colin. "Did you invite him?"

"I did, but he said no."

"Why?"

"He said he's too shy."

"Typical."

Jim said, "Who's Marty? You didn't tell us you have a boyfriend."

"He's not my boyfriend!"

"So who is he?"

"An immigrant!" Colin replied.

Upset, George set the record straight. "Marty was born in Canada. You know that, Colin. He's a nice guy, but his whole life revolves around his family."

"He should have life of his own. Don't you think, George?" Colin said, with a laugh.

On behalf of his mother and the family, Peter, the oldest son, formally welcomed the guests. When he was done, the kitchen doors suddenly opened and waiters erupted into the room to serve Mrs. Hong and her guests at the head table. The other tables had a designated number, and Peter invited one table at a time to go to the buffet table at the front of the room.

Behind the table stood an army of male servers in white shirt with a bow tie, waiting for the guests to choose the salmon, seafood, or braised beef, along with roasted vegetables sprinkled with rosemary and other herbs.

Mrs. Hong appeared on the big screen. "Your mother's not eating," George said.

"She's waiting for the desserts. Which aren't good for her."

"It *is* her birthday," Keith remarked.

"Tomorrow she won't remember a thing. You have to sit down beside her and tell her to eat. I'd better go help her."

George looked around. Half the guests were Caucasians, the other half Chinese, though they all seemed to be chatting in English. Christopher Hong, one of Colin's brothers, moved a chair over next to George. "What number are you?" George asked.

"In our family, we never called ourselves by numbers, the way they used to in the old days."

"What about your mother? Which number is she?"

"I'm not sure. Ask Colin, he'll know."

"What was it like to grow up on a farm?" George asked.

"I hated it. We all did, my brothers and I," Christopher replied matter-of-factly. "Hey, you don't have a drink. Come with me."

They walked to the table set up at the opposite end of the room. There was a wide selection of local and imported red and white wines. "There's even a Spanish wine," George noticed.

"Do you like Spanish wine?"

"Yes."

Christopher smiled. "We just came back from a three-week hiking trip in Spain."

"You and your wife?"

"Our daughter Christie came with us."

"How was it?"

"Come and eat with us at Mom's house tomorrow. I'll show you some pictures."

George's table was called to the buffet, and when he returned to the table with his plate of food, Keith was saying, "This isn't traditional Chinese food."

"Nobody's wearing traditional Chinese clothes, either," George joked.

Colin almost choked. "You can't be serious!"

Keith remarked, "You're the third generation and it shows."

George turned to Colin's American cousin on his right. "Do you feel Chinese?" George immediately apologized, "Stupid question, sorry."

The American cousin replied with a smile, "No worries. We ask ourselves the same thing."

After the main course, the guests were called in table order to the buffet for dessert. There were French pastries, flans, meringue kisses, crème caramel and, at the centre, several varieties of cheesecake.

"No wonder they gave us another dinner plate," Keith said with a laugh.

While the guests ate or waited in line, a large screen over the buffet table played a slideshow of old photographs. They watched as the birthday girl blew out two candles at the centre of a huge cake. Colin, now sitting next to his mother again, told her there was still one candle left.

"Oh, is that so?" The old lady bent forward and blew again. The servers took the cake back to the kitchen to slice it.

After a lengthy delay, someone called out, "What's going on?"

Peter Hong stepped up to the microphone and announced that the electric knife on site wasn't working properly. The caterer had been called and a replacement was on its way over. Everyone laughed, and Peter added, "On behalf of Mom and my brothers, thanks again for being here."

The guests stood up, applauded and sang "Happy Birthday." Several guests went up to the head table to kiss Mrs. Hong. One would stroke her arm and another would put an arm around her shoulder and smile for the cameras.

Keeping his eyes on the big screen, George commented, "Look how gracious she is with everyone."

George had heard many family stories about Mrs. Hong's life. She was the daughter of a Chinatown shopkeeper, and had often been the victim of racism. She used to be known as a wild creature given to yelling at her husband. Gone, too, was the woman who'd quarrelled bitterly with her mother-in-law for years, over cooking, raising children and tending livestock.

Colin said, "She's gracious now, but before, if she got her claws into you, you were dead!"

"She's turned into a very nice person," Keith said.

The big screen showed his mother dozing, and Colin stood up quickly. "I need to get her home right away, or she'll be too tired to walk." After he blew a kiss to the sixty-per cent gay table, Colin walked over to his mother's side.

The whole room watched as he gently touched his mother's hand. When Mrs. Hong got up and the two of them started walking out, the guests rose, sang "Happy Birthday" again and wished the birthday girl good night.

Chapter Fifty-Five

The Hong brothers and their families spent the weekend at the Surrey family house. While the adults reserved the bedrooms on the upper floors, the younger generation took possession of the downstairs, which included three bedrooms and an entertainment room.

Before closing his bedroom door, Colin shouted, "Good night, Mom."

A few seconds later, he heard a gentle knock. "Uncle, can I come in?"

Colin was pleased to see his favourite niece, Christie. He only saw her on special occasions, as she lived in Los Angeles with her parents.

"Grandma must be exhausted. It was a lot of emotion for her."

"She couldn't even undress by herself; the caregiver had to put her to bed."

The young woman burst into tears.

"What's wrong, Christie?"

"I want to go to Berlin, Uncle. Could you talk to Mom and Dad?"

"I know how much you want to go, but why there?"

"It's the place to go for music, real music. Listen to what my friend Madison just posted." Christie thumbed her iPad and played a clip from a concert in Europe. "Madison knows this cool guy from Berlin; he's a DJ."

Colin wasn't thrilled with the sound. "What kind of music is this?"

"Dance music, Uncle. Ever since I was a kid, I've loved this kind of thing."

"That's your genre?"

Christie corrected him. "I'm into sub-cultural movements, not genres. I don't like rules and categories."

"Like me when I create pottery."

Christie was hunting for something on her iPad. "Listen to this. It's a remix I did for the guy in Berlin."

Again, Colin was not impressed. All he said was, "You want to be a DJ?"

"You got it! I love underground culture."

"How do you make people dance?"

"By being myself a hundred per cent and showing them it's okay to be yourself. I try to feel the room and give them something that challenges them in the right way."

Christie couldn't stay still. One minute she was facing her uncle and swaying; the next she was going through the pages of his sketchbook.

"There's nothing... I'm not doing anything right now."

"Why not?"

"It's a long story."

"I love your pottery. It's out of the ordinary."

"Take as many as you want."

"Really?" she squealed. "Oh, Uncle, that would be amazing, thanks!"

"Stop moving, you're making me dizzy."

"Are you on Instagram?"

"What's that?"

"Do you have a cell phone?"

"I don't use it much. The caregiver has to remind me to turn it on when I leave the house. I'm supposed to have it on in case of an emergency with your grandmother, but I always forget and then she gets mad."

While he was talking, his niece showed him a picture of a blond teenager staring at the camera and making faces. "That's Madison. What do you think of her?"

"She's pretty."

"Come on, Uncle Colin. She's *gorgeous*, and I love her."

Colin took a better look at his niece: jeans, purple hair and a piercing on the tip of her tongue. "The last time I saw you, you hair was green."

"Which colour do you like better?"

"Either one."

"The whole creative process is about communication for me. What about you?"

Colin remained silent; his back was aching. He said quietly, "I wish…" He stopped in the middle of his sentence, for fear of upsetting his niece; Christie was the only person in his family he really cared for. What he wanted to say but kept to himself was that his antidepressants were killing his creativity.

Christie said, "I've got a grant. It covers everything, tuition and accommodation for two years. Do you promise you'll talk to my parents? I don't know what I'll do if I can't go. I don't want to be an engineer. Dad keeps saying, 'Keep the music as a hobby.' Please, Uncle."

"I'll do it, but it may work against you."

Christie rushed over and kissed him. "I love you. Why don't you come visit us sometime?"

Colin answered, "I can't leave right now."

"Why?"

"Because…" Colin paused. "What would you say if I told you I hear voices?"

Christie jumped up and down on the bed. "That's cool."

"My friends are the only ones who know."

Christie got up and opened the door; the two families were in the living room, watching TV and laughing. Before leaving, she turned back to her uncle, "So, for sure you'll talk to Dad?"

Colin woke up in the middle of the night. There were voices coming from underneath him. He quickly pushed the sheets away and kneeled on the floor to look under the bed.

He dressed and crept out of the room. He slowly and carefully opened the door to the underground garage. He didn't want to wake up the youngsters sleeping in the adjacent basement. He got into his mother's old Volvo and drove back to the city.

It didn't take him long to reach East Vancouver; traffic was light at that hour. When he arrived at his house, it was 2:22 on the clock. The street was quiet. He opened the gate and saw piles of newspapers scattered around the front yard and on the steps. He walked around the house, checking for signs of an intruder. Over the past few months, the hole in one of the basement window screens had gotten bigger. The voice was saying, *Give your money to the Natives.*

Chapter Fifty-Six

As soon as he came back from church, Marty went into the house without a word. The morning's Bible reading was still on his mind: "...a man will leave his father and his mother, and be joined to his wife; and they shall become one flesh."

He was on his way to the basement when his mother stopped him. "The dinner is ready."

"I won't be long. I have to check something."

"Don't make the family wait. *Tita* Ruby will get upset for the rest of the day."

Marty looked at himself in the mirror. The other day at school, one of his colleagues had suggested getting an apartment so he could have a life of his own. Now Colin was telling him the same thing, over and over. "You live in a woman's world," Colin said the other day at the Roundhouse. The nagging question in Marty's mind was, If I leave, what'll happen to Mom?

Someone banged on his bedroom door. "Bring your guitar. Mom wants you to play something."

Marty recognized Jimmy's voice. The man was so used to yelling when he was on a scaffold that he couldn't get away from the habit, even away from a construction site. Marty opened the door; there was his sister's fiancé, all smiles, with a can of beer in his hand. "For you," he said, thrusting the can at Marty.

"I'm not thirsty, but thanks."

"Then it's all mine. Cheers!" Jimmy laughed. "Let's go."

They climbed the stairs to join the rest of the family. The living room looked like a children's storybook, with its tall and well-branched Christmas tree, heavy with decorations. Christmas cards, like a row of *mah-jong* pieces, adorned the fireplace mantle. Others cards were stapled to a bright red ribbon handing from the ceiling.

The house was packed with relatives and friends, along with the two female students currently staying with the Puas. Marty's mother was in the kitchen, arguing with *Tita* Ruby.

Susan said loudly, "Mom, *Tita*, it's Christmas. Can we have a truce, please?" Everyone laughed.

"Wait till you get married. It'll be worse," Jerry Surla replied with a laugh.

Marty looked fondly at his sister Susan, who was leaning against her fiancé's chest as if glued to him.

"What are you grinning at?" Susan asked.

"Nothing." Marty suddenly felt embarrassed. No, ashamed, because he didn't have a "normal" life like Susan and Jimmy or Tomas and Sandy.

"Look at him. What a beautiful necktie!" Auntie Gemma said. Marty froze.

His mother, now in the living room, came to his rescue. "Gemma, stop teasing him."

As usual, *Tita* Gemma wouldn't stop there. "I know a young girl who likes a man who dresses well."

Soledad leaped to her son's defence. "Marty has plenty of time in front of him." She called everyone to the dining table, then she and Ruby went back to the kitchen to finish preparing the food.

Marty had always enjoyed the Christmas holidays. He was thinking about their annual trips to Hawaii for the Christmas holidays. Their father was there on business for most of the year. He said to his siblings, "Do you guys remember how we all cried on the way to the airport?"

"But your father wanted to be reunited with his family." For the benefit of the Sandy's parents, Soledad added, "His family was all he cared for and loved."

"I know, Mom. But anyway, when we got there, it was so much fun."

Tomas said, "Yeah, we all piled into *Manang* Rita's Lincoln Continental."

"Everyone except Dad, who stayed in bed," Susan said, laughing.

Soledad said to the ESL students, "Holidays were the only time for my husband to get some rest. He worked so hard." Soledad frowned at her daughter. "Your father worked too hard—no, don't interrupt me—it killed him. I feel like crying."

"Mom, please. It's Christmas!" Susan said. "Dad wouldn't want you to be sad." Jimmy tightened his embrace and kissed the top of Susan's head.

The two ESL students looked completely lost. Their heads bent, the girls fidgeted with the folds of their skirts. Marty thought they might be entertained by the custom of the *Misa de gallo*.

"After mass, we would eat outside; hundreds of parishioners, under large tents. Father Vince would always sit with our family, and we'd watch the sun come up. There were huge flowering shrubs all around the church and a soft breeze. Uncle Max would say, "I don't want to rub it in, but at this time of year, people in Vancouver have nothing but dark rainy days.""

"To go back to your father," Soledad said to her children, "your dad was so proud of each one of you." Marty, Susan and Tomas replied respectively, "Of course, Mom." "We know, Mom." "We're grateful, Mom."

With tears in her eyes, Soledad looked at her children and said, "Your dad, grandpapa, grandma, my sister...they are all gone." Soledad was now crying in earnest.

Tita Ruby said, "Christmas is a depressing time for the people who are left behind." Her wisdom was acknowledged with several nods.

Marty broke the silence. "Your noodles are delicious, *Tita*."

"Thank you, Marty. I know you like shrimp. Have more."

"I'm too fat already."

Soledad protested. "Don't say that. You are sturdy, and you take if from your father."

"You can't escape blood," Jerry Surla remarked.

Marty was struck by the fear of being cut off from his family. Sometimes in the West End, he noticed men staring at him. It made him uncomfortable. His mother had drilled into him that staring at people was rude.

The students sat together in a corner, texting, their heads down.

Pushing back his chair, Marty picked up his guitar. "Come on, wake up, everyone." He began playing a tune he had recently downloaded for a fee from the Internet. "After the holidays, I'm going to teach it to my kids at school."

As soon as Susan heard the first notes, she said, "I love it. Can you send it to me?" She was holding hands with Jimmy.

Marty strummed the last chord, then called out, "Mom, *Tita*, do you need help?"

An answer came through from the kitchen, "Don't stop playing, Marty. We are listening."

After dessert, Tomas and Sandy sat on the couch, holding hands. His brother and Sandy looked so happy together, Marty thought. If only they could have a child.

Mrs. Surla helped clear the table while the men relaxed, their eyes half-closed. At least no one was snoring.

The Korean students were all smiles as Marty played a few more songs. They clapped and bobbed their heads up and down in time to the music. "Good, very good!" they said in unison.

At around two, several families showed up at the door. The parents held pans of food and the children carried containers of fruit juice and bottles of three-litre bottles of Coca-Cola and Sprite. They were coming from the noon mass at St. Anthony's Church.

Jimmy and Tomas brought up another table from the basement to hold the extra food. Marty heard his mother whisper to Florfina, "I don't think I can eat anything else."

Florfina replied, "Jerry will eat, don't worry."

Josh Togonon, who worked for the Vancouver Philippines Connection, began photographing the food on the table: *pancit*, pork and chicken *adobo*, dried, deboned or steamed fish, even the cutlery wrapped in paper napkins. Noticing the statue of the Infant Jesus of Prague on a pedestal covered with a white cloth, he asked, "Why the colour white?"

Soledad replied, "White is the church colour for Christmas."

With this new piece of knowledge, Josh went back to photographing everything that caught his eye: the tree, the ribbon strung across the ceiling, with candy canes hanging from it. He got a shot of Father Antony, the parish priest, who was waiting to bless the food. Next to him was an altar boy with a blue spray bottle of holy water. Josh kept pushing his glasses up onto his head to peer into the viewfinder. Satisfied that he had the shot he wanted, he would drop his glasses back over his eyes and take the picture.

"Can you send me some of the photos?" Susan asked.

"Are you on Facebook? I promised Milly that I would post them there for her to see."

"She's not coming? Where is she?"

"She went back home for Christmas."

Soledad cleared her throat. "Father, would you do us the honour of saying grace?"

Father Antony asked everyone to bow their heads. All did, except Josh, who prepared to take another few photos. "In the name of the Father..."

"Mother of God, why me?" Soledad was kneeling in front of the statue of the Virgin Mary, on another pedestal in the living room. Two weeks from now would be the first anniversary of her sister's death.

As soon as she repeated, "Why me?" Soledad heard her sister's voice, *"You should never say Why me? Do you understand?"* So much had happened in Soledad's life.

Her sister's house in Victoria had been sold. With the Canada Pension cheque, and Marty's monthly rent money, Soledad had enough to live on. At Christmas dinner, Florfina Surla had suggested she invest in a time-share in Hawaii, but Soledad had grimaced at the thought of running into Carmelita's old friends at St. Philomena church. They'd want all the details of *Ate's* battle with cancer. "This would break my heart," she'd said to Florfina.

"Well, it doesn't need to be in Honolulu, Soledad; you could go anywhere."

"My place is here with my children and, God's willing, my grandchildren."

Her eyes closed, Soledad continued to pray. The phone rang, "Would you be kind enough to answer the phone, Ruby?"

One second later, Soledad heard Ruby say, "One moment..."

Ruby came out of the kitchen with the cordless phone in her hand. "For you." She whispered, "It's Aurora Munda."

Her mother tongue had the power to reconnect Soledad with her roots, her childhood. When Soledad heard Aurora's voice speaking Tagalog, she became the person she was meant to be. English might be the other official language of the Philippines, Tagalog represented Soledad's true identity.

Aurora Munda was saying breathlessly, "They can't stay with me, even though I would love it. You have been to my place, Soledad, and you have seen how small it is."

Soledad interrupted her. "You are going to have a stroke, Aurora. Take a deep breath and then tell me from the beginning." She heard Aurora sigh, and then say that Anna Embottorio had Skyped her from the Philippines the day before.

"She went back home? I didn't know. It seems to me that she went there not a long time ago."

Like she had done the year before, Anna had returned to the Philippines to spend two months with her husband and children in Iloilo. Then, shortly after she returned to Vancouver, the government of Canada had finally let her know that her husband and her two children could come and live with her in Canada.

"She must be so happy. Tell her that I am glad for her."

"They need a place to stay temporarily," Aurora said. "While she was in the Philippines she contacted one of her co-workers here, but the lady has not been able to find a place for them to stay. This shouldn't come as surprise. There is nothing to rent in Vancouver." Aurora had tears in her voice. "My heart is breaking. I would like so much to help Anna. Our mothers were cousins…"

"Anna will understand. Your condo is for one person, not a whole family."

"There is no way that I can accommodate them."

"When are they coming?" In a flash, Soledad found a solution. The idea came from *Ate*; it was the type of thing her older sister would do. "I have two bedrooms that are empty."

"What about your students?"

"They are gone. Too much work for Ruby." Soledad looked around her to make sure that Ruby had left the room. "Her blood pressure goes up and down. Six months ago, she had a minor stroke; I never leave her alone in the house. I am worried about her." She sighed. "We are not getting younger. Pretty soon, we'll need someone. Anyway, tell Anna that they can stay with me until they find their own place."

"They couldn't find a better place, but..."

"But what?" Soledad became impatient.

"What about Marty?"

"What do you mean?"

"When he comes home from school, he wants peace, I am sure."

"My son loves children." Soledad was thinking aloud. "So they will be four... Don't worry, they will have plenty of space downstairs, and all the privacy they need." Soledad was thrilled; there would be some rearranging and cleaning to do, but of course her children would help and some parishioners would no doubt lend a hand if asked.

"I must tell you, Soledad, Anna is pleased to have all her family with her, but it is not what she planned to do."

"What else can she want?" Soledad said impatiently. "Her family is reunified after many years."

"Of course she is happy, but she was hoping to bring her younger sister's baby."

"What happened to the mother?" Aurora said nothing. "Are you still there?" Soledad asked.

"The mother died last year." Aurora paused. "During her time in the Philippines, preparing to return to Canada with Boy and the children, she applied to adopt the child." Aurora sighed. "There was not enough time. She couldn't stay long, even though she has a good employer here, in Vancouver. She had to get her children ready for school, find a school for them, get the books, all those things." Aurora's voice changed. "Don't get me wrong. Anna is so happy, and the children of course."

"So the baby is staying with the father?"

Aurora snapped, "Are you kidding? He left her as she told him that she was pregnant. The child has an unnamed father."

"And then the mother dies. It's so sad." Soledad sighed. "Who is looking after the child?"

"Her older sister, but her husband is a pedicab driver, with no other means to support the children." Aurora became emotional. "Anna's mother is old and sick. There is no end to the misery."

Then Aurora seemed to recover. "I don't worry about Anna's husband in Canada. He is an electrician; he is not one of those lazy men who take their wife's money and do nothing. All those years that Anna worked and lived in Canada, he cooked, washed, took care of their two children before going to work and in the evening. He is smart. He will find a job quickly."

"Regarding the orphan infant, what will happen to him?"

"Her; it's a girl. Anna hopes to find a Filipino-Canadian couple who could later adopt the little girl."

"Can't she just raise the child?"

"Anna is pregnant. What will happen next? Anna has no idea. We are talking of months and months here. She may decide to keep the infant, after all."

"Oh, now I understand." Soledad thought for a minute, then repeated, "They can stay in my house all the time that's necessary." Soledad became excited, and barely stopped herself from telling Aurora about the idea that had just come to her. "How old is she, Aurora?"

"Nine months."

This brought a vivid image to Soledad's mind: her daughter-in-law Sandy putting a baby to sleep. This happy thought was crushed by the memory of Soledad feeding her first daughter Susan, thirty-seven years earlier. She suddenly saw see the child's tiny body lying crumpled on the street. Soledad gathered herself and said to Aurora, "We need the flight number and the time of the arrival. Tell Anna."

"I will Skype her."

After she hung up, Soledad rushed to the kitchen for the box of matches. She hurried into the living room to light a votive candle at the foot of the statue of Saint Thérèse of Lisieux. After the death of her child in Edmonton, the parish priest had suggested to Soledad that she go on a pilgrimage. "Not to forget," he'd said, "but to heal."

With her mother and Carmelita, Soledad visited the town in France where the nun had lived. When Saint Thérèse was dying, her blood sister who was in the same convent asked her, "Will you look after us from Heaven?" The saint had replied, "No, I will come down to you."

After wiping away her tears and blowing her nose, Soledad dialed Tomas's work number to invite him and Sandy for dinner.

Chapter Fifty-Seven

One evening, Keith received a phone call from Colin, who said he was in pain. He complained of back pain so severe that he couldn't lie down. "Can you take me to the emergency?" Colin asked.

"What's going on?"

"My whole body aches."

Keith picked Colin up at his home. When he reminded him to buckle up, Colin grimaced.

"What's the matter?"

With his hands over his ears, Colin shouted, "Don't talk; it hurts!"

On the radio, a journalist was reporting the latest news from Syria. "Turn it off," Colin shouted again.

"Sure thing," Keith said, refusing to be alarmed. He'd been here before, as this wasn't the first time Colin had called him in a panic, just when he was getting ready to go to bed. There was no point in arguing. He should have known by now to turn off the radio before Colin got in the car.

"God is talking to me." This was another regular feature of these emergency trips to Vancouver General. "The voice is telling me to give all my money to the Natives in Northern BC."

"I have my doubts about the wisdom of that, Colin. Waste of money, if you ask me."

Staring at the road ahead, Colin mumbled, "I want to see a priest."

"If I were you, I'd go to a Buddhist monk instead."

As usual on a late Saturday evening, the emergency room was full of patients. Colin and Keith waited more than an hour before the triage nurse showed up to interview Colin, who repeated what he had told Keith earlier: his back was killing him; he couldn't lie down; car drivers were honking for no reason; the children next door and their friends were making noise, jumping up and down on a trampoline late in the evening... The nurse left.

Keith said, "I have to take the dog for a walk. I'll be back in an hour."

When Keith came back he checked with the nurses and found out that Colin had been seen at three a.m. Keith was just sitting down to wait when Colin came out. "So?" Keith asked.

Colin looked puzzled. "I thought you went home."

"I went and came back. So who'd you see?"

Colin became impatient. "Let's go!"

"Do we have to go a drug store first?"

"Yes. I have a prescription."

After dropping Colin off at his house with a bag of new medication, Keith turned on the radio and headed home.

George was just finishing breakfast when Keith called to report on his time sitting in the crowded emergency room. He said, "Everyone knows what life is about, except Colin."

Colin's ability to pay cash to buy a house thanks to the inheritance from his father had never bothered George, nor did he mind Colin's idiosyncrasies, such as his huge collection of cactus or his irrational dislike of anything remotely Chinese.

"The guy's a spoiled child," Keith groused. His evaluation of Colin didn't come as a surprise, as Keith was a self-made man who'd worked hard all his life, while Colin had been given everything on a silver platter from day one.

"You're right. Partially."

"What do you mean *partially*? Why can't he be like everyone else?"

George couldn't bring himself to argue with Keith's habit of blaming the victim where Colin was concerned. Instead, he ventured, "Colin is sixty years old. It might be too late for him to learn new tricks."

"He keeps saying, 'I'm an artist,' as if it's some kind of excuse."

George was overwhelmed by sadness. Was it Colin's distress or Keith's worldview? He muttered, "Colin is alone."

"You always did have a soft spot for him."

George decided to ignore Keith's remark. He asked, "What medications is he taking?"

"I know a few of them...antidepressants to stop him from hearing voices, Ativan for his panic attacks and something called OxyContin. Oh, and some anti-inflammatories and painkillers."

George was outraged. "What are they thinking, giving him all those pills!?"

Keith interjected, "I forgot, he's also taking something for his tremors."

Still in shock, George said nothing. How could he tell Keith what he was feeling? He wished he could hold Colin in his arms and just cry and cry.

"Nobody has a clue what's going on with him," Keith was saying. "They're calling it *psychogenic pain*, whatever the hell that is. All I remember them saying is that whatever medication you take, not only does it does nothing; it actually makes the pain worse. Whatever."

As if suddenly bored with all the medical mumbo-jumbo, Keith exploded, "If something happens to you, deal with it! You can't blame anyone else." Out of steam, Keith sighed and said, "I think Colin's hit the wall."

The so-called *psychogenic* pain had taken possession of Colin and whatever that pain was, at that instant, George could feel it deep inside. Unable to put any of this into words, he simply said, "It's cold out there."

Chapter Fifty-Eight

Soon after she, her husband and the children moved in with the Puas, Anna Embottorio began teasing Marty for still being single. Finding Marty alone in the living room one morning, she asked him, "You don't have a girlfriend?" Without giving him time to reply, she cheerfully added, "You and my cousin Elda would get along, I am sure." She said her second-degree cousin had been looking after her father, who had recently died.

Marty kept his attention on his laptop and said nothing.

"How old are you?" Anna asked.

"Sorry, I'm downloading music. What did you say?"

The conversation between the two was in English, although Anna mainly spoke her Cebu dialect. "How old are you?"

"I'm thirty-three. Why?"

"My cousin is thirty-five but she looks younger. She is on Facebook. Are you on Facebook?"

Marty sighed inwardly. After closing his laptop, he walked toward the basement. "Sorry. I have work to do."

✳

The following Sunday, Soledad organized a family dinner. That evening, all three of her children were present, along with Sandy's parents, who were quite upset. Tomas had just told everyone that he had called the BC Ministry of Social Services and had been told that he and Sandy should be patient, as overseas adoptions took time.

Jerry Surla was indignant. "Bureaucrats! They are all the same everywhere!"

"Dad, please!"

Tomas gently stroked his wife's arm. "It's okay, honey, we're all frustrated. They say that we should adopt a Canadian child instead."

Jerry looked restless, primed for action. "They want money, that's all that is."

"Dad, please," Sandy repeated.

Tomas asked his mother, "Mom, what do you think?"

Instead of looking at her son, Soledad turned toward the portrait of her older sister on the dresser. "*Ate* will help us."

A few faces brightened up at the mention of Carmelita. Susan remarked, for the benefit of her fiancé, "Over and over, *Tita* would say: 'Where there is a will, there is a way.'"

Soledad said to Anna, "Can you tell my family what you already told me?"

Anna looked panicked at being the focus of everyone's attention. "Like what?"

Soledad provided some clues: the Inter-Country Adoption Board; the forms on the Internet; things that had to be done through the receiving country...

Anna's short answer came as a disappointment to everyone in the room. "A lot of paperwork and money."

Jerry looked at his wife. "I was expecting that. How much, Anna?"

Anna seemed to melt under Jerry's determined stare. "A lot." She smiled, embarrassed.

Sandy took Anna's hands. "I understand that you're in the process of adopting your niece."

After a nod, Anna said, "Yes, madam." Then she corrected herself. "Sandy. Since I am the guardian, it should go faster."

"Tell us, what are the adoption fees?" Tomas asked with a warm voice.

Anna stood up. "I have it written down. I will go and get the papers."

Tomas touched her arm as she went by. "You don't need to do that. Just give us an idea. Do you remember?"

Anna raised her head. Staring the wall as if the figure was written there, she said: "Two hundred US dollars for the application fees."

Florfina smiled with relief. "That's all?"

Anna looked at Soledad and Florfina. "Then you have the processing fees."

Jerry took out his iPad. "How much for those?"

Her head down, Anna muttered, "Two thousand dollars."

"US dollars, Anna?" Tomas asked.

"Yes, sir."

Soledad was stricken, unable to speak.

When Sandy asked, "Do you have the money?" Anna shook her head and said, "No!"

"What will you do?"

"I don't know." Though her tears, Anna said, "I will borrow money."

Sandy handed Anna a tissue. "Who's looking after the baby in the Philippines, your mother?"

"The baby is with my older sister." She sighed and added, "You have to prove a lot of things but I am lucky because I supported my sister's family ever since they took the baby, so it will help me a lot in my case."

Later that evening, Florfina asked Anna, "Is it true that you have a cousin who wants to come to Canada?"

Anna was cutting up rice cakes for her children, who were downstairs with their father. She put down her knife. Again, she seemed uncertain what to say.

Soledad said, "Anna, repeat what you said to us, to Marty and me the other day."

Marty stared at his mother, puzzled. "Mom, what are you talking about?"

"Oh, I remember now; you were not there. Anyway, Anna, would you repeat what you were telling me the other day about someone who wants to work in Canada?"

Anna remembered a conversation with Marty, but not with Soledad. "Elda?"

Soledad nodded, "Elda, yes."

Jerry jokingly interjected. "Did you hear, Marty? Your mother is trying to match you up."

"Dad," Sandy reacted angrily. "That's not funny!"

Soledad, "It's not for Marty, it's for all of us."

"My cousin wants to come to Canada. She has no one in life, since *Tito* Manuel passed away."

"She has to have an employer waiting for her in Canada, right?" Jerry interrupted her.

"She is a caregiver and knows how to drive."

Jerry shook his head energetically. "They don't want caregivers anymore. It's not as easy as it was in the Seventies and Eighties. Filipinos were welcome then."

"Jerry, she might not need to go out to work," Florfina replied. "Just in the family, she would have enough work. Soledad and I often talk about it. We are getting older."

Soledad remarked sadly, "With someone from the Philippines to take care of her, my sister wouldn't have died among strangers."

Anna left to join her family downstairs.

Florfina tried to reassure Soledad. "There will be someone to look after you, not to worry."

Soledad wiped away her tears and blew her nose. Sandy was gazing at her husband, their hands entwined. Susan was looking at her fiancé, who was nodding off; Jimmy had been up since 5:30 that morning.

"I have some marking to do," Marty announced, and left the room.

As the Surlas were getting into their car, Florfina invited Sandy to join her in the back seat. Meanwhile, Jerry said, "Tomas, come and sit at the front."

As soon as Sandy got in, Florfina put her arm around her daughter. "Your grandmother, my mother, was your age when she had me."

Sandy let out a sob.

The four passengers were quiet during the whole trip to the high-rise condo building where they all lived. In the underground parking, as the two couples waited for the elevator, Florfina broke the silence. "You used to regularly go skiing; Whistler has more snow than ever before, I hear." She looked at her husband. "Couldn't they take Friday off?"

Jerry said, "Of course. The children don't need my permission."

Chapter Fifty-Nine

As soon as he saw George walk out of the Waterfront SkyTrain station, Marty got out of his car. He waved his hands over his head and called out, "Uncle George, I'm over here!"

Rain was falling heavily. He watched as George looked around to find out where the voice was coming from. Both sides of the street were lined with cars waiting to pick up passengers exiting the station; drivers were peering between the rapid sweeps of their windshield wipers. George soon spotted Marty and quickly crossed the street. Marty threw his bag into the trunk as George got in the car. "Thanks for picking me up, Marty. It's really nice of you, especially in this terrible weather."

"How was the sailing?"

"A bit rough, but okay. Were you surprised when I asked you to go to a play?"

Marty smiled. "Maybe, but I'm looking forward to it. What's the play about?"

George had read an online review of a play at the Cultch Theatre on the *Georgia Strait* cultural magazine's website. The play was about a real-life mother and son, who lived in Toronto, and the clash between generations and cultures. "I'm looking forward to it, too. Also, it's nice to get away from sleepy old Victoria once in a while."

"Which hotel did you book?"

"I'm staying at Keith's."

It was now dark and the traffic was heavy. On the sidewalks, women were carrying shopping bags, holding children's hands and trying to keep everything dry in the downpour. Marty felt his nerves begin to fray. "Hey!" he yelled when a driver cut him off. He apologized for his outburst. "I don't drive downtown that often."

"Have you seen Colin recently?"

Marty sighed. Only his sister-in-law knew what he was going through. From the instant George got in the car, Mary had been waiting for him to mention Colin's name. George had provided the opening that opened the floodgates of Marty's torment. "He's avoiding me."

"Don't take it personally," George said, then reported what he knew about the decline in Colin's mental health. "He can't stand street noises anymore; people talking on the radio or TV, any kind of music, people wearing black clothes, his neighbours..."

Marty couldn't detect any warmth or affection in George's voice; it sounded as if he were describing a fictional character, not someone who was his friend, supposedly.

"He's not returning my calls." Neither Keith nor George knew about his sexual encounter with Colin. "I worry about him, a lot."

It took nearly half an hour to find a vacant spot near the theatre. "What time is it? What about the tickets?" Marty asked. He could feel the sweat under his arms, and hoped he'd have time to dash into the washroom before the performance started.

"Relax. Keith has our tickets."

As soon as George and Marty entered the theatre hall, Keith came up to them. They headed for the inside doors and after each was handed a program, the three men walked into the auditorium.

Just before the show started, the theatre manager indicated where the exits were located, named the show's sponsors and extended an invitation: "At the end of the show, there will be an opportunity for the public to meet with the actors."

Less than a dozen spectators stayed in the lobby for the Q & A session; the two actors appeared and sat, their backs against the bar with its row of liquor bottles of various sizes and colours. The mother, in her late fifties, was wearing a red sari with an elaborate pattern along the bottom edge. She was smiling softly.

"This is Mom, and I am Ravi, her son." The actor looked to be in his early thirties. He wore a pale shirt and blue jeans. "Mom, can you say a few words?"

"I came to Canada to fulfill my dream and start my own family. Every year, my husband and I and our two children return to India and stay there for two months. My parents were always asking me to come back to India, but I never wanted to move back. My sisters do nothing during the day, except discussing food and watching TV." She looked at her son. "Now it's your turn."

The play was based on fact. While Ravi was travelling in India with his best friend, his parents decided to introduce him to potential brides.

"When I met one girl's parents, the father asked me, 'How much did you earn last year?' I said, I'm an actor, I earn nothing.' Everyone in the room was shocked, my father particularly. The next day the girl and I met in a restaurant. We had a nice chat. As was the case for me, it was her parents' idea that she meet someone and get married. We laughed about it, but when I came back to the hotel, I exploded. I said: 'Mom, I'll get married in my own time and on my own terms.'" The man had since married.

When George asked if he'd found his bride in Canada or India, Ravi replied, "Kelowna, BC."

The mother said, "Thank you for coming to the show." Mother and son joined their hands and bowed. "We have to be at the airport early in the morning."

Once outside the theatre, George sighed. "It's a pity they had to go."

"Why?" Keith asked. "Do you like him?"

George reacted joyfully. "I'm an old man and he's young, with dreams that he's working toward. I'd love to hear about those dreams."

"Nothing else?" Keith asked, with a sarcastic smile.

George looked thoughtful. "All my life, I believed that every person you meet can enrich you somehow."

Marty stayed silent, as he had during the Q & A session. The play was about entrapment, and this was familiar territory: loyalty to the blood and the values coming from above or outside the individuals. He couldn't think of anything smart to share with Keith and George. The only thing he wanted was to be with Colin.

Outside the theatre, Keith suggested going to his house for a coffee. "Or tea, whatever."

"Sorry, I have to pass," Marty said. "Our band has a gig in two weeks and we have an early practice tomorrow—8 o'clock sharp."

"Too bad." Keith remarked.

"Could you open the trunk, Marty?" George asked, "I need to get my suitcase."

"Oh yeah, I forgot all about it."

Once in Keith's car, George said to Marty, "Keep me posted on what's happening with Colin, okay?"

Marty nodded. "I will."

"Good night, and thanks again for picking me up."

"Thank you for the play."

Keith started the car. "I didn't finish listening to the news earlier. Do you mind if I turn on the radio?"

"Go ahead. Maybe I should call Colin or just show up on his doorstep. What do you think?"

Keith shrugged. "If you're expecting to see him or even get him to talk to you on the phone, don't hold your breath."

He knew it was going to sound melodramatic, but George couldn't help saying what was on his mind. "I feel like my friend of nearly thirty years is being buried. I've gone through grief over people dying before, but this is worse, because Colin's still alive!"

Chapter Sixty

The next Monday, instead of going directly going home from school, Marty drove to Colin's house. He picked up the pile of junk mail on the steps of the porch and rang the bell.

"Go away," came the voice from the other side of the door.

"Colin, it's me, Marty."

"Why are you shouting!?"

"Can I come in?" Marty moved closer to the door. He heard Colin mumble something, so he slowly opened the mail slot.

"The garbage men knew her." Colin laughed. "She would talk back in her dialect."

"Colin, it's me: Marty."

"Sometimes a snake would move when we were in the middle of the shrubs..."

"I won't stay long, I promise," Marty said. He whispered, "Open the door, please!" Marty picked up a garden chair that was leaning against the entry wall and set it down close to the mail slot.

An old lady walked by with a tiny dog on a long lead. Upset by Marty's presence on the porch, the dog began barking. The lady stared at Marty for a few seconds. "Come, sweetie," she said. She pulled on the leash, but the little monster held his ground and kept barking.

Colin banged on the inside of his door and yelled, "Shut up, you god-damned dog!"

The old lady started. She scooped up her dog and walked away as quickly as she could.

Marty strained, but couldn't hear anything else from inside the house. Suddenly he heard, "Shh! The Japanese devils are coming..."

Marty heard the sound of a chair scraping the floor, then Colin's voice again, "Someone's calling."

"What is it, Colin?"

"Leonard was good at those things; he would have mentioned it to the realtor."

"I have to go, Colin. Mom wants me to drive her somewhere. But I'll come back day after tomorrow."

"What time?"

"After school."

Then the house became silent. Marty folded the garden chair, put it back where he'd found it and walked to his car.

While Marty was driving his mother to Walmart, he confided that one of George's friends—that how he always referred to Colin—was going through personal difficulties. "I'm afraid something bad's going to happen, Mom."

His mother didn't ask for details; she simply replied, "I will ask Father John to say a mass for him."

"Mom, he's Chinese."

"Then don't worry. His family will look after him."

Chapter Sixty-One

The next day, as Marty was entering the house at the end of his workday, his mother came to meet him. "Someone called you. It sounded urgent."

"Who?"

"Keith, he said." She pointed at a small piece of paper on the hall table.

Marty looked at the telephone number. "Did he say anything?"

"He wants you to call him right back."

Marty didn't even take his shoes off; he rushed down to his bedroom to call Keith. "Colin's in a psych ward," Keith said.

"I don't understand. I talked to him..."

"You saw him?"

"No." Marty didn't mention the mail slot; his heart was still bleeding from the rejection. "I was planning to go back tomorrow after school," Marty added.

"No point now, he's in Burnaby Hospital."

"How did you find out?"

"His older brother called me Monday morning."

"Have you seen Colin?"

"He called me. 'I'm fine,' is about all he said."

Marty repeated, "In a psychiatric ward! How long does he have to stay there? How is he?"

"He asked me to call George for him. They've confiscated his cell, so he can't make long distance calls."

"What does he want from George?"

"To come and see what it looks like. 'My situation would be interesting to a writer,' is how he put it."

Marty said, "But Uncle George lives on Vancouver Island! Why does he want to talk to him?"

"There's something I have to tell you, Marty."

"What, Keith?"

"This isn't his first time."

Marty almost shouted, "What?"

"It's an overdose of painkillers and antidepressants. Again." Keith paused. "There's nothing you or I can do."

Marty could feel Colin's loneliness, like something seizing him by the throat. "I need to get some fresh air."

"Are you okay, Marty?"

"Just tired; I've had a long day. I really appreciate the call."

"Listen, Marty, I know you care for Colin. I was hoping that…" Keith paused again. "I thought maybe you could help him get free of his obsession with Leonard. At least both of you are artists. Leonard was never a good match for him."

This was the worst day of Marty's life, yet in a strange way, the most wonderful. A door had suddenly opened, giving Marty a glimpse of a world he hadn't allowed himself to experience before. Colin had given him the key to who he really was. Things were different now, and there was no going back.

Marty had once heard a Filipino parishioner say, "There have always been men like that, back home." The man, who had just returned from the Philippines, added, "They dress like women, but it's for fun. They are not really gay, like those you see here."

Marty had touched a man's body and been touched in turn. He called Sandy as soon as he hung up with Keith. "Can I see you?" he blurted.

"Sure. Anything wrong?"

"I can't talk, I'm too upset."

"What is it, Marty? You're scaring me."

"Can we meet for lunch tomorrow?"

"Is this about Colin?"

"Yes."

"Tomas has a business lunch tomorrow."

"I only have forty-five minutes, Sandy."

"Do you want me to go to your school? We could eat in the park."

"Okay," Marty said, feeling a sob bubbling up.

"I love you, Marty."

"I love you, too," was all Marty managed before bursting into tears.

*

The following day, Marty waited outside the school for his sister-in-law. He got in her car and they drove to a small park near the school. They sat on a bench and unwrapped their lunches.

Sandy broke the silence. "So what's going on?"

Marty bent his head. He could feel Sandy's eyes on him. He looked up. "Colin isn't well, and he doesn't want to see me or anyone. But there's more. Please, don't tell anyone."

"You know I won't."

"Sorry...Colin's in a psychiatric ward."

Sandy looked shocked. "My God, what happened?"

"It's overwhelming." Marty told her what he'd learned from Colin's friends: Colin had been suffering panic attacks and hearing voices. "He hears voices, can you imagine? I didn't think much about it when he first mentioned it, but this is serious! I feel terrible, Sandy. During the day, I can't focus. This morning I sent a child to the principal's office because he was out of control. That's not like me."

"You have to keep your distance, Marty, for your own good."

Marty's eyes welled up. He felt a mixture of frustration and despair. Sandy added, "You have to protect yourself."

"I can't do that, Sandy. I love him. I still can't believe I did that to that child. I love teaching. It's my life."

"Can you take a few days off?"

"I can't stay home. I won't be able to keep it from Mom."

"Come and stay with us, then. Tomas won't mind."

"I'm gay, Sandy. Mom doesn't know, Tomas doesn't now, Susan doesn't know…"

"Are you sure about that?" Sandy asked softly. "What are you going to do, Marty?"

"Deep inside, I'm convinced that Colin will get better. I have no doubt about it. You see, he's not connected with his family, and that's the problem. But life can change for him."

"You mean… you can save him?"

"I have to try, Sandy. For my own sake, too. Do you understand?"

"We all just want you to be happy. We love you, Tomas and me. Remember that."

Marty reached out to hug his sister-in-law.

Chapter Sixty-Two

Colin's friends gathered at Lukas and Jim's condo to talk about what they could do to help. Marty came in with Keith, and Tom Williams, who Marty hadn't met before, arrived soon after.

"Have you called Haroon and Sigmund?" Tom asked.

Keith replied, "They're on a cruise." Marty breathed a sigh of relief. At least he wouldn't have Haroon hanging all over him.

"George is with us, too, on Skype," Jim said.

They all shouted, "Hi, George."

"Hi, guys!" There was a map of the world on the wall behind George. There was a brief silence, then he asked, "What's the news?"

"What's the family saying?" Tom asked.

Lukas said, "They want to help, but he doesn't want to see anyone."

Marty was following the exchange between these older men who had known each other for many years. When George asked if he had any suggestions, he said, "No, sorry!"

"Colin won't even accept help from the doctors," Keith said.

George remarked, "He's drowning."

"Don't say that," Lukas objected. "There are medications for anxiety, depression. Right, Jim?" Jim nodded.

Tom looked at Keith. "Do they know what the issue is, exactly? There must be someone who can help him."

Keith said, "They can't keep him against his will. It's against the law and he knows it."

Colin is an artist. Marty said nothing, but he was dying inside, and no one seemed to notice.

Lukas served them green tea. "It's from our food co-op." He went back to the kitchen to boil more water.

To Marty, it seemed that Colin had ceased being a friend; he was now a burden to these men.

Tom said, "Whatever issues Colin's struggling with, I'm not sure any of us can help him. We're all getting older—"

"So?" The question came from Jim's plasma monitor. George laughed. "Are you saying we all go crazy as time goes by?" His next words came as a pronouncement. "It has to do with being alive."

Marty agreed with George but said nothing.

"Colin has no one to rely on. What about a group home?"

Jim was fiddling with his serviette. Lukas asked, "Jim, what are you thinking?"

"He needs someone…someone who cares. A roommate, maybe, but someone who loves him."

George intervened. "Colin needs someone who will just hold his hand, nothing else. Has anyone ever done this for him?"

Keith asked, "What about Leonard?"

"Great idea," Tom said. "Has anyone contacted him?"

"I did, but we haven't heard back from him," Keith replied.

Marty wondered whether Colin would let him hold his hand. He decided to ask Uncle George on Facebook.

Once outside, Marty logged in on Facebook. His first message was, *Help me make sense of my feelings for Colin. I'm losing my mind.* After deleting a number of variations on the same theme, he simply wrote, *Can we talk?*

Within a few minutes, George's reply came back. *I'll be in Vancouver sometime this week. Let's meet for coffee.*

Marty was relieved. George was worried about Colin, too.

George was browsing through a box of old LPs when Marty arrived at the funky Prophouse Café. "They don't seem to have any classical music," George said.

"There's something I always meant to ask: How did you end up becoming my aunt's caregiver?"

Marty's question seemed to take George by surprise, but then the older man corrected him. "Your aunt and I were friends."

"But aren't you...?"

"You mean gay? She didn't seem to mind."

"Did you tell her?"

"No, I never told her about my sexual preferences, and you know what?" George looked at Marty, who was expecting some extraordinary revelation. George said with a laugh, "I never asked what she did in bed with the man she called her husband, either."

This isn't a conversation, Marty thought. The two of us are just circling each other. What he wanted to hear, more than anything, was the question: "Talk to me about you, Marty."

Instead, George asked, "Are you in love with Colin?" Marty nervously looked around to see if the couple sitting at the next table had heard. "Don't worry, most of the patrons here are gay."

"How do you know?" Marty asked, then he nodded. "Oh, right, the famous *gaydar* Colin keeps talking about."

"I guess so, Marty."

"I don't know anything about those things." Marty sighed.

"Have you ever thought of living on your own?"

Suddenly, Marty's suspicions about George melted away, along with his fear. "*Tita* Carmelita said I should."

"Your aunt was very perceptive. It's one of the things I loved about her." George continued, "One day, she left her country and never looked back."

"I always envied her strength." Marty told George about Anna Embottorio's cousin in the Philippines who wanted to come to Canada.

George burst into laughter. "For you to marry?"

Embarrassed, Marty shook his head. "Mom's considering sponsoring her as a caregiver; she keeps saying she's getting older and needs someone to look after her."

"Like your aunt?" Marty looked at him, intrigued. George explained, "She never really liked the staff from the Lighthouse Home Care Agency. She wanted to sponsor someone from the Philippines instead." George became emotional. "It was difficult… The idea simply didn't make sense at the time. The cancer was spreading… It was too late."

"She was strong-willed all her life," Marty said with a sigh.

"That's not all there is to it. Your aunt became strong because of the tough choices she made. Who you *want* to be is what defines you, Marty."

"*Tita* was right: you are a philosopher."

"I don't know about that, but I do know one thing: you aunt taught me to love life just as it is, and to enjoy every moment of it." George leaned toward Marty and said with a smile, "I used to be a professional worrier."

"I thought I was the only one."

George breathed deeply. "Sorry. I just vented." He suddenly got up and put his coat on. As they hugged, George whispered in Marty's ear, "Go away for a while."

Marty leaned back. "Where to?"

"Anywhere. It doesn't matter, Marty."

"I'm afraid, Uncle."

"Of what?"

"The unknown, I guess."

"When someone asked her how she was, your aunt used to say, 'As soon as I say I am fine, I start feeling better.'" Marty knew he looked puzzled, because George added, "Say to yourself: I'm not afraid, and you won't be afraid."

"Thank you, sir."

George laughed. "I thought I was your 'uncle'."

Marty apologized. "It's part of the Filipino culture."

"Stop, Marty," George almost shouted. "Don't use that as an excuse for not living your own life."

Chapter Sixty-Three

Soledad was experiencing a contentment she'd never known before. The house was full. Anna and her husband and their children had enriched her life in ways she never would have expected.

Sandy, Tomas and Sandy's parents had joined them for dinner.

"Spicy enough, but not too spicy," Florfina said for the benefit of the chef.

Soledad nodded. "With milkfish, Ruby is hard to beat."

As Anna got up to clear the table, Ruby objected. "Go and rest. You look tired."

Anna nodded. "I will go downstairs and lie down." Her husband offered to help with the dishes.

While this was happening, Florfina took Soledad aside and whispered in her ear, "Sandy thinks that she is pregnant. She doesn't want to tell anyone."

Soledad suggested a novena to Saint Thérèse of Lisieux, while Florfina proposed imploring Our Lady Mediatrix of all Graces, who had appeared to a Carmelite nun in Las Batangas.

"I don't remember much about her," Soledad said.

"Rose petals were falling from the sky. Crowds were gathering in spite of the parish priest saying the apparitions were not real. The Bishop said that if this was from God, no one could stop it. I have a video. Do you want to borrow it?"

Soledad nodded with a smile.

One morning, Soledad called Tomas at work to invite him and Sandy for dinner that day. She warned her son not to expect anything fancy. "Ruby has gone to the casino with her friend Lorina."

As soon as they were done eating, Anna Embottorio sent her children away. "Go and play downstairs." She took her husband into the kitchen to do the dishes. Soledad smiled her thanks as Anna closed the kitchen door, granting the family privacy.

Soledad dove right in. "Marty is being very mysterious these days. Can either of you tell me what's going on?" Without waiting for her son's reply, Soledad turned to Sandy. "You and Marty often talk together. Don't get me wrong, Sandy..."

"Sorry, Mom, what did you say?"

"Has he told you about all the meetings in the past few weeks?"

"Mom, you worry too much," Tomas replied.

Soledad became agitated. "Your father never shared anything, either." She switched to Tagalog. "It never crossed my older sister's mind to share her worries with me, or her thoughts." She paused. "God give her peace! Until the end, she kept things close to her chest. Your brother is up to something. I can feel it."

Tomas reassured her, "Mom, you would know by now if something was really wrong."

Soledad didn't feel they'd resolved anything. Tomas gave her a warm hug and said, "Take something to help you sleep."

When her company had gone, Soledad checked that the French doors to the patio were locked, then opened the closet in the corridor to get a new box of Kleenex. She headed for her bedroom, having made up her mind: she would not be able to sleep until Marty's return.

✳

Soledad snapped on her bedside lamp as soon as she heard the sound of a key turning in the front door. "I am not sleeping," she called out.

"Good night, Mom," Marty's voice came back. "I'm going to bed."

"I have something to tell you, Marty." In spite of herself, Soledad couldn't hold back the question, "Where have you been?"

Now standing at the foot of his mother's bed and facing her, Marty replied, "Mom, I'm thirty-three years old."

"You don't need to tell me; I am your mother. Am I not allowed to ask what is happening in your life? You have been out almost every evening in the past weeks."

"I already told you, Colin is very sick. His friends and I are trying to figure out how we can help him."

"Doesn't he have a family?"

"His mother has dementia."

Soledad became exasperated. "Well, sad to say, we all have our own problems. If the family is not *there* for him, Marty, there is nothing that a stranger can do."

"I'm not a stranger! We're friends, Mom."

"You are too good for your own good, Marty. *Ate* was right."

"Tomorrow's a school day, Mom. I'm a teacher, remember?"

As Marty walked out, Soledad felt as if she'd fallen into a well. From its depths, she shouted, "If you are looking for excuses to move out of your father's house, then go!"

Marty shouted as he walked back in, "What are you talking about?"

"Go... Leave! If this is what you want."

"Mom, please!"

When Soledad saw Marty, the baby she had given birth to, yawn in her face, she recognized the enemy in the room. "Are you some sort of social worker?"

"What about love, Mom? What about love?" Marty walked out again.

Soledad nearly fainted. She saw the abyss opening beneath her: another sleepless night.

Chapter Sixty-Four

On Friday afternoon, Dr. Andrew Sihota shared his clinical observations and recommendations with Colin and Peter. Colin's brother had been alerted that he could take Colin home. As the doctor spoke, Colin stared out the window over the psychiatrist's shoulder.

Peter thanked the specialist and everyone on his team for the care and attention they'd given his baby brother. When the psychiatrist asked if they had any questions, Colin stood up. "Let's go," he said, handing his brother the prescriptions Dr. Sihota had written for him. He walked out of the room as Peter shook hands with the doctor.

Once outside the hospital, Colin rushed toward his brother's car, saying, "The sun hurts."

His brother was angry. "You could have said something, like thank you, don't you think?"

"What for? They can't figure out what's wrong with me."

"How could they?" Peter pulled out his iPad. "You didn't give them a chance."

"The food wasn't bad, but the bed was awful. I couldn't get comfortable."

Between business calls, Peter stopped at a pharmacy. Colin just sat there. "Come with me."

Colin shook his head. "I'm tired. Don't be too long."

"I can't help it if there's a lineup."

Colin was shaking. "Don't talk, just go!"

Half an hour later, Peter came back with a plastic bag in his hand. As soon as he got in, Colin said, "Let's go."

"I'm taking you to Mom's house. You shouldn't be alone."

Colin shouted, "No! Drive me to my house."

When they arrived, Colin got out and walked off with his bag of pills, leaving the car door open. Peter leaned over and called out, "Don't forget to take your pills." Colin kept walking. He heard Peter say, "Call me if you need anything," then the slam of the car door.

That evening, Colin aligned all the little jars on the coffee table in his living room. He took one pill from the first jar and swallowed it with water. He took another one from the next jar...

He went to the hall table and picked up a bag. His mother's physician, Dr. Brunt, had given him some sample medications when Colin mentioned he'd been hearing voices.

I am an artist. Dr. Sihota was no better; he had no clue what was wrong with him.

Colin suddenly noticed a car parked in front of his house. "Idiots," he muttered, "they park wherever they want."

Halfway down the staircase to the damp and musty crawl space, he turned and went back to get a bottle of water. A pot of tea would have been nice, he thought, but that was as far as he got before descending to the basement again.

His grandmother seized his arm and dragged him toward her. With movements of her hands over her own body, she showed him what the Japanese would do to women and girls. His grandmother had been fearsome and as a child, Colin had loved it. Gesturing with her hand and eyes, the old woman, who had never learned English, urged Marty to drink some yellowish water that tasted of ginger.

Colin pushed more capsules into his mouth.

Chapter Sixty-Five

Marty picked up the phone. "I didn't want to call you at school—" he heard George say.

"How's Colin? I was planning to see him today."

"I'm afraid I have some bad news, Marty. Keith told me that Peter brought Colin home from the hospital, then went back to his office—"

"Couldn't he stay with Colin, give him time to readjust? Or at least ask someone to keep him company for a while?"

George replied, "Peter had to rush off to a meeting; he meant to come back."

Marty said, "How can you make excuses for him?"

"I'm not... Just listen to me, please!"

"Sorry, Uncle."

"When Peter came back to check on his brother." George paused. "It was in the evening, after he'd had dinner with his family. He found the front door unlocked."

"Oh my God! Someone broke into the house?"

"Please let me finish. Peter walked through the living room and the kitchen. There were blister packs of medication, all ripped open, empty. There were pills on the floor. He heard music in the basement, but the lights were off. He went down—"

Marty shouted, "Is Colin okay?"

"He was unconscious."

The hand holding the receiver began to shake, and Marty whimpered, "How is he? Is he going to be okay?"

"Colin is dead, Marty."

Marty sank onto the bottom step of the staircase. "Why did he do that? He wasn't alone. He had a family, friends..."

"Colin didn't know that he wasn't alone."

"What's the point," Marty meant to say: of living, but kept the words to himself, "if love is useless?" Marty became conscious of his mother's presence. "Can I call you tonight? I need to go to work."

"Don't go to work today, Marty," George said.

"I have to."

"Marty, is anyone with you right now?"

Marty looked up at his mother and replied, "Yes. Mom's here."

As soon as Marty hung up, Soledad took her son in her arms. "What happened?"

"Colin's dead, Mom, he'd dead!" He burst into tears.

"Cry, my son, cry all you want to."

*

After the pathologist's report came out—death from drug overdose—Colin was cremated. His name was to be added to a plaque that bore only his father's name.

Sandy took the morning off to attend the funeral service with Marty, whose head was resting on her shoulder. Colin's frail mother sat in the front pew, staring up at the stained-glass windows. She was flanked by her two remaining sons and their wives and children. Colin's gay friends sat further back. Keith, Leonard, Tom, Jim and Lukas, and George were all there. They were like three tribes, Marty thought, each one dealing with pain and loss that couldn't bridge the invisible and implacable divide.

After the service, Peter Hong invited everyone to his nearby house for refreshments. Sandy whispered in Marty's ear, "Go with your friends."

"Do you think I should?" Marty wiped away tears.

"Don't worry about Mom, I'll stop by before I go to work." As they hugged, Sandy said to him, "The two of you need to talk, Marty. You've waited too long."

As he stood wordless among Colin's friends, Marty now knew without a doubt that he loved men. There was no going back to his past life, to who he was or, at least, used to think he was. The terrible unknown remained: what was he supposed to do with this knowledge and certitude?

Chapter Sixty-Six

One evening, just as his mother turned off the TV and headed to bed, Marty asked her to wait a few minutes. She sank into an armchair.

"I'm taking next year off to go to the Philippines," Marty announced. "Mr. Bloom has already signed my request for leave without pay. He said the board would approve it, too."

His mother's face became tense. "Do your brother and sister know about this?"

"Sandy knows, and she's told Tomas."

His mother remarked, sarcastically, "Of course, Sandy knows."

"Mom, I need to get away. You know how hard the past few months have been for me."

Hi mother stared at him, then it seemed to dawn on her. "You mean George's friend."

Marty said, in the most neutral tone he could manage, "Colin was *my* friend, Mom."

"Doctors prescribe those drugs too easily."

"Keith says Colin fell through the cracks of the medical system." Marty waited, but his mother didn't say anything. "What do you think, Mom?"

"About what?"

Marty said impatiently, "My trip to the Philippines."

"What do you expect me to say? You just informed me." Soledad moved to the edge of her chair and looked her son in the eye. "I don't know your plans in the Philippines, but promise me that you will stay with *Tita* Adela. She knows everyone in Laguna."

Mother and son remained silent for some time. Then the mother wept loudly while the son stood frozen like a deer in the headlights.

PART IV

Chapter Sixty-Seven

Adela Orantes was a relative on Marty's mother's side, and the guardian of her colonial Spanish ancestors' heritage, which included personal pride and a disregard for what money meant to individuals who didn't have any. She lived in a two-storey mansion with two maids and a gardener. Apart from that, her only contact with the locals was through the window of her black SUV.

People in town knew his aunt. Marty watched one day as a store owner left his stall as soon as he saw her pull up. Adela gave the man her order; he fetched the goods and handed them over and she handed him the money.

"It's like a McDonald's drive-in." Marty said.

Tita Adela had asked him about his aunt Carmelita. Marty described his aunt's battle with cancer and talked about her love of life in general and food in particular, and about the big house Uncle Max had built for her that she hadn't wanted to leave.

Adela sighed. "She died too soon."

"When Mom heard that I wanted to come here, she said I had to stay with you."

Tita Adela remarked, "Six months ago, my answer to your mother would have been: 'He can't stay with me.'" As always when she talked, his aunt gesticulated, as if airing her flamboyant red fingernails. She repeated, "I would have said, 'No, sorry.'"

She repeated a story Marty had heard bits of before: a food poisoning six months earlier that had almost killed her. The event took place in Manila. "I was with my niece Gemma at the City of Dreams."

"What's that?"

"A casino. You must have seen it when you arrived; it's next to the airport. Anyway, there was an ice cream parlour. It looked very clean, so I told Gemma: 'Let's have some.' I ordered lemon, my favourite flavour. As soon as I put the spoon in my mouth, I started throwing up." His aunt put her hand on Marty's arm. "It was hurting so much. I said to myself, I am dying. The manager called an ambulance."

"Gemma went with you?"

"I said 'Gemma, call your brother Nando, tell him to meet me at the emergency.'"

"What happened at the hospital?"

"I almost died. I spent six days at the intensive care unit. It was a long time before I was better."

"Six days! It must have been awful. And you were in no condition to travel."

Adela had spent part of her life in Vermont with her husband, who had a medical clinic. Less than two years after he died, Adela sold the house, the business and their condo in Las Vegas and returned to the Philippines. "She lives like a princess," Marty's mother had told him before he left Vancouver.

Every time Marty needed to access Wi-Fi, his aunt insisted on driving him into town. Marty protested, "I can take a tricycle, it's only a few pesos."

"This is not Canada. You have to be careful. They know that you are a foreigner."

"*Tita*, who's *they*?"

"The locals."

While Marty checked his emails at the Internet café, his aunt visited the First Lady, the term she used for her old friend Amelia, who was the mayor's wife. Two hours later she would pick him up, saying, "I promised your mother that I would look after you."

About a week into Marty's stay, his aunt invited a number of people for a meal. As they waited for the food, Marty was introduced to Ben Morales, a retired engineer who belonged to an association called Couples for Christ.

"What's that?" Marty asked.

Junever, the engineer's wife, explained, "We build houses for poor families."

"Something like Habitat for Humanity?" Marty asked. He was intrigued, and mentioned that he had planned to do some volunteer work while he was in the Philippines.

Junever suggested that he work at a medical clinic.

"That should be easy for you," her husband said, "especially with all those medical people in your family."

When she heard Junever's idea, Adela became excited. She asked one of the guests to get Dr. Rhodrigo, who was chatting with a group in the next room.

Marty said nervously, "Wait, I don't have any training."

"It will be fine," Adela said. "Your cousin is one of the best doctors here."

Marty shook hands with Dr. Rhodrigo Opina, a short man who looked to be in peak physical condition.

"What do you think about me working at your clinic?" Marty asked.

Dr. Opina warned Marty, "Some may be upset with me for hiring a foreigner instead of a Filipino. We will see."

"I don't want to cause you any trouble."

Tita Adela smiled. "I told you that there would be something for you."

Marty wondered, "What if it doesn't work out?"

A bald man named Leonardo, who had been following the conversation, said, "It's okay, I know someone at the DSW." He shook Marty's hand and added, "I am married to a cousin of Ben."

Marty stayed silent. Within minutes, he had been introduced to a dozen men and women, all supposedly his *Tita* Adela's relatives, so they were his relatives, too. It took him a few beats to recall that Ben was Junever's husband. "DSW, what's that?"

"The Department of Social Work. Your aunt told me that you are a teacher."

After everyone had left, Marty offered to clear the table. His aunt said, "Hermenia and Wendy will take care of it."

"I'd like to give Wendy some money for washing my clothes, just a token of appreciation. What do you think?"

Tita Adela's terse reply came as a shock. "I am the one here who gives money." Then her voice took on a milder tone. "You would give them too much, anyway."

"Thanks for the wonderful party, *Tita*."

"Did you have fun?"

"The food was so good. I ate too much. And you found me a job!"

"Your mother will be happy."

Marty suddenly realized he had forgotten that he had a life elsewhere. After less than a week in the Philippines, thoughts of Colin rarely crossed his mind; there was nobody to mention his name to. How many times had he heard Colin say, "You don't know me?"

There had been a moment when Colin seemed to drop his guard. He told Marty about growing up in Surrey when the area was nothing but farmland.

"She was crazy," Colin said about his grandmother, who lived with them when Colin was a boy. "Before everyone else woke up, she would take me with her when she went through the neighbourhood garbage bins and picked out food, bottles and tin cans. I guess I'm crazy like her."

Marty asked, "When did your grandmother die? How old were you?"

Colin just stared at him with a blank look, like a sleepwalker. "That's a secret."

The clock in a gold frame on the wall indicated 11:00 p.m. In Vancouver, people were heading off to work.

By the following week, arrangements had been made for Marty to work at Dr. Opina's clinic. The Sunday night before he was to start, Marty asked his aunt, "How do I get to the medical clinic tomorrow?"

"I will drive you."

"That's very kind of you, but I could easily take a jeepney."

"All right, but Wendy will go with you."

"Are you sure that's necessary?" *Tita* Adela didn't answer.

Chapter Sixty-Eight

Marty soon discovered that Dr. Rhodrigo Opina, who was the youngest child of one of his aunt's nephews, was leading a double life.

During the day he was a family doctor serving mostly poor patients. The consultation was often free, but the medication was not. Marty's mandate was to help the clinic's assistant pharmacist organize and file records. The pharmacy was staffed by two of the doctor's female relatives.

In his free time, his cousin played volleyball with younger men. This was his other life. One day Marty met two players. His cousin told him the boys' parents couldn't afford to keep them in school. "They have no future."

His cousin's mates would come and go as they pleased at his house. After bowing and saying a quick hello, they would disappear into the living room to watch TV or play video games. Marty never talked to them.

Marty didn't see much of his cousin at the clinic, except for brief exchanges between patients, when Marty would enter the doctor's office to ask a question or get his signature on behalf of the pharmacist, who was busy filling a prescription. Even so, Marty learned a lot about his family tree and where its various members stood on the socio-economic scale.

"Did you ever meet your *Tita* Adela before coming here?"

"I vaguely remember seeing her at my parents' place. She doesn't remember. I was just a child then." Marty laughed. "She told me she never liked babies and children."

Dr. Opina laughed, too. "That sounds like her!"

"*Tita* Adela says you're a very good doctor."

"I won't be a doctor forever. I might decide to do something else one day."

"Like what?"

"It will depend on God's will." Marty had noticed this habit in other Filipinos since his arrival. He suspected that it was sometimes used as a cover for not knowing what they wanted, or not wanting to share their plans.

That Friday evening, Marty joined Dr. Opina and two of his teammates for dinner at a restaurant with a karaoke room. They found seats and Marty watched the amateur currently holding the microphone.

"I like music," Marty shouted over the noise of the speakers. "I play in a band with my sister-in-law." Rhodrigo nodded. Marty read the lyrics of the current song on a big screen. The video quality was quite poor. A pirated copy, he concluded.

Nasio, one of his cousins' protégés, chose the song "Teenage Dream" and began singing. The others were debating what the next song would be.

Forget my past
I am not doing anything
Nothing at all
So leave a message at the tone.

A man with the number eight tattooed on his right shoulder handed the microphone to Marty and said, "Your turn."

His cousin pointed at a bundle of sheets listing the songs. "Pick one you know."

Marty took the sheets and scanned the titles: "Let It Go," "I Don't Care," "No Rules for Me," "I Am Free." He asked the tattooed man, "What's your name?"

"Jay."

"Why do you have the number eight on your shoulder?"

"My lucky number." He was quite drunk. "Sing!" he said to Marty as if he were angry.

"I don't know the song."

Jay pointed at "Truly, Madly, Deeply" and said, "Enter the code."

As soon as Marty pressed the green button, the song started playing, a round ball dancing over the words on the screen:

I'll be your dream, I'll be your wish, I'll be your fantasy.

I'll be your hope, I'll be your love, be everything that you need.

Jay put his arm around Marty's shoulder and his head on his chest. Marty became aroused. "I don't know the song," he repeated.

His cousin laughed. "Don't worry, he doesn't know it either."

At the end of the song, Marty asked Jay, "Do you want to go for a walk?"

With a yawn, Jay mumbled, "Stay here. I want this song."

"I have to go." Marty rushed to the washroom. His erection was apparent, and his cousin had certainly noticed it.

As soon as he saw Marty coming back, Jay called him over. He was reading rather than singing the lyrics, as they were moving too fast for him:

When I think of you

I wonder

If you ever

Think of me

Unable to keep up with the tempo, Jay began making things up, twisting syllables around and jumping back and forth among the lines of the song.

Marty whispered to his cousin, "He's drunk."

His cousin nodded. "Alcohol is a problem in the Philippines." Dr. Opina announced, "Let's go," and the whole entourage stood up.

Marty said goodbye to Jay who didn't reply, the man was mesmerized by the dancing ball on the screen.

Dr. Opina dropped Marty off at his aunt's house and then drove off into the night with his protégés, passed out, hanging out the windows on either side of the car.

As the weeks passed, Marty saw that his aunt's protectiveness had diminished to periodic warnings like, "Don't buy anything from the street vendors."

This morning she cautioned him before leaving for the office, "Don't buy any of those frozen drinks. The ice will make you sick."

"But what if it's filtered water?"

His aunt laughed. "They are lying."

Over the months, Marty's jeepney rides to his cousin's medical clinic became an enjoyable routine. The vehicle would fill up with girls wearing plaid skirts that varied according to the school, and young men in white short-sleeved shirts and white polyester trousers. Even their shoes and socks were immaculate white. At first, Marty had avoided making eye contact with any of the passengers, but over time, he grew confident enough to initiate conversations.

On one day he met Joel Palma, who described himself as a community organizer serving the people of *Barangay 3*.

"What do you do exactly?"

"I find sponsors for events, print tickets, write reports..." Joel had manicured fingers and smelled good. He put his hand on Marty's arm and said, "My English is no good, sorry!"

"Your English is excellent."

Joel bowed his head. "Thank you." He added, "On Saturday we have an event for children, would you like to come?"

"I would, thanks."

"Here's my cell phone number."

Marty programmed Joel's phone number into his own phone. Joel got out of the jeepney and said, "Good bye, sir." Before crossing the street, Joel turned back and the men waved at each other.

The following Saturday, Marty went to the *barangay*. When he arrived at an outdoor stadium named Estradasium in honour of a congressman, the show had already started. Like an orchestra conductor, Joel was directing lines of young boys and girls through a series of choreographed movements. Rather than paying attention to Joel, several of the children, most around four or five years old, were trying to catch their mothers' eye.

"I like to see the smiles on the parents' faces," Joel told Marty after the dance had finished and the children dispersed. "That's my reward."

The festivities went on into the evening. Someone used the term honourable to refer to Joel, who explained to marty that he sat on the *barangay* council.

Marty commented on his cologne, and Joel said, "Versace. A present from Uncle Jonas in Canada."

"Where in Canada?"

"I don't know. Sorry!"

The two men met again the following week. As soon as he saw Marty, Joel asked, "Do you have something for me?"

Marty handed him an unopened sample of Yves Saint-Laurent cologne.

"I am honoured. Thank you."

Joel had trained in restaurant management. One day he confided to Marty, "I want to improve myself and help my parents. They are poor."

"Would you like to live abroad?"

"That's my dream."

"Why?"

"To help my siblings to go to school; I am the oldest."

Chapter Sixty-Nine

Since his arrival, Marty's main occupation after work was listening to Filipino songs suggested by *Tita* Adela's maid Wendy, an avid downloader. Her position on copyright law was that anything on the Internet was public property.

Wendy ceased being his chaperone. Marty increasingly ventured out on his own, though he was still struck with shyness on occasion.

On the jeepney ride one morning, Joel said he was organizing a week-long fiesta in *Barangay 3*.

"A whole week?"

"There is something every day."

"Like what?"

"First a movie night, then a basketball tournament and on Friday, a disco night. Would you like to come?"

"I won't know anyone."

"I will be your personal guide."

Marty turned up for the disco event. All evening, he watched a striking Joel wearing close-fitting black jeans and a tight white T-shirt. An image of a little boy with bruised eyes was on the front of the shirt, with the caption, *I am a good boy*. Joel's hair was dyed red.

At one point in the evening, Joel came up behind Marty and asked, "How do I look?"

Marty turned around to see that Joel was wearing makeup that made his face look whiter. Marty was speechless.

"You have nothing to say?"

Marty managed, "You look nice." Joel beamed.

The twenty-nine-year-old man came from a farming family. He was determined to excel at anything he took on, whether helping a teenager prepare for her prom or roaming the town in search of sponsors for the numerous prizes awarded at the end of the pageant. He told Marty that the first prize would be three thousand pesos, and twenty-five hundred for second prize, along with baskets of beauty products.

"The parents don't have to spend any money for the girls to compete," Joel proudly told Marty on their morning ride to town one day.

"How much money do you have to raise?"

"The total budget for this year is thirty thousand pesos." Marty mentally converted the figure into dollars.

Marty began helping Joel pull the events together, and Joel introduced him as his associate. He kept asking Marty, "Tell me what I do wrong." Soon Marty was editing Joel's speeches and the announcements he would shout through a megaphone as he travelled the streets of the town. Marty often accompanied him on these outings outside of work hours, and invariably, Joel would ask for feedback. "How was I?"

As Joel had predicted, Marty soon became an additional drawing card. "People love your accent." One day, Joel asked him, "Would you like to sponsor the Search Pageant?"

"What's that?"

"Another beauty pageant."

Marty burst into laughter. "You want me to sponsor a beauty pageant? Are you serious? You should go and ask your mayor or the governor."

Joel reassured Marty, "Not the whole pageant. You would only sponsor one of the awards."

"You have awards?"

"Of course." Joel listed some of them: "Miss Congeniality, Miss Photogenic, Miss Popular."

"How much am I supposed to give?"

Joel looked at Marty and smiled. "We need two thousand pesos for the fourth prize." Marty agreed to fifteen hundred.

The so-called Search Pageant's purpose was to select a queen from among seven contestants.

"How old are the girls?" Marty asked.

"Between fifteen and eighteen years. They have to sell tickets to their relatives and friends. The candidate who sells the greatest number of tickets gets an award and…" Joel paused. "Another favour, please."

"You want more money?"

Joel gently touched Marty's hand. "You will be our sixth judge."

"Now you want me to judge the pageant, too?"

Joel put his hands together as if he were praying. "Please."

"What do I have to do?"

"Don't worry. I will give you a sheet for each candidate. There are categories; you write your observations and your marks."

"Hmm. The same thing I've been doing for years as a teacher."

"Is this a yes?"

Marty nodded. Joel threw his arms around Marty and kissed him on the cheek. "You will be a big attraction."

Marty laughed. "Ah, now I see your real motive."

The beauty contest was a community event, with parents sitting on benches and chairs or leaning against the fence that divided the school playground from the rest of town, while kids sat on the ground close to the stage. As the emcee, Joel described the various competition categories—sunshine suit, casual dress, gown—and then introduced the judges.

When he heard "Mr. Marty Pua from Canada," Marty walked up to a table facing the stage and shook hands with the other judges, then took his seat. The judges on his right were a teacher from the Negros Occidental College and a municipal councillor, while the seats to his left were occupied by the owner of Ricky Reyes Salon and a fashion journalist from a neighbouring town. The last judge was a young man who listed so many types of work that Marty couldn't figure out if he was an event manager, an interior decorator, or a flower arrangement specialist.

"My sister works in Spain," the journalist whispered to Marty.

"Wow!"

The woman smiled. "She is coming next year to visit."

The teacher, Marty's immediate neighbour, introduced himself. "My name is Arel. You are from Canada?" He faked a shiver. "Oh, the snow. I would not be able to bear the snow."

"Ladies and gentlemen." Joel stood at centre stage. "As the haute couture legend Yves Saint-Laurent once said, 'The most beautiful makeup on a woman is passion.'"

Arel touched Marty's hand. He indicated the master of ceremonies with his head and asked, "What do you think of him?"

Marty wondered whether Arel and Joel were related. Before he could respond, Joel continued, "Let me introduce you to seven beautiful girls who have admirable personal qualities and unique skills. It won't be easy to decide who will be crowned Ms. Famy this year."

Behind the row of judges, the spectators applauded and laughed. Children ran in and out among the crowd, occasionally taking refuge in their mothers' arms. For each change of outfit in the six categories, the young girls wore high heels. As high as his mother's, Marty thought. Marty knew she'd enjoy hearing that detail of the event.

When Marty commented on the heels, Joel explained, "To make the naked legs look longer."

The salon owner, a woman in her fifties with eyebrows that were no more than crayon lines, asked Marty, "How long have you been here?"

"Six months. Time goes fast."

All evening, Marty focused on the contestants. He assessed their self-confidence, their personality, the quality of their smiles, and other attributes. He filled out the evaluation forms conscientiously. Leaning toward the young judge on his left, he joked, "This is like what I do back home—put marks on report cards. It's like I never left Vancouver."

Joel's hair was dyed orange. One minute he would disappear behind the stage, then reappear to chat with the commentators, a young man and woman no older than the contestants. Some of their remarks sounded familiar to Marty, who concluded that Joel had written the script.

Each candidate had to answer the question, "How can you express inner beauty?" Contestant number three took the microphone and said, "If I am beautiful inside, I'll be prettier outside." She beamed at the audience.

This is pure Joel, Marty thought.

Each candidate was responsible for providing the recorded music that was heard when she was on the stage; it became her theme. After a while, the spectators could tell from the music which contestant was walking onto the stage. Marty knew several of the songs: "Will of the Wind," "My Love Is Here," "Fixing a Broken Heart" and recognized the voices of Diana Ross, Ed Sheeran and other stars. He vaguely recognized one of the songs and asked, "What's this one called?"

"'Stay with Me,'" the teacher replied.

"Sam Smith is the singer, right?" She nodded. Sam Smith was Colin's favourite singer. Marty had longed to hear "Stay With Me" from Colin. For a moment, the contestants, the judges and spectators, even Joel with his orange hair, vanished, and Marty was back at Colin's memorial service.

"Colin couldn't let anyone to be intimate with him," George had said to Marty at the service.

"Why not?"

"There was no key, no door, Marty. He was lost to himself."

Marty was startled out of his reverie by a hand on his shoulder and the words, "I know that song." It was a relative of his cousin Junever. The woman pointed at the teenager seated next to her and added, "He is always listening to him." Marty looked at the boy, who had a friendly expression on his face.

"What's your name?" Marty asked the boy.

"Kim."

"Do you like Sam Smith?"

The boy's face metamorphosed into a smiley emoticon. "Yes. He is my idol."

"Who else do you like?"

"Sarah Geronimo, Regine Velasquez…"

"He knows them all," the mother remarked. Her expression combined amusement, pride and bewilderment.

✳

In the jeepney later that night, Joel whispered in Marty's ear, "Will you take me with you?"

Taken aback, Marty didn't reply. He kept his face forward. He wanted to love and be loved. Finally, he asked, "Will I see you tomorrow?"

"Would you like to see me?" Joel asked with a smile.

"We could eat together," Marty suggested.

"Do you want?"

"Answer me: yes or no?"

Without a word, Joel blew a kiss at Marty and got out of the jeepney.

✳

Contrary to what Marty had expected, the work at the medical clinic was taking less and less of his attention. The day Marty suggested replacing the old and shabby filing cabinet because none of the drawers were closing properly, his cousin laughed.

"Why? That would be costly." Rhodrigo didn't seem concerned about the general appearance of the clinic or the pharmacy. A graduate of the prestigious St. Luke's College of Medicine in Quezon City, he had rejected offers to work abroad. One day, with a mischievous look on his face, he asked Marty, "Do want to know why they all come to see me?"

"Because you're a skilled physician?"

"It's because they can't afford to go to a fancy clinic."

Between consultations, his cousin often logged on to Facebook.

"How many friends do you have?" Marty asked him one day.

Dr. Opina smiled. "Not that many."

Whenever he was invited to a party, the doctor would ask Marty to accompany him.

The first time this happened, Marty said, "Can you call and ask if I can come?"

"Relax. Everyone knows that you and I are relatives."

Among Rhodrigo's entourage, only one accompanied him everywhere—a young boy he referred to as his nephew. Junever revealed to Marty that the boy was no nephew at all; he was there to attend to Rhodrigo's needs. Marty never heard his cousin thank the boy. He wondered if he was the only one who could see the intimacy between them, or was it that no one cared?

In the company of his cousin and his entourage, Marty often had the feeling that he was less of a Filipino. "Is it because I was born in Canada?" he asked Rhodrigo.

His cousin shook his head. "You should live with the poor people in the mountains. Until then, you will never know what this country really is."

One day, Marty accompanied his cousin to a party hosted by a woman who must have been in her late seventies, a contemporary of his aunt Adela. The hostess was wearing a colourful dress—actually a wide piece of cloth draped artfully around her figure—and a pearl necklace.

When Marty complimented her on her dress, she replied, "It is a *malong* from Malaysia. Do you like the Philippines?" she asked.

Marty told her about his ancestors, his work in Canada, and his motive for spending a year in the Philippines. At some point he mentioned his aunt who had passed away. "So sad," the lady remarked, sighing.

Some older men and women had gathered around, apparently interested in the exchange. Marty was describing his life here away from his family, his work at his cousin's clinic and all the men, women, and children he had met since his arrival.

"The day of my arrival, I asked *Tita* Adela if the maids were our relatives." Just as he was completing his sentence, Marty felt his confidence evaporate, as if the ground had fallen out from under him. He mumbled, "I just wanted to know."

Rhodrigo was following the conversation. He came close and asked, "In Canada you don't have helpers?"

"They're called staff."

"Isn't that disrespectful? Interesting!" a man in his late fifties remarked. His white shirt and pants contrasted with his ink-black hair. "Here this is our way of helping relatives who are poor."

"You haven't been here long enough to understand our customs," Rhodrigo said.

Marty smiled.

Chapter Seventy

Upon Marty's return to Canada, the saga of Facebook chats with Joel began. They had arranged that Marty would get up early to connect with Joel, for whom it would be the evening.

One morning, frustrated after a thirty-minute wait, Marty wrote, "Where are you? I have to go to school."

Then suddenly Joel's name and profile photo appeared on the laptop screen. *Are you mad at me?*

No, but I have to get ready to go to work.

Sorry. Are you coming home for Christmas?

You mean the Philippines?

Marty had already sent his question when a second message from Joel came in: *Do you love me?* followed by another: *Say it, please.* Marty stared at the screen. *Are you there?* Joel wrote.

For Marty, such a declaration on Facebook would be like walking naked through the streets in broad daylight. A year ago he had fallen for Colin and since then, nothing. As if reading his mind, Joel's next message came through. *I will never be Colin.*

Marty typed, *Stop it. Please.* On the screen, the word *Please* looked like a shout. Marty shook his head and wrote, *This fifteen-hour time difference is killing me.*

The dots were motionless; Joel seemed to be waiting.

We have to be patient, Marty typed, to fill the void.

Joel messaged, *Have you told your mother?*

About what? Marty typed.

Christmas in Phil.

After a hasty, *I will. Bye,* Marty logged out of Facebook.

Marty dropped the bombshell the next day. He and his mother were having their usual late and copious Saturday breakfast and making plans for the weekend.

When he told her he wanted spend next Christmas in the Philippines, his mother had a meltdown. She seemed to be grasping for reasons why her son couldn't go. "Your aunt might have other plans. She might not stay home for Christmas or the New Year."

"Mom, I already asked her."

"Oh, I see. And you are telling me now?"

"Mom, please!"

"And? What did she say?"

"She's staying home for Christmas."

"All that money for two or three weeks?"

"The money comes from *Tita.* She wanted me to travel. Mom—"

"Why the rush, Marty? You just came back." His mother's facial expression brightened. "I have an idea: let's go together, the whole family, say next year."

Marty remained silent. There was no point in saying anything as his mother continued, "We could rent a family suite on Boracay Island and Auntie Adela could join us."

How could he ever tell his mother about his plan to sponsor Joel's visit to Canada? He was convinced the news would kill her.

Chapter Seventy-One

Marty and Joel were on Facebook again, chatting about the prospect of Joel coming to Canada. Joel typed, *It will not happen.*

We have to be patient, Marty wrote back. *The government is making it harder for people to come in on tourist visas. They're frightened that everyone will try to stay.* Marty waited.

The dots were dancing as Joel typed, *Could Lance come with me to Canada?*

Who's Lance?

My godson. You met him; he was on the boat.

Marty messaged, *Say hello to him.*

Can you sponsor him, too?

Marty barked a laugh. Are you kidding me? he thought, then typed, *One thing at a time, Joel.*

*

Months passed. Marty still taught at the Montessori school, while Joel did side jobs in the Philippines to supplement his honorarium from the municipal council. The town money wasn't enough for him and his parents to live on. One day, he begged Marty to send him money to buy rice. *It's planting season here.* He added, *It will not happen again.*

Okay, Joel, but remember, it's a loan.

After work, Marty went to a Western Union office and arranged for an electronic transfer of four thousand Philippines pesos.

Joel updated Marty on his application for a tourist visa to Canada. *A paper is missing.*

Which one this time?

Don't be mad, darling.

Stop calling me darling. Marty saw the blinking dots as Joel typed, *Sorry.*

No problem. So what's missing?

Your bank account information.

I already sent a statement. Okay, I'll email it again.

Are you coming home?

My mother wants to come with me. Marty didn't mention that his mother knew nothing about Joel.

Joel sent an emoticon of a laughing face.

Marty noticed that the dots were jumping. Joel was typing. His message appeared: *Can you bring me some new shoes?*

Marty thought he'd pressed the Enter key, but his vague response to Joel's request remained on the screen. A question came in, *Do you want a picture?*

Sure.

A few seconds later, the photo of Joseph's penis appeared on the screen, followed by: *Do you like?*

From that day, the exchanges became more explicit. The two men would write out fantasy scenarios. Joel excelled at writing the script.

When Marty logged in one morning, there was a new message from Joel, who was online: *Hi, darling.*

Marty was just about to reply when a photo came in. Joel was sitting on a mat, wearing nothing but a flowery towel around his waist.

Marty went to lock his bedroom door.

What are you doing? Joel typed.

Chatting with you.

Darling, you know what I want?

Marty unzipped his fly and he typed, *Take it.* He fondled himself, his hand picking up speed and his breathing quickening. Eyes closed, Marty ejaculated.

I want a picture, Joel typed.

Too late.

Chapter Seventy-Two

Marty constantly checked the clock on the wall. The family was gathered in the living room, nibbling on snacks. They were celebrating the twentieth anniversary of *Tita* Ruby's mother's death.

Tita Ruby had surpassed herself with the appetizers: *lumpiya* with dips, roasted peanuts, pork crackling and roasted corn nibblets.

As soon as he saw Ruby coming out of the kitchen with a large bowl of dried anchovies, Jerry Surla exclaimed, "Where did you get those?"

"From my nephew in Antique."

Jerry Surla took a handful of the silver fish. "There is nothing better than these!"

Marty looked around him. Sandy was pregnant. Susan and Jimmy, now married, were there, too. Tomas was discussing business with his father-in-law. Anna and Boy Embottorio sat off to one side, as always.

A petite and nervous-looking but strong-willed woman, Anna kept a strict eye on her children, reminding them, "Walk, don't run," or "No shout, please!"

"The house is big, let them play," Marty's mother said.

At three-thirty sharp, Marty excused himself. "Facebook time."

Soledad looked at the ceiling as if hoping for an answer from above. She sighed. "What's so fascinating with Facebook?" No reply came. She added, "When someone asks if I am on Facebook, I say, I don't have time to waste."

Sandy grinned at Marty; she knew about his long distance relationship.

Marty was halfway down the staircase to the basement when he heard his mother say, "Don't make us wait like last Saturday."

Sandy offered, "I'll come and get you when the food's ready."

Marty locked the bedroom door behind him. Joel was online and had already sent a picture: he and two other men, all three of them in drag. Joel's arms and shoulders were bare under a Madonna-style brassiere. The man on his right wore a long gown open open at one side to display his legs. The other one, who was rather fat, was in a bikini, with a yellow floral-patterned shawl around his hips.

Wow! Marty typed. *Who are they?*

Chrissel and Barbie.

Marty didn't know what to think or feel. Disgusted, maybe? There was no life *down there*. Like the lady boys he had seen in the Philippines, Joel was obsessed with whitening products, dresses and high heels.

You don't like me?

Stop, Joel. Marty typed.

Are you mad at me, darling?

Marty heard a knock at the door. "Dinner's on the table," he heard Sandy say. He quickly logged off.

When he came out of his room, Sandy took one look at his face and asked him, "Are you okay?"

"Things never work..."

"What happened?"

"What's wrong with me?"

His sister-in-law put her arms around Marty, who burst into tears.

Chapter Seventy-Three

As soon as Marty entered the café, George got up and walked over to greet him. "How are you?" he asked. Without waiting for Marty's reply, he added, "I didn't eat on the ferry. Are you hungry?"

"Not really, but I might have something. It was a rush at school; I ate my lunch while making photocopies."

The two men went to the counter, chatting idly as they waited to place their orders. When they were seated again, George got to the point. "On the phone the other day, you sounded upset."

"Yes."

"What's wrong?"

Marty remained silent; his hands were pressed together in prayer position, his elbows resting on the table.

"Anything to do with Joel?"

"Yes."

"Is he coming?"

"No."

George was getting frustrated with Marty's one-syllable replies. "Marty, the other day you said you couldn't talk about whatever's bothering you over the phone. Tell me what's going on! I'm here now."

"I'm thankful."

"Stop, Marty."

Marty lowered his head. "Sorry!" He paused. "It'll never work with Joel."

"What happened?" George asked. He paused, "How was it in the Philippines?"

Marty told him everything: their first encounter on a jeepney, the pageant, the disco night, the meals they'd had together, Joel showing him around the various places in the province of Laguna. "It was hard to say good bye."

"Have you met anyone else since you came back?"

Marty looked at George, surprised. "Of course not! I'm too busy, anyway."

"How is it on Facebook?" George got no reply. "Is he coming to Canada?"

"I don't like his friends."

"What's wrong with them?"

"He's like a different person now. When I was there it was only him and me. During the last weeks of my trip, we saw each other almost every day." Marty stared bleakly at George. "They wear makeup, dye their hair…"

George nodded. "I know, it's everywhere in the Philippines."

Marty's face became even sadder. "I'm in the worst and darkest period of my life." He looked George in the eye. "What kind of man was your partner?"

"Why do you ask?"

Marty stuttered, "Was he effeminate?"

George shook his head, laughing. "Do you mean a drag queen?"

Marty looked embarrassed. "Sorry." He said. After a pause, he added, "Do you have anyone in Victoria?"

"There's been nobody since John passed away."

"Do you still miss him?"

George pictured himself at home, writing. "Do I miss him? The answer is yes. Do I still feel pain? I wouldn't call it that. There's a hole inside me. After all these years, it's still there."

"I miss Colin. I don't know why; he never cared about me."

"You came too late in Colin's life. He was too far gone." George paused. "My heart aches when I think of him."

Marty didn't seem to hear. He added, "Can I call you *Kuya*?"

George had heard the word before, but couldn't remember what it meant in English.

"It means big brother."

"That's how you see me? Not like an uncle anymore?" George teased.

Marty had tears in his eyes. "You stayed in touch with me after Colin died. You're always there...to heal my wounds."

"I owed it to Colin, who was my friend," George said.

"Where can I go?" Marty blurted out the words, as if hoping they would make sense, that his listener would do the work of articulating his feelings for him.

"What do you want from me, Marty, really?"

"All I see and feel from you is good."

"I don't know what to say."

Later that day, George finally understood why no one had ever been able to fill the hole in his life. Others touched him in different ways, sometimes hurting him, sometimes bringing him a measure of happiness. He felt like the leaves of the old hazelnut tree on his property, which even a soft breeze could agitate.

During months, his old Filipina friend, like some sort of foreign invader, had controlled his days and nights. As if she were still directing him from the beyond, he realized that it was his turn to look after someone, to be the constant presence that Marty seemed to need.

As the weeks passed, George developed a great tenderness for the younger man, calling him little brother, while Marty continued to use the Tagalog word *Kuya*. They met almost daily on Facebook or Skype and talked about taking a trip abroad together. Marty took up residence in the warm space that John had left behind.

Glossary

Atsuwete	Small tree. The seeds are used as red colouring in cooking.
Ate	Older sister (term of respect for elders as well as within families)
Ati	Negrito ethnic group mostly found in Western and Central Visayas.
Balatong	Munggo (mung) bean
Barong	Transparent shirt made of pineapple fibres worn by men on formal occasions.
Barangay	Smallest administrative division in the Philippines.
Canadian	Term used by Filipinos living in Canada to designate Anglo-Canadians.
Cano	Nickname for any white foreigner. Commonly used in the Philippines.
Carabao	Water buffalo
Congee	Traditional Chinese gruel made of rice and water. The longer it cooks, the more "powerful" it becomes.
Dinuguan	Stew made from internal organs and blood of pigs.
EWTN	Eternal World Television Network, founded by Mother Mary Angelica of the Annunciation, Poor Clares of Perpetual Adoration.
Jeepneys	Modified US military jeeps from WWII.
Joe	Nickname for any white foreigner.
Kadios	Dish made of boiled pork, onions, garlic, jackfruit, and black pepper.

Kalamansi	Lime tree or small acidic fruit of such tree.
Lanzone	Fruit common in Paete, Laguna.
Lechon	Pork cooked over a fire and eaten at fiestas or special events.
Lei	Hawaiian garland of flowers worn around the neck.
Lola	Grandmother
Lolo	Grandfather
Lumboy	Species of native blackberry.
Lumpiya	Chinese dish consisting of meat or vegetables rolled in a rice starch wrapper.
Makapilis	Filipinos loyal to Japanese during the occupation.
Malong	Long wide piece of cloth worn by men and women in some Asian countries.
Manang	Any older woman
Manong	Any older man
Mestizo/a	Half-breed (Spanish or Chinese) man or woman
Muumuu	Long dress that hangs free from the shoulder (Hawaiian mu'u mu'u).
Nanay	Mom
Ninang	Godmother
Ninong	Godfather
Nipa	Species of palm. Its leaves are used for making thatch.
Pandesal	Slightly sweet yeast-raised bread.
Pilit	Sticky rice
Pancit	Rice noodles served with a variety of vegetables.
Pomelo	Giant grapefruit
Sinulog	Religious feast of the Infant Jesus (in Spanish, Santo Niño).
Tamarind	Fruit of a tall tree. The pods have a sour-sweet pulp.
Tatay	Dad
Tia	Aunt (Spanish)
Tio	Uncle (Spanish)
Tita	Aunt
Tito	Uncle
Tuba	Native coconut liquor
Valenciana	Dish with turmeric-flavoured rice and a variety of meats and shellfish.

Acknowledgments

Special thanks to Myrna Lowe of Vancouver, BC, who kindly offered to be my guide and hostess during my first visit to the Philippines. To the Emmanuel family, especially Isidoro, who lives in Victoria, BC, and Juliet Emmanuel Esmores, my cultural and social decoder during my sojourn in Igbaras, Iloilo. Thanks also to the members of the de Lara family, including JB for sharing his library on Philippines history and culture; to Myrna Plata-Munda and her husband Rey, for showing me around the University of Santo Tomas in Manila; to Norma Duy, for acquainting me with life in Paete, Laguna, under the Japanese occupation, and for her generous hospitality; and to Maria Navarro Andaluz and Amy Garside for sharing family memories. My gratitude to Mr. Anthony Achilles L. Mandap, Consul, Consulate General of the Philippines in Vancouver, for clarifying a matter of government policy in his country. My gratitude also to my Paete buddies, members of the Agravia and Iligan families; to my linguistic advisers, Joseph Evangelista Valencia of Oton, Iloilo and Frandy Nodado of Famy, Laguna; and to board members and friends from the Victoria Filipino-Canadian Association, for welcoming and feeding me more than once. Finally, I would like to thank Clare Thorbes for her attention to detail in the editing of this book and for her artistic intelligence.

CPSIA information can be obtained
at www.ICGtesting.com
Printed in the USA
LVOW11*1732131117
556109LV00007B/83/P

9 781773 028200